A Conversion for Hopeless Romantics

P. Charles

A Conversion For Hopeless Romantics

For Jen-Jen, who helped me not to become like Benedict, and Valerie, whom I always pray for.

"Tell me who admires and loves you, and I will tell you who you are."
-Antoine de Saint-Exupery
Part one: My introduction to women, and how they have affected me

ONE

I will profess, with the greatest honesty, that I do not understand, nor will I ever understand, the mind and the psyche of the woman. She is a mysterious creature. She gives me chills down my spine, and for me to understand her would indeed help me to better understand myself. I am a naïve creature, a sheltered, fearful and desperate shadow of a man. I seek her which I understand least- the woman.

How I long for the day when I find her, and in her heart, she recognizes an undying passion, an eternal love for me. Certain emptiness fills my mind, when I think of the fact that my life slips by, each second, without her. I have only the incompleteness that characterizes my train of thought. Completeness- the elusive state of being that I long for, seems to slip away each hour, and each time I pursue it, I end up more confused, broken and miserable than I ever have been.

I am at a venue in Tallahassee, doing what I do best- covering a show. First up are the Millimeters, a math-rock band from Jacksonville that is on the up and up. They are touring for their new album, *Give them an inch, and they take a Millimeter*. The band after them, Rotary Pilot, reminds me a lot of Radiohead's *OK Computer*, maybe with more acoustic guitars. The last band, though, I am supposed to be totally in awe of. When "Doctors of Labrador" take the stage, the crowd usually goes silent. I don't think they are that great, but my job dictates that I must pretend.

I find a corner and pull out my pen and paper. I remove myself from the apparent loneliness I feel, and begin to write about my impressions of these bands. I love the way music makes my spine tingle, and I love the way my emotions rise and swell with the guitar melodies.

I am a journalist. I write for a music blog called *The Indie Chronicler*.

This is the kind of job that has awesome hours, horrible pay and a great amount of panache. It's the type of job where you watch pretentious emo kids sweat their songs out on stage, and eat their lyrics with their body movements. It means writhing in agony with the chords of each heartfelt guitar riff, and digging into the real meaning behind music. And then I go home, and post it online. Rotary Pilot is up now. I follow them with my eyes, and in the interim when they are setting up, I retreat back to my thoughts:

Dear God, why do I feel so detached in public? What is this horrible, disconnected feeling that overwhelms me? It has the sting of a lemon on your tongue. It is warm electricity in my bones. It is the stirring of the Holy Spirit in my veins. It has no limit, and no trigger.

I see a beautiful woman out of the corner of my eye. She is memorable. My mind snaps a picture, and my heart creates an illusion to go with that picture. My mind plays out the wedding in picture frames, and I desire only to be with her. My life becomes diluted in the content of this fantasy, and I try only to control my thoughts. Of course, I see her boyfriend, that awful term- or maybe he is her *lover*- the one who means more to her than anyone. And then, as reality sets in, her beauty dissolves into thin air, and I get a hold on my thoughts, my heart begins to beat at a normal, healthy rate, and her beauty no longer overwhelms me. The music collides with the remains of my wedding fantasy that is winding down in my skull. The only thing that remains is the bride, and the bass line in quarter-beat measures from the song. Somewhere in the song, I could hear notes of the Sunday's Best while they are stringing the verses from beginning to end.

Music expresses hurt. God created it for joy, but humans take everything, and turn it into its opposite. Music was made for joy, but we have made it into a medium for expressing our darkest emotions. Only then, does it appeal to many of us. How often do you hear a joyful song at a show now? How many happy songs did Red House Painters, Nirvana, Joy Division, New Order, or any other really amazing band write? The best you can anticipate is neutral. There are a few exceptions- One Line Drawing, Death Cab, The Vines- Ok, the Vines are a long shot, but you see what I mean. You really have to think *hard* to identify positive bands. My seating position sucks, and my back is killing me. I am anxious for Doctors of Labrador to start playing, so I can get this over with. When they finally do play, a thousand pretty underage girls crowd the stage. The pretentious emo scholars look for a corner to hide in, and the band begins succession after succession of uninspiring melodies that I have heard a thousand times.

It occurs to me halfway during the show that I have seen them enough times to know that if they are going to play a new song, it will be in the beginning. I wait out the first three songs, and when they don't show me anything new, I head to the parking lot, hop in my blue Saab, and high-tail it back to Tallahassee.

My house- well, my place where I live, where I have roommates, in Tallahassee, is pretty cool. It is equidistant from Gainesville, Jacksonville, Pensacola, and maybe some spots in Georgia nobody cares about. It is near downtown, and I love the area. In January, with the Camellias in bloom, I go for lonely walks under cloudy skies, and it brings me the greatest pleasure. I am madly in love with this sort of incompleteness. It is the only permanence I have ever known, and the city knows it.

I am a little weird, mostly because I like weird music, I brush my teeth at random times, I like eating refrigerator-aged cheese, and I drive a Saab. Saabs are pretty strange cars. The ignition

6

switch is between the seats, and they look like alien spacecraft. My Saab is a 1978 99 EMS- The Electronic Manual Special. I have had this car for almost six years, since I was eighteen. It was a gift from my dad. It was ugly, and blue, and delightfully shitty looking, and it was fast. It also has an eponymous vanity plate, so that if anyone asks what it is, I point to it, and they say "oh, a Saab 99!" I would drive it around the back roads near Pensacola, listening to Penfold, on my way to and from college. In my time of melodic math rock, no first dates and utter nerdiness, the Saab was my hiding place. I take notice whenever I see a Saab. I feel that driving a Saab endows me with a form of credibility that other people will envy me for having. Or, if anything, people will know when I have arrived.

"Benedict, how was the show last night?" I am asleep on my couch. The person asking the questions is my roommate Kevin. It is ten A.M. and I am worn out. I fell asleep at five, after getting home from the show.

"Huh? What is it?" I was still exhausted from last night. Kevin was already gone when I opened my eyes. I slipped into a lucid slumber, only to be woken up again with Kevin asking me to move my car.

I crawl out of bed, becoming painfully aware of my stench. It feels super cold- maybe thirty nine degrees outside, and sunny. Welcome to Florida winter. With a bit of difficulty, the Saab fires, and I back it out of the driveway. Kevin drives off in his Datsun, and I drag myself to my computer to publish last night's notes. I burn off the haze with some old school Christie Front Drive, and check my Facebook.

Facebook is brand new. It has the ability to help you find people if they went to certain schools or colleges, and FSU was an early adopter. I acquired an email address from FSU after taking one class there last year (the failed start of a master's degree) and was assigned a school email. Then I promptly dropped out. But this amazing utility lets me find any girl I want to.

Facebook also has this annoying habit of ruining your day. It isn't just a social utility. It is a stalking utility. I use it to stalk girls I used to like. Now that college is over, and all of us are so uncool, it gives me immense pleasure to see what kind of guys the girls from college are dating. Or what kind of guys they are marrying. Every week, one of my 900-ish friends seems to be "just married." They should create a category on Facebook for lonely, fucked up, unattractive and miserable people, so we can keep track of each other. Instead, it rams all these beautiful women who want nothing to do with you into your skull, and you are tempted to look at them, and see how much better off they are than you.

I guess I should acknowledge my issue here. I do it every day, but acknowledging that you are undesireable and fucked up on a daily basis is really healthy if you want to fix yourself.

I pop in a CD from Sunny Day Real Estate and listen to the opening notes.

I can't look at pictures of beautiful women that I know. Notice that I said *beautiful*, not 'hot.' The word 'hot' inspires, or fills you, with lust. These hot women fill you with a disconnected desire to gawk at their pictures, but beautiful- that's different.

Beautiful is *sacred*. Beauty is purity. Beauty is to be *revered*. And in my unworthiness, my patheticness, who am I, a creep, to gaze upon the barrage of photos these beautiful women put up to show the rest of the world? "I cannot gaze into your eyes, for they torture me with their unobtainable perfection," I tell myself.

I have tried to confront this odd persuasion, made up of one part shame, one part guilt, one part self-awareness, and two parts unfulfillable desire. Why look at something- even consider something- so far beyond your reach? Because all of us are seriously and badly ruined people, we don't know how to get what we want. We get caught up in the wanting, without being able to pursue. The pursuit is so painful, because it is often curtailed by rejection. But Men are like weeds. They keep coming back, no matter how much they are rejected. And the rejection grows more outward, until you have been totally defeated. Those pictures and those two parts unfulfillable desire are so powerful because, when you see them, the woman is saying to you "you are inadequate, and I am too good for you. I reject you."

One part from the woman, and one part, knowledge on my behalf, that I will be rejected. The rest of those emotions are the bastard offspring of being rejected, and knowing you will be rejected. I cannot fulfill my desire for you. You will not allow me. What course of action do I have, then, but to hide my eyes in shame?

See, I am a hopeless romantic. But it isn't my fault. It's God's fault. It is fair to blame God in cases like this.

I get to work, and stop dwelling on my inadequacies long enough to write an article.

This silly blog has way too many followers. Most of them are under the age of eighteen, and I've become this elusive internet celebrity thanks to it. There is also a forum where people discuss this crap. They make it their whole life to sit down and bullshit about what I, and my colleagues write- it's like they can't enjoy the actual music. In fact, most of these bands I write about will be gone in five years, or they will get signed, go on tour, and forget about Florida. Whatever happens, I am entirely removed from it. I get paid to write about them, and work from home, and go to shows, and it pays something like three hundred dollars a week. I have to make five or six crappy shows a week around the area, and then write a blog entry about each one. I can only love my job, so I try my best to. Francisco, the guy who runs the thing, doesn't really care anyway. Once in a while he tells me to sound 'more excited' as I write. He is married to a girl who is a model of indie culture. I envy Francisco.

I get up and go make a sandwich, and then go back to my computer to check my email.

A little more than one year ago, I graduated from college with a degree in statistics. By the time I was done with all those classes, I hated stats, and I hated school. But I liked the environment at school- my friends, and the activities that took place. Graduating in December was total crap. Its like your senior year of college is cut short, and you miss all the fun stuff in the spring.

I look at my email. Nothing I care to read. Obstinate Records (they put on most of the shows around here) have emailed me their schedule for this week. I am expected to attend most of these shows.

I think about college a lot when I'm writing. My college I went to (It was a Catholic College, named for St. Mary) was nearly perfect. I mean, it had its shortcomings, but they were forgivable. I would rate the entire experience, with its challenges, emotional ups and downs, and its evils and strengths, a ten out of ten. I wouldn't trade it for anything. Being one of 4,200 or so was perfect for me, and I was so very happy with the whole ordeal. It was a typical private Catholic school, full of rich kids, and then a few who went there for its solid education. That's what my dad says. It wasn't as expensive as most private schools, and my parents could afford to help out. I wasn't stuck with student loans when I was done, and I left free and clear.

Francis (Sometimes I call him Frances, because I think he should have been born a woman), my other roommate, interrupts my deep contemplation about college while telling me it is time for Mass. Frances could tell you everything about women. That's why when he sits down and talks about college, he just goes "eh...it was alright."
People who get exactly what they want always fail to see the beauty in what they have, because there is no contrast, and they don't have to work for anything. Frances is cool, but he is like that. He had access to some amazing women. But of course, Frances and I are both upright gentlemen. We didn't sleep with any of them. The truth is he didn't choose to sleep with them. I never really had an opportunity to make that decision. So I just lie and say I stayed a virgin despite circumstances that could have compromised that state of being. Frances looks at me, nursing his lip with a paper towel. He can read my thoughts.
"What happened to your lip?" I demand.
"I hit it on the fridge. You left it open."
I smile, awkwardly. "Sorry, Francesca."
"Are you thinking about girls again?"

I like being his roommate. He doesn't ask. He just *knows.* He knows I think about girls, and marriage, and being alone, and college, and all the women that trampled over me, all the time. He also knows that when I am thinking about girls, I don't pay attention to anything.

"Benedict, you need to snap out of this phase you're in. It's getting in the way." Like I said, he just knows.

He's right, I think. He understands fully that I am currently distracted by women. The problem is, however, that I have always been this way, and I did a pretty damn good job of hiding it for years. It bothers me all the time, and I feel awkward and uncomfortable in my own skin. Recently, however, it really started to eat away at me, and now it has taken over. The incompleteness, that is. The feeling that you need someone there- that desperate longing.

"There's a party tonight at Kristen's house. You want to go?"

Frances interrupts my thoughts again. Kristen is like Jesus trapped in a woman's body. She is so perfect and holy, and she talks to me like I am a little child, like I am perpetually out of line with our beliefs. I looked at Frances and nodded before he even finished the question. "It's after Mass. Are you going with us? You should come, it'll be fun. Kristen says she hopes to see you."

Kristen and I have been friends since I was eighteen, and after all the shit we have been through, she still treats me like I am six years old. She says my foundations are in disrepair, and that Jesus needs to intervene in my life. In fact, she prays for it all the time, she says. But she doesn't really love me. She is just uncomfortable with me being in her circle of friends, and remaining as I am. That really bothers her. And when a person wants you to change, it really means they want to control you, since they believe their agenda is more pure, holy and perfect than yours is. I accept her for who she is, even though she irritates me, but I never ask her to change, or tell her she needs to modify her personality. I hope God keeps us separate in heaven, most of the time.

I do mean it though. We really are friends. She and I go on

retreats and mission trips with each other, and she and I talk when we see each other. Our lives have no intersection, though, other than what we believe. In fact, we believe the exact same thing, and practice it in totally opposite ways. She doesn't like the fact that I am in the world, and I think her perpetual sanctity is utterly fake and pointless. But unlike what she does to me, I never criticize her for it at all. In fact, despite my resentment towards her, I encourage her to be herself. I think she secretly resents me, too. And resentment is one of those emotions you can't block. You just have to accept it for what it is. It sits around for years, and I think there has been this sort of resentment between Kristen and me when she found out who and what kind of person I was.

It is five-thirty P.M. and I am sitting in Church, right before Mass starts. I'm wearing khaki pants and a red sweater. I cannot focus.

My mind shifts back to college. College is great because when I dwell on it, it brings back all these bittersweet memories, and bittersweet is the best. My nights in college were spent between being a wallflower at parties with normal people, and being a participatory Catholic. I led this kind of dual existence. One was centered on my faith, and the other was, well, I guess one word doesn't explain it. I think Frances could. Until he had his "conversion," a return to his faith, he was a party animal. I mean, he had a sort of ideal life, making out with women at bars and parties, and then he had what we call an intimate encounter with Jesus, and poof, he was changed. He and I were friends before he changed, however. I don't think we were close friends, but we knew each other. He got me to sign on to the lease with him, and I guess he acted like my best bud to try to get me live there. When you need roommates, you have to do what you have to do. Not that I think he lied, but I don't believe he really knows or cares about me as much as he says he does.

Ok, so the wallflower stuff. I made all these friends right off the bat, because, as all my platonic female friends put it, I am super nice, cutely naïve and unthreatening. So they would drag me to these parties, and get drunk, and then ask me to take them home if they didn't pick up some moose at the party to go home with. Usually they got their business done somewhere else. And they never directly "asked" to be taken home. I had to intervene when things got out of hand and drag them out of that inferno. It's kind of like an end of life agreement for a comatose person. 'If it looks like I am not going to make it, or I am really messed up, pull the plug. I won't know the difference at that point.'

There was one in particular that really damaged me. She damaged me because I loved her. Seriously, I did, and she knew it, and she kept using me by appealing to my love for her, so I could be her crutch. She knew I would protect her, no matter what, and I did, and when I would protect her, she would get pissed off, and be mad at me for a week, and then come back. We would hold hands- an utterly meaningless exercise of manipulation for her, and an emotional indulgence with a woman I was crazy about- for me. And then everything would be better. And then she would launch into orations about the guy or guys she liked, and she would wiggle her sexy little tongue while saying their names, and I would feel cold, naked and embarrassed. I would fall in love with every word she was saying, and my mind would boil over with envy for these losers, and I would quietly hold it in until she would leave, and I would lay on my bed, listen to Jets to Brazil, and imagine I was hers, and we were together. She was my Madonna, but in reality, my basic instincts said she was not the dulcis Virgo I wished she was. I am hesitant to call her a whore- That would be degrading her humanity. It would have been a title that suggested I did not truly love her, and I did.

Somehow, I have ignored the entire Liturgy of the Word thinking about this crap. I do it all the time. And right back into it I go.

I dragged myself through situations that would have been crippling to an ordinary man, and I kept coming back. True love knows only one thing- the object it seeks. She loved me also, she told me so, but she was also so corrupted that she could not appreciate the love that I had for her. If you are used to, and desire what is ruined, damaged and screwed up, how can you want what is pure, perfect and unbroken?

One night we were at a party in some guy's house, and there was this closet. She had disappeared, with some guy in tow, and I found myself lost in this house. This place seemed bigger to me, in the wee hours of the morning, with the loud music and the smell of smoke and beer everywhere. I disassembled myself, and dragged all my pieces through the halls, in search of the truth. The music got quieter as I walked through each room, and each corridor, and every subsequent space seemed bigger than the one I had left. It was like I was cave diving, and my light had burned out. I could not tell up from down, left from right, in the womb of the black waters. And then I heard her.

I turned and ran, angry and miserable at what had passed into my brain. No one here knew me, and something inside me had broken. I think about that moment a hundred times a day. Years later, I still find myself in that room, listening to her moving with his body movements. I forgive him for what he did to me. I can't forgive him, however, for what he did to her, even if she consented to have sex with him. I refuse to relinquish that bitterness, even if it makes me miserable.

The entire way home, she said nothing to me, and I am almost certain she felt my presence in that room, briefly, long enough to know that I was there and that I was broken. It was the longest drive home that I had ever experienced, and there was no one around for miles. I had found my life line, and I crawled out of the cave without her. Her body rested on the bottom, somewhere in one of those passages, cold and lifeless.

I have been damaged goods since that moment in time, and I have no idea what will mend me. It was in that moment, however, where I found God.

TWO

I am on my knees, watching the priest hold up the consecrated host for us to see. "My Lord and my God!" I whisper. In

14

this moment, he must be trying to show me something, but I am too far lost in the past to really see any meaning in it.

"Lord, I believe. Help my unbelief!" I think to myself. I am in a nebulous space constantly, somewhere in between the past and the future, drifting through the interim. I simultaneously plant myself in the present while gazing on the past with binoculars, honing in on every little fragment of detail that deserves to be amplified. I give myself a shred of credibility by starving myself of the fantasies that I have dreamed about for my entire life, and instead focus in on why I cannot reach these desires, and how unrealistic they are. The present is an altered present. If these events had not occurred, it would be different, better. I claw my way back and forth between what is happening now, and what happened to make now the way it is. I am lost in a dissociative fugue, trying to find that watershed moment where I was tossed into a sea of uncertainty and confusion.

I was not always lost, and I had a grasp on my desires and my life all throughout my adolescence. But as the evils of the world make themselves known to you, you end up with no choice but to break free from your childish thought patterns, and try to figure out what you're supposed to be doing as an adult. And here I am, trying to figure out how to heal the wound that growing up has inflicted upon me, and I think, well, I know, God has some sort of answer, some sort of truth, that He is aware of, and we are not.

After Mass, I go home, and Frances is waiting for me at the table. He is dressed in brown pants with a button down shirt that has pink stripes.

"Are we carpooling?" I inquire.

"That would be a good idea, I think"

"Well, Francesca, what if I wish to go home early?"

"I'll find a ride with someone else, Benedict."

I arrive, with him, at seven fifteen.

It's not really a convent, but we call it could be. The girls that live there are virtuous to a fault, and they are certainly bent on converting the rest of the world. These girls are not your ordinary girls. They care about others (instead of just themselves), and they are more interested in helping the rest of the world than their immediate friends. And this makes them more confusing than ever.

There are a bunch of cars out front, and it seems like everyone I know is here. But there's an odd reason for this celebration. Kristen throws these things every month for someone's birthday, or wedding, or God knows what, but this time it's supposed to be about something even more important. To me the only thing that could possibly be more important than any of this is that someone has decided to leave the normal world and take on some sort of celibate, religious vocation. I, of course, always wondered what that was like, but the degree of closeness that I needed from another person could not come from Jesus, no matter how much like Him that piece of bread is. I need a woman in my life. Amen.

I hate being in public. It really makes me feel awkward, and, whenever I show up, people always seem to eventually notice me, and then the questions come. I shrink down in the room, and I enter the house. I need a friend, fast. Someone to hide with. When you're engaged in conversation with another person, no one will disturb you.

I take a quick look around to see who is here. Kristen is at a table handing out name tags. Her roommates Theresa and Helen are in euphoric conversation with some of the more benign, theologically adherent men of our community. Deacon Steve is here-he's 26, and left FSU to go to seminary. He will be a priest next year. Then there are the manly men-Paul, Thom, William, Xavier, Jack, and this new guy that someone addresses as James. New people in this group are not rare, but this is the kind of group that attracts only one kind of person. I am looking for my friends, and I hear more voices out back. Judging by the number of cars –usually one car brings two people- there are at least thirty people here. In the corner of an outdoor patio I can see my good friend Patrick. He's talking to Francis and Kevin and our friend Nicole. I begin to move towards them...

" Benedict! Long time no see!" Kristen squeals. "Have you

been keeping out of trouble?" Trouble is apparently what I'm famous for here. Of course, the Catholic definition of "trouble" is not making daily Mass plus a Holy Hour every day.

"If you mean what I think you mean, I am currently in trouble."

"Ohhh, Benedict, you're too funny! You know why you're here, right? Go get a name tag. We are going to be discussing the formation of new study groups. It's going to be so interesting…seriously!"

"Ok, dear." I cautiously fill out a name tag. I don't ever put my first name on name tags. I put "Rad" on there. 'Rad' is a derivative of my last name. It's the only cool thing I have, unless you're into Saabs and math rock. That's what normal people call me. But here, I'm Benedict. And I'm always in trouble.

I make my way over to Patrick. He's in conversation, so I use the interim to scrutinize the new faces. I do not use this time to check out girls. Men who do that are animals. I would like to find a few guys like that, and put a chastity belt over their eyes. But I am still looking for cute girls, and I think I just might find some.

To the left of the patio, by the grill, there is a table. On that table, there is a stack of papers, and six people are sitting down, discussing something that seems very, very important. There is a priest there- Father Henry, from the Cathedral. And to the left are two uninteresting looking girls that I don't know. Then there's another unic, Sam, and then, this girl that I have seen before but didn't talk to- someone calls her "Madeleine"-and one of her friends. My eyes dart all over Madeleine, and within seconds I determine she is incredibly cute. I want to send her five dozen roses. I want to tell her how lovely she is, with a wax sealed letter, I want….

…The guy who just came up to her, who seems super comfortable around her, to go away and disappear. He's so comfortable around her, as a matter of fact, that she might just like him.

"Hey Radmeier, how the heck are you, buddy?" Patrick is now attending to me.

"I'm jolly. Just jolly."

"Have you seen any great new bands? I heard that there's this one group on the up and up that is Catholic, and they write music that is actually appealing to normal people!" He has just discovered Penicillin, you would think.

"Patrick, you mean *Army of Me*, right?"

"Yeah, that's it. They are amazing."

I like them more than most, and there is something very real about their music- it's heavy on theology, but most people don't know it.

Patrick and I shoot the bull about the show last night. I tell him how good Doctors of Labrador are, and how I wish they played more shows here.

"Patrick, who is that girl, Madeleine?" I ask sheepishly.

"Oh dude, she's super cool. She's getting her grad degree in journalism at Florida State."

"When did she move here, and where from?"

"I think," Patrick looks lost in thought, and then looks hard at her- "I think she came here from Franciscan U., maybe a month ago."

Then, I recall where I saw her. She had been at Mass with all of us for our friend Tristan's wedding a month ago.

"She's quite lovely," I whisper in a British accent. You can use British accents to diffuse awkwardness and inappropriateness at any given time. "Is she discerning?"

Discernment is very important. It's also overrated. It basically means that you are trying to convince yourself that you could do religious life for the next century.

Patrick giggled, and then put his hand on my shoulder.

"Benedict Radmeier, you ask me that about another girl every week."

He's absolutely right. But it never hurts to learn something from someone you can trust, and so I ask him, knowing he won't make fun of me.

"Ok guys, time to go have a seat!" There are chairs set up in the living room, and stacks of books. Kristen is orating from the front of the room. A quick headcount reveals that there are 32 people here. The segregation of the sexes takes place, with men sitting on one side, and women sitting on the other. No one tells us to do this- it's fully automatic. It makes me mad. Kristen commences her monologue. "As you know, we are here today to form new study groups. But the book we are studying is going to be monumental. It is going to change all of your lives forever, and ever. This new theology, which was pieced together from documents written in the Vatican in 1980, is the subject matter of a brilliant young theologian and his new book. This book is called *Redeeming Sexuality*, and it re-examines the importance of God's creation of man and woman, and why our culture has led it askew. The author, Joseph North, has planted in this book the seeds of a revolution that will enable the culture of life to proceed with new purpose and direction. It is a long awaited book that we have all been anxiously anticipating."

I look at the ominous stacks of books. This thing is at least 300 pages, and I bet it's small print. Good luck, finishing this Opus Magnus in 3 months. It might be a catastrophic blunder like *Humanae Vitae* was. However, if you ask the group leaders, Paul and Kristen, *Humanae Vitae* was an immense success.

"We have several copies of Mr. North's book, but you are encouraged to buy your own copy. They can be had on Amazon for about $35.00. I know it's expensive but it is worth it, I promise."

I am going to start a Catholic library. I have all of these volumes of books I have purchased for this stuff, and seriously, I never really read any of it. I just hate the awkwardness of being in a study group without the text. I really hate sharing books, especially when the book is not mine.

"In a few minutes we will have sign-ups for our new study groups. However, this time we are going to do something a little bit different. Traditionally, our groups have been based on documents from the Church, and have been divided into men's and women's groups. But *Redeeming Sexuality* is so important, we are going to have three different groups meeting each week that are co-ed. Pick the group that fits your schedule the best. We really want you to come to this." Paul ends his little oration with a sniffle.

I waited for sign-ups to begin. I carefully kept an eye on Madeleine, watching to see which group she's going to choose. I watched her lovely luminescence trail her to the sign-up table. I move out of my own body, and despite the nervousness, my fear stays frozen on the chair, and I glide across the floor to see what she is writing. I notice that there are three different groups- a Saturday morning group, a Tuesday night group, and a Thursday night group. Thursday night is always bad for me. It's one of those nights when there is always a show. Tuesday is good for me. No one plays on Tuesdays. And, luckily, I see Madeleine's name on the Tuesday group. My heart skips a beat, and I write my name beneath hers, along with my number and email address.

"Benedict! I'm so glad you're going to do this!" Kristen whispers over the group of people bombarding the table. "I hope you really grow from this book!"

I wonder how she knows that I am so screwed up. I mean, she addresses me with a passive hostility. She talks to me like a loving mother who wishes her child would change entirely, and anticipates a day when he will grow up into a nice young man, instead of a difficult man-child. I wish she understood me better, but she doesn't want to. I am poison for the mind of a saintly woman like her. It's not like she isn't beautiful. She's terrifically beautiful, but her beauty is overshadowed by her piety. She knows me better than most people do, though. My entire personality is overshadowed by the fact I am a fucked up, unhappy, insubstantial human being. Whatever substance is buried in there lies under a layer of shit so deep that only God can find the real me. But for now, I think Kristen is fully aware of the layer of shit. She is just not aware of the human being underneath it. One day she will leave for the convent, and I will find myself under the layers. What she doesn't get is that her condescending behavior will never fix me.

As is the norm, there are refreshments. There is a couch by

20

the patio door, in the living room. It is made of burgundy vinyl, but it feels like leather. I love that couch. That couch is *sexy*, and it feels out of place here. I can imagine myself having a conversation with Madeleine on that couch. But I sit on the couch with a bunch of my guy friends, and I feel great discomfort in my own skin. No one talks about *anything* interesting at all. The men here don't discuss women. They talk about Pope Benedict and St. Augustine. The women here talk about abortion and politics. I don't feel like giving a damn about this stuff. It's all extraneous, and, as they say, it's in God's hands anyway.

But part of me really cares, and part of me is in this awkward place that I feel so uncomfortable in for a really good reason. I'm not here to meet girls. I'm not here to incriminate the Catholic Church. I'm here because I believe that somewhere in this writhing mass of theology, God is present, and He is able to fix me. I don't know how He is going to pull it off, but I think the answer lies within these walls. I try to ignore the fact that I dislike most of the people that share the space.

An hour goes by. It's about nine o'clock, and there is Madeleine, sitting on a chair, saying good bye to her friends. She gets up gracefully, like a mermaid slipping out of the ocean, and migrates to the door. Her body language says she has had fun, and that she will be back. My affect quietly improves as result of this form of encouragement, and I slip into a lucid fluidity, where I feel good because I have come in contact with this beautiful woman. She walks out the door. I am in rainbows. I feel lightheaded, and my mind wanders from me. I look about the room, and it feels like it is turning slowly, with no specific order in mind. In the presence of beauty, I am quietly lured out of this virile depression that makes me ill and uncomfortable. I feel a sort of steady drive to improve, and suddenly, a little bit of me is healed. And my mind slips into that in between space between not caring and not having a care in the world...

"Does anyone own a tatty blue car?" This is the first time I hear her voice.

"I don't know what kind of car it is, but it is blocking me in…" Her voice trails off.

I smile, and my emotions bubble inside my tummy. I raise my hand, like I'm in first grade.

"It's mine, and it's a Saab."

"You're blocking me in. Can you move it, please?"

I get up and promenade across the floor. I am so proud of my little Saab for picking the perfect parking spot. I follow Madeleine at a cautious distance. The vision reminds me of the beauty of ripened fruit, and contains the essence of pure sunshine. It is only thirty degrees outside, and I fumble for my keys. I crank up the Saab, and on my slightly loud stereo, New Order's song *True Faith* is devouring the silence. Madeleine, smiling, shivers, and fumbles with her keys. She has a green Corolla, and it contains the scar of a slight accident on the driver's door. I watch her open the door from the warmth of my car. She gets in, hastily, and slams the door. She starts the engine, and within seconds, she is reversing away. I am in a trance. There is nothing to do now but leave.

The worst part of going home for me is the knowledge that I will wake up miserable and upset in the morning. I don't know why. It's just how I feel all the time. However, when a woman enters the fray, I am forced to look to something for hope. It isn't the conclusion, since the conclusion has not happened- it's the hope that this one *might* be the one. The hope that something may happen that is good. The hope that you will rise to the top of her list. But as I age, I realize all too often that the women I want do not want me at all. The infinitely desirable woman, the eternally perfect woman, has no eyes for me.

They say we are supposed to hope in God for all things. I have never had the one hope I have longed for fulfilled. I trust in Him, but He does not tell me what He is doing. The mystery is too complicated, and too overwhelming. Or perhaps, I am too insignificant to merit a response. Either way, I have waited too long for an answer, from a God I know exists.

Monday morning came suddenly. I had gone to bed early, and at eight, the sun became powerful enough to wake me up. The sensual reds and pinks from the colored curtains of my room reminded me that I was still alive, and in the distant rooms of the house, I heard Kevin moving around. When I wake up, I thank God for each new day, but, for some reason, it seemed harder today than before. It was never a hurried "thank you." It was always thoughtful, complete, and sincere. I would always say to Him "thank you for this day, and thank you for the life you have breathed into my lungs. I am grateful for the wonderful life you have given me!"

But this morning I *struggled*, like a dying person, who had the life running out of him through a wound. I barely got through it, and when I was done, trying to find meaning in each word, I felt as if I had swum across the ocean. And then, within sight of the opposite shore, I drowned in knee deep water.

I don't want to be received by God until I am received by the woman I love.

Today I have an objective. I plan to go on Facebook and find out more about Madeleine, buy a copy of *Redeeming Sexuality*, and cover a show tonight. There is a new band in this area. Supposedly, the lead singer is also a grad student at FSU, and is working with two other guys from the area. I have heard good things about them, and they are playing a show tonight in Gainesville at Spec's.

First order of business: Purchase my book. I toy with idea of also buying one for Madeleine, and saying "hey, I bought this for you, because I know how excited you are about it!" Fortunately, reality sets in promptly. She probably already owns this book. And me giving her a copy would make me seem totally creepy. So I go on Amazon, and buy the book for $22.00, which is way less than everyone else seems to be selling it for, and then I log onto Facebook.

The cultural phenomenon of the social utility has transformed the way we think of everything. Now, the line between private people and not so private people has been blurred. There are those who say they are very private and don't allow people to see their Facebook profile at all. And then there are those who are not private and let everyone see the entire world they live in. And then there are those who have no Facebook, because they don't want anyone to know anything about them. And then, there are people like me, who should not have access to Facebook, because we become so emotionally involved in everyone's life. There is no real substitute for human contact, but Facebook certainly braces you for the occasion of seeing people in real life.

Madeleine is my target, and using Kristen's page, I have found her. Madeleine's last name is Townsend. She went to Franciscan, as we thought. She will not share any of her information. Her picture is in front of an abortion clinic. Or what looks like one. Or maybe I am just slowly losing my mind. But, nonetheless, I decide to send her a request. So I check the box that says friend request, and then I think "maybe I should send her a message so she knows who I am."

My mind draws a blank, and then I start writing on a piece of paper:

"Hey Madeleine, do you remember me? I had to move my car after I blocked you in. I thought we should be friends."
"Hey Madeleine, I asked around about you after I had to move my blue Saab. I found out we share a lot of the same interests, so I thought it would be nice if we were friends on Facebook."
"Hey Madeleine, I'm the guy with the blue Saab that blocked you in last night. Would you like to be friends?"
"Hey Madeleine, You may not remember me, but I am that awesome guy who was cool enough to move his car for you."
"Hey Madeleine, my name is Benedict and I think you are really beautiful, and I want to be your friend."
"Hey Madeleine, my name is Benedict, and this week I am in love with you."
"Hey Madeleine, you can call me Rad, and we are in the same study group. I think we should be friends."

"Hey Madeleine, my name is Benedict, and I saw we share a study group. I sent you a friend request. I hope you accept it."

The last one is acceptable. In other words, of all my mediocre ideas, this one is the best. And by that, I mean that there is no wonderful, fun way to solve this problem. Introducing yourself to a girl is always going to be awkward and difficult, and all the more so when you have an ulterior motive attached. I realize that doing this will change nothing, and at least she will know who I am. I say a quick prayer, and send my paper heart out to the wolves.

I have some work to do, and so I put on my entire stack of Death Cab CD's, and start plugging away at my blog. And my mind wanders into the past constantly.

A long time ago, almost five years ago, when I was eighteen, and I shipped off to college, I was a happier person. I was optimistic, and I had something to look forward to. I had this lovely plan that I was going to go get a degree, a job and find the woman God had ordained for me. I mean, what a concept! All over the Bible, God tells us that He has things in store for us that are going to be good and wonderful. And He talks about the woman being one of the most important things for a man. The man who loves the Lord always seems to love his wife, and his wife is always this amazing woman. So if God has good things in store for us, one of these good things must be the perfect wife, right? I keep asking myself this, and it made me feel amazing to think that God had this awesome plan that I couldn't imagine.

One by one, I watched my friends fall in love with women that they said were amazing and wonderful, and it seemed to pump me up. It primed me, and made me even more excited. But by the time I was twenty one, I was wondering what God intended for my life. Right before that, a terrible event happened with the girl I liked, and that night, when I dropped her off, for the first time in my life, I wondered if God even had a plan for me, and if there was a woman for me. Why had God placed my heart in such a precarious position, as to love a woman that had no true love for me? I mean, when I really committed myself to God when I was about fourteen, I gave Him my heart. I entrusted Him with it, and then, five years later, I fell in love with this girl who had no designs for our future together. It was the worst type of love extant- the kind where you love for both people in the relationship, and all of your love is wasted. I tried to be happy after that night, but, like a pervasive illness, depression began to creep in. I lost sight of the anticipatory joys of waiting, and I really, slowly, began to think that God's plan of happiness did not apply to me.

But I did not lose faith in Him. He made me, and I know He is real. I just don't believe He has a plan for me that involves a woman. But, if God doesn't have one, I won't know unless I try, right? I mean, He helps those who help themselves doesn't He? When I was a kid, my dad and I used to go to this candy shop. To keep little boys from snatching candy off the shelves, they made them really high. So my dad could reach the candy, but I couldn't. So, dad would say "Point to the one that you want, and I will get it for you." And, I would point, and he would give it to me. If I didn't like it, I would get mad at him, and he would say "Benedict, this was your choice. All I did was hand you the one you chose."

God is like that with women, I think. You ask, and then He places the one you want in your presence. And then you get to know her, and you decide if you like her or not. And if you don't like her, you feel like you wasted your time and God's time praying for this to happen. But if you do like her, something worse happens.

She doesn't like you.

Candy has no free will, and cannot choose to stop you from eating it, but the woman does, and this compounds the difficulty. Free will screws everything up. Every bad decision I have made, I have decided to make. Every bad piece of candy I picked out was my choice.

It boils down to this: There are plenty of wrongs, and there is only one right. Only one decision you will ever be happy with. Only one woman who will ever really love you, and only one piece of candy in the entire store that is actually better than all the rest. In fact, that piece is so good, that all of the other candies suck compared to it.

To make things worse, God is also giving these women the man of their dreams. I see no quality in my being that a woman would find really desirable. Let's be realistic. Women have more control than men do. Men are easy and they will settle for anything; their standards are fast and low. I do know our standards are very contagious. If a woman gets used by enough men, her standards become fast and low, too, right? I hear stories about women that will sleep with anyone, but I have met lots of these supposed women (a few of them were close friends, I think) who would never dream of having sex with me. So the truth is that some men are infinitely desirable to women, and some aren't. There are some women who are more desirable than others, and the ones that are not desirable, well, I guess they feel like me.

Of course it doesn't stop there. A good number of these desirable women are plagued with insecurities. They think they are ugly, and they are not likeable, and then they starve themselves or sleep with anyone, or starve for approval and get drunk when they don't get it, or kill themselves.

But when a man shows up who truly cares about them and loves them, he is usually not handsome, drunk or confident enough to win them over. So they feel like shit because they deliberately throw themselves at attractive, desirable men who treat them like shit.

I want to save all of them. I want to clean up everyone else's mess. Unfairly, in our awful world, one asshole can ruin a woman in a few weeks, and ten nice guys over the course of ten years who love the woman to death, and will do anything for her, cannot undo the damage. I believe that love is temporary, but damage is permanent. The only permanent love is God's love, and we do a pretty damn good job of cutting ourselves off from it. As for those ten nice guys, that asshole will indirectly damage them, too. It's contagious, and those ten nice guys will be transformed into assholes that ruin every woman they come in contact with. Misery is the reward of the man who chooses not to be an asshole, as hardly a woman desires a good and kindly man. The men I knew who found and married those perfect women must have been really great people who God made exceptions for. I think there are exceptions, but exceptions are special. I am not special, and thus, I cannot hope to be an exception. I am not exceptionally religious, and I am not exceptionally kind, responsible, intelligent, and handsome or anything good. I am exceptionally naïve, but no one gets a reward for being an idiot, unless they get killed doing it. Only a naïve idiot should really want to fix a broken woman. After all, unless you're God, it's not really possible. But I am quite stubborn, and at the back of mind, I am always willing to attempt this again.

It is later in the day after I have finished a number of entries, and I am going to have to leave for Gainsville. It's a long drive, and I leave at four. By the time I get to Spec's music, there are a bunch of people already there, and there are some bands playing that I don't really care about. I take a flier that I can post online, and scope out a wall in the room I can take notes from. I look at the playlist. There are just two bands here. The first one, Miracle Whip, I know nothing about, and hardly care for. The second band, though, is on my radar. "Archie and the Listers" is the creative project of this guy, Jim. He works with two other guys I haven't met. But I emailed Jim to let him know I wanted an interview with him for the *Indie Chronicler* and he knows I am going to be here. On the flier, the band is spelled "ArchieandtheListers," as it appears on their album. I listened to it once, and I liked it. It had kind of a racy feel, with sticky guitar hooks and crunchy, compressed rhythms. Jim has a distant, austere voice, like the guy from Interpol, and he has contemplative lyrics that talk about how confusing life is. I have never seen him in person, but I'll know who he is when he starts to play.

Miracle Whip sucks, as I expected them to. They sing about girls, and beer pong, and they use power chords that I have heard a hundred times. But they are having fun, and I am jealous, because I know women like this sort of crap. I sit down in the corner, listening, and trying to pretend I am in an empty room.

So, finally, Archie and the Listers come on, and I am forced to acknowledge how full the little music shop is. I take a good hard look at the band. Jim, the lead singer, looks familiar to me, but I can't place him. The lighting is dim, and the guitars begin to chatter as they warm up on the tiny stage. The other two guys look kind of gnarly. One has a huge beard, and the other dreds, and they both look like they are tired. The bassist, the guy with the beard, has a really loud voice. He yells to the sound guy to turn up his bass amp. The sound guy yells back that if it's too loud, it will drown the guitar. The bassist shoots him a finger, and tells him to turn up the bass. A few seconds later, the bassist hits his notes, and it is clear that the sound guy did what he was told to do.

The drummer is nonchalantly setting up his snare, and he doesn't seem to mind that he has a tough job. Jim is tuning his guitar, and hiding from the light. But as soon as he stands up, I see the outline of his face, and realize that he was the new guy on the couch last night. I wasn't totally sure, and I tried to convince myself it was not true, but I had the feeling that my first guess was dead on.

Their first song is called "*Alias, Activated*," and it drives you along with a steady, aggressive guitar riff. In person, it sounds a lot worse than on the CD, but I can still follow the song pretty well, and it makes me think of how much I hate the sound quality at most of these shows. I write down a lyric that stands out to me; 'Everywhere there is someone looking to find you, hide yourself fast, or activate your alias.'

His other songs are just as interesting. After four more compositions, something tells me that Jim has put serious amounts of time into his music. He has careful, catchy riffs, and I feel like I am in the presence of someone who has promised not to have any bad songs. I strongly anticipate my time with him.

After their set is over, at ten, I wait for The Listers to break down, and stand at the stage. Jim is putting away his cables, and looks over at me, standing there. You can tell he is older, maybe twenty eight. He stops for a second. "Can I help you, bro?" He inquires.

"I'm Benedict, the guy who is supposed to interview you for *Indie Chronicler*."

Jim thinks about it for a brief second, and then he sizes me up. "Give me twenty minutes, and then I'll be ready."

"Jim, can I help with anything?"

"Umm, sure. Carry this box of cables out to my van. It's there by the door." He points to a plain looking Chevy cargo van on the street. So I carry that box out, and he hands me an amp, and then a guitar case, with instructions to place it in a specific part of the van. Then, after I carry his stack with him, piece by piece, he goes back to the stage to check for any missing bits, and I follow him around like a lost child.He sits down on the back of the van, and he asks me to come over. "Where are your other two guys?" I ask.

"Oh, they are probably talking to girls, at a bar. I don't like attention, so I let them have all of it. That's our agreement. They play what I want them to, and they get to have all the attention."

Something tells me this guy has a story- the kind of story that shouldn't get posted online. I have a feeling this interview is starting, so I try to keep the questions focused on the music.

"Jim, before we start, please don't tell me anything that you don't want anyone else to know."

He looks at me, and laughs. "First off, I'm gay. If you want to, Benedict, you can leave now." The silence is awkward. Then Jim laughs.

"I'm too much of a womanizer to be gay. You can leave now if you want!" He's still laughing.

"Why would I leave? I saw you the other night at our meeting for the new book we're reading."

"Well, I didn't see you there." He looks at me again, hard.

"... So when I talk about my music, I have to talk about my faith. Most guys are not interested in associating the two, and a lot of the meaning is under the table. The guys in this band aren't religious, but they like working with me. Either way though, it's their decision, not mine."

"So, Jim, what inspires you?"

He looks at me again. "What kind of stupid-ass question is that? I just told you what inspires me. What inspires you?"

I have never had the question turned back around on me in any seriousness, and I struggle to come to an answer.

"Come on Benedict, we're waiting."

I choke. And then it comes out. "Nothing inspires me to be creative except when I see a...beautiful woman."

Jim looks at me with familiar hostility. "What do you mean?" He grumbles. The look on his face suggests he finds me immature and pedantic.

"The mystery of the feminine. The desire for a woman. It inspires me to do everything. It's like, it gives my life some kind of meaning."

I suddenly realize what I said, and I feel very, very awkward. It sounds so juvenile, and I feel like a pair of hands is now at my throat.

"Sounds like you're trying to find a nice way to say that you want to get laid. A *polite* way. We all find ways to grow out of it..."

"Oh yeah, why?" I stammer, suddenly feeling relieved.

"This is about me, not you. Let's talk about my songs."

He smiles a little bit, but it is a loaded smile. It was on his face to hide something else. But I honor his request.

So, at about eleven P.M., I left Gainesville, and headed back via I-75 and I-10 west. I was intrigued by Jim, and his songs. Even more intriguing was that he had openly admitted to being like I was, and then he grew out of it. He wasn't hung up on women. He was doing something besides sitting around writing songs about how girls have pissed him off and made him feel inadequate. But the mind of a fool drifts back to the follies that he has indulged in. All I think about is my current state. If there is a future state of happiness for me, where I am stable, content and my life has meaning, I can't see it happen. I drive sleepily back to Tally, listening to Pavement plus my noisy muffler. I was home by two A.M., and I passed out. Tomorrow holds great expectations.

In the morning when I woke up, I couldn't be at my computer fast enough. I had to see if Madeleine accepted my friend request.

The moment of anticipation burns inside you, like a slow heating coil. You're nervously hungry, but your appetite is gone. You want a drink of water, but you feel like you're drowning. You really want to know the truth, but in reality, what you need is a sweet, comforting lie. I am friends with a lot of girls, and I had the same amount of nervous anxiety before becoming friends with the ones I really liked. And, honestly, this one is no different. It's just that all of those missions failed miserably when these girls were clued into my motives. Girls are oblivious; it seems to take them years to figure out that I like them. Or maybe they like the attention (but how would I know?).

I bite the bullet, acknowledging that there are only two possibilities: she has accepted my request, or she has not. I brace myself for the moment, log in, and go to my wall.

"Congratulations, you are now friends with Madeleine Townsend," I tell myself.

I go to my message box, and find she has returned my message. Of course, it is not what I hoped for. What I really wish, and hope for, is that she sends me a message that says "I have been waiting for you to friend me ever since I saw you that night. I think you're really cool and I can't wait to get to know you better!"

Instead, she leaves a brief note" "Hey, I'm glad you're interested in our group. Hope you get a lot out of it. God bless, Maddy."

Women are amazingly dismissive. Of course, when they say something so cordial to you, there is always a cryptic meaning that they are too afraid to blatantly spell out to you, because it is "rude," or it "isn't like them."

What her message really says is as follows: "Hey weirdo,

only a guy as creepy as you would friend me after moving a car for me. You need to come to our group, because you have serious problems, and hopefully, you will reform yourself. This is only possible through divine intervention, and you need Jesus very badly in your life."

Based on the tone of her message, I can clearly see she is unexcited about my desire to befriend her. Now, I bet she's asking everyone else in that group if they are friends with me also, and if she needs to be careful around me.

I look at my phone, and the time is later than I thought it would be. I have to post a report on the show, and I am late by about an hour already. So I start writing about Archie and the Listers, and Jim, and how cool he is, and why his music is going to go really, really far. I anticipate a major breakout for his band, and hopefully I am right. I talk about his faith, and how it gives him an excuse to write. And then, when I run out of things to write about, I go back and edit everything, and go eat something.

I have this great idea: my Saab looks awful, and the high today is sixty seven degrees, so I am going to wash it. It's this gray-blue color, with a black vinyl interior. It has funky wheels and on the back it has two stickers: A Pixies sticker on the rear hatch, and 'Northeast Florida Saab Owners Club' sticker on the bumper. I love this car. I would fold down the rear seats, open the lift-back up, and give the girl from college I liked back rubs. We would lie down and look at the sky when I would go see her, and I would bring my guitar, and play songs I wrote for her. She would giggle, and ask for more back rubs, and when I would offer her my hand, she wouldn't take it, but she would allow me to hold hers, and she would not hold back. And after I found out about the first guy she slept with, the Saab was where I would turn up Jets to Brazil, and sit there and feel miserable. I would drive up and down twenty-seven into Suwanee County, and brood, and listen to more good music, and turn around and go home. My life in college was a wonderful, austere and miserable experience. And I lived it out in the back of my car.

33

The gray dirty water from my roof, hood and trunk runs off in streams. It reminds me of my own vitality.

Three
A short introduction to Lucia

I shouldn't really tell you her name, and I don't really even think of her name when I think of her. So, when I am forced to acknowledge she exists, still, and she has a name, and a life, and an identity, she is immediately back in my frame of consciousness, and the ups and downs of our life together become even more evident. She comes alive at shows, at mass, in my dreams, and occasionally in the shower. She jumps out of my favorite songs, making me cry and teasing me with her insufferable beauty. I look back on a crystal clear past, and treasure the memories I have of her. They are all I have, and they are all I will ever have.

She was Lucia, and occasionally I would call her "The Princess," especially when I think of the times that she hurt me. The more miserable I felt, the more she rose up on the pedestal. The more royal and venerable she became, as she ruined me bit by bit.

I met Lucia in my first week at college. We had seen each other at orientation, and I had not forgotten her. She was lovely, with her long, dark brown hair. She was five-foot four inches. She wore glasses that concealed her dark eyes. She had this goofy smile. It was filled with pride and laughter, like she was having fun all the time, and she was very confident. She had a beautiful body, with heavenly curvatures. I spent many nights thinking about what it would be like to make love to her. I still do.

Many men desired that body, and she, despite her solid, Roman Catholic faith, also desired them. She said getting drunk wasn't really a sin, but that it impaired her judgment, and she made bad decisions while she was drunk. But she made those decisions when her full decision making faculties were not available, and thus, she didn't have the ability to discern right from wrong when she was drinking. In the grand scheme of things, that worked out pretty well for her, however, she would wake up next to those guys, and she would be sober again the next morning. She always told me what happened the night before, but she never, *ever,* talked about the morning after. "That's very personal," she would stammer, almost like there was a secret ritual she engaged in to make meaningless sex more meaningful.

Anyway, I must have sent out some kind of signal to her during that orientation, because when I saw her two weeks later at the book store, she looked at me and smiled. I looked back at her, asking "It seems as if you remember me. Is that *possible*?"

She giggled. Her nose was a little bit bigger than I recalled it being, but other than that she was the angel I remembered, and I was ecstatic.

"Who are you?" I gently inquired.

"I am Lucy, but my full name is Lucia Capella. And you are?"

"I'm Benedict. Benedict Radmeier, I guess."

"Are you lying? Do people ever call you Rad?"

It was the start of a beautiful downward spiral. Of course, there was that three month grace period, where she was innocent, and I was discovering her mysteries. And, of course, the start of college was my number one priority. But I left that first encounter with a phone number, and it was like an adrenaline shot to the heart. It was the drug induced stupor I needed to look forward to things, and I would not want another introduction to college.

When we hung out the first time, she had this cunning beauty about her that drove me mad. There was no touching among us, initially. Just a hug or two, when we greeted each other or when we were departing. I knew she was attracted to me, but I never understood why. She never really built me up, but she said that I was funny, and I had this gentleness about me. She also said she enjoyed the time we spent together, which, according to what I later learned, means she loved the attention that I gave her. Among the ironies was that if she had actually told me that this was the only reason we were friends, I would have gladly accepted it. I was more or less smitten (or doomed) from day one, and at night, when I look back at these illusory correlations of attention and romance, I realize I had no choice. They were merely one and the same.

One day, she placed her hand next to mine, and I began to touch her lovely fingers, and then her palm. I studied the little lines on her hand, and the valleys that formed between her fingers. I looked at her painted nails and her excellent finger tips. I touched these little parts of her body with the greatest delicacy. I loved her right hand especially, and it became clear that I was allowed to *hold* it.

Please be aware of my naivety before I say this. Women, like Lucia, are looking for two things: a man to be a romantically involved source of conflict for them and a man to shower attention on them. In other words, they want to pursue and repair an imperfect man, and then run into the arms of man who does not threaten them, very much like I was for her. In my simple mind, I was hoping that one day she would see the benefit of being with me, and thus change her mind. Matter of factly, as we spent more and more time together, and would go on things that looked like dates, I began to wonder if we were in a relationship, or if the opposite was happening, and we were drifting further from being in one.

We spent those first three months staying up late at night, holding hands, going on picnics, talking on the phone, going to movies and studying together. It seemed substantial- we would talk about books, and films, and our future. We had little in common in the music department. She much preferred rap and reggae to my indie rock, and it almost seemed like she was about to be infected by the culture of college. Her innocence had evaporated like gasoline. She was showing me the last puddle of it. But part of the mystery of each woman is the secret life she lives. Lucia had slowly found, in the limelight of her high school after glow, that part of the college experience which no amount of "innocent, nice guy being madly in love with you" can distract a girl from.

The trouble started when we were out one night, on a date, or something like a date. We drove into downtown Apalachicola, and we were gazing in the windows of the little shops. It was so damn cute, like it was painted in watercolors.

Lucia and I were holding hands, and walking slowly down a side street, and she seemed unnaturally excited and frustrated at the same time. In a few seconds, I knew she would admit that she had something to tell me. It wasn't the something one would anticipate; we had already had that conversation. But instead of taking it slow, this was the moment in time that defined my hopeless pursuit.

"I have something to share with you," she said.

Translation: "There's something I have been withholding from you for a while…" I nodded for her to continue.

"But I can't really tell you right now. I just want to enjoy tonight with you."

Translation: "I am about to redefine the nature of our relationship with what I am about to tell you, but I am enjoying the attention right now, so I will wait until later to emotionally castrate you."

Suddenly, I am right back in that moment and I am touching it with my fingers.

I ask her if it is bad news. She says that it will not change our friendship. We walk back to my car. I do everything to hide my frustration, and mask all of my feelings.

I am suddenly alone, and I pretend that she is a ghost, and I am a machine, and neither of us has feelings. I start faking my moves. I smile, open the car door, and then close it gracefully. She says something and I detect a bit of nervousness, and then I pretend nothing happened. I start the Saab's engine, and put on Coldplay, and carefully select my gears. I rev the engine high and long. I keep smiling at her, telling her that I really enjoyed our night, and that I like being her friend. She never really said much besides "I told him about you. He's fine with it."

When I look back on it, I know that I lied through my teeth, in my actions and in my words. In that moment I was falling apart and miserable. I felt like my entire relationship with her was in failure mode. I was relieved when I dropped her off, and I hugged her like you would a greatly disliked relative at a funeral. What I should have done was stand up and give her an ultimatum, or declare my love for her, or cry...something, anything, really.

For a few hours the next day (when it was too late), I sat around and thought about it. My first resolution was to never call her again, and I followed it up by destroying her phone number. My second resolution was to tell her how I felt about her, if she did try to reach me again, mostly because I had nothing to lose. My final resolution was to find out who this guy was.

I sat around for another twenty minutes or so, and then (because I knew her number by heart), called and asked her how her day was going. I had to tell it to a voicemail because she didn't answer the phone. I seriously thought about leaving her a voicemail that said I was in love with her, but I figured that was taking the easy way out. I didn't want to get rid of her- I wanted her to love me.

By five I was at student dining. I hadn't eaten all day, and it was Saturday, so student dining was vacant. Those October afternoons in Northwest Florida were hot as hell. I sat there in a white shirt and gym shorts eating a turkey sandwich, trying to pretend I was hungry. Evenings were quiet, because I really didn't have enough friends to keep me entertained, and at our little Catholic school in Apalachicola, everyone was busy getting drunk on Saturday. I needed to find out what was going on, and why it was bothering me so much.

By virtue of fate, Lucia lived in the apartment complex very near mine. She had two roommates, one of which was always at her boyfriend's place, and another who was always studying. I could drive down Bluff Road, turn into her apartment complex, make a quick left, and see whose cars were there. I wanted to see her apartment badly, but it wasn't visible from the road. I saw a car there, though, that looked like a car a guy would drive. No girl would be driving an '88 Caprice with ugly wheels and a bright red paint job. It was right in front of her apartment, and I had never seen it before. I drove home, silently, feeling like I had just violated her privacy. I had no other reason to be in that apartment complex.

Everything was pretty quiet until she asked me over on Monday to help with her math homework. I was quite good at math and science, and she used it to her benefit. So, I went over there, resolved to tell her how I felt about her, and still not really knowing what to say. I felt like she was up to something by now, but I had no way of knowing what it was. I was too emotionally involved to care anyway, and I figured that the only way this could end was badly. So I pushed through, and when we were done studying, we lay down on her floor, talking about meaningless things. Then she did it. She gently placed her hand on the carpet, next to her body, fingers open.

"My hand hurts from writing too much. You should make it feel better," she whined in the cutest way.

This was the subconscious signal she sent out when she wanted me to take her hand, and often I would wonder what it really meant. So I waited a few minutes, and then, gently, like a thief, I stole the space between her hand and mine.

"Why do we do this?"

It was a hard, stupid question, but I needed to ask it. She looked at me suspiciously. "What do you mean?"

"Does this mean anything to you? I mean, do you believe that there is any significance in us holding hands?" I was struggling to be calm.

The woman's number one defense statement was launched.

"Benedict (notice that she used my name- she was talking as directly to me as she ever had), we're just friends."

"Just..." It didn't hurt her at all to say that. In fact, I think she enjoyed it. This statement is as lethal as a curare-tipped arrow, and as venomous as a scorpion.

That statement indicated that she A) knew I liked her, and B) she wanted to define the relationship we had.

I dragged my arm away from her hand, across the carpet. I was limp and paralyzed. I needed a strong drug to cut myself off from reality. Being friends was not good enough for me.

"Why?" I looked at her and mouthed the word without feeling myself say it. It was as if someone else had asked for me. She looked at me angrily, clenching her teeth.

Her answer was as predictable as it could have been. Girls never have a new explanation for anything. They have learned how to ignore boys and tell them off. They have learned to use terms like "just friends" and "I like things the way they are" to control boys like me. But there is one word that really sticks out in my mind, like a festering wound.

Chemistry. Fucking Chemistry, the magic word that signifies inadequacy. It's the only excuse they can come up with, because it's the only thing that matters to them.

"Benedict, we don't have chemistry. You're my friend. I feel safe with you. I like being your friend."

Her plan was to make me think that it made her supremely happy to be my friend, but I was aware of her trick.

"Lucy, does it make you happier that we are friends and not in a relationship?"

She nodded.

"Lucy, does it make you happier to be friends with me than in a relationship with anyone?"

She looked at me blankly. My jealousy was burning on my tongue. We were both angry- she because there was no way that she could keep using me for unattached attention, and me, well, because I knew the truth.

"Lucy," I whispered awkwardly. "Lucy, can you tell I like you?"

"It just needs to be what it is. We shouldn't talk anymore if you feel this way."

"There's someone else, isn't there?"

Her eyes burned. She was trying to look as ambiguous as possible so that she could avoid answering my question.

"Fuck you, Benedict. That's not the issue here."

"Have you kissed him yet?" My world was still innocent. People didn't fuck. They kissed and maybe slept next to each other. "It doesn't matter." Her expression suggested that what she had done with this guy was much worse than I thought it had been.

The fire in her eyes burned brightly, and she clearly wanted me to leave. She needed time to cool down, and I needed time to figure out what my next move would be.

It's amazing what men will do for a woman they love. They will stoop to utter acts of self defamation, just to show that they do, indeed, wish to please her. I was in downtown Miami one year, in the summer. There was a man on the street, selling wilted roses, on Lincoln Road, down by the clubs. I stopped and asked him, very politely, if men ever bought any roses from him.

In his broken English, he responded that he would not be there if no one was buying them. A few minutes later, I watched an intoxicated man buy one that he promptly gave to an immodestly clad woman that was wearing the layers of a long night of clubbing and drinking.

A certain type of man is willing to do this, and, given the conditions, it very well could have been me. If I *thought* Lucia would love me if I gave her one of those damn wilted roses, then I would have bought one without question. But what woman would fall for something so juvenile? It simply wasn't good enough, humiliating enough or embarassing enough.

I had no real idea what was going to fix my situation with her. I felt stupid making assumptions, but I think that our instinct guides our assumptions, and instinctively, I had a sense that she was seeing someone else. But even more so, it wasn't about her seeing someone else. It was about her rejecting me.

I believed, and still believe, that Lucia felt the following way about me:

-She found me acceptably attractive, but not in a way that really got her heart going.
-She felt safe with me.
-She had no idea what she truly wanted.
-She did not see us ever being romantically involved, short term or long term.
-She did not appreciate me.

This way my first taste of feeling grossly inadequate. I had felt inadequate before, mostly with girls in high school, but the majority of these girls from my high school did not interest me in the least. I was focused on getting good grades, and I had a job at Publix stocking shelves. Girls were nice to me in high school. I was nice to them. I liked some of them, but I was busy trying to get everything in order for college.

And then you get to college, and you're like "Now what?" Your parents no longer control your life, and you have some liberties you didn't have before. Now girls can come in to your room, and you can get closer to them physically. I think the closer you get to a woman physically, the closer you get to her emotionally. And of course, that's when you begin to evaluate yourself.

Inadequacy begins with a question from one's self. "Am I adequate to love this woman? Am I good enough to make this woman happy? Is she happy with me, and who I am?" The woman never says to the man "I am going to enter into a romantic relationship with you as soon as I determine whether or not you are adequate."

I don't even know where the question came from, but it has plagued me ever since I realized I had a fear of being inadequate. That night, when Lucia told me I was good enough to be her friend, but I wasn't quite the material her boyfriends were made of, made me feel this gross level of inadequacy.

Four

Our study group convened at seven thirty, and I got there just in time. No one had their books, except for the elite of the group. I was still humming the tune to Interpol's song "Say Hello to the Angels." Everyone looked at me like something was wrong, but I took a seat on the white cloth sofa against the wall. Madeleine had not arrived yet, and I prayed she would sit down next to me. In fact, most people had not shown up. I sat up straight and tried to look inviting and comfortable. I felt like someone had knocked the wind out of me. I had an expectation attached to my presence, and if it was not to be fulfilled, I would be unhappy the entire night. I kept watching the door, and looking beyond it. I would get the shivers, seeing headlights. When would Madeleine come? Was she going to ever show up? Was she afraid of coming? Did she know I was going to be here? Did she change her night because she knew I was here? My friend request must have ruined everything.

I believe that when you nervously wait for something to happen- when you burn with anticipation for it- it extends the amount of time it takes for it to actually happen. God does not give us what we want when we really want it. He seems to know that we will react with too much emotion to it, and so He drags it out a bit, until we get tired of hoping. Then, when we stop expecting it, He allows the girl to walk through the door, and we are able to control ourselves when she does.

It is now 7:45, and Madeleine has not shown up. Kristen opens the meeting in prayer, with a meaningful, introspective narration about how important this book is. She goes on to ask God for guidance about what to do, and then closes with a Hail Mary.

She opens the study with a question. "What do you guys think God's original plan for human sexuality was?"

I take a quick look around. There are six people here. Kristen is here, of course, then Xavier, and then Sam. There's another girl who is sort of plain, and then there is Alaina, who is cute but unavailable. And then, here I sit.

At 7:48 Kevin walks in. He sits right down next to me, and takes up the rest of the couch. I look at him, earnestly. "Can you please move?" I ask him nicely.

Poor Kevin, I just threw him under the bus. But you know how these things go. He gets a chair while Xavier tells us how God made man to love the woman unconditionally. I am not paying attention. Instead, I am quietly seething inside because Madeleine has not shown up.

At 7:51 P.M., my fears are relieved. I am flipping through some photocopied notes about Joseph North (He is from England.

England!), and the door cracks open, and Madeleine shuffles in. She looks around the room, seeing if seating is available. She sees the open spot on the couch next to me. There are no chairs left. She looks even harder at the seat on the couch, and then looks at me quickly.

"Hey, Kristen, Do you have any more chairs?"

"Look in the kitchen, dear."

I can't believe what just happened. She made a conscious decision to not sit next to me. She thinks I am a bad person. I feel a tinge of despair. My hand shakes as I turn the pages. Kevin looks at me, with a smirk on his lower lip.

Of course, I have no choice but to follow the dialogue in the room. It is Kevin's turn. "I think God created sex as a way of helping the man and the woman, who are committed to each other, to become open to each other in a very special way. Sex is the pinnacle of closeness. The summit of intimacy lies within it."

Kristen smiles at him. "I have a feeling that J.P. Two would agree with that."

Now it's my turn. I get to be honest. "I believe that God created sex, and then made it our deepest desire. He uses this deep desire to control us, so that we are forced to trust in Him. He attaches conditions to it, so that we are always worried about offending Him if we violate these conditions. So the man finds himself struggling for approval from the woman and from God if he is to feel fully satisfied with this deep desire for God-given love and intimacy."

Kristen, and more so Xavier, were not very happy with my response. It was written all over their faces. "Radmeier, don't you think that you're being a little bit short sighted? God didn't give us sex to torture us." The thing I hated most about that statement was how Xavier stared right at me when he said it. I would have accepted his response if he had not addressed me so strongly.

"Xavier, I think you're wrong. If sex wasn't mean to torture us, why do we, as a society, have such an uncontrollable desire for it? I mean, if you're addicted to pornography, don't you think that if your desire for sex wasn't torturing you, you could just get up and

44

walk away from it?"

"Let's try to remember that this is a co-ed event!" Kristen says gently. Her comment pisses me off. She wanted me here, and she knows what comes with my participation.

I keep talking. "Sex tortures us because is a strong desire that we rarely have the opportunity to fulfill. Of all our desires, it is the most pointless, the most destructive, the most productive, and the most elusive. It controls everything, it is everywhere. If something you want badly is being shoved at you in all directions, and you can't fulfill your desire for it, how would you feel?"

"Rad, are you saying that sex has a greater presence in the world than its creator does?" Alaina asks. I thought about her question. My desire for God has never been as strong as my desire for sexual intimacy with a woman.

"I am, and the desire for sex, at least when you're a typical man, is far more real and present than God is."

"Don't you think people just ignore God?" Xavier comments.

Kevin chimes in. "God's presence is greater- I think your priorities are all out of line."

I am forced to retort. "I am talking about our society, not necessarily myself! Why do you have to make it seem like I am just talking about myself?"

Everyone seems quiet. Then Madeleine speaks up. "He's right. Sex controls the secular world. It is a beautiful creation of God that has been perverted by the culture of death."

"Your view is supported by the text" Kristen assures her. It was okay because she said it. If I had said it, at least in my own way, no one would have listened. I shut up after that.

For the rest of the discussion, I didn't open my mouth. I watched Madeleine out of the corner of my eye. She didn't look at me the entire time. I mean, she might have glanced in my direction, but there was nothing deliberate in her gaze. These sorts of things only serve to drive me insane anyway.

The meeting is over at nine, and I try to get away. I am tired of hiding in the cracks of the couch, and I look at the door, hoping to make an escape. I am still nervous. People must be contemplating my statement earlier. They are cold and unfriendly, as if I violated their trust and committed some sort of heresy. But finally Kevin says something. "Radmeier, it's not that I disagree with you. I just think that there are better ways to say the things you said."

"Ok Kevin, I'll publish a 300 page encyclical about why sex governs our economy, our homes, our relationships, etc."

Kevin can see the bitterness in my expression. He softens a bit. I continue. "This is the ugly truth. If we can't be comfortable talking about it here, how are we supposed to really fix anything? We need to get over the inappropriateness of it, and have a discussion like normal people do."

No, Christians are not normal. Real Christians have something different about them, and depending on the circumstances, that something can be both good and bad.

Kevin looks off into space. This is more than he bargained for. These silly Catholics, they clearly know what the problem is, and they are too afraid to say a damn thing about it. The greater difficulty, however, lies in understanding the problem, not just knowing what it is. I know what all my problems are, but I don't understand them at all. Maybe Joseph North understands me.

Madeleine is sitting on her chair reading. She just got done talking to Kristen, and now she is glancing at the little packet Kristen gave her. I pretend that this is not reality, and I disconnect myself from it. I take six generous steps towards her, and ask her how she is.

"Oh hey," she glances upwards at me. I smile back, like an idiot.

"How's your blue car?"

Indeed, she recognized me. I feel a bit more relieved. "It's cool. I hope I didn't offend you with my comment." I smile at her again.

Kristen announces something, but I am only half-listening. "Feel free to keep a journal as you read, so you can share your thoughts with us."

I look over at Madeleine. She isn't smiling.

"I want to ask you a question, Benedict."

I nod for her to go ahead with it.

"Do you really believe that sex is greater than God?"

In my heart, I knew that I had always given women more attention than I had my Lord. I wondered what that meant, and why I was like that.

"I believe that men desire sex, and they don't know they need God." If that wasn't the truth, I don't know what the truth is.

The expression on her face indicated that she understood exactly what I was trying to tell her. I was too nervous to say anything else, and I was hoping she would respond. I am more afraid of her than I am of anyone in this room.

My bitterness about human sexuality doesn't stem from unfulfilled desires. It stems from the way people fulfill those desires, and what we (and I have been) forced to do to fulfill them. You can't snap your fingers and hope it goes away. Every time I looked at porn, for example, I knew I was doing the wrong thing, but there was almost no other choice. You're stuck with this drive- this urge- that you play a back and forth battle with. One minute you control it, and the next minute it controls you, and it makes you do things that you truly regret. While pornography is bad, it certainly doesn't hold a candle to having drunken anonymous sex, raping someone, or even getting into a relationship with someone just because you want their body.

Every time I go to confession and have to discuss porn, and all the actions and ideas that go along with it, I don't exactly rejoice. There is no nice way to say "I abused the gift of my sexuality," but to a single man, who is a shameful devotee of the porn industry, sex is not a gift. Instead, it's an unwanted burden. Then, of course, people at church tell us over and over again that God wants us to use this desire responsibly. How can you use something responsibly when it controls you? When it controls an entire country? When everyone is fine with it having the power it does? Fighting your sex drive means fighting a losing battle.

In all honesty, the root of all my prayers revolves around this distressing "gift."

"God, when will you send me the right woman?"

"God, please make me good enough for her."

"God, please tell me what You're doing."

"God, please tell me why You're allowing me to suffer like this."

"God, take this away from me or fulfill it."

"God, I'm sorry I did what I had to do to deal with this."

"God, why do I feel so miserable? I couldn't control myself any longer."

"God, stop torturing me with this desire. I hate the way I feel when it's not fulfilled, and I hate the way I feel when I try to fulfill it. Why don't you send me a sign of hope? At least the promise I will find a woman in the future, so I can hope for the fulfillment of it?"

And no answer comes. I pray these little prayers over and over again, in great, deep honesty- and nothing comes of it. I don't look at porn all the time. I seem to trade off between having two good weeks and one bad one- or vice versa.

My assignment for Wednesday is simple. I have to interview "Drive-in Movie," an emo band with a small following that's playing a show at FSU. I don't have to cover the show, though, so I just show up beforehand with my media pass and see if they have five minutes. One of the security guys (Or at least that's what his shirt says he is) alerts the band that I'm here for an interview. The bassist says he has a few minutes, and the keyboardist says he will be there in a bit. They have a new, self titled album. I ask for a comment on what the album is about, and the lead singer gives up thirty seconds.

"Our album is about our childhoods, and how the world has changed as we have become adults."

As meaningless a statement as any, but I wasn't asked for a good statement, just a passable statement. In the music world, mediocrity is often veiled by pretentiousness anyway. The way the lead singer said it, he almost made it seem as the world changed because *they* all grew up. Of course, listening to the album, it was really about girls growing up into women, and continually breaking boys' hearts. The bassist and the keyboardist both spewed the same crap all the other victims of a giant ego-turned-lead singer spew. They play music for the fun of it, and like being on the road, and it has its difficulties, but, you know, blah blah blah. I carefully record all of this meaningless crap and then vomit it up into my blog that evening. This was just another entry like any other.

This job has left me perpetually bored. I think sometimes that if I had a fulfilling job, I could turn my focus away from women and I could solve problems that had actual solutions. When I graduated with my degree in statistics last year, I had it all planned out: I would land a job that would connect me with real people, and I would record life in ways that matter, ways that I could observe. Then, my love of music made me want to write for publications that cared about music, but those sorts of jobs were elusive. And by some miracle, this job came along, and now I hate it.

The next day, I am checking my email, and I notice a short message from Francisco, my boss. I open it, not expecting what is about to happen.

Benedict,
It is unfortunate that I must inform you of this. I have hired a new blogger to replace you who has a more enthusiastic writing style. Your posts, as of late, have been more and more dismal, and they are not helping to attract readers and advertisers. I think you will be happier doing something else, and I am going to encourage you to accept this without being upset. I feel you have outgrown the Chronicler *and it is in in your best interest to find a job in your field.*

Best of luck,
Francisco Menendez

Not only do I hate my job, but it is no longer my job to hate. I try to see things objectively, and I suppose all of my sour feelings about writing are paying off. I hated all the bands on the scene, and now I don't have to see them anymore. Now I need to think about how I am going to pay my bills.

It wasn't the sort of job I could raise a family with, anyway. It showed no promise, and it was just something to keep me entertained and sheltered. Now I don't have to wake up at twelve P.M. and go to bed at four A.M., all the while smelling like smoke and beer. I suppose I am fortunate to lose such a great job that most people would kill to have. I also think that the guy who is getting this job will hate it just as much as I did. He will just need a few months.

I can't solve my job issue right now, so I begin to read Joseph North's book. As I anticipated, it's thick, and the print is tiny. It smells like a missal, and the pages are slightly glossy. On the cover, there is a picture of Michelangelo's *David*, but instead of an exposed midriff, poor David has had his genitals pixilated. The cover has a sort of comic appeal to it, much less serious and flowery than I had expected it to be, almost like this book was written as a joke to the conservative American Church. I turn it over to the back, and I see a nice picture of Mr. North holding a pen, dawdling over a pad, and looking very contemplative indeed. The blurred picture heavily conceals the smirk on his face, and, in true British fashion, he cites C.S. Lewis as his inspiration. He has dedicated the book to his wife, Jessica, and, somehow, it was granted a Nihil Obstat. The Imprimatur was given by a bishop in England, and there is a small picture of Pope John Paul in the corner. Below it, the aging pontiff provided a tiny quote: *"The future starts today, not tomorrow."*

I turn to the first page. Mr. North has written the reader a note:

"In our present culture it is ever more worrying that the

50

entire purpose of God's plan for sexuality be wiped out, and a new zeitgeist of rampant indulgence be installed in its place. I am not saying this to alarm anyone, but rather to inform all of you that your personal decisions are going to either stop this change or give it forward momentum.

God created our sexuality to be enjoyed and cherished, in such a way that it gives us immense pleasure and stirs the deepest desires of our souls. Truly, the creation of human sexuality can easily be argued to carry the most significance of any of the attributes to humanity that God has bestowed on us. In short, sexuality is the pinnacle of God's creativity. It is no wonder that Satan has tried to destroy it with this so-called culture of death.

But who are we to exercise control over God's plan for humanity? We, as Christians, have been so afraid of this gift that we don't talk about it. We have thrown it out, and trampled on it, and now, this most mysterious, significant creation is left to rot. The devil has found this little treasure, centuries ago, and has been converting it into a means to ruin the plan of salvation that God has intended for us.

My brothers and sisters, it is ours, and we MUST take it back.

I invite you to leave your comfort zone, as I do my best to explain this secret mystery that so many in the Church have been afraid to share, and so many others have devoted an immense amount of time to understanding. I am fully aware of the consequences of putting forth such a doctrine, but I assure you, all of this has its origins in sound Roman Catholic doctrine. My job, as ordained by God, is to bring it forth into the world. God is love, and He wishes for us to experience love, not just between Him and us, but between man and woman, between families, between strangers, and across the entire world. In order to do this, we must understand His plan of creation, and how it culminates with the redemption of human sexuality.

The book certainly carries some sort of weight (other than its dismal physical mass). I had always believed that, down to the tiniest detail, human sexuality was creative and brilliant, and more so, it was the most brilliant thing God had ever done. Why would men think about something worthless every few seconds, and why would entire corporations make a fortune off of it? Beauty in a woman would be almost meaningless without the added element of sex, and sex would be meaningless if it was not so difficult to attain. Truthfully, it is getting easier, and, as such, it has become more worthless by the minute.

Now that I am jobless, I have decided to divide my time between reading and looking for a new job. It seems like a good idea, so that I won't wait in suspense for whatever item comes along next. Admittedly, the job I had never felt like a job anyway, and it will be hard to adjust to normal life with a boss, and a schedule, and all the crap that goes along with it.

Five
I take out a notebook, and write "journal" on the cover. I draw a small cross, and on the bottom of the cover, I write a small quote:

"Those who are well do not need a physician. I have come for sinners, and not for the righteous." This simple quote is how I know Jesus actually loves me. I open the journal, and begin to write.

Day one
I have always believed that God made us to be miserable while we were single. Mr. North went on and on about the Garden of Eden, and how Adam had everything, and at the end of the day, all he wanted was a woman. So, contrary to the idea that Eden was perfect, it wasn't, because deep down inside, Adam was lonely. He was missing something huge.

My life isn't perfect, and I know I am also missing something. Adam was willing to leave paradise to follow his bride, so that means he either really loved her, or really loved sex, but no matter what, he couldn't live without Eve.

Despite the horrible reactions I may get from the people in this group, I think Eve performed some sort of wild, crazy sexual act on Adam to get him to eat the apple. I am not suggesting this to be sacrilegious. Rather, I think Adam had to have some extraordinary impetus to drive him to take the forbidden fruit. Other parties might say that he ate it because he wanted so badly to be with Eve. He knew that because she had eaten the apple, she would be banished. He wanted nothing more than to follow his bride, so if she were banished, he would banish himself, for her sake. Even in his sinfulness, Adam was Christ-like. The big question here is 'was it the right thing for Adam to do?'

We always seem to give up something great to get some sort of short term reward. As people, we do it all the time. Imagine how healthy and skinny we would all be if we never ate ice cream, sugar, cereal, cookies, etc. Or imagine how much freedom someone would have if they were in prison and they hadn't done the stupid thing they did to get there. If my theory is true, I bet Adam was thinking "Man, this looks like it would be a lot of fun!" and didn't perceive the seriousness of the situation or the consequence. I am more than certain that Adam and Eve were unpleasantly surprised when God asked them to leave.

Mr. North says that Adam loved his bride too much to leave her. He would rather be miserable with her than miserable without her, and honestly, I feel the same way. I am glad Adam left Eden for Eve. I would have done the same thing he had done, down to eating the apple. Paradise is meaningless without true love and even hell could be enjoyable with one's soul mate. Even in his sin, Adam was still being a perfect husband.

I loved Lucia enough to stick through the worst of it with her. There were times when she was drunk and throwing up, and I was with her, making sure she didn't pass out in her own vomit. She never appreciated it, but even on those awful nights, I believed she was my soul mate, long after she had bitten the apple of sex and lust.

I never really had a chance to share that apple with her, like Adam did with Eve, but if she had offered it to me, I would have taken it. I always felt bad for being an innocent little virgin while she was off with all those guys. She made me feel bad about it, but there was nothing I could do but love her all through it. We never had an Eden, and I had never known my Eve. But I know under the circumstances, I would have done the same thing. Long after the near Eden, when the shallow, surface-perfect friendship I had with Lucia soured, I stuck by her side despite all the pain. When she would yell at me for being so perfect and good, I would think of that apple she ate, and I would say to her "my goodness is not goodness. I want you, and I want to take all of your sins, and assume them on myself. I will give you my innocence."

But in a world where blood can be transfused in minutes, and money can be wired in seconds, guilt and innocence cannot be exchanged in equal parts. Lucia never felt my love for her. Her guilt, or her lack of caring, or whatever it was, blinded her from seeing the beauty in me. I stuck through it all the while, and she never saw me as worth anything. I wonder what Mr. North would think about my situation with Lucia?

Reality is a state of being that is concerned only with what is possible. In my reality, I would very much like to rectify three impossibilities:
1. *I wish to make Madeleine Townsend fall in love with me.*
2. *I would very much like to have a job that I like.*
3. *I would like to get over my past, and its difficulties.*

We waste so much time as human beings trying to make impossible things happen. Why can't we just acknowledge that they are not possible, and focus on getting the most out of the things that are possible? It seems that my main focus is on making impossible things seem real. I am so tired of this train of thought, and there is nothing I can do about it.

Wednesday is nearly over. I slept in until noon, and spent three hours reading and journaling. It's four, and it's cold, so I don't feel so great. The temperature is about 49 degrees, and I put on an ugly sweater, and decide to go look for a job. It's getting to be Easter in a few months, so I figure that seasonal work might be possible until I can find something better. But it's Tallahassee, so everyone else has the same idea. I hate this crowded, ugly city sometimes. The dearth of college students here makes this place unbearable. At my old job, in Apalachicola, I had tons of fun because no one who went to our school worked, and finding a job was easy. I worked at a small coffee shop in town, and all of the kids from the different campus ministries used to go there. Christian kids and coffee were inseparable. "Let's go get coffee together." That's what they always say to each other. Normal people go to bars on the weekend, and Church kids hit up the local coffee house.

It's Florida. And it's too hot here for coffee (most of the year). In the 49 degree weather, I go for a walk with a pad and paper and think of the kinds of places I would like to work at. I start my list as 'places where I would like to find a job:'

-*Somewhere with lots and lots of cute girls*
-*Chik-fil-a*
-*A research lab*
-*A bakery*
-*A laundry-café*
-*A bar or a club*
-*A place where lots of cute girls work*
- *A bike shop (lots of cute, athletic girls come to bike shops)*
- *A flower shop*
-*Publix (last resort)*

I look up at the sky. It's overcast and it's unusually cold for winter in Florida. But I like the weather. It's brooding weather and I enjoy brooding. Now I need to find a list of places I could get hired. My love of Publix and my past employment there put it last on the list, and I have no idea where to find a laundry café. I wonder if they even exist anymore.

Tonight is not very exciting, but I figure that since I am brooding over this girl, I might as well say something to her. Men put way too much thought into these sorts of things, but it doesn't matter, because the woman will not answer, no matter what the question is. As I look back on the following mundane sequence of events, I realize that I was acting out of necessity, which essentially means that there was only one choice I had.

I sat down in front of the computer and went to Facebook. I opened up Madeleine's page and proceeded to send her a message. I thought about all the things I could do to make sure she wouldn't be too suspicious.

1. Put yourself in the friend zone so she doesn't have to do it.
2. Don't seem excited.
3. Don't make any real plans, just suggestions.

"Hey Maddy, I was wondering if you were free sometime this week. I really wanted to sit down and discuss the book with you. I think it will help me to understand it better if I talk about it with someone. I'm free most nights this week, and I was thinking we could go get coffee or something, and talk about it."

I went through all of the potential responses in my head, but essentially the words "yes" and "no" never seem to really make their way into a woman's vocabulary unless she is overwhelmed by something that has pushed her to her limits. In my specific case, and in the present, I believe that a woman will tell you why she won't do

56

something before she actually agrees to do it. Simply put, I won't convince her with just one message to see me. She will make it hard, asking me what my motive is, and why I feel the need to talk to her. If, in fact, she is seeing someone already (which I never really considered as a possibility until now), she will give either no response at all or a very polite dismissal. Anticipating failure makes it easier to accept when it happens. The likely outcome here is that she will never respond, and there isn't anything I can do about it. By now, I was too exhausted to give a damn about women anyway, so I hit the send button and accept whatever fate determines as an outcome.

I have this royal peeve about girls with boyfriends. They talk about their boyfriends constantly, almost like they are trying to convince themselves that the guy they are seeing is the one for them. I didn't always notice how much it bothered me, but it seems the more I make contact with girls, the more of them I meet that are with someone else. They sort of rope you in. The really cute ones will befriend you, acting like they are available *and* interested, and phone numbers flow, and they hug you and flirt with you enough to where you can't stop thinking about them. As soon as you actually sit down on the phone, or Facebook, and have a real conversation with them, they notify you that there is no chance. "Oh, my boyfriend is just like you…We've been together for two years…he is *really* smart…I am super *happy* with him!"

It leaves you in this spot where your bitterness is carried like a concealed weapon, making it hard for you to actually see the good in people without being suspicious. Women rob themselves of their own mystery by telling you that the mystery is unavailable to you anyway, because some prick has already capitalized on it.

Jim, from *Archie and the Listers*, left me a voicemail asking if I would like to get together and have dinner with him.

Before calling him back, I check Facebook one more time. Nothing. I phone Jim, and we agree to go to Fazoli's. He is in town for tonight, because there are never really shows on Wednesday. I drove over in the Saab, smelling pretty awful, since I don't see a need to shower to impress a guy. Jim meets me at the door. He's wearing a cardigan with some ugly, badass shoes.

"What group are you in, for our book we're reading?"

"I'm doing Thursday, so I haven't had the pleasure yet."

"You're going to love Kristen. She is super fun. She will make sure that the conversation is kept free of any questionable material."

"That's ok, I want to talk about the book, not stir up controversy."

"In order to discuss the book, you have to talk about controversy, though."

Jim pauses for a second. "You mean like porn, and sex, and that kind of thing?"

I nod, sort of feeling embarrassed. One of the perks of Christianity is that we have a great system of code words that sound more appropriate than the things we are trying to not say, but are desperate to talk about.

Jim orders a chicken parm (euw, chicken!), and then looks around the room to make sure no one is really paying attention. He is getting ready to grind my comment into the ground.

He looks up with his left eye, and starts to say something, and then he stops. "Are you reading this book to understand what needs to change about our society, or are you doing it to solve all of your own issues?" Jim asks hard questions. I order my food, and keep thinking.

"If you're in this group to find the answer to all your own problems, then I think you need to look somewhere else. I think you need to work it out with God."

"On what kind of basis?"

"On a man to man basis," Jim laughs.

I look kind of down, so he changes the subject. Or maybe I am just *that* insufferable.

"I think I remember you from somewhere else. A long time

ago." I grab my food from the counter. I think about where I saw him before.

"I used to be in a band called *Photo Collage*, do you remember them?"

I think about it briefly. "I think so. Did you play guitar?" *Photo Collage* was an old school emo band, from when I started school back in 2001. They were loud, and they had some really great songs. I remember the girls that used to approach them. They were just like any girls in the emo scene- pretentious and stupid. And, of course, desirable. They made great music, but, just like every other show I used to go to, I was loathing with envy for them.

"You had a different look then, didn't you?" Jim smiles, and then rolls up his sleeve. Under the sleeve is a tattoo of a unicorn, and another one of the lyrics to a song. They were instantly familiar to me.

I think about it for a second. Photo Collage had disappeared suddenly, and I never really thought about it. "Where did you guys go?" I demand. "I remember you guys left suddenly."

There is some silence, and then Jim smiles a little bit. "Do you remember our second album, the one that had a unicorn on it?"

I remembered the unicorn vividly. It was stereotypical, but for the fact it looked sadder than a stereotype of a unicorn. The album was simply called "Caliope," and it was really good. But the band never supported it. As soon as it came out, they disappeared, for no real reason at all. Photo Collage was a mystery, to those of us who cared about music of that variety. No one had ever known Jim's name, either, as he and the other members had conducted themselves in secrecy with pen names, aliases and the like.

Jim continues. "In 2002, when we split up, I met this girl, who was quite a bit younger than me. But I think she really liked me, and we tried to be all badass, and hardcore, and we got married. We thought that it would be fun, but no one thinks of how difficult marriage is when they are drinking, and being idiots. They just think 'I will have this hot girl around, and we'll have sex, and when I feel lonely, I will have somebody there.' "

"Did you stop because you got married?" My eyes dart at his fingers, looking for a ring. But something told me it was a decision that had to be unmade.

"I didn't stop because I got married. I stopped because I could not be married and be in a band. It just didn't feel right."

"Was it because you were on the road all the time and you couldn't spend any time with your wife?"

"Marriage killed my creative spirit. Once you're married, things sort of become ideal. And if they aren't ideal and perfect, then you are doing something wrong. At least that's what she expected. I would write songs about being hurt, or being in love, or something, and she would get mad. She was always asking me if I was unhappy. What could I say? I guess if something unhappy made me want to write a song, I ignored it. It's marriage, you have to be happy all the time, you know? Unless someone dies or something."

"So, I guess you left her?"

Jim looks at me ruefully. "She left me. She had a set of ideals I could not ascribe to. The adventure had lost its mystery. There was nothing left for me either, and I suppose her leaving me was smart. It absolved me of the guilt."

I was about to ask another question, and then Jim charged at me. "I don't want to tell you anymore about myself. Let's hear about you, Benedict."

Jim was a bastard.

I love to share my problems, but I hate to talk about myself. I look at Jim again, this time with a bit more frustration. "All of my issues are nothing compared to yours. I am just an unhappy guy that wishes he could get married to a woman he loved. And that would be the perfect life." I felt bad about saying that. Jim mocks me a bit, making me feel guilty for being naive enough to believe in such a thing as perfection.

"What do you want to know about me?" I was scanning Jim's face, but I had a feeling that he probably has me all figured out. He is in his late twenties, and I am a child.

"Benedict, what do you feel you would bring to the table to

make a perfect marriage?"

Jim suddenly made me question myself, and I really, really hate doing that. It's not that I don't feel I am free of any wrongdoing. I just don't like to think about my shortcomings.

"I don't know. I would be totally devoted to the woman. She would be my one and..." I stopped short. I sounded like a kindergartner. I am very concerned at this point, mostly for my dignity. Jim already knew I was an idealist.

"How come you aren't married yet if you're so noble? Don't any of the girls you like know this about you?" His tone is unmistakably caustic. I get a bit bothered by his sardonic undertone.

"They did, but they were always interested in assholes. I was about as useful to them as a twenty dollar bill in the woods. All you can do is burn it to make fire."

Jim looks at me remorsefully. "Guys always say that, but really they are just pansies. They don't say what's on their mind."

I turned the idea over in my head for a moment. It's funny-when you like a girl, it's almost a crime to say it. It's like you offend them by telling them that you have any sort of feeling for them. I remember, on one occasion, there was this girl I liked, and she knew it. So one night, we were all out at some church thing, and I promenaded up to her, and I said "I want you to know that I'm glad we are friends, and just friends." She approved of what I said, because from that point, she was normal towards me, until she found out I had lied to her. It was as if she was personally offended by the fact I found her attractive. Of course, silence is the worst form of negativity. It implies "NO!" with a sort of quiet, irresolvable force that dooms you to whatever state you are in with the woman.

Jim looked at me again. "Why do we lie to women? Why do we never tell them that we like them?"

I thought about it for a minute or two, and then I blurted out my response. "We have too much to lose by telling them we like them. We have this fragile, little, meaningless liaison to the women we like. Of course, they are content to keep us in this meaningless state, and whenever we try to advance, they push us away, and we are so attached to them that the termination of this utterly meaningless relationship is viewed as a dreadful punishment. We would rather have the pithy lie than the awareness to move on. But they are all the same, so you become content with pretending." I take a deep breath.

Jim was still trying to figure out what I had said. "I can see where you're coming from. We have all been there. But you're especially pathetic because you pursue women who are out of your league. There's not very much that's impressive about you. You don't put up a front of any sort. You're whiny little Benedict. Once upon a time, I was just like you. Then, when our band hit big, I hid behind our music and pretended I was cool. My ex-wife didn't screw me for who I was- she just wanted to have sex with a guy in a band."

I was clearly hurt by this clairvoyant message that struck at my fairly naïve and simplistic core. Part of being naïve is not knowing that you're naïve. Part of being naïve is believing too strongly in one's self.

Now back in my room, Jim has clearly made me aware of my worst problem- me. I usually feel better about things after I look at porn, but today, it isn't helping. My mind is not numb. The women aren't the ones who ruined it for me all these years. I ruined it for me. I sabotaged my own relationships. I was never super fond of myself. I mean, I don't think that I am the greatest, most handsome guy in the world, but I certainly perceive myself to be better than other people, under certain conditions.

Hypothetically, let's say I am interested in a girl. So is another guy. This girl is cute, and funny, and insecure. And she has my attention. But she is checking out the other guy. Now let's say this guy is white. Really white (I'm really white), but he has a bad hair cut, and his pants are hung low. He's a sort of a white trash gangster. He has no job, and he has a couple of meaningless tattoos. He says all sorts of sweet, empty things that indicate his desire to get laid. His penis is masterminding his plan to have sex with this girl. And he is utterly worthless. He listens to shitty music, thinks shitty thoughts, and doesn't read. He drives a shitty car. He has accomplished nothing. He is a piece of shit. And, some how, this girl, this beautiful, enchanting female, gravitates towards him. I care about her, I want to know her, I want to build a sustainable relationship with her, I want to listen to her and be there for her, but while I am thinking of what kind of flowers to buy her, shithead is imagining her naked in the back seat of his '88 Caprice.

Why do women want this sort of thing? Hypothetical situation two: I am invested in this nice, sweet Catholic girl. She goes to Mass five times a week, and prays often, and dresses nicely, and has discerned the religious life. I like her, and she knows it. But she's looking at the guy next to me, who is holier, maybe not as handsome, and possibly whiter than I am. He is as unbadass as a Styrofoam cup. Actually, he is the whiteness of white. And she is crazy about him. He is certainly a better human being than I am. I am not good enough for her, but based on situation one, she should gravitate towards me, the greater of two evils. I know what will happen though. The holier than thou guy is primarily invested in God. He doesn't see the entirety of her beauty. He doesn't care about her enough; he is willing to satisfy the principle of marriage, but not to give the woman the desires of her heart. Shithead and holier than thou have one thing in common- they don't give a shit. They have a set of personal ideals they need to fulfill. Shithead wants to get laid and have a good time. Holier than thou wants to show off his nice Catholic family, forty kids and holy wife, and then die and go to heaven for being a good husband. How can you not care about someone that appeals so strongly to you?

I was told by Jim, during that lunch hour, that I put the woman ahead of God. I now understand that I idolize her. If a woman idolized me, I would be ecstatic. Of course, women feel comfortable being ignored and deprived of care and attention, so it seems, so that makes me, the caring idolizer, look like a creepy stalker. They idolize the guys that are the most distant from them. I have a checklist to support my theory.
Guys who women idolize:

- *Guys in bands*
- *Celebrities*
- *Wanna-be thugs with spinner rims on their cars*
- *Meat heads, or other popular high school-ish sports or entertainment figures*
- *Generally speaking, guys that they like who don't give a damn about them because they are too busy being assholes.*
- *Guys with British accents*

Guys who women do not idolize:
- *Nice guys*
- *Best guy friends who are always there for them*
- *Religious figures*
- *Nice, decent gentlemen with good heads on their shoulders*
- *Gentlemen, in general*
- *Nerdy, well intentioned guys who like them*
- *Guys who have found their thing in life, and are happy doing it*

It has been my personal experience that I end up on the bottom list. I can safely say that there is not a woman in this universe who idolizes me. It's not like I want a slough of them. I just want one. I want one woman who perpetually adores me, and makes me feel like I am the greatest man ever. The narcissistic facet of this is obvious, but I can assure you that we all have a desire to be idolized.   No body admits to it, but we do.

The sun dips below the horizon, and night time comes. I feel filthy, and in need of my favorite sacrament. I need Christ in this moment. The only thing that brings me back to God is knowing that I am unfulfilled without Him. And I do despise being in this state of perpetual failure.

My phone rings, and in my mind I wonder if Madeleine is calling me. She has no way of doing so, but I wonder, and anticipate, and hope for it. Of course, she won't be doing so, but there is at least the possibility.

FOUR

I still have friends left over from college, and I know I don't really bring them to mind very often, but there are a few. Before I began this trend towards melancholia, I thought about them often. They consumed a real part of my life, and I was happy to spend time with them. I have this one friend who has always stuck by me. He lives near Camilla, Georgia. His name is Stephen Poff, but he will always 'Poff' to me when I am being rude. Or Poff, when things are serious, or I am thinking about him. I see him several times a year. He works for the school board in Camilla, since getting his degree. We met in college over something totally silly. In a certain realm, we are kindred spirits. We are about as normal as we have to be, and our weirdness seeps out of the cracks. If you haven't guessed by now, we are both Saab owners.

I was in a parking lot near the school one day, feeling crappy and walking up to my car after class. There was sort of a tranquility about things, like something important was about to happen. When I got to my car, this goofy looking blond kid with the biggest glasses ever- I mean they were huge- was sitting on the front bumper of my EMS.

"Is this thing *yours*?" It was like I was driving a Ferrari or something. He was hellbent on finding the owner of the Saab. When he saw me walking up to it, he went on this tangent about how the 99 was the greatest thing from the seventies, and how nice mine was, and how there was nothing cooler than a vintage Saab. He was absolutely stupified when I asked him if he was crazy or not.

"Me? *Me?* Of course I'm crazy. I drive a Saab too!"

It was like he and I had the same father, or something. He was anxious to introduce himself to me.

"I'm Steve- er- Stephen. Stephen M. Poff. I drive a 1971 Saab 96." I liked his last name, and I don't think he was

ever completely Stephen to me. I had never really seen a
Saab 96, much less met someone who owned one. Funny
though- over the next few weeks as I got to know Stephen, I
found out he and I actually had things in common that most
people did not understand. Being that we went to a Catholic
university, we were both Catholic, but Stephen Poff went
about it more pragmatically than I did. Anyway, back when I
used to be cool, and things were fun, the campus ministry
would set up these exciting retreats.

I convinced Poff to go on one of these with me. We
had friends who were girls, so we shoved all of them in my
EMS (there were five of us) and headed to this retreat center
in Niceville. One of the funniest things about the retreat, that
I recall, was how inappropriate (and wickedly funny) Poff
was the entire weekend. It bonded us as friends for life, and I
often think back on that entire weekend as if it happened
yesterday.

Retreats are a funny thing. At this time, I was a
sophomore. My one-sided dependency with Lucia had boiled
down to a writhing, hot mess, and I was somewhere between
wanting to leave her and wanting to leave God. It's silly- I
should be bothered about world hunger, or the number of
abortions committed every day around the world, but this is
the first world, and I'm a selfish little prick. Poff knew I was
down, so he invited some cute girls he knew to come out. We
were all young and silly then- no one was doing anything
really bad. It's just that in our big, ugly apotheosis of a
Catholic college, the principles of religion did not stick.
You'd think it was a public school in New Jersey. As we
piled out of my car, and the three girls ran off, chit-chatting
together like small animals, I could see the sun eating up the
gulf in Niceville, and suddenly I felt like God existed again.
Here, the water was clear and calm. The smell of the gulf
permeated my nostrils, and I looked at the hoards of young

Catholics from our school filling in the ranks, and bustling, churning, forcing their way into the building. There were kids here from FSU, UWF, and maybe some other places. I grabbed my stuff, and made a place in the crowd. It's time for the magic sentence: The MC yells "Girls are blue, and Boys are red- no purple!" I am not surprised, but Poff is already looking for a retreat girlfriend. It's easier to be on one of these excruciatingly long weekends if you have someone to share the 'fun' with. Needless to say, it's 2002- people are doing worse things. I scoot over to him. We are forming small groups, so we have a forum to discuss all of personal issues, and I shake with well-intentioned anticipation that an attractive female should be present in mine. Our groups are based on the color of our name tags, which we did not select. They were handed to us. I'm positive that before the retreat, they preformed the groups based on colors. "Blue" would be the cute girls group, "Pink" would be the super holy clique from FSU, "Orange" would be for creepy stalkers, like me. Or, in Catholic terms, those who "Jesus wishes to bless on this retreat."

I am not a bad person, but retreats make me feel that way. Once they have subtly slipped in the notion that you need Jesus to fix you, you wish to be a better person, and so you open your heart up to the Almighty. Poff and I did not buy into this retreat Jesus, who seemed to be bipolar and difficult. In real life, Jesus had always been a wonderful guy. I needed a special favor from Him on this retreat. There was a dark shadow named Lucia that was destroying my brain, and I badly needed some sort of divine apathy to cure myself. Another possibility presents itself- the possibility of escape. The prime accomplice for such a task is another girl, who will hold my attention as strongly as Lucia held it. Given the male-female ratio here, being apathetic would be too hard. Plan B was far more inviting.

As soon as the gaggle of girl scouts that rode with us

dispersed themselves from our car and went to their cabins, and we had our first talk, I began the search for my retreat girlfriend. Poff, in all contrariness to his nature, was vivaciously taking notes on the talk that one sister Teresa was delivering about Catholic mysticism. Poff, in awe of Mystics like Padre Pio or Marthe Robin, was having the time of his life. I, on the other hand, was cleverly scanning the room to see if there were any women that caught my eye. Unfortunately, the archetype of Lucia permeated my inspections, and I was left frustrated that this one female who had wronged me and hurt me for so many months was permanently burned into my brain.

Small group time creeps up on us. Poff is in a different group, which looks more exciting than mine, and I start looking at the faces sitting in a circle around me. Right across from me, the kid who is now my roommate, Francis, is introducing himself. He is a junior, and I have seen him before- perhaps in some sort of loathsome state at a house party that I took Lucia too, or a bar, or something. He mentions it's his first time here, and he is really excited. I would give a finger to be excited about something. Surprisingly, there are two nice looking girls in our group. I count two more girls I am not attracted to, and two other guys I dislike for some reason or another. I'm sure the girls find me to be ugly, and these guys don't give a damn about me either. Everything is fair. In fact, I want for them to dislike me.

My solitude is disrupted. One of the plain girls is asking me a question. "So, er, Benedict, why are you on this retreat?" I respond by employing a plethora of anti-truths to hide my secret. The best one is "I am here to seek a deeper relationship with the Lord." The girl who asked me looks at me lovingly, but bleeding through that love is an affect where she knows that I both dislike her and I lied to her. I am a male college student. My brain is rotting with thoughts of sex and damaged romance. I am here because this is the only place I can meet a girl right now.

Reasonably attractive girl number two answers the same question. "I'm here because I feel that God is calling me to be here." She goes to FSU. Her name is Kristen. She is being honest. Reasonably (more) attractive girl number one answers. "A bunch of my friends invited me to come, and so I am here because they really wanted me to be here. That being said, I am very excited." The circle around me emits encouraging noises. She seems to know Kristen. A tiny bit of midriff reveals a navel ring. Thank God for the possibility of mystery. I am forced to listen to the ramblings of these people, and then I contribute on occasion. I do wish I really wanted to be here. I wish my mind was not polluted with ulterior motives. Then, and presently, I wish I actually, truly *loved* God instead of just believing in Him. The difference between me and all of these people is that they all had some form of love for God, and I, for some reason, because I am not a wonderful human being, force myself to love him. But instead, my fickle mind is eaten with thoughts of an unfaithful lover who does not love me, and a glistening navel ring that might hint at a past that beckons accessibility.

Our group is told to end its discussion, and we split up to prepare for Eucharistic Adoration. Adoration is only fun when you love Jesus. When you believe in His presence, it is still difficult to sit through. In a way, it is sort of like swallowing raw garlic. You do it because it is good for you. Every minute is corrective, and you are forced to pursue something higher. I take a glance over my shoulder. Poff is merrily chatting up an attractive female from his group. It seems she has taken a shining to him, because as the group gets up and leaves, she stays right there by his side. I walk towards him. He smiles at me like a fox (a fox!), and I mouth the words "you bastard" as I graze his side like a bullet. I smile blindly with envy, and he continues chatting up his new (very pretty) friend. I wonder how he manages to be such a ladies' man. For a minute or two, I hate his guts. Our friendship only grew from there.

That retreat failed to change my life. Just like every retreat, it contained one or more interesting females, and I was smitten with them, but as soon as the weekend drained itself, I squatted back down on the latrine of self loathing, realizing that I was both a horrible human being and a depressed one. Poff could smell the stench of wallowing, and he stuck it out with me as needed. It's easier to be holy when girls like you, when your finances are in order, and you're not sick of the people that surround you. Here I am, several years later, and holiness is even more elusive.

Five

Stephen Poff is on the phone. He is visiting everyone and wants to know if he can stay with me. I consent, and then, in my mind, I harbor a hope that he can turn on the charms and get Madeleine to pay attention to me. As usual, he is somewhat up to date. I can hear him rambling now- "Benedict, it's not that these women dislike us. It's that they don't trust us. They stopped trusting all of us when the first guy lied to them. Madeleine has no reason to trust you at all."

I nodded, even though he couldn't see me. All women have been hurt by something, so once we figure out what that something is, we have parameters to work with.

I need to quit being a weenie and come up with a plan to get Madeleine to trust me. I'm quiet for a bit. "Hey! Rad! Are you still there?" I snap out of my Madeleine-induced coma. "Rad, we will sort this out tomorrow when I arrive."

Mr. Poff arrives Thursday at 7:30 PM. His Saab looks so odd next to mine in the driveway, and I stare awkwardly at him. He gives me a quick man hug, and then marches inside. It is thirty seven degrees outside and cloudy. I follow him in.

"Poff, I made us something to eat. Want anything?" I take a tray of fish sticks out of the oven, a jar of tartar sauce, some velveeta and some white bread. When I see Poff, we have our customary Fish Stick sandwich. It is our way of commemorating how much fun college was for us. We sit down and drink soda and bullshit like old people in a nursing home somewhere down south. Poff looks at me and tells me stories about all three girls that live in Camilla, Georgia, and how some guy who though he was a badass tried to run Poff off the road with his F350. Poff pulled off into the dark, and followed the guy to where he was going. Turns out he was going to a bar. Poff slid under the truck and drained out all the transmission fluid from the guy's truck, and disappeared.

Another time, Poff met this girl at a gas station. She was cute and stuff, but she had worked there for the past five years and didn't really know what else was out there. Poff asked her if she had ever seen a Saab before. She liked his funny little car so much, she went on a date with him. He didn't say if anything happened on that date or not, but knowing Poff, he was only a good Catholic when it really, really mattered. Otherwise, his interest in the mysteries of the Church kept him involved. I can only stare at him enviously, and live through him vicariously.

Poff had somehow found out that a group of people were getting together after the study. No one had called me, but I suppose they didn't really want me there. I might talk too much. He suggested we go, so we quickly finish our sandwiches, and drive to the pub where everyone is supposed to be meeting, and take a look around. As if it really mattered who was there, anyway.

I heard that Madeleine was coming, so I kept my eyes peeled. I take a small table with Poff, and, oddly enough, Jim was there- and we all got Newcastles (Poff paid for mine since I'm broke) and for the first five minutes we talked about things that didn't really matter. I keep looking around, straining my neck towards the door, as if my neck muscles have some invisible hold on the universe that will bring Madeleine here.

Women are hopelessly unreliable. Cute girls never show up on time, ever. It's like they know that every guy in the room will stop missing them if they are actually reliable, and when they do show up, they show up in a way where you never actually see them walk in. They are essentially operating off of the basis that everyone wants to see them, and that makes being late excusable. I wasn't even invited though, so who am I to open my mouth?

New Castle brown ale is like Natural Ice, but from England. It doesn't taste good, and it has food coloring. I sipped mine lightly, for fear of it staining my teeth. Poff chugged his like it was going to get taken away from him.

The Thursday night group barrels in the door, simultaneously. I am uncomfortable now, and there are too many people here. Poff is bombarded by all of the people, some of whom are new faces. The funny part is that they all seem to know him. He presents as a damn good Catholic, though. Maybe it is because he owns up to his shortcomings, and actually had some changes to make. I will never see him as a religious person, but then again, I don't see myself as a religious person either. This must be an example of my own short-sightedness, as one girl once called Poff a male Mother Teresa, and me, well, she had nothing for me. I am on my second Newcastle when Madeleine walks in with some girl who was still beautiful, but less attractive than she was. If you asked me to explain why, I would just respond by telling you that I am a chauvinist pig. I always go after the prettiest girl, the most beautiful girl, the most charming girl- with no chance of success.

It would be useless for me to see Madeleine and not

inquire about the Facebook message. I instantly confess everything to Poff, and Jim hears me rehash the whole thing.

"So, listen, I need to let you in on something. See that girl over there?" Poff nods, and smiles. Like a fox, always. He motions for me to continue. "That's Madeleine, and I sort of asked her to get coffee with me, and stuff. As friends." He laughs at me, and Jim is entertained as well. "I haven't heard back yet. What should I say to her?"

"Don't say anything at all!" they yell above the noise in the bar. Jim is sitting next to me with a plate of potato skins. I take one, and then begin to chew on it, slowly. Poff goes off to socialize, and Jim goes back to wherever he came from.

In my head, I try to make lists:

"Hey, I was wondering if you got my message."

"Hey Madeleine, I was wondering if you got the message I sent you on Facebook."

"Hey Maddy, I was wondering if you like coffee."

"Hey Madeleine, I was wondering if you ever check your Facebook messages."

"Hey Madeleine, I sent you a Facebook message about going out for coffee. Is that ok?"

"Hey Madeleine, I'm too afraid to ask you anything because I am afraid you will just say no."

"Hey, Madeleine."

I just sit there and watch her. There is this guy that is always in her personal space. I saw him at our first meeting when we started this book, and he is still here. Supposing it has only been a little less than two weeks, I am not surprised. Our friend Tristan, and his wife, Amy, who just got married, seem to know both of them and greet them like they are another couple. I am slightly scared, and a bit suspicious. What did I miss?

Jim comes back. "You know, Benedict, she is not

going to come over here. All these girls have been conditioned to receive homage from men. Better go pay yours so you can get rejected now instead of later. Or just buy her a drink." Jim doesn't smile, so he must be as serious as he sounds.

I hail the waitress and ask her to take Madeleine's drink order. She goes up to Madeleine and asks her what she would like to have. Madeleine tells her nicely to ask later, so the waitress walks back up to me. Evidently her radar is on.

"She doesn't want anything yet," says the waitress as she saunters back to me. I fight for words. "Um, err, can you, well, do you, have any *red wine*?"

"What kind of red wine?" The good-natured *serveuse* asks.

" Like a Cabernet, or a Pinot Grigio?" I plead intensely. "How about a Merlot, or a red Zin?" She asks. I don't know anything about wine.

"One of those sounds fine, miss. Surprise her; she likes wine (all girls like wine, right?)."

Poff hears what I just said, as he comes back to the table to grab his New Castle. He is with some other guy, Hamilton, who isn't friends with the Catholics, but seems to know Poff well enough. Hamilton goes off to order a cider. Poff looks at me like he's just seen me naked.

"You're an idiot, Radmeier. A dork to the point where it's funny. Wine? *Wine?* At a *pub*! I can't wait to see this. Oh, and Pinot Grigio is not red."

In two minutes the waitress gets her a glass of red wine, and hands it to her calmly.

"Umm, miss, I didn't order this," she says dismissively. "One of your friends is, er, surprising you." Or so the conversation goes in my head.

Madeleine sets it down on the table that she is standing next to. I hide my face, like a small child who has done something really bad. I feel her staring at me, wondering how pathetic I am. Any normal girl would have thought I was at least trying. But Madeleine, exceptionally beautiful and perfect Madeleine, knows better. She sees me for the pathetic little minion I am. Poff is laughing his ass off, discreetly. Hamilton returns. Out of pure chivalry, Poff stops laughing and refuses to tell Hamilton what happened. I look up, half-heartedly, and stare at the glass of wine. It sits there for almost five minutes. Then it sits there five more minutes. Madeleine walks away from the table, abandoning my meaningless little gift to her. I try to wish the glass out of existence, but there it sits, a tribute to my awesome manliness. The velvety texture of the light in the room makes it look like a glass of blood, and I wish fervently that a vampire would come up out of the darkness and consume it.

Poff resumes giggling when Hamilton leaves, and Madeleine floats about the room, as would a fairy in her forest. She loves this dark room, with all these glowing people. She smiles with an effervescent smile, and she breathes lightly. She is like glass, solid and transparent, containing an unknown substance that is liquefied being. Her perfection is beyond any human perfection. If she is aware of my presence, I will certainly be amazed. I am so madly captivated by her, and so wild about her beauty, she will have to see me.

Flatly, she paces towards the group of people whom she calls her friends. One of them notices the wine glass. If only I could read lips, I could see what the other girl is asking her:
"Who got you that glass of wine?"
"Where did that glass come from?"
"What loser bought you that glass of wine?"
"When did you get that glass of wine?"
"Why did some loser buy you that? He seems like an idiot."

I'm sure it was one of these. There could be nothing good said about that glass of wine. I love too strongly.

The waitress walks by, and sees the glass, and puts it out of its misery. She comes over to me. "I won't charge you. I see what happened."

I feel stupider than ever, but at least it didn't cause me to lose money. I am very afraid of the result of this, though. Poff taps my shoulder. "Go over and say hi to her. What are you afraid of?" Poff taps on the table. "Do it or I'll do it for you!"

Out of fear, I pull myself together, and take tiny steps towards Madeleine. I am studying her, relentlessly. She glances sideways, in my direction. I turn around again, and take a step the other way. She senses a movement in her direction. I walk up to her again, and smile at her. She smiles back, nervously. Poff is watching me and I am terrified. Poff smiles an evil smile, with no room for compassion. He understands very little about what I am struggling with. I want to marry this girl, and he thinks she is expendable. There is no other Madeleine Townsend. Once she understands, and thusly makes up her mind that I am a loser, she will never want to be with me, and well, that's it. I am not certain about what I should do. I need to bite down on something.

"Hey Madeleine."

"Oh, hey Rad."

"How do you know my nickname?"

"Everyone knows your nickname."

One of her female friends dashes in and heroically saves her by dragging her away. It didn't matter anyway. Nothing was going to come out of my mouth.

It's amazing what sort of dichotomy this presents. I am unaware of how pathetic my words are, and I am also unaware of how meaningless this sort of dialogue is in the first place. My interaction with Madeleine is 99.9 percent analysis, and .01 percent actual conversation. The content of the conversation is meaningless, and thus the analysis is also inconclusive. My brain is in love with a figure of speech, really. It is in love with the idea of what I say Madeleine is. Madeleine that my brain thinks of is not real at all. Madeleine applies none of my dreamy, self centered thinking to herself. She exists in a conditional cerebral vaccuum that I have to deal with every waking minute. Her beauty is the catalyst for all sorts of irrational thoughts. My insecurity is the breeding ground for all of my failures. These two things, her beauty, and my insecurity, will ensure that she is out of my league. The roller coaster hits bottom again.

The morning after the bar, I have a headache. Poff congratulated me for saying all of eight words to Madeleine, and drowned me with another round of cheaper beer. He said that we weren't celebrating; we were just looking for an excuse to drink. This all took place after the Catholics left. I was too tired to even really drive home, so Poff, who has a whale liver, drove the EMS back. I was grateful for his sobriety. Maybe things could be worse.

I need a job, and I have maybe three weeks of money left until things royally tank and I will have to live with my folks. Frances helps me find a few gigs. One stands out to me: this really old Publix in Lakeland needs an associate customer service manager. I might have a chance, since I worked at Publix for a century. It was so pleasant, and neutral. I could eat chalk at work, and no one would notice. There could have been a buffalo at my register, and I would have never gotten a look. If possible, maybe I should pull myself together enough to leave.
"Leave Tallahassee?" Poff screams. "Why? Why the heck would you want to leave?"

"Why did you leave, Stephen Poff?"

"Your life will only suck more if you leave."

"Poff, I am at rock bottom. It's a good idea."

I fill out the application, and submit it, and then I go and submit more applications. Poff goes back to sleep. We wake up at one, and realize that college really is over, and we need to be serious about life. Poff agrees, and then reminds me that he has been serious about his job. I have been the one who has kept the college thing going. My logic is not only pathetic. It's also dangerous, in that it makes me look dumber than I am. But something in my life needs to change, and I don't want to sit around waiting for that to happen. I could die of old age in the process.

SIX
Lucia, manipulatrix

I was suspicious that Lucia was sick and tired of me. But she was unwilling to drive to these parties by herself, as she might get a DUI or wreck her car. She was deathly afraid, and I was madly in love, and fear kept us together. Her fear of messing up something expensive, and my fear of losing her. She and I were at opposite ends of the spectrum. I wanted her more than ever, and she just wanted to be rid of me. But, if there is any way to fool a man into thinking a girl likes him, it is by getting him to do stuff for her that she knows no one else will do. In my case, it was even worse than that.

"Benedict...Ben-e-dict...I need a ride out tonight." She would sing my name, like a siren. "Are you able to take me?"

I would honestly try to say no, but that answer failed to move her. "Do you not care if something happens to me?" she demanded. Suddenly, I was responsible for her. She was my problem. I was no longer able to relate to the Benedict that said 'no' anymore. If she changed her mind that night, and something happened to her, then it would be my fault.

"What time?"

"9:30."

She liked to party late. I would pick her up at her apartment, which was just starting to explode with life, and I would go up to her door. She would come out, dressed in high heels and revealing shirts that showcased her uppers, and made her seem irresistible to me. In my pathetic ineptitude, I would try to hold her hand as we walked down stairs. Sometimes she would allow me to, but she never held mine back. Sometimes she would brush it off. Those were the nights that I knew she was going to end up in someone's bed.

There was that one night, though, that changed everything. It was about nine, and she was wearing this dress that made no sense. It was so revealing, and I kept asking myself "why would a woman bother to wear this unless she was looking to remove it?" There was no pride in being seen with her, as everyone knew I was just her driver. Tonight, however, we went somewhere different. We drove to this house that was really, really big, and freakishly fancy. It was on the water. There were a bunch of cars there, and a good number of them had all of the right stuff- the rims, and the tint, and the audio. They were expensive cars, too. Lucia had a certain look on her face- I didn't understand it at the time. There was some seriously loud music playing, and I was going to turn into the driveway. But she stopped me. "Park out here," she commanded. I dropped her off, and then she looked at me with a stern face. "Now leave" and she smiled, and marched off in her heels. I instantly felt shitty, and I knew something was really up. She wanted to party like a big girl. "Call me if you need anything, OK?" She didn't even hear me.

I was trying to find God in this mess. He must have been moving somewhere in that big house, with all those cars, and those ill-intentioned guys. I saw some things in the background that scared me. I only prayed that Lucia would be safe. I parked my car, and thought long and hard about what I should do. I felt hot and cold all at once, with no serious idea as to why. My hands and feet were falling away from my body. I couldn't feel anything but sadness.

And yet, at the same time, I resented her. I loved her inability to care, and I loved her lack of compassion. She lived at the center of her own universe, and for some reason, I was stuck there. If only I could have this universe to myself. But I am an asteroid, sucked in by her gravitational pull. As I get closer, I will burn up, and turn to dust. My own body was on the verge of combustion.

That night I decided that there was something in there I needed to see. At eleven or so, I hid the Saab behind a tree, down the road. In fear of losing my keys, I hung them on the inside of the bumper, and I ran down the street. The lights were on in the yard. I didn't want to be present there- I only wanted to *watch*. I felt so detached from this mediocre setting.

The first thing I noticed was that all of the kids here were ostentatious pricks. They had expensive cars (carelessly parked on the lawn), nice shoes, big watches and bad hair cuts. They had all of the class of a *Chandon* with none of the appeal. They lived lives of desensitivity, with an epic egotism that drowned all of us. I walked into the house, trying not to go deaf in the stereo, and found a place to hide. From my seat in the foyer, I nested behind an excuse.

"Hey kid, what are you doing here?"

"I'm here to do one thing only- watch for cops. That's my job."

"Right on."

Fuck him. If only he knew what he would be in thirty

years. The universe is a wonderful place to watch people get what they deserve. From this little foyer, there is a window into the living room. I can still feel the fall air on my neck, blowing through the doorway, while the smell of alcohol and the scent of cologne and perfume linger around me. There is a girl sitting on the couch. She is poorly dressed to my pious eyes, and her body is shapely. Her eyes are empty, so she is either drunk or spiritless. She is like a piece of meat in shark infested waters. I wonder why she is here. I feel like I'm thirteen in her presence, and she notices me watching her for a second. There is a mob of people dancing on the floor. I watch their bodies writhing and grinding, and it is very painful for me. I am caught somewhere between a repressed desire and a broken promise. I watch the hands of the boys touch the bodies of the girls, and I see the little flashes of electricity streaming off of their fingers. I am in awe of how their guard has fallen. I am amazed at how they touch each other. I am flawed because I can't be there with them. I am in shock because this is real. In the corner of my eye, and just the corner, I see Lucia moving with a male body. His careless motions suggest that he has been drinking. His aggressive gestures show that he has a destination. His imagery is offensive, and his touch is unappreciative.

But somehow she receives *all of this*. She takes it in with pleasure. There is a smile on her face, and she moves her little body with him. Her navel ring flashes in the light. Her innocent glances are gone. Her beauty waxes insolvent. Her skin is melting with his, and, as she dissolves, his body engulfs her. She wants something he is forcing at her. I take a step back to analyze how that sort of thing looks. I have no idea where this monster came from. I want to kill him, and let him know how angry I am. But I shouldn't be here, so I go back to watching the writhing mass. I am so tired, suddenly.

I have a beautiful idea of what it means to be in love. The beauty of this is the magic of getting to know another person, and the tiny interactions that define what you mean to them, and they to you. You want for them to know you so badly, and you want for them to love you for the things that they know about you. You beg for a certain connectivity, that generates more connectivity. You look for those golden opportunities to connect with that person. You relish the intense sadness that you feel without them. You feel a vast lack of inner peace, and you are aware of how alone you are. You think about what it would mean to hold them at night, and to make them the center of your world. You long to touch them, and know how their skin feels. You want to cry, and feel comforted in the same second. Of course, what do we know?

We know nothing. This state of being is a near lie, and love never happens so gently and so perfectly, with such coordination. We never feel the closeness we long for. We just cry and are never comforted. We sleep alone. We see no moment of opportunity. No connections are made. We remain lonely. We are bitter. The sun rises and sets on another day of unhappiness. Our youth is wasted. We are closed off. We become terribly bitter, and we feel hopeless. The one thing we feel we were created for has failed us with no hope of change. We keep struggling for it, looking for the last light of hope, and we find darkness. Our sleep turns into sleeplessness, and our dreams turn into fantasies. And we find ourselves with bad haircuts, nice cars, and money at parties. We find ourselves trying to get laid for one night, and enjoying none of it. We find ourselves stuck in a place where there is no magic. The beautiful idea is becoming an anachronism.

But it still exists vibrantly for me. I refuse to trade it in for something so alarming and cheap. I refuse to substitute the lie for the truth.

My Saab has a sunroof, and I always dreamed of

looking out over the gulf with my lover, and kissing her. And then, someone will take a picture, and we will have arrived. This is my dream, and this is the dream I still have. As long as I can dream, I will always understand what it means to be happy. I may not be happy in my waking life, but at least, as I sleep, there will be a destination. It may not be Lucia. But I can dream, for now. In the mean time, I will do the only thing I know how to do: reverently chase the impossible. I return to the car for a bit to take a nap.

Asleep behind the wheel of my (parked) car, something wakes me up, instinctively. The lack of Lucia's presence makes me almost frightened for her. The woman that I love has vanished into this evil place. And I must save her. In my mind, I am continuously in this and the following moments, and they are present in my mind constantly. I walk (I stumbled, perhaps) into the house. It was about 2:30, and things were darker, and more evil. There was a lingering stench of drunkenness, and those who remained looked disillusioned and tired. Where was my lover, my one and only? Did the depths of this sarcophagus swallow her up? I tried to hide from all of these shadows and these lies, but the only way through them was to meet them face to face. What was she doing here, under the cover of darkness? In my nervousness, I ran into a girl who was incoherently dancing by herself in the living room. I made eye contact with her, and she failed to notice me. Her gaze seemed to be miles deep, like the ocean, and only after 30,000 feet would I hit bottom. The endless wasteland in her mind seemed to be revealing itself to me through her eyes. She noticed, in that brief second, that I was studying her, and she moved away. For the first time that night, I wondered if something else was going on that I didn't realize. If there was so much evil in the world, I needed to stand for the good that could defeat it. If there was so much evil in the world, there had to be a certain goodness and purity that would be its undoing. The opposite of all of this chaos and confusion was, and still is, God. He watches with a solitary glance, and we fail to notice Him. The girl in front of me, whose nakedness had been revealed, moved to a far corner of the room, and she died another tiny death in her soul.

I begin to feel urgent, and in my mind, I try to figure out where Lucia is hiding. I am alarmed that she is not on the first floor. My mind looks around the corridors, and I see a staircase. It is magnificent, but in a dark and sensual way that makes me afraid of it. There is no hope at the top of that staircase, and in my soul, I know where my soul mate is. I climb the stairs, step by step. In my mind, I am Sir Edmund Hillary, climbing the impossible steps of Everest. He had an easier time breathing than I did, and I feel I am ascending a stairway to the sky, where the air is thin, and cold. My lungs are burning for lack of air, and my body is trying to collapse. I keep going back to this moment in my mind. I have no idea what is at the top. For Hillary, it was the sky. For myself, something much more dreadful. And this is how I discovered it.

I was thinking to myself "this is how women end up with emotional scars and unwanted pregnancies, and STDs, and things that are unpleasant to talk about."

So one by one, I kept climbing those fucking stairs. I was not about to give in to my fear, and run away, but it was having an overwhelming drag on my sense of being, in that moment. Melting like ice cream, I reached the top. I looked to my left, and I saw a hallway full of bedrooms (Oh, the possibilities!). It was scary, and dark, and slightly cold. There was a stale stench in the air. The evidence of what had happened here before was disempowering, and unpleasant, and lamentable. My own sexuality was paralyzed with terror, and my spiritual depth, from the smallest, tiniest place in my heart, began to seep outwards through the cracks.

"God, are you here?" a little voice in my soul whispered. As a young man, this was the most *questionable* place I had ever ventured. I felt more and more uncomfortable by the second, eyeing each door, wondering what was behind it. The implicit nature of closed doors in a full house suggests only one thing: that there is something that the door is protecting, or hiding, because it is either delicate and valuable, or shameful and disgusting. In big houses like this, if it were not for human sexuality or materialism, there might not even be doors. I fingered the locks, and the sides of hallways, wondering what sort of bad decisions had been made here. In my naïve, Catholic mind, there was a lack of identity that stemmed from being so dissociated with these sorts of decisions and settings. The mystery of this place haunted me perpetually, and I needed to get out of here. But I loved that girl, and I needed to find her and see if she was alive.

When we are in places like this, we sense the presence of a human being in another room. I felt Lucia's heavy breathing seconds before, and I detected her vitality within a few feet of the door. She was not *alone*, as I recognized another presence with her.

The heavy breathing of a man. The sound of a woman in orgasm. The distaste of discomfort. The image of penetration. The violation of what God made sacred and Holy. The anger at sin in the world. The watershed for a falling out. The disproportionate amount of evil in the world. The apple leading us to bad decisions. The feeling of being rejected for something of lesser value. The inverted tube of our skewed perceptions. The inventive nature and genius of lying. The truth versus our fragmented, abnormal, imaginary reality. The wild nature of the repressed human spirit. The excuses we give ourselves when we allow ourselves to fail.

I opened the door. I lament the fact I looked at

pornography the night before. I wish I had gone to confession just before seeing all of this.

The confusing scream of sexual ecstasy. The discharge of common sense. The rebellious act of fucking. The invisible nature of sinfulness. The complex lack of feeling during the sex act. The ironic exchange between man and woman. The horrible thought of being inadequate. The curious positions we put ourselves in to accomplish the same result. The repetitive thrusting towards a few seconds of dopamine. The contamination of our brain with delusions about the opposite sex. The willing female who has cast aside all of her rationality. The veiled shame that is taking a backseat to the willful urge to continue this awful trajectory. The infinite wisdom that has no answer. The dark night of the soul. The empowering sense of being in the moral right. The thankfulness that I am pointing the finger...

I see her naked body moving in the dark. There is a man behind her, and they are in a corner of the room, left of the door, away from me. She is a stranger. There is something wrong. This is awful. This is evil, extracted from its veiled presence in the world.

The awful feeling of having nothing left to give after ejaculation. The guilty satisfaction of failing again. The triumphant return of the need for reconciliation. The visible choice of wrongdoing that was made. The easy decision that we over-complicate. The desire to reach the same level that the woman has. The implosion of self worth. The satisfaction of judging a lesser man as a lesser man. The intoxication of speaking with moral authority and condemning another human being in place of God. The contortions of truth we use to justify our wrongdoing.

I turn and run away from her. I leave that place, but the image remains in my mind.

The visible retreat. The sensitivity to light. The conflicting feelings of self loathing and wallowing. The disconnect from feeling what you should feel. The invisible barrier between right and wrong. The discard of ideals and hopes and dreams. The cruel intentions of our egos. The wishful thinking that all women are perfect. The Madonna-whore complex. The perilous last rites of a happy ending. The discreet fact which you knew but did not want to prove. The imagery of a descent. The filthiness of rock-bottom. The horrific gestures that we desire so badly. The lack of understanding that fills the human mind. The state of detachment, and our desire to reattach. The confusion that leaves us hanging.

The complex psyche of the Catholic female. The end of hope.

Seven

At 3:47 A.M. I heard a knock on the window of the car. I was huddled in a fetal position in the car. Apparently Lucia saw my Saab out here. She was pissed. She never spoke in complete sentences when she was angry. I was willing to accept any command she gave me.

"Leave."

That was all I got from her. It made me want to kill her friend that I caught her with, but it more so made me want to vaporize myself, or drive off alone, into the night. I don't think she knew that I saw her, but I calmly sobered myself. I fingered for the keys. They were in the ignition switch, between the seats. I started the engine, and didn't even look at Lucia. She marched back into the house. I drove home, in the dark, and went to sleep, feeling awful.

I got a phone call at Eleven A.M. I had risen from bed a few minutes earlier. I hadn't slept. My body felt like it was frozen. My mind was still carrying the shock of something that it could not accept. In the daylight, I wondered if what had happened before was even real, and in my highly irrational brain, I leaned into the dichotomy that there is a daytime world, and a nighttime world. In the nighttime world, what is unreal in daylight is very real at night. And what should not happen in the daylight happens at night. The sunlight reached the depths of my soul, and I was able to move, albeit with a great weight I could neither ignore or cast off. I was safe, and then, as I began to move, and look at myself in the mirror, the phone rang. I ignored the first ring. I was protecting myself, but I knew who it was. It rang again. Saturday morning bore down on me in the form of a cross. Benedict falls the second time. The phone rings again. I fumble for it. The number is odd. I feel a sensation in my stomach that could be a tumor. I answer the phone.

"Benedict, come get me."
"Where are you?"
"You've been here before. The house on Palmetto."
"I remember."

I hated that house. This would be the second occasion that I had picked her up at this shit hole. I put on a flannel shirt, and I found my keys. Some moments are just too heavy for words. I dug deep into my CD case, and put on Saves The Day. Being unable to stand the sounds, I drove in dead silence. Half way through my commute, this question came to me. "Who the fuck is this guy, and why is she sleeping with *him*?"

Women make all sorts of awful decisions about who they sleep with, and we, the kings of chivalry, have to pay for it. In my heart, I feel compassion. In my mind, I feel complete disillusionment, at least when I think of the possibility of meeting someone who has actually made good decisions her whole life. I was one step away from turning back around, but my compulsive desire to repair Lucia was keeping me in this pink and gray zone of ambiguous commitment. When she was away from all of these men, she loved me. She held my hand; she gave me little kisses on the cheek. She would lay there while I drooled over her sacred body. She tolerated my imperfections. I would absorb all of her faults. And yet, somehow, in every line she spoke of love, and of what a good relationship was, there was nothing in it that she attached to me. I was a "good guy," and a "good friend." How can you tell someone who considers you their everything that you are just a good guy and a good friend? I told her, repeatedly, that she was my *princess*, my *sunshine*, my *perpetual virgin*. I longed to be her *knight,* her *lover*, the *object of her desires.* But her desires were filthy, and wasted, and as beautiful as she was to me, I could not convert this substantial physical beauty into a lasting purity of heart. The worst part of all this was that I needed her. There was no way, at this point, to tear her away from me (I felt she had consummated herself to me, somehow), as I was invested in her to a degree of madness. Even now, years later, in the present, the question of what to do to detach myself from her remains.

I stare at the Blessed Sacrament, wondering what happened to make me cling so tightly to this femme fatale. I often ask Jesus why I cannot cling so tightly to his mother. I often ask Him what made me love Lucia. The answer came to me in much the same way as it does to those of us who are looking for *any* answer. Any answer to the thing that drives us insane. If only I were to stop loving her, then I would see her for who she really exists as, and there would be no attachment. If only God could cure me of my attraction to her. Of course, we must choose to love Jesus more than these, right? We must, mustn't we?

I would sooner have burned that house, but she was inside it, so my inner angst would have to be bottled up and fermented, so that no one could see it until it was ugly, and passive aggressive.

She walked up to my car, slowly, looking guilty as hell. I kept my mouth shut, and stared anxiously at the road. We were listening to Jets to Brazil. When she tried to say something, I turned it up.

This was a repeat of multiple incidents. The first time I picked her up after one of these one night fiascos, I had no idea what had happened. Not until the third time, really, did I catch on to the fact that these were residences of men with well executed ulterior motives, and that this was the executive suite of their darkest desires. One time, I got so mad at her, that I stopped the car and told her to walk home. But as she was getting out, she took a sharpie from her purse, and wrote the words "thank you!" with a smiley face, on my arm. I felt so rotten. I started to cry, and she climbed back in the car.

"See what you get for being mean to me, Benedict?"
I should have been meaner.

Morning. I have no idea what day it really is, but Poff is there on the couch, in his underwear. I go outside, into the emerging sunlight.

From the time I was a child, I believed in an ocean in the sky. This ocean was visible to me from the time the sun rose until 8:00 in the morning, and during the evening, when it got dark. I could see its rolling waves and their swells at night, when I would watch the sky. The stars were not stars, but the illuminated mystery of the celestial sea.

As a child, I named it the 'upside-down ocean,' and where it met land, there was always a cloud beach. Of course, as I aged, it became the Celestial Sea, the Inland Ocean, or the Heavenly Ocean, or the Gulf of Rainbows. But sometimes, the upside-down ocean is just that. I would go for drives on those early mornings, and in the chill, I would open my sunroof, and watch the cloud beach roll in. I felt these immense feelings of loneliness and smallness, watching the ocean swallow up the rest of the sky. I wondered what lived in its depths. I would love the days when it would rain at dawn. I would get up, and sit there, and watch it. Occasionally, a thunderstorm would stem from the gulf, and the evenings would light up with the beauty of a new creation. I grew older, and harbored the belief that the Inland Ocean (my favorite title for it) would comfort me when I felt sad by glowing rose colored. Or by showering in the morning, it told me it was feeling melancholy, and I would listen to Copeland (they are from Lakeland!) and get lost in the sky. Human connectivity has failed us, and we don't really communicate anymore. Fortunately, God knows me, and He uses this glorious celestial body to communicate with me. In these early morning hours, I don't feel simply alone, but instead I feel lonely and *glorious*.

My friend came outside. "What are you looking at?" He asked this question routinely, and I answered him the same way I always did.

"If you could see the things that I see, even in the ordinary, you would be amazed and staring, also."

"Rad, you have a hangover."

When people don't understand you, they are certain you are drunk (like on Pentecost in Acts of the Apostles!). And for those of us whose lives are empty and meaningless, they are only so because we chose to see them thus.

People's personalities are vicious and unrelenting. They are heavy, and they weigh down on you. Stephen called some people, and soon we were in his Saab heading to breakfast. It was about 10:00, and I-hop was fifteen minutes away. I listened to the thrumming of the German V-4, and looked around at my city. If such a thing were to happen- such a thing as me leaving my city, I always wonder how I would make new friends. I wonder if there is a magical city where people are truly happy, and nice, and hopeful. My friends here don't really like me, and I am unhappy with them. One day I will understand why people are so closed off, and why they use religion as an excuse to look down on people who are not just like them. I might even understand the thin line between pretending to love someone and actually loving them. I have no role models (except Jim) among these.

"Madeleine is on to me, isn't she?" I ask Poff. He just laughs for a while. We drive on and on through the traffic. I had a brief thought, about what it means to a woman when there is a man who likes her. The issue was that Madeleine was not really my true love, she was just another replacement for Lucia. I didn't even know it, but I was looking for the sweet, innocent Lucia that I had met early on, who had sort of fallen to pieces in a short time. I never really got to know her in that stage of her life, but I am suspicious that my mind is playing tricks on me again. It fills in the cracks, you see, with the ideas that it holds on to.

"Before Lucia turned bad, she was looking for someone like me."

"Before Lucia turned bad, she was excited to be near me and around me."

92

"Before Lucia turned bad, she aspired to meet someone like me."

"Before Lucia turned bad, she was perfect."

"Before Lucia turned bad, she was Madeleine."

"If I fall in love with Madeleine, I can redeem Lucia."

My mind is like two pieces of land divided by an abyss. All of my unexplained tendencies- my weirdness, my inexplicable failures, all of their truths and causes lie in this abyss. Somewhere in this abyss, I am trying to use Madeleine to get back to Lucia. Furthermore, my mind is merely placing the false attributes it created about Lucia onto Madeleine now. Neither of these women really exists in the form that I love them in. The physical appearance of the woman is a blank canvas onto which I tack on the false attributes. Perhaps they can sense this, and perhaps this is why they don't love me.

Poff interrupted me.

"You say 'on to you' like you're committing a crime. Do you feel guilty for liking her? Do you feel like you're trying to harm her?"

I was taken aback by his comment, but when I thought about it long and hard, it really did make sense. I felt guilty for liking her, and I felt guilty for liking Lucia also. Who can blame me?

Poff continued. "Women want you to feel guilty for liking them anyway. That's why they invented the friend zone. It's like a form of punishment for men who feel anything that is deep and sensitive and meaningful, and happens to include them."

Now I was really puzzled. Did God give us these odd illusions about women in the first place, when all of them were truly evil and wanted to punish us for liking them? I had no clue, and I really needed help sorting out this complicated mess. I wondered why God made all these beautiful girls so heartless and defensive. I only knew that whatever I approached them with, besides total silence, was wrong. God forbid you call them out on it. They hardly even know what you are talking about. Everything is unacceptable.

"How should I approach her?"

"You idiot. Ask her lots of questions."

"About what?"

"You're girl-retarded because all you do is talk about yourself. I never noticed it, until I actually listened to you."

My brain began hurting. I felt like a man waking up from a coma. I was so wrapped up in the illusion that I never bothered to get to know the victim.

"Stephen, how do you ask girls questions?"

"Rad, you're a complete moron."

"I mean, what's the *in*? What is the catalyst? How do you ask someone a question that doesn't sound weird or suspicious?"

"Rad, your issue is that you don't really want to get to know them. You are trying to push reasons for them to like you. You don't really want to get to know them to ask a question; you need to want to get to know them. Does that make sense to you?" I look at him angrily. He was certainly right on, and I was strange. There was no good way for me to communicate with a woman whom I only desired to possess. Without a doubt, all of our relationships should be mediocre and watered down, shouldn't they? And if you love a person, why should you get to know them? Because you want to, right? It is a natural compulsion of those of us who harbor an attraction to a woman to want to get to know them. The problem is that we still harbor the delusion of perfection, and we cannot reconcile ourselves with it.

Breakfast was quiet. We talked here and there, and we were all a bunch of guys with nothing to do on a Friday. I should have been at work. My life was one, long, boring weekend. The idea of marriage looked like a solution to this boring weekend, but I had a feeling I would miss these doldrums once the currents were moving me along in matrimony.

At breakfast: Two pancakes, a cup of coffee. Some of Poff's friends that I knew. An ugly feeling in my stomach when I was done. Plans for Friday night. Boredom.

I had no idea what to do with Friday. Thankfully, Poff has enough people who want to see him, and I am forced to tag along. I feel awful never being the person that people want to see. There are those who want to be the center of attention, and those who don't mind making the center of attention. After years of girls stealing my universe (and using the mind tricks to hold me hostage in theirs) I would like to be the center of my own universe, and have a few visitors.

I had to go to Publix in the middle of the day, about two. I felt like I was on food stamps, shopping so frugally for little things that I felt would sustain me. When I was nearly finished with the shopping excursion, I had a gallon of milk, four boxes of cereal, some cookies, a gallon of orange juice, some bread, and some peanut butter and jelly. It was like I had never left college. This basket of groceries belonged in a Stephen Malkmus video. We would survive off of bagged cereal and milk. When we were done eating the equivalent of ten servings (from a giant salad bowl), we would look at ourselves, and then go back to pretending to study. Or talking about girls, perhaps. It was the only free entertainment we knew of. Our little college town was so quiet, and so serene. I wish that I had made more time to enjoy Apalachicola, and not been caught up in these stupid things. I love Publix because the cashiers are cute. I also love Publix because everything is bright and colorful. When I feel down, I go there and it lifts my spirits. A feeling runs down my spine this time. I can sense that I am going to see someone here that I will know. The peanut butter shelf gleams before my eyes. Then on to the cereal shelf. And from there...

I am getting one last thing, and feeling pretty good about not spending too much money, and then, from the other side of the freezer, I see a face that draws me in.

Madeleine is walking by unpretentiously, filling her shopping cart with healthy things that make me feel guilty for eating cereal, and milk, and such. Her twenty two years old seems so much more substantial than my twenty four. I am looking at her. I am struggling. I wish I was doing something empty and meaningless, like brushing my teeth, or napping.

She turns around as I approach her. I pretend not to notice, and wait for her to see me and say something.

Dead silence. Screw me for thinking that she would notice me. I follow her from a distance for a bit, and then I go to the check out. Forcing yourself to give up is almost as hard as reaching for your goal. Of course, it was time. The lady in front of me is having a hard time with her check. I look to the left, and Madeleine is pulling her shopping cart into the lane. It is quite full. This is the moment that the universe has allotted to us. It may never be repeated.

I try to use my brain. She looks over at me and smiles an awkward smile. I look at her with a look of apology. "I'm sorry for being here, at the grocery store, while you are also here."

She and I lock eyes for a split second, and I remind myself I am insane. We finish ringing our groceries up. It occurs at just about the same time, but I am done first. I stand there, sort of watching her, and thinking.

"May I help you carry those out?"

She looks at me, and starts to think. You can tell what she's thinking. She wants to say no. She really does. But somehow, out of the corner of her mouth, she feels a tiny bit of complacency, and struggles.

"Sure." She agrees, which surprises me. I pick up her

grocery bags and put them in her basket.

"You know, I did this for a while in high school," I tell her. She looks at me indifferently. In all my years carrying grocery bags, it seems like she is the least grateful. I felt good about my little deed of chivalry, though, and it motivated me to keep trying. I look at her groceries. She really was a responsible dieter- there was whole bag of spinach, and she had everything in paper. I looked at my paltry plastic bags, and I felt bad. But I swallowed the feelings of inequality. She speaks up. "Benedict, I parked on the other side of the parking lot, away from your blue car. "Are you sure you want to do this?" She had noticed my car. Inside, I am beaming. "It's cool. I am enjoying it…"

Poff had told me to ask lots of questions and listen carefully. "So, Madeleine, how far in the book are you?"

"I'm on the third chapter. What about you, Rad?" I didn't want to tell her I was still finishing chapter one. Fortunately, someone invented lying.

"I am also on the third chapter, but just barely. I am trying to read it slowly and carefully, you know?"

"Yeah, it's a good book." I stop at the cross walk, to make sure no one was going to run us over. I push the cart slowly towards her car. She was not paying attention to me the entire time, but suddenly she stops.

I can feel her starting to say something. The words don't come, but I have heard it enough times…

"I feel like you want something from me." She doesn't quite say it but I can put the words on her lips. I know she wants to ask me something like that. I approach the car quietly and take the bags out. I slip them in the trunk. She looks at me again. I find the courage to open my mouth.

"I want to be friends with you." I just said it. Wow. I just told her something that I wanted. She almost didn't hear me. She looked hard at me, and couldn't seem to process what I had said to her. She seemed almost *offended*. I am breathing nervously. I might as well stop now.

"What do you mean?" she demands, gently.

I am struggling for words. "We should spend time together. I think you would enjoy being my friend," I say to her slowly. My confidence is faltering. She looks at me with a certain amazement. I was in shock, and she was unhappy. I was not sure what sort of speech she was about to give me.

"I don't think it would be right for us to be close friends." Her statement stings me deeply.

"You seem to think I want something from you, don't you?"

"I think you like me." Her tone is accusatory.

The words roll off my tongue like melting ice.

"I am not interested in anything more than being your friend." Lying is so damn easy.

"I need to go, Rad. Maybe."

"Maybe? What does that mean?"

She unlocks the car and tries to ignore me.

"It means that I am not going to say 'yes' just yet. I think you like me."

"I don't, Madeleine, I swear." She looks at me, and shakes her head.

"You don't believe me, do you?" I ask.

"No, No." She continues to shake her head. Her face morphs into a look of unfriendly sarcasm.

"If I do like you, why is it such a problem?" I am getting frustrated. She opens the car door, slightly pissed off, gets inside, and waves. "Thanks for carrying my groceries out." Her tone is ungrateful. I am now upset. She pulls her car out, and she drives off with some sort of unmasked vigor. "Women are narcissistic bitches," I mutter to myself. The heavy burden of honesty has won. I don't give a damn. She, like most girls, will not change her mind. I load my groceries, and drive back home.

When I arrive at the house, Poff is sitting on the couch, talking on the phone. He is making plans. Nearly thirty of us are going to the bars tonight. It will be like college. The group of friends he introduced me to is called "the mob." They are shitty people, but they know how to have a good time. Lemonheads are on the stereo. I sit down next to Poff, after I put the groceries away. I am ready to cry. Poff finally finishes. He looks at me, and he can tell that another girl has said something hurtful to me. "Grow up, Rad."

I go read some more of this worthless book.

Day 2.

Dear Diary on Joseph North's book. Screw you. This book, in the first five minutes of reading the first chapter, has made me feel like shit. North goes on and on about how his experiences with women were awful and horrible, and how he magically prayed to God, and God fixed all of it. Somehow, this super Catholic British dude could get any woman he wanted with his British accent. I constantly get rejected when I do try. Why is it that those of us who try more often get rejected less, but those of us who try carefully- the ones who make calculated and well intentioned, brilliantly thought-out proposals to the women we are attracted to, always get shut down so quickly. It is unfair, and that is the only word. I won't hurl myself at average girls I am not attracted to. Of course, now Joe has a perfect, beautiful wife. I bet it took him five minutes to win her over. This guy doesn't know my pain. He can't relate to me. I dislike him.

However, the problem, for him, was never the woman. It was himself. Just like me, he had an issue with pornography, and an issue with being happy. But he wasn't a virgin, either. Girls were interested in him. So... what does one do when no one is interested in you? It's like there is no hope at all. What can I do here? Keep asking God to send me a woman who is going to decide she hates me as soon as she comes in contact with me? Send me a false hope that will not pan out? Who knows?

In the second part of chapter one, North talks (in sparse detail) about how he was almost pressured into making out with girls at parties in high school by his friends. North was an awkward teenager who had moved to the United States from England with his parents. Then he meets this group of friends who put him in situations where the girls were provided and willing. I don't know what I would have done, but it is clear to me that sleeping with one of these girls was but a step away, when you went to a very secular school, in suburbia, with girls who were used to sleeping around. I knew girls like that in high school. It almost seemed like it would be harder to get them to sleep with me than with some other random dude. They were different than nice girls- their candy colored lipstick, their excessive fingernails, their multiple earrings and their see-through clothes. Of course, that was the nineties, and we were all kids then. I examine the situation with disdain, and I realize that these girls did not feel beautiful at all. Their gaudy trinkets and overdone make-up, see-through blouses, spaghetti straps and short skirts were all signs of a greater issue. According to North, it is a sign of a lack of understanding the implicit dignity we are created with. It is beyond low self esteem, or insecurity. It is beyond being loved. It is a total negative valuation of ourselves. It is the outward expression of feeling like we have no dignity except that which the captain of the football team bestows on the undignified girl while he is undressing her.

*Maybe I am not meant for a woman. While my first reaction should be one of intercessory agreement (*Oh Mother Mary, help me to submit to the will of God, that I might be celibate for His kingdom!*), it is really, in my opinion, a divine occlusion (*Oh God, I don't see why, in Your divine will, I must carry the cross of celibacy! Can't you change your mind?*). I will not beg the intercession of the saints and angels to help me undertake what I believe would be an error on God's part. And the error would be Him making me desire a woman, but not giving me one. However, feeling this way changes nothing. When I am done with this entry, my life will be the same.*

The first chapter of this book, in all of its complicated language, simply states that everyone is wounded, and we all try to close the wound by restoring our dignity, and hoping it will bring us healing. By what means we restore our dignity is irrelevant- there is only one, and it is through Christ. However, what fascinates me is how our dignity got depleted in the first place, and how to keep it from happening again and again. Dignity is like a sink full of water. When you have too little of it, the sink is empty and useless, but when you have too much, it makes a mess. Dignity is always leaking out of something, or overflowing from somewhere. And all too often, it is tainted. I suppose I will eventually figure it out. For now, I need to deal with this issue concerning Madeleine.

Poff is getting ready, and I am telling him about my afternoon with Madeleine. This was our conversation:

"You should have just stopped trying. Girls are narcissists, and if you give them enough to work with, all they do is prove that I am right." I was not going to argue with Poff.

"So how come you are able to make headway with them?"

He laughed at me insolently. "Because I don't care."

I eyed him suspiciously. "Where is the fun in not caring?"

"I don't know, Rad. It just seems to work." I fumed. I did not like his ambiguous, half-assed answer. It was like there was a secret he was guarding.

"Poff, where is the fun in not caring?" He would answer me the second time. Poff shrugged his shoulders.

"Stephen Poff, answer my fucking question! Where is the fun in not giving a shit?"

Poff grew indignant. "There is no fun in caring way too much, like you do. All you do is torture yourself." If only there was a button, and if only it could be pushed. I would explode.

We are in the car, and there is silence. We are two best friends of equal standing- peers, if you will. Finally, he looks over at me. He sees right through all my bullshit, because he is a Saab owner, and I am a troubled teenager in a young adult body. "This girl, Rad, why is she special?"

I had never asked myself that question, so I ask him for a period of time to figure it out. "You probably harbor delusions about her, don't you?" He continues.

I am silent. He is mostly right. I also borrowed some delusions from my infatuation with Lucia, and inadvertently pinned them on Madeleine. But I am only partially acquainted with this truth. I am not happy with the reasons that I like her, but I have never really had a good reason for liking a girl.

After a bit more silence, I give Poff my answer.

"I just do, man. I just like her." Poff knows I am lying to him, but he accepts the lie, and doesn't judge me. "I think that's realistic."

We are listening to The Weakerthans, and continuing our awkward silence. Poff looks over at me again for a second. He is sizing me up. He doesn't say anything, but I think he is trying to figure out if I have the potential for impressing this girl. I think he is trying to figure out if he can help me. I hold onto the armrest, and look straight ahead. I am running on borrowed time. No one likes a failure. I twist and turn. Poff is exhuming my soul from my body, and examining it with his logical, rational brain.

We park the car in one of the garages, and we walk downtown. The more devoted members of the mob are standing by the Supreme Court building. It is about nine O'clock. We head down a few blocks to a divey bar. They all know this guy who has a band. The previous band, a college-ish punk outfit that should have left Tally a long time ago, is leaving the stage. I remember them- at the time they were called "The Sheep," now they have a new name. But it doesn't matter. The guy that heads the second band, Billy Hollis, is familiar to me because one time he and I got in a scuttle at a party in college. I was up at FSU visiting a friend of mine, and he said something to me. I tried to beat the crap out of him, but I have never really been any good at that. He gave me a nasty bruise on my upper chest. Lucia had left me by then, and I was aggressive all the time.

It surprised me later to know that Poff knew him. Poff had heard, as a matter of fact, that Hollis had bruised my collar bone during that altercation. Hollis did not recall who I was. Perhaps this was for the best.

Hollis' band, "The Burning Drugs," were not really that great, but they were having fun. When I interviewed Hollis for *the Chronicler*, he told me that having a band wasn't about making good music; It was about making music that would make women listen, and want you. The drugs' first album, *The Burning Drugs smell like Flowers*, made a couple of heads look up, but those heads weren't inhabited by strong minds that had good taste in music. He was drunk during that interview.

I sit down next to Poff while he is getting a beer.

"Radmeier, how do you want things to go?"

What ever was he asking? "What are you asking me?" I yelled at him, but it was not really noisy.

"How do you wish things would play out with Madeleine?"

"They won't," I muttered. I shook my head to reinforce my pessimism. I took a good long look across the room. I am silent for a minute or two, and then Poff interrupts my silence again.

"Who cares if you are being realistic or not? How do you want your relationship with Madeleine to go, if it were going right?" He has just asked me a question that I am ashamed and embarrassed to discuss.

"If you want to know how I think they should go with Madeleine, then you will have to understand how I wish they had gone with Lucia."

"Ok, Rad, how do you wish it would go in general?" This was a better question, as it allowed me to be rampantly idealistic.

"If things went the way that I wanted them to, I would meet a girl, and we would instantly hit it off. It's like she would be *drawn* to me. I would approach her with confidence, because I could see her light up whenever she saw me. There would be no question of whether she liked me or not. She wouldn't come out immediately.

She would watch me for weeks, quietly, escaping from my view, in secret. She would catch on to the fact that I felt unwanted and unloved, and want to fix everything. She would feel a closeness to me. After watching me for weeks, she would approach me, smiling, shy and quiet, but glowing gloriously, in an inconcealable joyfulness that clued me in to the fact she was in love with me. She would be beautiful beyond question, and I would be happy to be near her. It's like my life would erupt in color and everything so far would make sense."

Poff was laughing as I finished my sentence. "Neither Lucia nor Madeleine will ever do that."

It's funny. I had not talked to Lucia in nearly three years. It made me wonder why my mind returned to that dark place.

"Terrific. You asked me how I wanted it to go." I felt very nerdy for sharing all of this with him. Poff stopped laughing long enough to order another beer. "Rad, here's the deal; girls don't stalk their prey. They order at the drive-in. They take whatever is available and looks good. So you need to be available, looking good, and not giving a damn. The stuff in the drive-in isn't good for you either. But you, you're a fucking pastry. Not only are you bad for the girl; you have no substance. All you do is bitch and moan, whine and cry, because you aren't man enough to say 'O.K., next!' when a girl rejects you. You don't get attached before the relationship. Madeleine blew you off because she knows what is best for you."

A fucking pastry, dammit.

The Burning Drugs started their first song, *Chatterbox*, and so our conversation was drowned out. I studied the girls in the mob. They were not really the most attractive girls, but they were friendly. I was always mesmerized by the cliques of very pretty girls in down town. They often dragged these benign retards with them that wore pink shirts, with perfect hair. These girls were the stuff of legend. A chasm of something invisible separated me from them in college. I always wondered what it would have been like to be cooler and have girls like that in my life.

I look over at Poff. He is right about all of it, every bit. I do not understand how I miss the bus, constantly. Relationships happen between normal guys and pretty girls. How is it that this keeps passing me by? Again, because I can't find myself in these situations, I assume the presence of a personality flaw that is blocking me from them.

Part Two: Chemistry, and why it should be destroyed

"Beauty is unbearable, drives us to despair, offering us for a minute the glimpse of an eternity that we should like to stretch out over the whole of time."
-Albert Camus

Eight

The Psyche is the face that you show the world, and the face you show the world is who people think you are. These girls have perfectly developed psyches. Between them, and the men they like, it is perfectly fine to comply with the following behaviors:

1.   *It is justifiable to ignore a man who pays attention to you.*
2.   *It is justifiable to say "maybe" but really mean "no."*
3.   *It is justifiable to lead a man on, but not for a man to lead you on.*
4.   *It is justifiable to be a bitch. No one will call you out on it.*
5.   *It is justifiable to be really religious and God-fearing one minute, but as soon as you leave church, to be rude and dismissive.*
6.   *It is justifiable to pretend you are more religious than you actually are.*
7.   *It is justifiable to turn down men based on their appearance.*
8.   *It is justifiable to make men feel inadequate.*

Somehow, they have engineered the delicate balances between being a hypocrite, and looking like a perfect Christian. It is the elaborate act of appearing to be one, while being entirely the other. However, no one has to pretend to

105

be a hypocrite.

There is a disconnect between men and women. Men are not deceitful enough to be both great Christians and great hypocrites. They will eventually get caught. Women seem to be successful at hiding this shit for their entire lives. What motivates this behavior? The few women I have met who are genuine and kind are a breath of fresh air. The problem is that they are so uncommon- so atypical, that it is impossible to recognize one when you first see her.

None of us are perfect. It's just that we shouldn't be so imperfect to other people. The most exciting people (er, women) are the ones who are always kind to you.

Poff grabs my arm and shakes me out of my stupor. It is very loud in the bar, and some of us are going somewhere quieter. We split off into a smaller group. I can see faces that I know. I am still uncomfortable and tired, and maybe slightly pissed off, but I can't find a reason for it. Someone is asking us what we want to drink. I don't even know how I came to like beer, but I am drinking it. There is a girl across from me who is kind of cute. I haven't seen her before. The way the guys in this group are reacting to her, though, suggests that my perception is erring on the side of conservative. They are chatting her up, and she seems to relish the attention. I don't feel particularly good about it, as I am stuck here with Poff and some people I barely know. I feel like it would be a bad idea, but I really want to talk to her. The big question is "how?" How does one approach a total stranger in an atmosphere like this? I don't know where to begin. Of course, I never know where to begin.

Poff, like a jackal, senses what I am trying to do, and whispers in my ear: "Don't."

"How do you know what I'm trying to do?"

"I can see you staring at her. It's awkward."

I think that Poff is telling me that I look as desperate

and pathetic as all of these guys here. Maybe a bit worse.

I make an attempt to listen to what she is saying. Initially, I have a hard time hearing her. I begin to put two and two together, and pick up that she is talking about some guy she used to date who had money, or things, or something like that. I can sort of smell the conceit dripping off of her. She goes on and on about herself. There are a lot of people smoking in the bar, and so I go out for some fresh air. As I walk out, I look back at the table. There is a circle around it, and my place gets filled in quickly with moving bodies. No one really cared that I was there.

It often dawns on me that I would like to be in a place where I am significant. Not important, or powerful, or feared, but just somewhere that people want to see me. Somewhere that I can go, and be welcomed, and where my presence will be enjoyed. In every group of people, my presence is sort of a burden. I am too boring to synchronize with the rest of them. Now I am here in this shithole, and I feel so out of place, and awkward, and stupid. Everything I have learned about how to behave in public has been all wrong, and none of it is working.

My friend father Phillip told me that I was too negative. He told me that the secret to being a good and happy person revolves around letting go of everything that upsets you, and *choosing* to be happy, and to live your life by looking for ways to help others. If only I had a good reason to choose happiness. If only I wanted to help others.

And then there is that abyss between my brain and theirs. All of it boils down to something on a chemical level that I have not figured out. It wouldn't really matter, but for the fact that at the core of this lays the woman, and the woman is what I am after. Sometimes I wonder if it is because I am a Christian and many of them aren't. But I am a pretty bad example of a follower of Christ. They *should* like me- after all, I failed the "go, and sin no more!" test, just like they did.

Lucia, Master Chemist

Lucia would always tell me that we had no chemistry. The morning after, when I drove over to *that* shithole and picked *her* up, she was sitting in *my* car, looking sort of guilty. She welcomed my presence as a return to some sort of normal, after the insanity of the previous night. The engine hummed loudly as I shifted through the gears, and every once in a while I would glance over at her, trying to force a smile. Naturally, there was no smile to force. Later on, when she commented on my expression, she said that I looked deathly pale, as if I were very afraid. I felt my way through the gears, and tried acknowledging how these sorts of things are devoid of meaning anyway. But her guilty expression, her semblance of deception, and the *fact* she was hiding something from me, forced me to have a conversation with her that I did not want to have.

I parked my car on the curb. I looked out across the street to her apartment.

"Thanks for picking me up," she murmured sheepishly. I had to say something. I was tired of her hurting me all the time. Perhaps if she knew that I loved her, everything would be ok. Perhaps if she knew that I loved her, she would start undoing the damage that she had done to me. Perhaps if she knew I loved her, she would change her mind and love me also. We always tell ourselves that if someone else changes, everything will be perfect.

"You know how I feel about you," I blurted out, distressed.

She looked at me, as if she had no idea what I was

talking about. I was uncertain about what to say. "Don't tell me you don't know," I stated vehemently. A light bulb glimmered in her eyes, and she elicited a response. "Yeah, I see what you're talking about." The words were clumsy, and forced.

I got angry. She could at least speak openly about the fact that I had feelings for her. She didn't want to acknowledge it, and I had wasted so much energy throwing myself at her. This whole eight months, from the beginning of college, to this point in time, had been an eloquent and pointless offensive towards an unattainable goal. I should have told her this within the first five minutes I saw her, and I knew that the answer was the same. She had always felt this way about me, and she had no plans of changing her mind.

"Benedict, we don't have *chemistry*."

If my life were a line on a graph, it would have been perfectly straight, but for that moment, where there was a disruption. After that, the line continued in a skewed trajectory, towards this present that I know. And that was that. She hugged me, and got out of the car, and stumbled to her apartment.

She had skewed my graph. I would never feel good about myself ever again.

What if we could invent an excuse that kept us from looking at the real reasons for things?

The dialogue usually goes like this:

"I like you, do you like me?"

"No, I don't like you like that."

"Why don't you like me like that?"

"We don't have chemistry."

"What is chemistry?"

"Chemistry is what makes people like each other."

But I would argue "Chemistry is what people feel when they like each other."

So what comes first? Does chemistry define the

relationship? According to Lucia, it did. If chemistry was not present right away, then there was no opportunity for anything to happen. Chemistry was a major prerequisite for her to even consider being involved with a guy.

At night, from my house, I watch this couple say good bye to each other sometimes. They meet down the street, by their parked cars, and they talk for hours. They don't kiss, but they seem to really like being close to each other. Sometimes I want to walk up to them and ask them if they feel they have chemistry.

Lucia left me hanging. Was chemistry an ingredient? Could it be added to something to make it perfect? Could I somehow build it into my personality? Does it ever expire? I felt like I was fighting a useless battle with women. They had invented this unknown substance, and told certain guys they had it, and certain guys that they did not.

The truth, at least as I know it, is that chemistry doesn't exist. It is the greatest conception of a lie that I have ever seen. It is a universally recognized code between women. It is an imaginary justification for their decisions. It is weightless, but all the weight is placed on it, so that nothing real will matter. Instead of placing the burden of proof on real definitions of compatibility, it is placed on nothing.

Of course, it doesn't matter, because chemistry was the most sympathetic of rejections. There were many other reasons to reject me, and I encompassed all of them. However, if I had one wish I could fulfill, I would make it illegal for someone to reject someone else because of chemistry. In the least, they could be honest.

Outside it was quite cold- maybe about thirty-five. I began to walk down the street, looking in the windows. Tallahassee is mostly college students. I still feel like a college student, but I feel like the majority of college kids are stupid and naïve, and I am a bit ahead of the curve. When I was in college, I felt stupid, also, and I certainly was.

I saw a group of kids that looked a bit older, maybe five years or so than me. There were three guys in the group, and four girls. The guys had really dolled up for this occasion- two of them had nice pink shirts, and benign haircuts, like they may have been in a fraternity before, while retaining heavy doses of alcoholism and metrosexuality. The girls were made of plastic. When I see people like that, I wonder what it would be like to be one of them. I can't imagine it without a personality overhaul, but I think it would be fun to be tepid and handsome, and have sex with plastic girls. I don't really wish that it would happen, but sometimes it is fun to think about. Maybe I would know what the missing ingredient of chemistry feels like. I keep walking down Gaines Street for what seems like forever.

Presently, I come to a slightly more upscale pub, in the All Saints district, after walking for a good quarter of an hour. I am sure Poff wonders where I am, but I have the keys, and he can get a ride home if needs one. It is still dark and smoky, but I feel like I should go in and have a look around. The air is thick and it hangs around me. I feel unsettled and nervous. I look at my shoes, and my coat, and decide I am well dressed enough to go somewhere classy, instead of languishing in this place. If I stay too long, I might get sick. So back out into the cold I go, planting my feet on the sidewalk and shuffling back to my car.

There's a coffee shop that all my friends hang out at. It is in the All Saints district, also, and on my way back to the car, I decide to stop in and see if anyone is there. There is a band playing there that I haven't seen before, and I see a few familiar cars out front. I open the door, hiding in the heavy atmosphere, and inspect the premises for a bit. In the far corner of the rectangular room, laced with 70's-esque furniture and lava lamps, I see a cluster of people. Before I can hide, Xavier walks up to me, and shakes my hand.

"Hey Rad, what's going on?" I smile, and distract myself by continuing to observe the group. I follow Xavier back to the alcove in the back. Thom is there, sitting on the couch with Frances (I usually expect him to hang out with the Catholics). Kristen sees me coming next, and she runs up to me. Her friend Paul is with her, and this girl named Heather, who is sort of plain, is also present. Heather waves, and Paul smiles and nods in my direction.

"Ben-e-dict! I've missed you!" squeals Kristen. She hugs me, sort of. Sadly, all this is not important to me at all, because in the far right quadrant of the trapezoid the Catholics occupy, sitting on a couch, is Madeleine. Next to her is that guy that annoys me so much. I walk up to Frances. "Hey buddy, what's his name?" I point at Madeleine's couchmate decisively, and make a distinct gesture in his direction.

"Oh, that guy? That's Anthony. I think he is seeing her."

"How's that? I demand rigidly.

"They are together a lot. I think she is interested."

Sure enough, he was occupying as much of her personal space as he possibly could. She wasn't doing much about it, and I was pretty upset about the whole thing. I kept asking myself if I was mad enough to fix the problem.

Kristen patted the seat next to her, and signaled to me. She was warm and glowing, and she indicated that she wished I would sit down next to her.

I reached over and helped myself into the chair.

"So Rad, are you enjoying the book?"

"Yes, I am. I feel it has redeeming qualities for humanity." She beams with delight. Her hair is straight, and her skin is white. She has brown eyes, with distinct eye brows. Her arms are hairy, but her fingers were delicate and feminine. She has a smile that looks well rehearsed, but it gives me immense comfort and joy. I feel both judged and loved simultaneously, and I try my best to deflect all of my negative emotions into Kristen's halo. In one minute she was nothing to look at, and in the next, she was distilled aesthetic perfection. But of course, in the world of perfects, Madeleine is more so. I carry on small talk about the book with Kristen, while I hatch a plan to intervene in the conversation with Madeleine and her friend. While plotting my invasion of her couch, I see him put his arm around her briefly, indicating that he is also planning on doing something tonight.

This question comes to my mind, and it is unprecedented. *"Am I being a follower of Christ right now?"* It stings my insides. I don't really know how to follow Jesus in this situation, because Jesus never had feelings for a woman, and he never had to compete for one. I am not being a follower of Christ. Christ would have dismissed this sort of thing as petty bullshit, and told me that I needed to concern myself with more serious issues. He would have said to me, "My son, I will deal with this for you at a point when you are ready. Stop taking matters into your own hands, and stop trying to be in control." I am the beggar outside the temple, blind from birth. I have Him to help me with these things, and I have prostrated myself before Him. He has done his part for me. My eyes are still closed though, and although Jesus has smeared clay all over them, I am still too blind to find the pool of Siloam.

I struggle again towards the center of all of this. "Why do I want to intervene?" I ask myself in a tiny voice. This is not the sort of thing nice people do.

For all I know, there is no reason for me to. She will not like me for walking over to her, throwing Anthony off the couch, kicking the shit out of him, and walking away. And I will most likely be arrested for it. I am not "Benedict Radmeier, the Bad Ass Hero," and I am not rescuing a woman from someone who is trying to injure or kill her. I am simply serving my own interests in this circumstance. My motive is not love; it is jealousy. For all I know, I am the most jealous person in the universe right now, and it is because, in the billions of square miles of space and time and earth and stars, there is a couch in a coffee shop, with a girl, and I am not occupying the space next to her. My brain starts to stray from its trajectory of violence (isn't violence the first reaction for many men?), and I wonder what else I can do here. I look right at him, and he doesn't see me, He is absorbed in Madeleine's smile, and she is fanning the flame. I am forced to sit here, and watch. I have no ability to remove myself from this situation, because I am too self-interested to do so.

Xavier goes over to join in the conversation with them. He sits down on a chair, facing across from Anthony. He is engaging Anthony and Madeleine equally, indicating that he is not cock blocking, and just catching up with friends. I sit silently next to Kristen on my right as she engages other people in conversation. I sit silently next to a wall on my on my left, and I feel super awkward. Kristen pulls away from me a bit. She may have smelled alcohol on my breath.

I look for my in. *"What could I possibly accomplish from some sort of invasion of their personal space?"* In my brain, I list all of the bad things that could happen:
1. Madeleine will now not only think I am a creeper, but also a rageaholic.
2. She will know I am controlled by jealousy.
3. She will never want to be my friend.
4. She will never change her mind.
5. All the Catholics will hate me and I will alienate myself from the only friends I have.

114

I make a list of all the good things that could happen:
1. I will blow any chance I have with Madeleine, so I will be forced to move on.
2. I will make myself feel better, since I took a bold step.
3. I will show Madeleine that she is worth fighting for (or over).
4. I will avenge Lucia.

I am not burning a bridge here. Instead, I am blowing up a minefield. I just need to make sure that I am not standing on top of a mine.

I brace myself for impact. I check my apparel to make sure that I don't have a shirt on that is inside out, or a pair of socks that don't match. I start to get up, and then I remember that I need to rehearse my lines. In my head, I go over the sequence of events, in slow motion, and then I inch towards my goal.

1.Stalk your prey. My selfish passive aggressive brain follows his movements, and analyzes them slowly, with contempt. I watch him put his arm near her, then around her. I watch him looking off into outer space while his hand consumes the space between it and her fingers. I am not afraid of him, but I am afraid of what he means to her. I get the odd feeling that this is a suicide mission. I am losing nothing, though, as this woman loves me as much as she loves acne, or red wine. She has eyes for Anthony, and so my motive is to embarrass him, and nothing more.

2. Make eye contact with the enemy: He turns towards me, and I smile in the most honest way that I can. He sort of nods, without smiling. He turns away rapidly. His affect is arrogant, and he has no idea why I am looking at him. I want to take him out, strip him of his clothes, and leave him naked on a highway. I only hate him because

he has what I want.

3. Approach the target. I go and sit down in an open seat right by their couch, and look right at her. I wait for her to greet me first. In the two second space, I freeze time, and she notices me. I open my eyes, and feel unsettled. She lifts her head, and her hair falls in just the right places. My heart beats faster than I like, and I can feel myself stutter, even though I have not said a word.

"Madeleine, how are you?" I ask her. She smiles, which surprises me, and looks at me with a glint in her eye. "I am having a great day, thank you." Her response is strained and somewhat cold. It lacks the warmth that a friend would receive you with.

In a second, the silence passes away and she makes an ambiguous gesture towards Anthony. "This is my friend Anthony," she quips. I am trying to keep my face bright and happy. I think the feeling is on the surface, but she will not believe me.

"Anthony, this is Benedict."

Anthony extends his right hand, and shakes mine. He dips his head and says a meaningless hello. Clearly, she feels awkward. He is older than I am- at least twenty eight. I dislike him more and more each second. I finally become anxious, and say something.

"So, Anthony, how did you make your way into this group?"

He smiles cordially. "I met Madeleine at Mass, and she invited me."

Of course it had to have been this way. Here he is, the whiteness of white.

"Have you been reading *Redeeming Sexuality* with us?"

"I already read it, actually. It's quite good."

"What do you do for work?" He chuckles a little bit at the last question, and bites his lower lip.

"I'm an attorney."

Damn it. He's an attorney. The rift of comparison swallows me in, and I am suddenly more insecure than I have ever been.

"That's cool. What kind of attorney?"

"It's nothing," he says. "You'd be bored by it." His false modesty is making me even angrier, and all I need now is some sort of response that will knock the wind out of me.

"No. Tell me," I growl impatiently like a five year old who is about to get a birthday present.He waits for a second, and then he smiles. I cannot tell if it is prideful, or if he genuinely loves his job. Here it comes…

"I work for the Diocese of Pensacola-Tallahassee. I'm in the family and life office."

My face falls. I can't hold up the façade any more. His job is to protect unborn children.

"I see…" I murmur.

"Why do you look so down?" Madeleine asks. She saw my face melt, so she knows something is up. I appeal to God for a lie.

"It's just sad to think about abortion, you know?"

They both agree, fervently. My affect is deteriorating visibly, and I lack the composure to really say anything meaningful. Here it is, right in front of me, and it has all become a shit show.
"There's no way you can sabotage this one," I say to myself quietly. This guy works at the pro-life office, and I sit in front of my computer and look at porn. We both pray to the same God and that's all.

I sit there in silence for ten minutes while all of them share small talk about things I hope to never care about.

Anthony looks over across the room. Aside, he mutters something to Madeleine, and she gets her things together. He stands up and helps her off the couch. He is so dainty, and pathetic. She offers him her hand, and he pulls her up. She walks ahead, in front of him. He turns around, and takes his first step.

My passive aggressiveness has reached its zenith, culminating in me putting my leg out right where the bridge of his foot will pass. He is too oblivious to see it.

Anthony is stepping. Anthony is making contact with my foot. Anthony is suddenly realizing he has lost his balance. Anthony is falling. Anthony is struggling while he is falling. Anthony is grasping for something in thin air. Anthony is seeing the coffee table in front of him. Anthony is smacking his face on the coffee table. In a few seconds, a small rivulet of blood is visible.

I quietly tuck my feet under my chair. "What happened?" Kristen shouts, anxiously.

"I think he tripped on my chair leg..." I mutter. I rush to his aid, handing him paper towels to coax the blood away from the furniture. Anthony is nursing his bleeding upper lip. Madeleine begins to sob. I apologize to him about my chair being in the way, and he looks at me, surprised, but too disoriented to do anything. I feel like an elementary school pupil who has just committed an outrageous act of violence against another student. When we make references to immature children who never grew up, and became immature adults, those references are relevant to me.

As I am straightening up the mess, Xavier mentions something about Anthony's teeth, and a recent corrective surgery. I listen in, realizing that I did something that was very wrong indeed.

Anthony gets up of of the couch, as the bleeding subsides just a bit, slowly, while nursing his lip. Madeleine helps him out of the coffee shop, and they leave. I stay for another five minutes, trying my best to appear remorseful. I let Kristen know that I feel bad, and she says that it is not my fault, and that I didn't mean to injure him. If only she knew the darkness of my heart.

Nine

I dismissed myself, and walked back to the Saab. I felt mildly ashamed of what I did, But I knew that there must be some justification for it. I hardly knew that Anthony had knocked a tooth loose on the edge of the table, and would require at least six stitches.

I also didn't know about his years of painful oral surgeries to correct a serious overbite, or that he had a thing about having scars on his face. All I knew was that all was fair in love and war.

I drove by the pub where Poff had been, but he was long gone. It seemed almost too quiet in there, and perhaps I should have stayed, but the lack of resolve in my soul carried me away and into deeper trouble. I flicked through the gears on the way home, trying to dodge the efforts of my conscience to make itself heard.

When I got home, Poff was sitting on the couch in a drunken stupor. I needed to get to bed before Frances got home, or else I would be in deep shit. He looked right at me when Anthony fell over, like I was responsible for it.

So I am sitting on my couch, looking for an excuse, and my dear friend Francesca walks in.

"Hey Rad," he says.

"Hey, Frank. Is Anthony still alive?"

"He needs stitches. Madeleine drove him to the ER. His face was a mess." He looks at me with a glint of accusation

"I promise I didn't mean to trip him," I state, trailing off towards the end.

"Well, I suppose that you had a motive. After all, you do like her."

"No I don't." My objection is adamant.

"What else are you lying about?" He asks.

Poff comes in from the guest bedroom, and he is starting to be coherent. "What are you guys talking about? Did Rad get in a fight and kick someone's ass?" Poff has no clue what happened to us.

Francis answers. "You know that girl Madeleine? The one Rad is in love with?"

Poff summons all his faculties. "The one he bought a glass of wine for?" I nod, sheepishly.

"Rad tripped her friend Anthony at the coffee shop."

I got mad. Of course, what can one more lie hurt? "I didn't do shit to him!" I yell at the top of my lungs.

Francis continues. "I saw him trip Anthony. He fell onto the corner of a wooden coffee table, and knocked a tooth out, cut his lip really badly, and bled everywhere." I stood there genuinely feeling shitty. "…And he had to go to the ER," Frances adds.

I leave the room, and go to my quarters. I would go to confession the next day. I pick up Joseph North's silly book, and read a bit of chapter two.

Chapter two: What all of us are afraid of

I tell people quite often that happiness is a state of freedom where we don't feel threatened to be who we are. Happiness is when you have fully realized yourself, and no one is trying to destroy you. So why is it that when we are with the person we love, we feel so threatened? One minute, we are afraid they are going to cheat on us, and the next minute, our sexuality is not good enough for them. Then, when we profess insecurity, instead of being received with compassion and understanding, we are left in neglect. And the cycle perpetuates from one partner to the next, and we are unhappy. When we are unhappy, we start to take things for granted, and nothing is beautiful, and everything loses its value. At the string of this worthless endeavor, we rip the value out of family, friends and finally, love and romance. One caveat- while this does not apply to everyone, it is becoming more and more common.

I have a theory about where one night stands originated from. A one night stand is a thinning and paring of all the components of love that are truly meaningful, until the most intense ones are removed and exercised in the course of a short period of time. Once you become attached to this short term ecstasy, you miss the little, smaller things that define what love truly is, and you confuse it with a series of sensual arousals that bring only short term satisfaction.

This all started with us feeling unhappy, and our unhappy

feelings came from us being threatened, and feeling insecure. Our insecurity is so pervasive that we can't separate ourselves from it. So how does one rid themselves of feelings that will ruin their happiness for the rest of their life?

People will settle for anything. We are so desperate and so pathetic, yet we forget we have a creator who sent His son to die for us. But we stand for nothing, and we will look for those untrustworthy tangibles- sex, emotional dependency, orgasm, sensuality, as our things we need to be seeking. We really ought to be seeking faith, wisdom, temperance, spirituality and a host of other beneficial intangibles, but who wants to do that? I realize that it is unrealistic for us to constantly seek holiness as the Holy Father, or Mother Teresa seeks it. We have to seek holiness to live a meaningful life, whether we like it or not. But at the end of holiness is happiness. A spiritual foundation is not rocked by someone telling us we are sexually inadequate, or by a woman telling a man he is physically unattractive. Holiness is a form of security, a shield from feeling inadequate and hopeless, from feeling insecure and vulnerable. Only when our center lies in a stable being like Christ, can we embrace the possibility of a complete and lasting happiness.

In my youth, I was often perplexed at what "being holy" truly meant. I was so unhappy with myself, and with others, that it seemed that this fabled religious lifestyle I had heard so much of meant about as much to me as the frozen foods section at the grocery. During my summer after high school, on a trip to England, I became involved with a girl about my age who seemed a much happier person that I was. She would often tell me that she felt connected to God, and when she was disconnected from Him, she was unhappy. Although I dismissed her feelings as nothing more than a security object, the memory of what she had shared with me lingered. In later years, I became intrigued at how many Christians I had met that shared something similar with me.

Since we have been asked to journal, and I am feeling truly awful, I pull my notebook out.

Dear diary on Joseph North's book:

Why is it that we do not have the ability to love when we need to love the most? What drives us to be such evil, uncaring figures? Why is it that we hold women so high above God? I should be excited for things like the Resurrection, the Eucharist, and the Holy Spirit. Instead, I wait for some theoretical preordained day of my life where God may introduce me to my soul mate. That day may never come. Instead of being prayerful and patient, I am spiteful and destructive, trying to eradicate love that is not directed at me. I quench my soul with the septic waters of pornography in hopes that God will one day magically turn my dark desires into some kind of love for Him. I hope that in this love, I will find my woman. But alas, while I know He has the power to completely change me, I do not know if the opportunity for change exists. I am a soul unredeemable.

Perhaps North is right (as usual). I feel so insecure and pathetic because I am disconnected from God. This awkward hatred of chemistry binds me, because I am a slave to the approval and disapproval of women. They hold the keys to my security, and they hold the cure to my insecurity. In my own world, I am praying to goddesses who cannot hear me, do not know my heart and do not care about how I feel. Why do I forfeit a loving God for something I cannot change and have no control over?

When they approve of you, they tell you that there is chemistry. I have erected a dais in my heart, and placed Lucia- and now Madeleine- upon it. I am addicted to their very movements, or the movements that Lucia made in the past. I could blame God for not moving more evidently in my life, or giving the burdens of sexuality and desire to cope with. How am I not to idolize women when my desires lead into such feelings? And how can I not feel insecure? Is it possible for me to even desire to be *holy*? We are not wired for holiness! We are wired to give and receive love, and even more so from a significant other! And yet, God has the *audacity* to ask that we try to be holy. When we can't have the one thing that we need and desire so badly, how can we even focus on anything else? Anyone who acts like they are comfortable with it is pretending.

But North is right, and here's why I think he is right. In the middle of chapter two, he says something that really stands out to me.

If God has given us everything we need, and we are lacking nothing, what is keeping us from being holy? Holiness remains a primary pursuit even for the very poor. In fact, in many countries where poverty is a way of life, we often find outstanding examples of holiness. Meanwhile, in our first world bliss, where everything is beyond the "perfect" that some impoverished third world citizens think about often, we find very few examples of holiness in comparison. Our first world distractions are intimidating. They complicate our lives to the point that we lose sight of the benefits of being holy. When the desire to find food and shelter is replaced by the desire to buy a new car and find a date for Friday night, we might lose sight of God more easily because our first world incomes and connections are supposedly supplying us with our needs, rather than a prayer to the almighty for our basic necessities. When we are too wrapped up in our own insecurities, our own failed hopes and our own little dramas, God has severely limited room to work in our lives. In this limited view, Satan has enticed the world with various substitutes that have immense amounts of sensual appeal. This chaotic first world life style is the gateway drug to all sorts of negative feelings.

The man who is searching for water in the desert has only one thing in mind- to find water. The man searching for water in a gas station can't even relate to a man in the desert. He is on his way somewhere important. He is not dying, or suffering. He is just looking to solve his slight problem of thirst, so he can now dwell on all his other slight issues.

I'm sure all my readers are wondering why a book on sexuality brings into itself such a heavy discussion of poverty.

We all want sex, and the desires for love, sex, romance and the like are not first world issues. They apply to all of us. Otherwise, the poorest places in Africa would just have famines, and not HIV epidemics. Satan has taken this inversion of God's gift of sexuality and used it to keep us from being holy. It has become a preoccupation for us, because the end goal of every human being is to not be alone. Everyone who is human at some point experiences a need to be loved. This is a very beautiful and God-given need, but when you saturate this need with the inverted sexual distortion that our society has become absorbed with, suddenly the desire to be loved isn't good enough. Just like our first world pursuits of material excess, a happy lifelong marriage does not cut it.

No, we are so confused that we pursue pornography, casual sex, sensual gratification in the form of prostitutes and nude dances, and then claim that we still want a happy lifelong marriage.

This is a hard statement for me to make, but I need to make it. If you are bent on fulfilling the desire for love, happiness and sex, you need to eliminate the distractions. How can a man pray for a good wife when he is spending time looking at pornography on the internet? If you didn't have the internet, and you were looking for food, you would be asking God to help you not starve to death. But instead, your fridge is stocked, you have a computer, in your apartment, where all your bills are paid, and you are so comfortable that you decide that it won't hurt to spend a bit of that extra money on a pay-site.

Those of us that have the excess should have nothing to complain about. God has given us everything, and thus, we now have the means to focus on Him. Imagine if you lost everything. I bet you would pray fervently to God to restore all of it, and promise never to lose sight of Him if He did. It's funny, as He gave all of it to us in the first place, and we fail to thank Him. We didn't even have to ask for it.

After reading this, I think to myself: *"If only I could destroy chemistry. Then I would not be distracted from serving God thankfully."* But chemistry is really a bitch. It's a virus. It's that one little thing that is elusive and intangible that messes up our entire

124

focus. What North is telling me is that I should toss that desire and focus on all the great things God has given me, In a way, I bet he even feels sorry for us citizens of the first world. We are too distracted to do anything but become paralyzed by our meaningless desires.

Suddenly, I feel guilty for injuring Anthony, and at the same time, completely insensitive. This desire for chemistry with Lucia led me to having unfulfillable feelings for Madeleine, and those feelings led me to an act of passive aggressive violence. If I were starving and living in a refugee camp in Serbia, I might have beat the shit out of someone to get a bite to eat, but somehow I feel that the act would be justified.

When I first became friends with Lucia, she seemed to transcend all things. I would have loved her, starving or not. I would have cared for her if she and I were socio-economically hopeless. I wanted a small apartment with her, within a walk of the gulf, where we could make love all day, and eat goat cheese, and not give a damn that I was a financially insolvent music journalist, and she a Publix cashier. Our lives would be meaningful because we would have meant everything to each other. Of course, when you feel like I do now- emotionally wrecked, sexually disturbed- and your brain writes everything in shorthand because you are merely observing things until you fade away, you are waiting for the next empty shred of hope.

But what is this book doing to me? Is it forcing me to change? Do I want to change? This thing is written for serial daters who have no concept of stability, right?

I want this book to restore hope in my life. But I don't believe in God enough to do it, much less Pope John Paul the Second, and I'm laughing about some British guy who wrote a book about what the other two were trying to explain.

Ten

The sacrament of reconciliation is a cross that the serial sinner carries. After a pretty dull Saturday morning of sitting on my ass watching movies that make me feel nothing, and listening to Kevin listen to Juliana Theory (which, in my post-masturbatory coma makes me cringe, as I feel separated from God), I resolve to go confession.

There are several reasons that I secretly go to Reconciliation every Saturday (besides the fact I look at pornography quite often):

1. I don't want any of my friends to see me not receiving communion. They might ask questions.

2. I don't like feeling shitty, and Confession is about the only place I can actually feel God making me not feel shitty.

3. I like pretending that I am never going to look at porn or masturbate again.

4. I like the feeling I get after Confession. It is euphoric and beautiful.

Of course then there are the negotiations I go through about why I shouldn't go.

1. I do this nearly every Saturday, and keep resolving to change, but I never seem to follow through.

2. Most priests I deal with about this sort of thing are not very nice about it. They treat me like I have a *serious* problem.

3. It reminds me of the fact that I am a relative failure in all areas of my life.

Confession always brings with it a certain relief. This is rooted in the fact that I know God still loves me. This whole business of needing to go to confession every week is temporary anyway, and when I meet the right woman, I will stop being lonely, thus eliminating my need for pornography. However, there is no guarantee that God will send me that person.

Therefore, if I keep up this filthy habit, it will be His fault.

I have always wanted a relationship with God based on something meaningful. He and I have never quite seen eye to eye on things. When we talk, it is defensive, and full of anger and bitterness. I identify with Jesus more. Jesus seems to understand what I am looking for. I don't know why he can't appear to my future bride, and tell her to love me.

Today, I am going to seek out a new church for confession. I am tired of being judged by the priests of my parish, and I really hate the idea of being scrutinized by them repeatedly for failing in the same way over and over again. I remember, once, on the retreat, there was a really nice priest, Father Phillip, from a church called Mary, Queen of the Sea, in Gulf Breeze. I had befriended him, and we had a number of deep conversations. He had moved to a smaller church in an area on the outskirts of town.

I must find this church. He understood everything about what I was telling him- when he heard my confession, and he really heard it, he could relate to me. There was a woman he truly loved at one point in his life. Leaving her was the hardest thing he had ever done, but he understood that these sorts of decisions are made with the head, not the heart. Anyhow, I will find him.

I gingerly wake Poff up. Poff is in his pajamas, as it was that cold outside. He had been nesting on the couch all night.

"Hey buddy; can you do me a favor? I need you to find out where this priest is that I want to see today."

"Why can't you find out?" He seems confused.

"Because I don't want to talk to the Catholics right now. They might find out about what I did."

Poff recalls all his faculties, and then it hits him. "Oh, you tripped that kid last night, huh? "

I feel mad, but I hold my tongue. "I didn't trip him. He fell." I pout with such pompous reserve that I am starting to believe my own lie.

Poff looks at me ruefully. "If you lie long enough, you start to believe your own lie. Besides, who is to say that I would not have done the same thing? I can be bitter and difficult too. You just had an episode." Poff has just taken my grave sin and turned it into an incident of insignificance. Really though, consulting Stephen Poff on matters of right and wrong always yields a gray area that most of the Catholics have issues with. Poff continues nesting on our couch. "Well, Poff, are you going to call someone?" Poff gets up, gracefully, and waltzes to the phone. "Rad, what is Kristen's number?" "You don't have it?" I ask. "I do, but it's not like I take it with me when I travel." I'm such a creeper that it's a miracle that I have any phone numbers at all. I hand him Kristen's number, and he dials her. It is relatively early (eleven-ish) and she answers the phone after it rings for a bit.

"Hey Kristen, This is Stephen." "Oh, hey Stephen!" She says with elation.

"Rad had some girls over last night, and he had a ménage a trois, and now he needs to know where Father Phil is working so that he can go pretend he's sorry." I angrily punch Poff in the arm.

Kristen is not laughing at his joke, but she immediately notifies him that Father Phil has been appointed parochial vicar at St. Paul the Apostle in Madison. I grab my phone book, and look up St. Paul while he and Kristen share small talk.

"Ok, you bastard, get off the phone!" I yell to him after a few minutes. I rampantly dial the number to St. Paul's, and wait for a recording. Surprisingly, someone actually answers the phone! This never happens at Catholic churches. You always get a pretty nonchalant recording. The lady sounds friendly.

"May I help you? "She asks sweetly.

"Does a Father Phillip work at your church?"

"Why yes, he does."

"Is he hearing confessions today, per chance?"

"Let me check," the nice lady says. "Give me a few minutes." I wait on the phone nervously. I really need for this to come through.

She comes back after a brief eternity. "Hey there, I *think* he is going to be hearing them. We usually start at two, but today he has a baptism, so he will be hearing them early. Maybe one in the afternoon?"

I thank her, and hang up. It is eleven thirty now, so I look up the address on the computer and write down directions.

By now the temperature outside has climbed into the forties, and it is sunny. Inspired by the outdoor scenery, I am forced to acknowledge the beauty of God in the world, and while I feel bad for looking at pornography, tripping Anthony, using foul language and being such an unhappy person, I am also forced to feel a shred of hope.

Lucia had a fairly odd relationship with this sort of thing. One day, I selfishly criticized her behaviors and told her that she needed to go to confession before receiving communion. This was way after our friendship went off the deep end, and there was no hope left for it.

Instead of finding Jesus in the confessional, she stopped going to Mass altogether. After I said that, she didn't show any anger, but there was a guilty look, and then a sharp word back to me, spoken gently, but with an underlying bitterness. We barely talked after that, as if I telling her she needed Jesus was the one thing that she did not want to hear. For the longest time, thereafter, I prayed for her return to the church fervently, hoping that she would come back to the Lord, clean up her act, and start to love Him again. But the worst thing was that the only reason I was praying for her, confessing my sins on a regular basis, and trying to be so devoted to Jesus was that I hoped Lucia would return for me. It is only human to want someone back so badly that they control all of your deepest desires. I would have given part of my body to have her back in my life, and in the Church. But of course, we possessed no chemistry, and this sort of thinking was irrelevant.

I arrive at St. Paul's at 1:05 P.M., and the church is dark. I have been here once before, now that I recall. All of my friends are familiar with this church, and they have also talked about it before.

I wander among the dark, hardwood pews, and gaze upon the giant crucifix at the front of the church. The church is somewhat cold inside, and seeing dying Jesus, right there in front of me, I feel immensely sorry for every sin I have committed. Slowly, I find a hidden corner and kneel. I look upon Jesus with the sort of sorrow that a man who has lost everything feels. I want Him to reach down and touch me, and heal me of all these awful desires. I want Him to absolve me of all of my faults, and take away the conflicting feelings of desire and lust. I want Him to erase the scars Lucia left, and erase the ones that she still carries. I want Him to help me care for Madeleine as my sister, without any expectation. I want Him to look upon me with love, and compassion, and empty me of all of my weakness. I want to feel His love for me. I want to feel good again.

The lights go on in a far corner of the church, and a figure in a white stole glides across the floor. No one is here but me. I can speak freely, and no one will hear me. I get up, and venture towards the door, with a shameful gait. The door is wide open, and there is a light emanating from it. I slip inside, and in front of me, is a strange priest- not Father Phillip, who is looking right at me, and motioning to take a seat. He is a big guy, somewhat older, with a beard. He looks very serious, and I am a little afraid. I sit down nervously.

He begins by crossing himself, and then he waits for me. This is the part I really hate- how to tell someone for the millionth time that I have an issue with something really bad. It would be much easier to walk into a confessional and say "father, I have a drug problem," or "father, I am an alcoholic." These are normal sins. They involve things that we get sucked into where there are treatment programs. They are things we read about every day, so we are entirely desensitized to them. So while they are still bad, it is "more common" to see someone with a substance abuse problem. No one popular chronically looks at porn, and it belongs to a dark underworld of sins that Christian society does not accept very well. I imagine it could be worse. I could have had sex with another man (but oddly enough, sex with a woman does not seem to be nearly as bad as pornography).

I begin, nervously. "My last confession was, er, a week ago. Since then I abused the gift of my sexuality by looking at pornography and masturbating. I also entertained inappropriate thoughts about women. And there's one more thing..." My voice trails off, and diminishes.

There has to be a way that I can explain this to a strange priest so that he understands it. I wonder if he has ever been in my shoes, overcome with jealousy because of what another man has. I certainly hope so, because if he hasn't, I will look even worse. I catch my breath. "I like this girl. I ran into her at a coffee shop with a bunch of my friends, and her date. I was really jealous of him, for being on a date with her, because I really like her. So when he got up out of his chair, I tripped him. His face hit a corner on the table in front of him, and he got a serious wound. He had to go to the hospital. So anyway, I want the Lord to know that I am sorry for that."

Father was somewhat upset by my comment. "My friend, The Bible tells us 'Thou shalt not kill', and in that all acts of violence towards other human beings are included. It is not up to us to decide when it is just and when it is not- it is never right to hurt another person when you are jealous of them. You need to find him and apologize for your action."

Father's delivery is abrupt, and painful. I should have followed the age old practice of praying for my confessor prior to confession. Who is to say that it is not just? If he was twenty four years old, and he was in love with a girl who didn't give him the time of day, what would that mean for him? What would he do? Still, there remains another part of this whole fiasco I must disclose to him. I look at the floor. "I'm not done, Father," I murmur.

"Go on," he says.

"I lied to him, and all my friends, and said it was an

accident."

The priest looks right at me. I can feel his eyes penetrating my soul. If this has never happened to you, it can be very uncomfortable. "I think Jesus would expect you to tell him the truth."

Unbreakable silence for an eternity looms over me. I just sit there.

He absolves me, and I say my act of contrition, slowly, and trembling: "Oh my God, I am sorry for my sins... In choosing to do wrong, and failing to do good, I have sinned against you... because you are good and deserving of all my love. I firmly intend, with the help of your grace, to confess my sins, to do... penance, and to...amend my life." I struggle with the word "penance."

Father looks up, and says "For *your* penance, I would like for you to apologize to him."

This means that if I fail to do my penance, then this confession is worthless. It means that I am not sorry. My regular confessor usually gives me a Divine Mercy chaplet. I pray it fervently, and go back to my life of sinfulness. This is different, though, as it will force me to be accountable. Not really what I want, but what I need. I need lots of things, but the easiest one would be for Jesus to magically fix me.

Father speaks one more time. "Please do it in person. I absolve you from your sins, in the name of the Father, the Son, and the Holy Spirit. Amen."

Now I have to confront Anthony, look at the scar on his lip, accept the fact that it was entirely my fault, and then apologize sincerely to his face.

I quickly thank the priest, get up and leave. I am now faced with the unenviable task of finding Anthony and asking his forgiveness. I struggle towards the door, realizing how hard this task is going to be for me. There has to be a way around all of this.

Immediately regret floods in. If I had been thinking like a Christian, and not a sexually depraved zombie, I would have had the courage to just leave. I could have gone home and wallowed in my misery, without any burden of guilt. Considering that wallowing is what I do best, this should have been the appealing alternative.

A strange feeling catches me. Usually, after confession, I feel like a burden has been lifted off of my shoulders. I feel light, and good, and free of sin. But this time, I do not feel this way. I still feel every bit as awful as I did before. I kneel down and think about this odd sensation for a bit.

After about ten minutes, it dawns on me that I will not *feel* forgiven until I have done my penance. Forgiveness will be withheld from me until I go out and find Anthony and tell him I am sorry. I have no idea if this is theologically accurate, but it sure *feels* that way. I look up at Christ, crucified. I think to myself "Holy crap, you're real." I quickly feel bad about saying "crap" in church.

I drag my feet out to the parking lot to my car. It is the only one there, with the exception of a green Acura. As I get closer, I see a bird has defecated all over my windshield. I go to the trunk and get a bottle of soapy water and a rag, and clean the bird shit off.

I get in the Saab. Legend has it that in 1978 there were no blue Saab 99 EMS's, and they were all silver or burgundy. But the man who purchased this car new owned a Saab dealership in Atlanta, and the company made him a special silver-blue EMS, with a sunroof and air conditioner. I really liked the amazing back story of this car, as it suggests to me that anything is possible with the right combination of ingredients. Now the car is faded, somewhat, and the interior is sort of tatty, like an old couch, and last week it rolled 250,000 miles, but I feel like the man who ordered this car new really and truly loved it, and would be happy it was being looked after so well. The black vinyl interior was like a second home for me, and I knew all of its imperfections very well. When Poff, that loon, first saw my car, it was like he had a vision in the middle of the parking lot. Everyone loves a tidy older Saab, but Poff had an infatuation with mine. Likewise, his Saab 96 had captivated me. He still owns the old 96, and enjoys its charms, but his "modern" car is a Saab 9000. It is cool, but not nearly as cool as the 96.

I drive back home. Today is Saturday, meaning that there is

no way I can go out with the Catholics tonight. I need new friends. I need friends who are cool, and not weird and judgmental. I need friends who actually like me and want to be around me. No one ever calls me and says "hey Benedict, I really want to see you!" Perhaps if I had friends who really liked me, I would not have been so mad and angry about Anthony, and I wouldn't have tripped him. No, one of those imaginary really good friends would have convinced Maddy that I was a stand up guy, and she would have consented to get to know me. I was enthusiastic about all of my friends at first, in college, but they turned out to be too perfect. I did not try to become perfect. All I wanted to be was myself. They were uncomfortable with who they were, and I was uncomfortable with them. They were also uncomfortable with me, and there were numerous occasions where our leadership would cite me for some sort of inappropriate behavior. I was almost always the black sheep, but I got used to it, and eventually became content with my role. There was something almost scandalous about it, an intoxicating notoriety. It was as if all of the Catholics expected me to fuck up, so they could secretly compare themselves to me, and say "at least I am not as bad as Benedict."

I always expected a discreet heavenly reward for carrying this cross. I figured that Jesus knew what was going on, and He could identify with me. After all, the Pharisees had the same opinion of Jesus. They saw Him as a trouble maker, and as an insurrectionist. My friends are nice people, but they remind me of Pharisees. I even saw Xavier wearing a baseball cap with a Bible verse upon it the other day...sort of like those giant headdresses the Pharisees wore that had the law written on a role of paper that was displayed upon their forehead for everyone to see.

I still love my faith. My friends just make it harder for me to show everyone that. I suppose that one day we will all grow up and see past the weaknesses that are such a challenge to all of us.

When I get home, Poff is still laying on the couch in his undies. "Poff, did you go anywhere today?" I ask. It is now almost three P.M., and he is lying right where he did before.

He looks at me, and realizes I asked him a question. "Huh?"

"Did you get your ass off of that couch yet?"

He laughs. "Sorry, I'm not a serial porn addict, so I don't have to wake up at five in the morning on Saturday and go to confession." Poff is just as bad a human being as I am, but he deals with it better, and hides his spiritual failings from all of the other Catholics.

"Are we going anywhere tonight?" I look at Poff. His chest is blond and hairy.

"I think so. " He yawns in the middle of his sentence. "There was some talk about the Catholics doing something."

I cringe. I suppose I will find Anthony there, and he will be all bandaged up. This needs to happen soon, though, so I get ready for this highly unpleasant form of spiritual healing. In the interim I pick up Mr. North's book and read more of chapter two.

Eleven

In my own experience with fear, I realized that I was scared of a lot of things that slipped under the radar of my faith, so to speak. Before I got married, I was constantly in search of a woman that I had feelings for. When I did meet these women, instead of being overjoyed to find them, I was suddenly afraid of them. I asked myself repeatedly "where does this fear of love and permanence come from?" I duly noted that if I ran off with the first woman I met, I could not be with the second, unless I was unfaithful. And I was also afraid of being unfaithful. What I was experiencing was a fear of commitment, which is right in line with the rest of our society. What does one do when they are afraid of being alone and also afraid of making their entire life about another person?

135

God did not create marriage for us to feel alone and insecure. Marriage is an example of something much greater- a foreshadowing of the love that we will feel with God in heaven. What more could we ask for besides this? Somehow, we have forgotten about love being a Godly thing, a gift. Instead, it has become a series of dramas that drags us in and spits us out.

This entire passage riveted me, as it shows how our entire lives are controlled by fear. Again, North has read me like a book, and now I look like a genuinely bad person. I desire only the best woman in the universe, and I look at the situation with this sort of assurance that she will be mine. The problem is that when a good one comes along, I always think "I can do better…maybe." The main issue that I forget quite often is that the majority of these women have no desire to be with me at all. What good are ten women who have no desire for me? There is nothing there. I am afraid of committing to a person who hasn't even identified the possibility of commitment. What good are a hundred women when you are trying to pick the best one, and none of them give a damn about you? The fear of commitment isn't really a fear for me. It is a lie I use to keep myself busy.

I have never had a woman want me, or need me, or have any sort of feeling for me. It has always been me, pouring my heart out into an unquenchable vacuum. Where these energies go, I have no idea, but I believe in a discard pile, somewhere in the universe, for wasted efforts and lost causes. I have a feeling that I will find myself there.

If only I had something meaningful to pour my heart into. If only I met someone that would accept it.

Towards the end, North says something brilliant:

Those of us that find love too soon may also be caught off gaurd. It is better for a man or woman to mature spiritually, so that they can bring this attribute into a relationship, instead of making mistakes with romance early on.

Funny, as it sounded just like Lucia.

Lucia in Love

It was the end of my first semester in college. Lucia was seeing someone, and my love for her was breathing its dying breaths. He was taller than me, and he was sort of shady. He was twenty two, and he was from Miami. I followed him home one night from her apartment. His name was Alex. I saw her kiss him on the stairs. It was not a romantic kiss. It was a filthy, dirty, lustful kiss. It was as if he swallowed her, covered her in his saliva, and then threw her up. She humbly accepted being covered in his bodily fluids. He walked off, and got into his Navigator, like he didn't give a damn. His bass was always at its loudest, and he was always trying to be a gangster. He wore Enyce, and Southpole, and he always used foul language. He lived in a trashy set of apartment complexes near the college, the kind where you see some asshole smoking at nine A.M., and beer cans on the five square feet of front lawn. I don't know what he was *doing* in college. I only spoke to him once. He said "what's up" to me, when Lucia introduced us on an odd afternoon before things got serious. I returned his greeting with a "hey." And that was all I ever spoke to him.

Lucia had met Alex at a party in April. Before Alex, there was a string of guys that she would sleep with. They were usually assholes, and they would prove themselves so almost immediately, so that Lucia would find another one, sleep with him once or twice, find out that he was completely rotten, and then move on. But Alex was different.

She seemed to really grow fond of Alex, and when she and I saw each other, she talked about him with this excessive, half-guilty smile on her face. She would tell me how much she enjoyed "cuddling" with him at first, and how he was cool, and sexy, and had big ideas to promote hip hop groups, or open a club in Miami Beach. She would tell me, eventually, about how much she enjoyed staying

137

the night over at his place, and how she felt "safe" with him. She shared all of her little gifts she would purchase for him and things she would do for him. She never made any mention of things he would do for her.

Alex was about five foot nine, with a fade cut. He looked almost Hispanic, but he wasn't. Lucia would hang all over him. He often wore wifebeaters. He worked out a lot, and I felt like a wimp when I saw him. He smoked weed too, and I was pretty sure I saw him pick up one time with Lucia in tow. Long story short, he fit the stereotype of an asshole.

My perception of the situation was such that he was still an asshole, but less so than the others. Or sex with him was *just right,* as Lucia hinted to me once. She had begun to see him often at the end of April, and I noticed that she spent less time with me. The sad fact was that all we did together by then was fight- I fought myself trying to tell her I was in love with her all the time, and she was fighting with me for acting like a jealous prick (these were her own words).

I would often drive by his place and see Lucia's car there, typically at three A.M. or so. I would listen to Jeff Buckley, and just be still. I would imagine them sleeping naked together after having sex. I would imagine them getting high, and not giving a shit. I would imagine ripping Alex to pieces during the chainsaw solo in *So Real,* and feeling good. I felt I must liberate Lucia from him, and make her come to her senses.

At the end of all of this madness was an event. I must have been by his house twenty times. On several occasions I would get up at two thirty, unable to sleep. I would work on my statistics homework for thirty minutes, and, restless, I would eventually lose focus. I would wander to the car, and tell myself that I was not going to drive by his house. I would then drive by her house, just to give myself the assurance that she was home. She was sometimes home, and then I would drive by visitor parking at her complex. From visitor parking, I could see her bedroom window. If the light was on, it meant she was there and alone. I only saw the light on when her car was there and his was not. I knew Lucia was uncomfortable with the dark, and preferred a light on when she slept alone.

If Alex's car was in the parking lot, as well as hers, the light was off. I hated to think about the meaning behind all of it.

In the event that her car was gone, I would drive to Alex's house. Her car would usually be parked right in front of his den, and the lights would be off. He had roommates too, but they were usually out. I never stayed long. I would simply wait in front for fifteen minutes, visualizing, and trying to convince myself to leave.

There was one night, in May, where she was at his house, sitting outside and seemingly drunk. He was with her but they looked unhappy, almost like they were saying unkind things to each other. I parked my car a safe distance away, and watched from afar. Disheveled Lucia, in her tangled web of drunken disparity, got into her Acura after making some visibly angry gestures at Alex. Alex yelled and screamed, and called her names like "bitch" and "slut." She drove off in anger.

I wasted no time in driving home. As soon as I got back, I called her, under the pretensions that I "couldn't sleep," and that I was "thinking about her."

When I called her, she was crying softly. "Benedict, is that you?"

"Yes, dearest, it is."

"W-w-where are you?"

"I am at home. I was thinking about you, and I couldn't sleep."

"You were thinking about me?" She stammered endearingly.

"Uh huh. What's wrong, Lucia, why are crying?" I asked gently.

"I don't want to talk about it."

"Can I come over?" I requested. She sounded so sad, and in that moment she was my Eve.

"I would like that," she whispered, underneath all of her tears. I hung up, assuring her that I would be there soon. You see, this was my last chance to win her over for myself. I wasted no time in getting to her.

I never told her about my late-night excursions, fearful of shredding the last bit of hope I had for her. I would go through lists of things that Lucia had done, and reasons why I would take her back. I would consider everything a possibility, and then accept it. But now, here was my chance to prove that I truly loved her.

Every man has this prom night fantasy, where the girl he loves sees him on a dark dance floor after she has been stood up by her date. She falls into his arms, and cries softly into his white shirt, leaving a soft palette of running make up, and left soaking wet with tears. It is the moment where the man is made aware of his worth and is rewarded for being there. As they dance in each other's arms, there is an unspoken promise of permanence, such that one will not leave the other, for anyone else, ever again (or at least in the near future). The incandescent glow of the night surrounds you, as your are left holding each other to the last song, and when she has pulled herself together, she looks up, and kisses you as softly as she has cried on you, upon your lips. You hold the back of her head, ever so gently, and stroke her hair until it is soft again. You dance perfectly to classical music, and you watch the hem of her gown twirl in the dark. Suddenly, you feel older and more significant, and you realize love is here to stay. And that was how I felt this night.

When I got to her apartment, the door was unlocked. She was lying on her bed, and wearing a spaghetti strap shirt with pink sweat pants. Her hair was a wreck, and she smelled like alcohol. She rolled over, and smiled at me. I could see that she was visibly distraught. I sat down next to her, and she sat up and gave me a hug. She rested her head on my chest, and she, in a visible sign of her comfort with me, reached up and removed my glasses. She did it so tenderly that I wondered if I had ever been mad at her at all. This gesture was significant because she had never done anything like it before. I was always the *initiator*. I took her hand and held it to my chest. It was cold, possibly lifeless. I had touched her hands so many times, but for once, I felt a quivering response from her, and she *held* my hand for the first time ever. For some odd reason, and as tainted as her slight clinging was, I felt more in love with her than ever before.

I lay down next to her, slowly. She collapsed down next to me, and I collapsed down next to her. I put my arm over her tiny, shivering body, and kissed her on the cheek. She stared up at the ceiling. I propped myself up on my shoulder and watched her eyes move.

"So what happened?"

She responded as if she were talking to herself. "He called me a whore. He told me I was an awful person and a terrible girlfriend."

"Why?" I think she was avoiding telling me about the iniquity that instigated the whole thing, most likely his offense.

"Well, he was with someone else. He got drunk at a party and this other girl and him were makin' out."

"And then?" Her improper grammar bothered me more than Alex's offense. In my mind I was cheering him on, hoping that he committed other transgressions with this other girl. I wanted to meet said other girl, so I could thank her for making Alex appear as the ass that I always believed him to be.

Lucia sucked on her tongue for ten seconds or so, and then uttered a response. "She gave him a blow job."

I was ecstatic inside. This might be the event she needed to endure to see that my love for her was invaluable.

"How did you find out?"

"He was acting weird, so I asked one of his friends what was up, and he told me it was not my business."

"So who told you?"

"He told me after I had sex with him tonight." Instantly, I felt more irreparable damage. I was thinking of ways to kill him, but all I knew how to do was ask more questions.

"How did you coax that out of him?"

"I told him I loved him, and he felt bad, so eventually it came out in pieces." I removed myself from her, slightly. I wanted to leave.

She continued. "I mean, he was drunk, so it wasn't like he *intended* to cheat on me. When I was first seeing him, I kind of sort of did the same thing."

In the absence of God, there is chaos. A mushroom cloud follows a blast of emotional destruction somewhere on the landscape of my soul. But deep inside, I felt nothing but love for her. How does one cast his precious angel out of heaven? How does one stop loving the only woman he has ever felt love for?

We fell asleep together, in each other's arms that night. She whispered to me at 4:30 AM. I really didn't believe what she said, but my heart *wanted to* so badly that I accepted it. Her cold hands on my warm skin felt so real. Her hair smelled like it was made of lilacs. Her body could have been Socrates' ideal form of woman. Her breath felt sweet and pure. They were the words that I had wanted to hear.

In the tiniest voice, she said it: "Don't ever leave me."

I went to class that morning in a state of ecstasy and elation. I shook off tiny, tired Lucia and left her house at 8:13 AM. I stopped at my place to grab my books and calculator. I was eight minutes late to my composition class (given the circumstances, I should have stayed right where I was). I had calculus after that, and then I could go home and be with her. My life had revolved around this moment and this action since I had met her.

After being in a romance coma all day long in class, I went back to my place, cutting through the surreal fog of what turned out to be a false victory, and called her. She did not answer, and I had been expecting her to be waiting by the phone. She did not answer the second time, or the third time, or the fourth time. Or the seventh, or the thirteenth. I decided it was time for a field trip, so I got in my car. As I flicked through the gears and listened to Matthew Sweet's *Evangeline*, I began to wonder where she had gone. She was not in class. Class was not until three or so for her, and she usually skipped. I was disturbed by her lack of desire to see me, and felt it was wrong for us to be so close one minute and so apart the next. I was being eaten up by a cancerous nervousness. It attacked my brain at its stem, and left me with a highly unpleasant nauseous sensation. The whole anticipation of seeing Lucia had created a massive expectation of happiness that *had* to be fulfilled. This uncompromising notion that I must see her had me in a death grip, and it was gnawing away at me. Of course, I refused to lie to myself. I knew where she was.

Like layers of a dream, I slipped back into my multifaceted fantasies about Lucia. On one occasion we were in a hot tub. Her body was perfect. I embraced her and held her, and right as we were about to have sex, she disappeared. I was left with an austere sentiment that bothered me after I woke up. The awful empty space was growing inside me, and I needed to find her so we could fill it. She needed to *finish* last night. She could not leave me for Alex. She could not take something complete and trade it for something incomplete. She could not take something good and accept something bad instead. She could not take something pure and trade it for something so tarnished. She could not take someone like me and leave him for someone like …Alex. But this is all I get.

No one realizes that there is a version of the prom night fantasy that women have, too. While it is not a total inversion, where the man runs into the woman's arm and cries all over her, it does involve the return of an unfaithful partner. In this case, the man comes back and begs forgiveness for his transgressions. I imagine Alex pleading with Lucia for forgiveness, and in her dark heart, she takes him back. There is some crying, and some emasculation, but the man only does this knowing what benefits are in store for him.

What happens next horrifies me. They don't stand there under the lights dancing. No, instead they have wild, passionate sex, where the man engages her entire body and pleases her on a carnal level and a neurological basis, feeding the sex addiction-based chemistry monster. There are no bright lights that come on as they walk away, hand in hand- together (as in a couple). No, instead, she leads him out, and they run away together, and they leave the building. She takes off her shoes, and giggling, they run to the car, where they cannot keep their hands off of each other. Wild kissing ensues, and I can almost feel myself, watching through the window, looking on pathetically.

And there I was, robbed of my fantasy come true. And what is to blame? Chemistry, damn it.

I drove straight to Alex's, knowing that was where she would be. Knowing that only the wrong thing can happen, and knowing that if things did go my way, it was only because they would become more strongly opposed towards me later. My car idled softly at the entrance of Alex's apartment complex.

In hindsight, I should have savored that tiny moment with her when she slept next to me for four miserable hours. If there was a better moment in my life, it could only have been so if I had not known her at all.

But in the gross reality of things, there was her Acura in his parking area. There was the sun, high in the sky, and the cold air circulating around me from the north. I wanted to go look in Lucia's window, and see myself sleeping there. But in my heart of hearts I knew that I would only see a wolf in bed with her.

I have multiple theories as to what had happened:

Theory one: Lucia went to Alex's to retrieve her "things," whatever those were. She had mentioned a number of personal items the night before. He told her he missed her, and after some persuasion, they reconsumated their "love," or whatever fucked up version of love they shared. She forgot all of his sins, and he kept doing what he was doing.

Theory two: She wanted to get back with him, but she was too careful to admit it to me. She just wanted a little bit of sympathy. Her idea was never to leave him, but rather to spend the night with me to get revenge. She went to him, telling him that she had been with someone else (me), and now they were even. I would like to think that they did not have sex, or some version of it, immediately thereafter. I like this theory the best, because I get to be an accessory.

Theory three: She awakens, realizing that she just spent the night with *me*, whom she finds repulsive. She runs back to Alex because she is used to him (and likes being used by him). She feels that she has to love him no matter what, simply to prove that she is the better person. He begs her for forgiveness, like the guys in a boy band would in their songs. She consents. The sex is wild. While she is having sex with him, she does not even think of me at all. I hate this theory, but it is entirely likely. This is my least favorite theory, even though it is also most likely.

The pointless question that I keep asking myself is "why did I *stay* through all of this?" Why did I keep hanging on for dear life to an idea that was never going to arrive at any sort of fulfillment? How was I supposed to make anything good come from this sort of self-destruction? She hurts me. I stay. She makes me feel inadequate. I stay. She makes me feel miserable. I stay. She chooses not to love me. I stay. She meets someone else. I stay. She pushes me away. I stay. She tells me things that kill me inside. I stay. She makes me stop loving *myself*. I stay. She makes me wish that I felt nothing. I stay. She makes me feel worthless and unlovable. I stay. She leaves. I am still here.

In several vague dialogues with her after that, I brought up the night we spent together, hoping that, like Alex, I could manipulate her into returning to me. But each time I brought it up, within a few seconds she could sense the intensity mounting in my voice, and she would irreverently silence me. She never allowed me express to her how I felt. The entire time, she expressed the feelings that I had for her to Alex. I have no idea what sort of darkness existed in the ravine that they had carved out for themselves, but I longed to kill him and take his place there, in Lucia's dark and sexy little heart.

In life, all moments of change boil down to just that- a moment. I was with Lucia, and it was early summer, in June. We were eating lunch together at a small restaurant in town. I was bored, and I called her up.

When I say that I was bored, what I meant was that I was

lonely. When I was lonely, what I meant was that I longed for the presence of someone. That someone was Lucia and Lucia only. I called her several times. She finally answered, curious about why I had called her so many times. I told her that I hadn't meant to call so much, and I wanted to see her. She finally agreed, after I pestered her for five minutes. She was sweet, and she agreed to meet in an hour. I got ready quickly.

I will never forget June 10th. It is the anniversary of my defeat, and the saddest day I can remember. This was when Lucia inflicted her deepest wound upon me.

I drove out to this café near downtown, and we sat outside. It was the sort of place you would expect for Apalachicola. It was hauntingly perfect for us, and since it was a weekday afternoon, it was almost vacant. I understood that when I would see her, I would be too uncomfortable to eat, and I anticipated feeling sick at my stomach. We had scheduled for one P.M., but in Lucia's typical fashion, she was late. Five minutes past the hour, she still did not show up. Ten minutes after that, still nothing. Every minute without her felt like an eternity. Every minute with her felt like it was slipping away in frames.

I have this idea about what it means to really want someone. When you miss them when they are not there, and your bed feels empty in the morning, and you think about them all the time, you truly *want* them. I still woke up every day thinking about Lucia, and feeling pervasive sadness that she was not there. The times she would come over for breakfast in the morning, and we would eat together, I would feel completeness. I lamented the fact that I never felt complete, like I felt complete with her, in my relationship with God. I would sit in my living room, the sun streaming through the windows, holding her on my couch. We would listen to the birds outside, and she would quietly acknowledge that she felt safe with me.

But not so, anymore. The quiet little angel-turned-devil

appeared to me in my state of melancholy twenty minutes later than she said she would. She alighted from her Acura, with her large purse. She wore big sunglasses, and a tank top that showed too much. Her hair was a mess, and when she approached me, I duly noted that she smelled like a mixture of male and female scents. I quietly looked at heaven, and asked God to give me the strength to just get up and leave. But Jesus never left the Cross, and so I must stay here too, and die for the sins of Lucia.

I stood up out of my seat, and hugged her. The anger inside of me melted down into tears, she squeezed me for a brief second and then sat down. The waiter came to us. I don't recall what I ordered, but I only took small bites. She got a salad of some kind, and upon receiving our food, ate in silence for a bit.

I had a hidden purpose in this meeting. I needed to tell her how I felt- all of it. It was not that she didn't know; she just did not understand *how much*. She had heard a hundred times how I wished I could run away with her, in some sort of subtle filibuster. She had seen me gesture towards her in ways indicating my feelings, and she was used to them. She had seen the insurmountable desire manifest itself already. The feeling she did not grasp was how much I needed her, and how I suffered for her. It was not enough that she let me hold her hand, and kiss her on the cheek. I needed her heart, and her mind. I wanted her to be dedicated to me. This was what she *must* know.

When we were nearly finished, and I had struggled to consume half of my meal, I looked right at her and began to study her. The skin that used to be pale was now a radiant orange. The sunglasses on her face hid her eyes. Her hair was a hot mess. Her chest was robust and beautifully sculpted, and her arms were bare and shiny. Her stomach had one little role in it, and the outline of a navel ring was visible beneath her upper garment. This was all I could see of her. Her hands darted quickly, and I remembered what it was like to touch them. I slipped my foot out of my flip-flop, and slowly glided under the table to hers. I needed to touch her for a second, just a second…

She jumped. "Sorry, I didn't mean to touch your foot!" she exclaimed.

"Oh, that's fine. " I whispered. I wonder why she didn't like it when our feet touched.

She began, again, to finish her food.

"Lucia."

"Yes, *Benedict*?" She emphasized my name.

"I don't know if I can ..." I struggled for words, and after a second, she sensed the seriousness of my unfinished statement. "I don't know if I am able to" –I stopped. I needed a new introduction.

"Lucia, I don't know how to tell you that I am sad without you. I wake up in the morning, and I miss you. I go through my day, and I think about you. I struggle to consider anything else."

"I am with someone," she said gently, lovingly. "I don't know if us being such close friends would be OK with Alex."

How typical of Lucia to never even consider leaving him to be in a relationship with me. I sat there for a bit, and became frustrated.

"Why do you have to be with *him*?" I heard my voice, and I sounded snotty.

"I can't be with both of you," she hissed indignantly.

"I am all that you need! I love you more than he does!" I could not hold it in any longer. Her face changed, and I could see she felt threatened and uncomfortable. She removed her sunglasses. I could see storm clouds breaking.

"We talked about this!" she cried. "We have talked about it for an eternity. What is it that makes you forget?"

I sat there, feeling excessively ashamed. She never talked to me about this. "I have never had an opportunity to express to you how I feel."

"Benedict- I am starting to believe that our entire friendship was a mistake."

"A mistake?"

"You are never satisfied with anything. You and I should not have been friends." She began to nervously collect her things.

148

"But you found me! Our friendship was *your fault*. You started this. You were cute, and charming, you slept with all those guys and I had to watch..." I ran out of breath.

She was unsexy, in her belligerent rage towards me. The pure and beautiful feeling of love that I was trying to express to this intelligent, heavenly body made her travel further out of my orbit. I had angered her to the point of an explosion. She got up and marched towards the cash register. She fumbled for her wallet, and paid for her salad. She was smug and closed off.

"You used me!" I yelled. "Over and over, you *used* me, and you knew I loved you!" I was making a scene, but I didn't care. She did not listen. She walked up to me, and then she said pulled out the knives:

Benedict, you are such a selfish, pathetic little fuck that no one will ever love you.

Those of us who do not possess chemistry possess anti-chemistry. This is the substance that makes women angry when we say we are fond of them. This is the substance that relegates "best guy friends" to their status of unending celibacy. This is the substance that I possess. If the value of chemistry is so immense to a woman, then the value of anti-chemistry is unfathomably worthless. More repulsive to a woman than being cheated on by a man she feels chemistry with is the idea of being with a man who possesses anti-chemistry.

As she walked away, I stood up and tried to yell her name, but the fresh shockwaves of her immediate outburst silenced me in my tracks. I watched her drive off, and I kissed her good bye in my mind. And then, she was gone. I was a mistake to her. There was no way to blame her for anything. It was all my fault.

The Pathological Model of Infatuation
"The fruit that ripens early, spoils early."
-The Author

12

If my desire for Madeleine was overwhelming right off the bat, it seems like it should have subsided, because my very being should not be able to handle such a drawn out process of enamorment. However, these are merely the symptoms of something even worse.

I have been infatuated with several women since Lucia, but I try not to think of them, since all of them were virtually the same, down to the bitter end. It was like falling for the same Lucia in a different body, each time. Each bout with infatuation was shorter than the rest, but this time I know that I have caught a new strain.

Tonight is Saturday night, and I need to find a way to get in touch with Anthony. Anthony is an ugly figure to me now, dark and precarious, and because I sinned against him, his disdain towards me will be justified. I must find an opportunity to do this with no repercussions, in secret, so that the darkness of my heart will remain hidden.

Poff summons me from my day-terrors about Lucia. It is almost six P.M., and I am told that we are going to going to a movie night at Xavier's house. I am a little bit confounded that we are not going to be consuming alcohol.

"Why are we going to a movie night?" My curiosity is boiling over.

Poff smiles. "There are going to be girls there."

"Girls?"

"Girls."

His smile is poetic, with a certain glow to it that promises an expectation that might be fulfilled. "Girls" is the magic word. The few times that I have interacted with women who thought I was fun and cool, they were always those girls that showed up at movie nights. Movie nights were always *fun*. I donned my best pair of tight jeans, and an unrealistic wish for lots of casual physical affection. I shower, and I struggle about whether I should masturbate or not. If I masturbate, I will go with my expectations defeated. If I do not, I will hold onto the precious bit of reconciliation with God I achieved earlier today, until I fail again. I imagine what it would be like to have facial hair. I make a promise to God that I will be good tonight.

I exit my shower, and I pull my Motion City Soundtrack shirt out of my closet. It is a faded pink color. I look super nerdy. I feel sexy. I grab the keys to my car, and I strut to the front door. Poff is waiting on the couch, and he nods at me. We walk to the car. The engine turns over three times, and catches. My thermometer that I stuck to the dash reads forty one degrees, and I reach into the back seat and pull out a hoodie.

Xavier's house is not very far from ours. We live on Alban Avenue, in Woodland Hills, at the corner of Maple Drive, in an aging Three-two. Xavier lives south of us, down Seminole Drive. You wind through the woods to Sumter Drive, and Xavier lives in a similar residence with a long driveway. The last strains of sunlight vanish as we drive through the neighborhood. There are cars out front in this unusually quiet area, full of old houses that are all close together, so we assume that the first house with cars in the front yard is Xavier's.

As I pull in, I fail to notice the automotive demographic- A newish Mercedes, a Porsche, an unusually nice older Volvo, a Lexus and a very stately looking BMW. Poff and I get out and walk up to the door of the fairly noisy house.

It already dawns on me that I have selected the wrong residence, and I am getting ready to turn around and walk back to the car, when I see a sign in the window.

Help wanted. Waiter. Must be culturally fluent and highly intelligent. No college strudents. Apply within.

So I knock on the door, and in a few minutes a man answers. He is tall and reserved, with a large beard and glasses. He wears a checkered dinner jacket. He smells like butter.

"Do you have a reservation?" He asks with consternation.

"No, sir, I don't. I was intrigued by your sign." I glance out of the corner. Poff is hanging out by the car.

The gentleman who smells like butter looks at me indignantly, and then demands my name.

"Benedict, sir. Benedict Joseph Radmeier."

He looks at me with even greater scrutiny. "What is the capital of Portugal?" He asks.

"Lisbon." I answer, quickly.

"How many different types of Paella are there?"

I think for a second. "An infinite variety?" I am so unsure of myself that I pick the most general answer.

The man nods. Again, he quizzes me. "Where do the best tomatoes on the North American continent grow?"

My grandmother in Canada used to send me tomato sauce from Ontario. They were good. "Ontario?" I ask.

"Why?" the man asks breathlessly.

"Because the sauce my grandma made with them was better than anything else."

Poff is now walking down the street.

"Name five great impressionist painters!" I used to hang out with this kid in high school that liked art. I did my best to remember his impressionist idols.

"Will four work?" I plead.

"They had better be good," he retorts.

"Monet, Toulouse-Lautrec, Renoir and Matisse."

The man looks at me again, and asks me to come inside. I enter what appears to be a nice living room, but there is noise drifting from another room of the house. In the corridor ahead of me, the smell of something strange and delicate pervades my nostrils. I take a look around.

In the far southwest corner of the room is a large globe that has several handwritten notes on it, covering various places. A large shelf of books sits to the right, and a smaller shelf of bigger volumes is to the left of the globe. A framed portrait of a very hairy man with a large moustache is hung on the wall. On the mantle, on the southeast corner, is a collage of wine bottles. I know nothing about wine, so this fascinates me. There is nothing on the eastern wall, and the western wall is permeated by a corridor entrance that I hope to go down. The north west corner of the room contains a large grandfather clock, and the corner to my right has a coat rack. There is also a very vacant couch.

The man asks me to follow him. He leads me forth, and I notice a sign over the corridor:

Maison de Gourmet Rosengart- Vendredi, Samedi

The sign was fascinating, and I am sufficiently intrigued. "What is your name?" I ask the man.

"I am Henri. Henri Rosengart."

He doesn't say "Henry" like we do. He says "Ahn-wree," sort of like he is yawning in French. And now I can see that he has a tinge of a French accent.

Henri stops me right before we enter the room that the noise is coming from. It is now clear that I am in some kind of restaurant, but it is nothing like I have ever seen before. It almost feels like the setting for Richard Olney's "French Menu Cookbook," or the dining hall for a duke during medieval England. The smells were now intoxicating, and I am ever more drawn to the atmosphere here. It stirs something deep inside of my soul that makes me forget about women for a moment. Down the hall there is an ever more potent conversation, and it is growing. I touch the wall on my right as I walk down the hall, feeling the vibrations as they resonate from the inner room. The smell overwhelms me, and I am gently enveloped in a pleasant disorientation. The artwork on the wall becomes alive, and it starts to throb with life. A nude woman wearing a large hat, in a very surreal picture, smiles at me. I return the smile. My steps are calculated, and the floor beneath me guides me forward. I take a deep breath before I round the corner to the next room. I take the temperature with my finger. I swallow hard, anticipating something huge around the corner.

13

The only way that I could describe this was as a cacophonic chorus of whimsical elderly voices. They seemed to be debating, but it was unclear what exactly.

"Guillaume died in the Spanish Flu Pandemic in 1918, in the prime of his life…"

"But do you ever wonder if he wanted to die, then? Do you wonder if he would have died in another way, somehow? Maybe in his surrealist illusion, he felt that he had an identified time!"

"Nonsense! Apollinaire was an excellent example of how those who are truly valuable to society die young. Instead of contemplating the mystery of his death, we should contemplate the body of his unfinished work!"

"But don't you see, fifty million people died in that pandemic. Why should we focus on Apollinaire! I find it absurd that we spend this time talking about him. Why are things so slanted towards those of us who write some bullshit that the masses consider memorable? I am more than certain that a multitude of those who had done more good for society than Apollinaire had died in the pandemic!"

"Apollinaire's work looks mediocre today, but he was truly a transcendent soul for his time period! I mean, how can we consider his version of reality unimportant? It shaped the face of modern art and literary movements towards the present day."

"And what of these modern movements? They are garbage! Apollinaire was a pervert. His primary sustenance was the erotic novel. His ambition was to feed the Parisian scum their shit. Somehow, he collected his thoughts enough to produce a meaningless treatise on surrealism. But really, the *Surrealist Manifesto* was a great example of why we had world wars and massive genocides. People were so busy being occupied by this garbage that they were not minding the state of society. If all of these highly intelligent thinkers had done their part to stop tyrants like Hitler and Stalin from killing thousands of people, perhaps in our current time of peace we could focus on these silly abstractions today, and have fun with them."

"Hitler was one of those deviant thinkers!"

"It is not Apollinaire's fault that these things happen. I doubt he wanted to become famous- he was just discussing that which is on his mind. I mean, he is no Kafka, really, but he certainly is a man with a valid point of view. But nonetheless, we should applaud him for leaving us with a memorable body of work, especially in such a short period of time!"

"Apollinaire cannot defend himself against an ogre such as you. Perhaps you should liberate your creative spirit. Or has teaching rattled your brain too long? If you were of the same fabric of genius that Guillaume was cut from, you would have written the material that was used as a contemplative literary work!"

A glass flies across the table, and Henri begins to laugh. A white bearded gentleman ducks, and the glass hits the wall and shatters. The guests begin to smile and laugh, and the heated conversation about the surrealist movement and Apollinaire is dismissed.

The eclectic body of the large table is eager for the second course. Henri stands me against the wall, below a picture of a group of men playing cards. The room is huge, and well lit. A luminous chandelier is hung from the ceiling, and the main table seats fourteen people on each side. It is elegant, and made of some ancient cellulose that bleeds history and romance. The guests are as well dressed as any woman or man who would have frequented the Louvre in our modern age. But the tenants of this strange house were beyond any I had seen, but for books and movies. They were not all old. There was a smattering of men and women, some married- some seeing each other, some from that divergence in society where brides are found and bachelors are made- permanently.

There may be twenty-five people at the table, not a small number, but not out of control. Apparently, these folks are of the upper echelon of educated western society. Taking in their dialogue for a few minutes, I find that they are both incredibly full of shit and also highly vocal- a trait that I tend to enjoy about the well-influenced. I have been nowhere in my life, and this place feels like somewhere. These people feel vibrant, and intelligent. Henri runs between the seats, grabbing plates and cups and glasses, and balances it all perfectly until he deposits it on a small cart, and then he buses it to the entry way to what I assume is a kitchen. A pair of hands grabs it, and moves it back into the place it came from. This pair of hands is delicate and feminine, but it is too dark, in the corner of the room by the door, to discern what she is. I am in a state of trance now, and have determined that every place like this houses a girl of extraordinary beauty. The lights dim, and Henri sits me down at the table, and introduces me. "This is our new server. We need a figure for him. He will be replacing our mutual friend."

All of the *ubermenschen* look at me, nod and applaud. They begin to talk amongst themselves. Henri continues. "He is a scholar of the post-impressionist movement, and also is fascinated by Cubism and Diego Rivera. In his spare time, he studies Spinoza and Descartes. He is also fond of Rimbaud and Baudelaire."

Henri continues to lie about me, with unsuppressed enthusiasm, while I sit there and cringe. If these people ask me anything about what I believe, I will keep my answers as general as possible. I have no idea what Cubism is, or who Rimbaud was.

An older gentleman to my right looks at me. "What do you really like?" He asks.

"I fancy cars and music," I answer sheepishly.

"Henri is a bullshitter, so don't feel like any of those lies he told about you will have to be proven. No one gives a damn about Cubism, or Rivera, or Trotskyism or Pilsudski, or Perigord, or *Le Spleen De Paris* or any of that nonsense. We only discuss it because we are old, bored and uncommonly educated."

I laugh a bit. "Who are you?" I ask, now less inhibited. The older man smiles at me, looks me in the eyes, and laughs. "We are a *Societe Anonyme* – We do not use our given names. We take the name of famous persons from the past, and live out our lives on these nights as if we were that person."

"So who are you? I must know."

"I am D.H. Lawrence. And now, I have spoken for my dead writer. Who will you be?"

I thought about it for a minute. "Why were you guys arguing about Apollinaire?" I ask.

"Well, he isn't here to defend himself!" The elderly man exclaims. And the chorus of dead literates bursts into laughter. Lawrence addresses me again. "I am sure Apollinaire worked as a server, also!" And the body of literates goes on to discuss other matters. Henri then hoists up a glass, and calls for the second course.

The room is dark, and cold, suddenly. There is a shadow in the corner, and it grows bigger. The smell of something strong, like vanilla mixed with incense, floods the room. Suddenly, I am at my wedding mass. Suddenly, there is a figure in the room, an energy that surpasses my own. I am powerless beyond my own ability to breathe. I know that smell. It has manifested itself in many forms throughout the course of my life, but each and every time, a smell that elicits this reaction brings me only to think of who is bearing it. And there is only one truth about such a powerful olfactory sensation- *it belongs to a woman*. I feel myself being infected by her pheromones.

I repeat to myself. "I am my own person."

She takes a step into the light, and I see her outline.

"I am my own…"

She manifests through the shadows, her body beautiful.

"I am…"

She looks upon us, and she smiles like the Blessed Virgin.

"I am yours. I will pray to you, and if I am worthy, you will love me."

She is beyond the words I have been conditioned to use to describe a woman of such splendid visual appeal.

Henri stands up, and begins to disperse the plates among the guests.

I stand, also, not having a clue on earth what I should do.

"Who is this?" the cherub asks.

Henri looks at me. And then, it clicks.

"I am Apollinaire, writer and poet."

"…And server," Henri adds, shoving a plate at me. There is a goose flank sitting on it, and I hand it to the nearest person seated. He addresses me aside. "V*oici, le fruit interdir de ma maison.*" He then shoves another plate at me. I had no idea what he said, but I can assume it pertains to either the girl, or the goose.

"Mr. Debussy has distaste for the skin. He will have this flavorless bit," Henri says as he gesticulates towards a man in his fifties, thin and tall. I am handed a piece of goose *sans gras*, which Henri directs me to place in front of the Debussy proxy. Another piece, large and heaping, with extra shallots, is given to a Mr. Camus. A woman who is known as 'Madame Bovary' is handed a very normal looking plate with equal portions of fat, gooseflesh and vegetables.

Picking up where I left off, the lovely creature is distributing real glasses around the perimeter of the table. With the goose, a small flute of Chandon California Brut is served to each guest. In a gesture of fluent familiarity, Henri pops the cork on a bottle. The rose-gold Chandon travels through the neck of the bottle, into the world of slobs and gluttons, and tumbles into the flute. It struggles to try to escape, and return to its clear glass womb, but it is overcome by gravity, and after bubbling in protest, accepts its journey to the bottom of the intestines. I watch with a half-starved smile as she covers the body of the table, quickly pouring the forbidden substance. Four bottles are emptied in nearly eight minutes, as I study her and Henri as they engage in their distinctly different pouring styles. If only it were absinthe...

When it is over, she approaches me again, and smiles. "So, Mr. Apollinaire, are you going to assist me in my work here?" Her lips move daintily.

"I am sure I can be of assistance." I mumble in reply. "So who are you?"

"I am Nanette." She smiles.

"That's super cute, but what is your real name?" I demand.

"I am forbidden to tell you. Here I am Nanette, and that is all you should know."

"So I can't talk to you outside of work?"

"That's the beauty of this job, friend. No one needs to know anything about you at all."

"Do you do anything else besides this?"

"Maybe," she laughs. "Or maybe I live in a trailer and get high all day with my three kids." Her last statement sufficiently disturbs me. The only way that you would make a joke like that is if you associate with those kinds of people. I wonder why there is no contact allowed outside of work. It really upsets me, as this Nanette is beyond any kind of beautiful I have known before. She quietly pushes the cart into the room as the guests sit quietly and wait for the fun to begin. As they hoist up their glasses, their voices rise into strains of laughter. The light flickers across their faces, and I begin to pick apart their expressions. They look at each other in an element of unrestrained interest. I wonder if any of them have broken the rules. I wonder why this no contact rule exists in the first place.

Henri breaks up my train of thought, and he pulls me aside. "Are you enjoying our little piece of the absurd?" he inquires with a gentle smile.

"I am. She's..." and I point towards the cherub.

"Are you enjoying my little sunshine, Miss Nanette?"

I smile sheepishly. I can't say yes. That would be obvious.

"You know, she is only twenty-four. She has been through quite a bit for twenty four. She has been here six months. She is the forbidden fruit of my orchard."

I stand there and nod slightly. I wonder why he is telling me about her.

"She loves this job. It is her favorite that she has had."

I continue to listen. "What was that scent she was wearing?"

"Oh, her perfume? That's vintage Shalimar."

"It smells like the inside of a church. A Catholic church."

Henri smiles slightly. "Don't stare too hard. You can't give a woman like that what she is used to having."

A cold chill runs up to my medulla, and back down, and then out to my hands and into my fingers.

"I must begin to incite discussion among my guests. Please pass these out." Henri hands me a passage from Simone de Beauvoir. He looks back and nods. "There will be a point in your life where a woman you will have considered physically undesirable in your youth will blossom with the fullness of beauty in your old age. Keep that in mind."

I wonder why he said that to me. I am a bit curious about Nanette, so I follow her to the kitchen. I look back at Henri. He is in the throes of reading a love letter from Sartre to Beauvoir. I stand and watch him for a second. I look at Nanette. The words 'forbidden fruit' fit her well, much like the title 'rotten egg' might fit me.

"Should they be edited or should they not be edited?" He asks the madding crowd in regards to the letters.

I follow my desires into the kitchen, where my dear Nanette is preparing the dessert. I watch her with eager eyes, from the doorway. She does not notice me as she burns a fleur de lis on top of a small cake. She then takes the top off each of them, and fills it with custard. After that, Nanette takes several berries that are covered in syrup and plants them into the custard. She gently places the top of the cake back on it. She gets some of the Berry syrup onto her fingers, but instead of wiping it off, she dips her other finger into the custard, and puts them both in her mouth at the same time. She smiles to herself, and I move slightly out of sight, so that she cannot see me. The threshold of light into darkness hides my face, and I am content to stand here and watch. She places each cake on a tray, and on each one she attaches a mint leaf. She drizzles them with a vanilla and cream cheese icing, and sprinkles almond flakes on the top. She blows them all a kiss, and instantly, I feel like I want to be on the tips of her fingers. I have no words in this moment.

And then, as light as she could possibly be, she looks up. "Hi!" I stammer, startled.

She smiles at me. He body is transparent. I can only see through her, but not into her.

"Henri must like you." She says.

"Yeah, I sort of just showed up here."

"That's cool. I heard him talking to you in the front room."

I de-escalate myself just enough to carry on a functional conversation with her. "I made a wrong turn and ended up here. I should actually be at a movie night right now."

"That's nice. Who was at the movie night?"

"My friends- you know…"

"My friends and I don't have movie nights," she said endearingly.

"What do you do instead? Do you have game nights?"

Nanette chuckles to herself. I notice her blonde and brown hair and her perfect body. "Well, sir, I don't have a ton of friends." She wears a smirk. It always confounds me when beautiful women say this sort of thing. I don't know what they mean. I don't understand how it is possible. I want to be her friend. Her *only* friend.

She touches her hair, prompting me to make a comment. Her eyes are transparent, and medium sized, and fiery.

"Why don't you have many friends?" I ask.

"Well, I don't want too many. I don't know. Are you trying to find something out about me?" This girl has already peeled back my thin disguise. I was wondering…

"I don't know. Maybe?"

"You won't." She giggles, and pats me on the shoulder. Then she walks right by me, out into the dining room, to make sure the guests have what they need. On the way out, she turns around and asks "do you know how to wash dishes?" I nod. She points to the sink, and I do as instructed.

And there it was: the introduction. I still barely understand the introduction of man and woman. I don't really see how these things mesh. I see woman as a heavenly body that collides with man. Man is earthy, made of soil. Woman is ethereal. When God made woman from Adam's ribs, she was only a tiny bit of flesh- the rest of her was divine. God took the most beautiful idea that He created- the woman- and gave her life. I still believe to this day that woman carries the substance of God inside her. Her nature is more celestial than human. Perhaps the essence of woman is hidden in the mysteries of God.

But what she shows us is uglier. I do not equate women with kindness. I rather see her as hostile and apathetic, shutting out men who do not appeal to her. Who can blame a woman for shutting out a man who is less beautiful than she? Beauty merits beauty. Of all men who are earthy, I am like sand. I slip through the cracks. I am grainy. My composition is uniform and boring. I am honest. Digging through my layers reveals nothing more than more sand. Why would woman, the divine incarnate, wish to waste her time digging through something so meaningless? Why would I be able to reach something so heavenly? Why should I bother to introduce myself to such a beautiful individual when I am so worthless and boring?

The dishes are slowly getting cleaner. Henri steps over to me and instructs me further about how to clean the champagne glasses (warm water, but not too hot, with a special cloth that has a funny texture), and I steal glances out of the corner of my eye, as I hear Nanette reading to the crowd from a little book by Jean-Paul Sartre.

Henri shows me a few more things about waiting on tables, and then asks me to come in tomorrow at two. He shows me the wine cabinet, and the inside of the freezer. In the freezer, a fish sits in a clear plastic bag. It is marked "*Fugu.*" The packing script is mostly in Japanese, and it catches my attention.

"What is that?" I ask, pointing to the fish.

But the old man ignores my question, and points to the thermometer instead. "The freezer must always be at 28 degrees."

I exit the kitchen, back to the dining room. I watch Nanette as she moves in the dark. She looks at me and smiles. "It was good to meet you."

I wonder how she can mean that, but her smile is so inviting and so perfect that I want to bow down and worship her. She reminds me of a line from North's book:

"If a man can sufficiently understand the beauty of woman, he is in danger of falling down and adoring her.

In danger of becoming an idolater, I wave goodbye to her, and run towards the Saab.

It is eleven forty one, and a dim light is cast over the shadows of the chapel. I am deeply in prayer, and focused solely on Jesus…I think. Every few seconds a quiet image of Nanette steals my attention, and I lose my focus. There is a pretty picture of the Blessed Virgin to my right, and to my left a picture of the Sacred Heart. Jesus is present in the room; I can feel Him. He manifests His presence with a warm sensation. He places His hand on my forehead and reads my thoughts, my feelings. He gently confers on me a sense of wisdom. His hands are warm on my face, and my body is renewed with the vigor of a beautiful day. He is filling me with His love again. This week of sinfulness that I indulged in melts, and I feel perfectly good and pure.

And then I remember- I must apologize to Anthony for my transgression against him. The warmth immediately disappears, and I feel nervous and frustrated. I must make good on my assurance to the priest that I would perform my penance with bravery and full confidence.

But the image of Nanette steals my attention again. I can feel it, suddenly. I do not even know her real name, and the pathogen of her beauty is infecting me in a way where I cannot control it. She begins to push and pull her way into my soul, competing for importance with the Almighty, ruining the spirit of consolation that I experienced a moment ago. I turn my eyes to heaven, and plead with God. "Do not let her destroy me, Jesus! Do not let this girl make me feel ill and helpless again."

Infatuation is a heady disease. It has its origin, the appearance and mannerisms of the beautiful one being impressed upon you. The subtle contagion of the woman is exposed to you, and your body not only receives it, but *desires* it with no inhibition. The contagion makes its path, infecting first your eyes so that you notice her, and then your ears, so that they hear everything that she says to you. It infects your fingers, so that you are overwhelmed with the desire to make physical contact with her, and it infects your olfactory system, so that you smell her in your dreams. Then everything around you becomes impaired. The sunshine becomes a yellow blur in the sky, and even worse, it will begin to rain. It rains for days. The upside down ocean recedes, and moments later, a deluge of water from the sky nourishes your depression.

The contagion grows no weaker- it infects the brain with no impediment to its intensity. It occurs in such a manner that you are forced to acknowledge the woman at all times, taking your thoughts and destroying them slowly and mournfully. You lose your ability to focus on anything else.

The contagion of woman, the bacteria of infatuation, proceeds to fully infect the brain. This is a most complicated thing to explain, as the contagion becomes the influence behind all of your actions and feelings. In the clearest way, I can only explain it by saying that you become a product of the pathogen. The terms 'enamorment', 'fixation', 'obsession', 'preoccupation', 'fancy' are all sub-derivatives of the state of existence that the infatuated person dwells in. He has no power to *not* be enamored with the woman, no ability to shake off the fixation, no desire to combat the obsession, nothing else to be pre-occupied with, and no one else whom he fancies. He is chained to the person's very existence. The substance behind the pathogen of infatuation is that it exercises itself over the entire life of its victim. It influences all of his actions, all of his thoughts. The modifier for all of his actions is that they in some way should affect the way that the woman feels about him, notices him or perceives him. He is not able to change his focus.

It is Sunday morning, and I am at Mass. When I enter the church, I immediately notice that Anthony has sat down five pews ahead of me, alone. In my pocket, I finger my meager tithe, and stew about how hard my apology will be. "I hate you, Anthony" I think to myself.

I will have to do this, even if it kills me. The ironic part is that it is killing me not to. I no longer look at him and feel envious. Rather, I realize that I am practically a murderer for allowing myself to pursue the carnal urge to inflict such a wound on him simply because a woman loves him. If I were in his position, however, I would secretly feel accomplished, having attained the love of a woman whom other ordinary men are willing to kill for.

The priest begins mass with a greeting, and we all turn around and acknowledge each other. I am fearful that Anthony is going to turn around and see me, but he does not. His neighbors in front of him keep him busy. This must be his regular spot. I see Xavier walk into the church, slightly late and join him. A few pews further up, I see Paul and James. The best way to deal with this scenario would be to hold mass at some ridiculous hour, where these prudes would be too afraid to come. I love the ring of it- mass at midnight, every weekend. There must be some indie cred to it. If I ever became a priest I would go to the middle of some huge downtown, and hold mass at midnight, or in the wee hours of the morning. I would hold confessions right before, so that everyone could witness the spectacle of receiving the Eucharist amidst all the noise.

The opening hymn begins. I really hate church music. I know that it is "good" and it is "nice" but it certainly is not holy. Rather, it is a mockery of all forms of good and nice music. On one hand, you have Gregorian chant, the finest version of religious music in our time, and on the other, you have these amazing secular bands. Church music doesn't even fall in the middle. It is cheesy, and riddled with anachronistic symbolism that may have fit the blinded, problematically ignorant church of the eighties, but does not mesh very well with the church of the new millennium (which I hope is waking up). The pope needs to dump all of this garbage and force us to come up with something better. Post Vatican two music is devoid of all expression and emotion. I don't understand why we sing songs that inhibit our expression of love for Jesus, or why we use our talent to write songs that are not meaningful, and unpleasant, and ugly. If I was not Catholic, but I was visiting a church like this, I would leave. If I were Jesus, I would make them all go deaf.

The liturgy of the word passes by quickly, and I empty out all of my thoughts. A perfect light casts itself over the congregation, as I listen hopelessly to the story of Jesus and the woman at the well. If he could so easily forgive this woman who was regarded as an adulteress, how then can he not forgive me, the passive aggressive, sexually misaligned little boy struggling to make it in this world? In Mr. North's book, the text states that " *...it is unnatural to sin. It was not God's intention to begin with. He understands this, and wishes to save us from it.*" We stand up and begin the Nicene Creed, and from memory I recite it with a passivity that can only come from years of being exposed to the same thing. It doesn't mean I dislike it. It only means that I know it. In the space of the church, I am made aware of the fact that I am unfocused on everything that matters. If my life were normal, let's say normal like the lives of these normal Catholics, I would probably have a much better grasp on the virtues of patience and observation. I would be eating up every word, and not thinking about it. But I am an inferior being, with an inferior intellect. My brain is riddled with tiny thoughts that grow in size as they approach the center of my intellectual capacity, passing like meteors, sometimes, making landfall and exploding, creating a distraction that wipes out any previous thinking I had. Such is my prayer life- A tiny, weak little outpost in a desert that struggles for life, with a meager supply of happiness. I fight, hour by hour, for this little planet, and then something will come along and destroy it, and I will start from scratch, working about the crater, getting things back in order. As soon as I am somewhat confident of my direction in life, the order that I have established is destroyed by a large chunk of something from out of nowhere, and I am forced to start over again. It has been this way since my spiritual conscience first came into existence.

And now the priest asks us to kneel, and we kneel, and I think about Anthony a bit more. He holds the consecrated host up for us to see, and I wonder about whether or not I am going to be able to receive. I look again at Anthony. I have no idea if an incomplete penance would deter me from receiving. "*Lord, I believe- help my unbelief!*"

In the middle of the consecration, I develop a plan. I am going to take care of this before communion.

The priest asks us to stand, and we pray The Lord's Prayer, and some people hold hands, and some do not. I keep my hands folded in front of me, like a traditionalist, and count the isles. There is just enough room for me.

The priest signals for us to offer the sign of peace to each other, and I make my way past each consecutive isle. Anthony is shaking hands with the person next to him. I stand there waiting for him to finish. He turns around after a second, and is startled to see me there.

"Benedict!" He exclaims. I speak. "Hey buddy. I need to tell you something!" I try to look nonchalant.

"What do you need to tell me?" He still looks startled.

"I will tell you more about this later, but I am sorry that I tripped you."

"Oh, that sort of thing happens, er, accidents." He still doesn't get it. Lawyers are hopeless, even if they work for pro-life organizations.

"No, stupid. It was d-d-d....*deliberate*."

He pulls back in disbelief.

"Like I said earlier, I will explain why later, but you need to know that I am responsible for your injury. It was not the right thing for me to do." I study his face, and the bandage. He reaches out, and shakes my hand. "Peace be with you, Benedict."

I exchange the gesture with him. I still dislike him, but at least he knows that. I race back to my pew, with hurried steps. My genuine interest in making things as painless as possible seems to be paying off. The sunshine peeks through the windows of the church, and I feign sufficient reverence to receive Jesus in the Eucharist. I watch Anthony as he gets up to receive, and I get up soon and walk with my hands folded to the front of the church. I bow, and then move on to the cup. After taking the cup, I pass right by Anthony, and I nod and smile. He returns my glance with a stern gesture as he kneels down. His face says "Right now is the time to be serious. I just received Jesus. Don't smile." I am now fuming mad, notably because all of these damn Catholics do that. You smile at them at the wrong minute, and they don't smile back. No wonder I am so calloused. Of course, they know how I feel.

One time I was at mass with the Catholics, and this one guy, Rick, who was really serious- too serious- was praying afterward. We were going out for pizza after mass, so I walked up to him, with the intention of inviting him to dine with us. I greeted him with a smile, but instead of returning it, he stared back at me with this soft, pretentious frown. Visibly irritated, I returned the gesture to him. "Can't you tell I'm trying to pray!" he yelled at me. "Fuck you!" I yelled at him. "I'm so sick of you and your fucking holier-than-thou condescending stare. I was just trying to invite you out for a fucking pizza, ass."

The Catholics who heard that were horrified. Our little chapel was silent for a long fifteen seconds. Then one by one, they left slowly, like I was holding a gun or something ominous. I think it was a bad idea in hindsight to have yelled at him, but I really dislike unhappy people. For now, I had satisfied the demands of my confessor. I at least had something to be happy about.

14

Resplendent in my new job as a server, I went home from Mass triumphantly. Anthony had received his apology in an orderly and proper fashion, and I was now free of the guilt that I experienced. This whole thing, however, did not absolve me of my attraction to Madeleine. Even the gleaming presence of Nanette, and her illustrious beauty, did not help me to shake my desire for a pure Catholic woman to take the place of Lucia.

Alas, it is Tuesday again, and our review of Joseph North's book has become less important to me. I was asked to glance at chapter three, and discuss chapter two. North's elongated rant about the issues in our society, and how they clash with God's intended purpose for man, is all too familiar to me. North mentions the issues of people using other people for sex, and the issues of abortion, divorce, homosexuality and such. He also cites these things as behaviors that our world accepts because it does not know Jesus. But what about those behaviors that we have become caught up in when we do know Christ? What does the drug addict do who has a physiological addiction that is stronger than his desire to pray? How does the woman who has had an abortion come to the Lord and "put it right." How do I, in my struggle with lust, stop being lustful? In the presence of these friends of the Lord, we open the discussion in high spirits. Madeleine sits in a corner next to her posse of righteous teenie boppers.

Paul leads us in prayer. " In the name of the Father, the Son and the Holy Spirit. Hail Mary, Full of grace..." I drown him out, and I contemplate how I can make this a real discussion. When Paul is done praying, he sits down, and reads an excerpt from the third chapter.

"In this world, brothers and sisters, Christ was never accepted. Instead of being received by the people, he was crucified for preaching something different. The Gospel is not a message of revolution or crime, but rather a call for us to love each other without any of the reservations that are so normal for us. So how is it that we have adopted these practices- abortion, casual sex, pornography and others? Do we, as followers of Christ, accept these as normal? Many Christians seem to, maybe not intentionally, but certainly passively. If we don't fight the battle against them, then we are for them. It is as simple as that. Do we make allowances in our lives for the things that are destroying our sacredness as human beings? Are we passively accepting the ideological flaws in the thinking of the culture of death? Is there anything in your personal life that is blocking Christ from working in you? Do you find hope in Jesus? Chances are every single one of us will answer yes to all of these. If you do not answer "yes," I beg you to reconsider. Have you

appealed to Him with a plea for help yet? Do you feel He can help you?"

Slightly disturbed by the passage, I laugh to myself. There is no one here who would ever admit to looking at porn, hooking up with strangers, supporting planned parent hood or anything like that. No, certainly I am the black sheep among this crowd of lambs.

Naturally, Paul waters down the discussion as much as he can. "Do you feel that Jesus has helped you resolve issues such as these in your lives?" He asks us. They all look like zombies, their brains failing to process anything on a meaningful level. They stay silent for nearly a minute. I laugh, silently, trying to imagine Paul hooking up with a girl, getting her pregnant, and then asking her to have an abortion. I shudder after that- what a thought.

Kristen speaks up. "Spending time with the Blessed Sacrament has made me a more sincere person. I used to struggle with insincerity." Her remark agitates me. She is still insincere. I go to adoration, too, and I am insincere. Adoration can't fix a personality flaw. Her overall issue is that she is currently being insincere to herself. Xavier pipes up about the same topic. "I feel that if more people spent time in adoration, many of their issues would be resolved. If adoration was a more common practice among all people, we would see a dramatic reduction in the number of evils in this world."

Further appalled by his sanctimonious babble, I utter a small prayer to God. "Lord, help me to be honest."

And then something very funny happens. He *responds*! *"Benedict, are you for me, or are you against me?"* This is a bad situation for a question like that, but I suppose I should challenge these fools to accept the truth about our flawed humanity.

"I go to adoration pretty often, about once a week, and I don't feel like it has fixed me at all. I go because I love the Lord, but I haven't gotten anything out of it."

"Why Benedict, of course you have!" Kristen exclaims. She always does this crap. At every group meeting, I will declare something about myself that is very real, and that I know for certain, and it will

170

make her uncomfortable, and she will shoot it down in the most loving and confident way that she can. "Sorry, Kristen. I'm pretty sure I still use colorful language and -"
"Remember, there are women here, and we don't want you to be disrespectful," Paul warns me, with a distressed look.

"Look guys, it doesn't matter what the sin is. All I am saying is that it works for you, but it doesn't work for me. I never said that the Blessed Sacrament doesn't contain the fullness of Christ, or that there is no possibility of Him changing you when you adore Him, but it has not worked for me. And I think some of you are overestimating how it has worked for you. I know that I am not in your shoes, and I have not had your experience, but all of you have always been this way. This is who you are, the good and the bad. Even my vices are part of me. Even if I lived in the adoration chapel, they would never go away. I would just be focusing on something else, in this case Jesus, and they would take a back seat for the time being. I am for Him, believe me, but I am a sinner, and so far, years of adoration have not made me love Him enough to give up that one vice which constantly drags me down."

Out of the blue, Madeleine raises her voice. "What vice are you referring to?" She inquires.

"Its unimportant. Besides, Paul asked that we be respectful." The entire room eyes me with suspicion. I am sure that Martin Luther would have been more gladly received. The room is silent for a bit, and then the tide of the discussion shifts to something more benign. After twenty minutes, we take a short break.

Kristen approaches me, "Benedict, I didn't mean to upset you. I was just trying to help you see that here has been growth in your life. I have seen it."

"I think you are exactly the same as you have always been. And I feel that you and I are not truly friends. I feel like you think I'm just a wayward soul who needs Christ. Until I am perfect, like Paul, or Xavier, or the seminarians, you will never accept me. You unconsciously judge me every time you see me."

Kristen is disturbed by my comment, and she reaches out her

hand. "I never meant to make you feel that way," she says. Her unintentional insincerity shines forth, like a headlight in my face on a dark road.

Presently, we resume our seats and begin to discuss the book again. I sit near Madeleine, taking in her beauty and struggling to keep from looking right at her. I keep thinking to myself "I really should not be attracted to this girl. She is out of my league."

And then, so why? Why is it that I have this never ending desire for the perfect Catholic woman? Who put it there? How did it originate? Part of my struggle stems from knowing nothing else. Somehow, my upbringing in the church has taught me that there is nothing else to strive for but a good and holy woman. A secular woman is trouble; a worthless endeavor that will only end in misery. But these women we have been taught to strive for and desire nothing less than a man of equal goodness. There is no fun in this pursuit, though. These perfect holy women do not accept their humanity. Instead, they see themselves as being better than the men who desire them. Only the most handsome man, the smartest man, the wealthiest man, the most interesting man, the *godliest* man- is worthy of them. I am left to strive for the impossible, as none of these attributes so much as crosses my shadow.

Madeleine notices that I am sitting near her, and she looks uncomfortable. I deliberately turn my head away from her, but my exaggerated motion draws attention. Paul is now rambling on about how our bodies are sacred and holy, and should be treated as such. "Modern culture seeks to downplay the beauty and mystery of the human body..." he states. I watch Madeleine's feet. What am I aspiring towards by watching her feet? Maybe if I watch and stare hard enough, she will move them close to mine, and play footsie with me. Maybe she will start to love me if I study her long enough. She flips through her copy of the text, following along as Paul reads through more passages that I have limited interest in. I continue on my depressing trajectory of thought, struggling to find something to grab onto in this meeting. As soon as I feel that I am starting to see meaning in their dialogue, the meeting ends. The Catholics begin to chatter amongst themselves, and I am left sitting on the couch...

But not for long. As I look about the room, preparing myself to get up, Madeleine walks up to me with a sort of inquisitive and demanding look on her face. I would normally react to this approach with a feeling of elation, but a feeling deep in my stomach tells me that she has questions. This is not a very good encounter. Her beauty almost becomes a detractor, as I wonder what she wants from me. She sits down next to me, and addresses me with a firmness in her voice.

"So Anthony told me what happened...and how you apologized to him." I feel my hands shaking. "What did he tell you? Oh, and by the way, it's nice to see you too."

Madeleine's vocal inflections have changed from the normal passive, apathetic dismissals that I am used to hearing from her, to an accusatory tone that I suppose all women have, but men never seem to think about. She disregards my previous comment, and jumps right in.

"Apparently you tripped him on purpose, and you also ran up and apologized to him in the middle of Mass, giving him no opportunity to discuss the matter with you. I can't believe-"

"Can't believe what? That anyone would do something like that to a pro-life attorney?"

Madeleine is speechless, and looks at me with anger.

"What do you want from me?" I ask.

Madeleine sighs for a second, and her anger winds down. "What made you do that? Anthony never did anything to you."

"I know. But it was a momentary thing. I was jea-" I stop myself out of fear.

"What were you?" She asks.

"You already know what I was. The drink, the groceries, wanting to be your friend."

"I really don't."

Girls always say this crap. They like to pretend men are not interested in them.

"It's unimportant, really. I had no *good* reason for it."

"I still want to know why you did it."

"It was more about you than him." I am already throwing myself under the bus.

"It was more about me?" She demands. "You're evading my question. Answer me. Why did you do it?"

"Are you guys together? Is he your boyfriend? Do you like him?"

"That's not important. Why! Why aren't you telling me?" She yells, and some of the Catholics look towards the couch.

"I will tell you, but we have to go outside, so no one else can hear me." I whisper, and I am embarrassed.

"Seriously?"

"Otherwise, you can figure it out yourself."

She gets up, walks across the room and opens the door. Now the big one- should I lie to her, or should I tell her the truth? I have at least four lies I can tell:

1. Anthony was being impersonal and it made me mad. I didn't like the way he talked to me, so I tripped him.
2. I heard he was married, and he was covering it up, and trying to date you. Obviously I was wrong.
3. It really was an accident. I felt bad, so I took responsibility for it. I don't know.
4. I just did it because I was having a shitty day.
On the other hand, there are five versions of the truth I can tell:

1. In the moment I felt jealous, so I did the first thing that came to mind.
2. I thought that by tripping him, I would put on a show of manliness and you would want to be friends with me.
3. I like you, and men do some weird things when they like a girl.
4. I was a little drunk, and that night I saw you and wanted to do something to make you notice me.
5. I'm obsessed with you, and if I can't have you, no one deserves

you.

None of these but the last is truly honest. In a situation like this, telling the truth is too hard. I get up and walk through the door, into the chilly night. Madeleine is standing by my car. "OK, let's get this over with," she huffs.

"I tripped him because I was jealous."

She glares at me with skepticism. "You did that because you were jealous of him? Why were you jealous?"

"He was with you."

She nods, and looks at me for a moment. She does not smile. She turns and walks back to the house. She takes ten angry steps to the door, and goes back inside. The night air bites my skin, and I stand by my car. She could at least have given me a reaction, or something! I don't know what to think. In a situation like this, I cling on to any detail I can. The fact that she gave me no response at all was ambiguous. When she nodded at me, she certainly was not smiling. I was hoping her lack of response was a sign that she was at least a little bit flattered by it. I don't need Madeleine anyway. I will ignore the fact that I am drawn to her. I will also ignore the fact that she probably really hates me.

Lucia, in the Twilight

In the aftermath of my last confrontation with Lucia, I anticipated that I would never see her again. That first year in college was rough, thanks to her. My optimism was depleted, and I had nothing to do really but hang out with the Catholics and study incessantly. I made it a point to go to adoration and pray often, and for a time, my desire to look at pornography subsided. Once in a while, I would even say a tiny prayer for Lucia. Despite my bitterness, I would often see a moment of clarity in all the mess, and my spiritual life, for a brief second I would blossom. To this day, I do believe that God still has some form of consolation for me. As silly and ephemeral as my desire for marriage is, I believe God has it in store for me.

I would venture back out into the world, and into our small college town, and I would become discouraged again. I would look up at the sky, and the sun, and wonder if God could see all of the parties, and the abused sexuality, and the immodest clothing, and the dirty dancing. I wondered if He saw all the drunkenness and the drug use, the lack of sleep and the guilty consciences. I was no better than any of these people, really, and for all I know, they were much happier than I. It was in this prolonged atmosphere of depression and gloom that I saw Lucia one last time. By this point in college, it was 2002, and it was May. Classes had ended for the semester, and I was living a low key life while I ramped up for my birthday (May 29th) . I was at the grocery store. The summer was quiet, and the majority of my close friends were home with their families. I didn't really want to go home and be with my parents. As an only child, I should have given them more of my time, but they were fine. They were really like strangers to me. I didn't know them that well, but I really believed that there was nothing to know about them. They were

176

completely empty-minded, well-intentioned people. They entertained guests, had a nice house, went to Mass every Sunday, saved for retirement and had their hobbies. My dad's car hobby made things interesting at times, but really, when he gave me the Saab, I was saving it from a life of sitting in our garage.

So I was at the store, looking at the frozen stuff. The liquor isle and the frozen crap isle were next to each other, and the main isle in the store contained a large island of a freezer. I was looking selectively at things I shouldn't eat, and thinking about nothing. You can say that at that time, all that was on my mind was the lonely summer, the stagnant heat and the lack of excitement. My mind was *empty*. There was nothing here that made me think of anything.

And then I heard that siren's voice, that damn melody signaling my demise.

"Ben-e-dict....*Benedict Radmeier!*"I looked up, and forward and I saw her there. Her hair was short, and there were strands of pink in it. Now she had a nose ring. She was skinny, and she was wearing (surprise) a revealing top. She smelled funny, nearly nefarious, and from the olfactory analysis, I surmised that she had amounted to nothing. She ran out of the liquor isle, and ran up and hugged me. I wanted to wash her off of me. The infatuation, in the twelve months since I had last seen her, had turned to disgust, and finally, I stopped thinking about her. She was gone, and I did not want her back at that time. She was worthless to me.

And yet I missed her. I extended my arm, and she grabbed it, planting her head under my shoulder. I felt her hair, thick, and oily, yet sexy and mysterious, with its dark glow. She removed my glasses and kissed my cheek, and I wondered what I had done to merit this display of affection. She glowed all over me, and she made me feel so serene, with her cherry smile, and her little universe.

I looked up from our eternal embrace, and saw the abandoned cart. She pulled back, and stood in front of me, smiling. With the cart was a guy- a man, really. He was tall, and he was dressed in clothes that looked decent, at least at one point. But beneath his short, red hair and a little bit of facial scrub, there was something about him that alarmed me. His eyes were distant, as if he had no perception of where he was or what was going on. He had a tattoo on his arm that was tribal. I disliked him instantly. All of the stereotypes- controlling, jealous, possessive- I applied to him, knowing they were accurate. The dissimilarities that I identified about her now, as opposed to then, were entirely his fault. He was the reason she had deteriorated into this mess. In the shopping cart was the proverbial tanker of cheap vodka, coke, beer, and some other stuff.

I snapped back into reality, wishing I could just run away and wash myself. "Who's that?" I asked.

For a second she didn't seem to understand what I had asked her. Finally, she came to, and realized that I was trying to ask her a question. "That's my boyfriend." I wanted to ask her if she was sure, but I could tell that for some reason, she was not thinking clearly.

"What's his name?" I asked, slowly and carefully. "Oh, yeah. Robbie." And she beamed with delight, like she suddenly remembered something. "Robbie," she said again slowly, with a smile.

Alarmed for some reason, I charged back with a question that no one asks. "How did that happen? How did he become your boyfriend?" She looked at me, puzzled, and then motioned for him to come over. "Answer me, Lucia. How?" She shrugged her shoulders and grabbed him by the arm. "Ben-e-dict, this is Robbie." And Robbie acknowledged me. I acknowledged him back with a muffled "hey."

"What are you guys doing tonight?" I asked.

"You know...hanging out," she said.

"Cool. Well, I need to go," I told her.

"You don't want to hang out with us?" She asked.

"Not really."

She looked at me, with big, sad eyes, behind her thick glasses. I saw a lighter in her purse. No one carries a lighter with them for any good reason. Lighters are trouble. I really couldn't place the smell on her either, but it wasn't good, and she was trying to hide it.

"How's school?" I asked.

She just laughed, as I turned around and walked down the aisle with my shopping cart. I didn't need to do this to myself. And this time, I didn't want to either.

If infatuation itself did not rot inside of us, and incite repulsion towards the infatuee, we would never move on. Unequal attraction is a heavy yoke. You can only carry it for so long, before you either cast it off, or collapse underneath it. But the seeds always seem to survive, and again they bear unobtainable fruit in new soil.

15

If Lucia had a dizzying effect on me, the one created by Nanette was more so. Nanette had a very enigmatic glow that made me wonder where she had been, and who she was. Henri had me drive over to his house to learn a bit more about my job, and so after I had gone to noon mass on Wednesday, I went home and changed into more provincial clothing(a white shirt?), and then headed back over to his residence. The Camellias were starting to fade a bit, and there were leaves falling. Japanese magnolias were relinquishing their blossoms, and I listened to "We have the facts and we're voting yes" by Death Cab for Cutie. I was charmed by the scenery and the music at the same time, leading to a powerful feeling of separation from everything else around me. I pulled up to Henri's while I was listening to "405." In the driveway was Henri's Citroen DS Safari wagon, presumably for hauling cases of champagne. Next to it was a car that I had seen the night before, but had not paid any attention to- what I had written off as a boring Japanese car was actually a Mazda RX7. It could have been as late as a 1994. I had always liked the RX7, but they were too expensive to buy and maintain. The Saab was actually too expensive, but for the fact that my dad and I kept it up. The RX7 was bright red. A hairbrush in the front seat suggested it had a female proprietor. I was a bit intrigued by it, since I had never seen an RX7 owned by a girl. Henri had said it would just be me and him, but I wondered if someone else had joined us, unbeknownst to me.

I climbed the steps to the house and knocked at the door. "Henri! *C'est moi!*" I yelled out. Henri heard me in a few minutes. "*C'est vous Benedict? Entrez!*"

I went through the door, and towards the dining room. Henri was hunched over a box, pulling out some photos. On the chair next to him was a copy of Camus' *The Stranger*. He mumbled in French while I stood near him and glanced at the pictures on the wall. It seemed like an eternity, as he got past the pictures and started sifting through handwritten and typed scripts that looked quite old. "What are those?" I asked. Henri ignored me and continued looking through the manuscripts, stroking his gray beard intermittently with a peculiar grin on his face. Finally, after his beard became several hairs poorer, he took hold of a small stack of typed papers and another manuscript written in fountain pen, and leafed through them for a bit. "*Voici!*" He exclaimed. Then he noticed me, finally, and held out his hand. "I get lost, sometimes, in boxes. My whole life, my story, is in boxes."

It seemed like an eternity that I stood there, but here I am, at least a half hour later, watching him. He speaks slowly, looking for simple English words. His mind is thinking in French, I can tell. He will form a word on his lips, and then stop, and then struggle to form the word again, but in English. He speaks in a low, deep voice, with lots of pauses for heavy breathing. " *Camus et moi*, we are friends, in a way. His son and I were friends when we were young, and when he was killed, I made it a point that I would know him…how do you say it? After someone dies…."

"Posthumously?" I couldn't help but finish.

"Yes. That!" Henri responds with faint enthusiasm. "You are a bright and sharp young man. Do you speak French?"

"I believe I told you already that I do not- it is unfortunate really." I touch my lips.

"These," says Henri, "are manuscripts from college. This is

my essay on *The Adulterous Woman*, which I wrote in 1964. We are going to discuss Camus' writings next week. Have you read him yet?" He looks at me with hope, that people still are aware of these things. I paw at the ground with embarrassment. No one has ever wanted to know if I read Camus before, but it seems as if this is the most important thing anyone has ever asked me. "Has Nanette read Camus?" I respond. Henri laughs at my question. "Is this your way of begging for an intercession?" He counters. "If Nanette wrote *L'etranger*, would you have read it? I suppose not." Henri extends his hand to me, and I take it. He leads me, carefully, to a room in the house. We walk down the hallway, until we arrive at a door. He pulls a key from his pocket, and unlocks an antiquated padlock. He pushes the door open with his hand, and flips on a light switch. "Your lady friend is in the kitchen. She has been in here before, but you are not to discuss it with her at all. These are my photos, from my youth. If anyone ever finds out about these, they will steal them."

And there they were- a picture of Beckett signing a copy of *Molloy*, De Gaulle's funeral, Algerian protesters, The millionth French-production 2CV right at the assembly line, Jackie Kennedy, angry Basques, Sartre and Beauvoir together, The Facel-Vega that took Camus, a classroom in Provence, a man hunting truffles with his pig in Perigord, and Pope John Paul II in 1981. Pictures were everywhere, and there were albums to boot. Copies of French newspapers in stacks kept company with magazines. I was amazed. It was as if the entire twentieth century in France after World War Two was laid out in this room. My hands shook, and my face turned numb. The smell of paper and past events filled my nostrils and ignited my mind. There was so much that had happened in just sixty years. And here I am, thinking constantly of women. Henri looked at the wall ahead of him. He brushed the dust off of the picture of Beckett. "An odd book," he mumbled under his breath. I gazed, speechless, at a picture of Chanel Number Five. It was a magazine advertisement that was done immediately after Marilyn Monroe had died.

"Who are you, and what did you do?" I slowly and carefully

ask the old Frenchman standing to my left.

"I was a photographer. What the hell else would I have done to accumulate all of this horse shit?" And he laughed unceremoniously. I grab his wrist with my long, white fingers, and I stand there for a good five minutes. It was as if this old man, who I had barely seen, and hardly knew, had merged his soul with mine, and given me the substance that I had never known. "Did women like that you were a photographer?" I ask.

"You are at that age," he tells me, "when women are all you think about. Graduating from college does not lead to eloping with Polish blondes. You will do better later. For now, do something meaningful. Don't ask an old man to repeat his sins. If I could do it all over again, I would have become a priest. But to be fair to you, they were fascinated by my camera. I even slept with a few of them."

"How did you manage to accomplish that?" I demand with moon-lit eyes.

"It was easier then." He leads me out, and shuts the door, locking it with a quick and defined action of the wrist. "Protect yourself, my dear friend."

Nanette greets me from down the hall. She smiles with a little half-drunk smile, and she is wearing a revealing shirt. Her sculpted body betrays a few bruises and red marks near her chest, and I wonder what their origins are. Her shalimar is intense and heady, much like Jeff Buckley's Lilac Wine. Her nails are done in a pattern of soft hues, and her make-up palette is extruding from her pocket. Her blue jeans are faded and adventurous, and her white blouse is simple and elegant. She walks up to me with a graceful step, and extends a delicate hand towards me. Not sure of what to do, I am so nervous that I take it and squeeze it, but I realize that it is her left hand and I should not shake it. As she withdraws it, I grab it, and draw it to me, kissing it with a certain awkwardness. As I draw her hand in, I try not to glance upward. My gesture goes far beyond being polite. I am acting on a craving for her flesh, and begging for a tiny bit of attention. Henri watches me as I erect my stature, and Nanette smiles at me with a renewed holiness. I feel so much better, and so much worse. She giggles with a passive gaiety, and then turns around and heads back to the kitchen. If she had spoken to me, I did not hear it.

"Come, my friend." Henri grabs me by the arm and leads me back to the door. He opens it for me, and for a second. I thought he was throwing me out for kissing Nanette's hand.

But no, instead he led me to the hatch of the Citroen, and lifted it. "Champagne," he says, "does not carry itself in. I see you as a light drinker, so none of it will vanish. If I had her do it, it would go missing." He points to Nanette's car. I am not really a light drinker, but I will do what I have to do to please him.

I smile in the direction of her car, and he thrusts a case of Chandon in my arms. I take it and carry it to the door, and he jumps ahead of me. He opens the door decisively and makes sure that I do not hit anything as I enter. We turn around and head back to the Safari, and we repeat the process. After six trips, we get to the last case.

"Who is she?" I ask Henri as he closes the hatch. Henri derides my question with a blank look. He bends over and ties his shoes laces.

"Who is she?!" I ask, more aggressively.

"Who is who?" Henri responds geriatrically.

"Who is Nanette? What is her real name?"

"What business of it is yours?" Henri asks.

"What do you mean? I work with her. I deserve the right to know."

"I won't tell you but if it is so important to you, you might ask her."

Suddenly I become docile, realizing he could just fire me. "Is that alright with you, Henri?" I feel I should thank him for giving me permission. Henri ignores my gracious gestures and points to the door. "The champagne must be put in the cooler for our next dinner.

Allez!" I march to the door, and he begins to remove bottles from their cases. They were the prettiest cases I had ever seen. Henri stops me, half way through. "After you talk to her, you may ask me a few things but only if it is fine with her. She is my priceless pearl-so smart that she is irreplaceable. I understand you must work with her, and mystery only leads to useless distraction. But I must also warn you that I cannot have an open wound seething with infatuation at work in my kitchen. I do not wish to see you pining over her, when there is a goose on fire in the oven (I imagine the oven going up in flames when he says this, as I dawdle over Nanette's barely exposed upper body)." He snaps his fingers to regain my attention. "See her all you want, make love to her, run away with her in spring, but do not carry your baggage into my kitchen. She is a girl not given in easily to affection. She has a tendency to not give a damn about men, and the men here are well dressed and intelligent. Do not expect her to give a shit about you. You are in the company of people who have come of age. She is among them. You are not. Please put the bottles in the chiller." To offset the harshness of his intonation, he pats me on my back and exits the large kitchen. I watch as he slightly limps, and then removes himself from my sight. As soon as he vanishes, Nanette sticks her head into the door from the main dining room. She has headphones in her ears, and she is singing to herself.
I signal to her to remove the headphones, which after some vigorous gesticulations she understands. She turns towards me, and looks at me inquisitively.

"Did you hear my conversation with Henri?" I ask her.

"No. All I heard was *Smashing Pumpkins*. Why?"

"It was nothing, really."

"I'm leaving. I'll see you Billy. I think we have to be here tomorrow. He is going to send us shopping."

"I like your car."

"My RX-7? Yes, I like my car, also. It's pretty sweet. I saw your car. It's cool, too."

"Thanks.!" And as I look up from my work, she has vanished. I hear her tiny feet on the floor, and that's that.

I hear her car fire up, the struggle of the engine against the clutch, and the strains of a strong exhaust. Dear God help me, I am infected.

Men are divided into two groups- those hold their emotions prisoner, and those that are held prisoner by their emotions. I know nothing of the former, as the only life I have ever experienced has been under the tyrannical rule of feelings. Feelings inhibit you from actually accomplishing anything. I have never quite figured out how to obtain the objective of the feeling- to find a way to make the woman love me, rather than just longing for her. But I am trapped in the feeling of longing. In the real world, be it Nanette or Madeleine, or even Lucia, there is and was no way to convince the woman that my feelings towards her are meaningful and desirable. All they are are messy compulsions that occupy my feeble mind. If I were to describe to Nanette what I actually thought about her, it would come out as tears and whimpering, followed by an accidental orgasm. What woman would be drawn to that? The manifestation of feeling is unsexy, and what human being desires something that has no sexual appeal? Women used to describe me using useless superlatives, such as "pleasant (Kristen)," "nice(Lucia)," "terrific (Kristen)," "sweet(Lucia)"- and no woman actually wants a guy who fits those superlatives. These superlatives aren't really superlatives- what they are instead are *positive derision*- a type of complementary language that has no reward behind it. It is no more than a cleverly masked bitch-slap to the heart. No woman wants to sleep with a "sweet" guy. No woman wants a "nice" guy to take her to bed. Women only truly value men of this sort when things are bad. Lucia never called me when she was having a good day. She called me when things were going to shit. Then she was sweet, and she would tell me I was sweet. I would be a fucking mess, and it would mean nothing, but when Lucia was a mess, God forbid that I should not be there. I could lose my string of derisory compliments should I fail to appear in her time of need. It was imperative, therefore, that she keep me in this compromised position, lest she get my feelings riled up, and then it would be over. I would feel horrible, and receive the double whammy of feeling like I let her down, plus the insufferable longing that I dealt with already. You could say that if my feelings were holding me prisoner, she was the guard at the gate.

I have often wondered what I could do to rectify this situation. The typical impulse is to perform copious acts of kindness, supposedly with no ulterior motive. However, these acts of kindness are in vain. The only thing they will earn are more vacant superlatives. However, I keep forgetting that if initial attraction does not exist, then all I am doing is setting myself up for failure. The worst part is that if the woman should discover these underlying motives, the punishment will be compounded. And, of course, the punishment is often watching the victor do absolutely nothing, and still capture the woman's heart. I have determined that there is no rest to this condition. In my heart of hearts, I know I should not tolerate this unfortunate repression, but what else is there? My brain cannot liberate itself from the pattern of failure, and my emotions are in full control.

How does infatuation tie into all of this chaos? Well, the compulsory action *associated* with the pathogen is the desire to perform an excess of kind deeds for the woman. The lack of honesty, and sheepish *excess* to which these deeds are performed hints at an ulterior motive. The issue at hand is that the executor won't even admit to it. Ultimately, we are ashamed to admit that we like them. Unfortunately, the typical admission of the man is that he is doing these altruistic tasks because he is the woman's friend. When your feelings hold you captive, this is the best you can hope for, so you know no better than to cite it as your impetus.

Being in the group of men who manifest control over their emotions (and thus realize their objective, or make a heroic attempt to do so), is an enviable position. I have never figured out how to make the transition from being controlled to controlling. Some people cling to various vehicles to mobilize the transition from one to the other- having more confidence, being *cocky* in some instances.

But myself, and some of the rest of us, continue to be handicapped by infatuation. So what if you actually turned your fantasy into reality? The inequality of infatuation is the most humiliating quandary one must deal with, but the inversion of the typical result can be just as scarey. Say you were to win over the woman you have become infatuated with. She will still never love you as much as you "love" her. Infatuation comprises a set of unrealistic expectations that can never be fulfilled. My "love" for Lucia was so unrealistic that the truth is, if she had fallen in love with me, I would have exploded. I think about how this all works- you love someone too much, and the relationship is doomed before it begins. On the other hand, you can have a "normal" relationship, where you and your significant other start by not caring about each other very much, and then slowly work towards giving a damn. You might even fall in love, if you try hard enough, and the chemistry doesn't evaporate.

So, you either fall in love with someone who doesn't care about you who you care *too much* about, or you marry someone you don't care all that much about, compared to your past lovers, or, in my case, infatuations. And there's one other option- you can choose someone who loves you whom you are not crazy about, and end up on the other side of the equation. Which one would I choose? I have no choice. No one is presenting themselves to me as an option. Damn the mutual consent part of love and marriage. I have had lucid dreams before where my beautiful dream was a reality, and where I became united with Lucia. She loved me as equally as I loved her, and we were together, and complete. But then, you have two people with massive expectations. What could be worse than two people who have massive, open, bleeding hearts for each other? I suppose God allows for the existence of children to offset the inevitable explosion that would take place under these circumstances.

I often wonder what it would be like to spend two weeks in mutual infatuation with another person. We could both be crazy about each other, until we exploded. I have never had the pleasure of experiencing such a terminal attraction, so I can only assume that it is worse to have an unfulfilled infatuation fizzle out than have a fulfilled one create mutually assured destruction for both parties. It makes me wonder how marriages even last. I thumb through North's book, and I see all these indications that marriage is holy, and mirrors Christ's love for the Church. However, the reality is that I can't fathom being part of something so good and so perfect. I would mess it up, instantly. If only there was a way to demystify it, and experience it, without actually have to accomplish all of the necessary tasks that allow courtship to actually occur.

16

Fully under the spell of infatuation, and completely annoyed with Madeleine, I find myself unhappy and blissfully content at the same time. Years of this sort of depression have bonded me to it, so that some sort of dramatic fixation needs to be present in my life in order that I should enjoy it.

Poff calls me from Georgia. He tells me how he is doing, and how he and some of his friends up there had a bonfire and almost burned down his house. I ask him how the ladies are; he just laughs, and says "you know, the usual."

I wait for him to ask me how the ladies are, and he does not, so I just start talking. He groans and does his best to listen, but instead of giving me advice, he just makes fun of me and tells me that I should have no business telling him about more pointless endeavors, especially this one. I tell him how my new job is going, and how interesting Henri is. Poff has to get back to work, so I return to my task of doing nothing at all. Thus far, Henri has ordered me to read the *Surrealist Manifesto* and *The Stranger*. Thanks in part to my simple mechanical inclinations, I also listened to French language tapes while assisting Henri in replacing the nitrogen spheres on his Citroen DS. French is a very rich language, with a way to express anything, it seems. Henri liberally uses both French and English, but not on purpose.

It is Friday. Mysteriously, the weather has changed, and is now true to the Florida lifestyle that I enjoy so much. I have become intoxicated with the spring air. The Camellias are breathing their last, and the late varieties are blooming. Henri's yard has become a plethora of beautiful new and dying blossoms, and I have taken several walks there. He has agreed to pay me for all my time I spend at his place assisting him with his *maison*, but when there is not much to do, I go outside and I take walks. It was here that on Thursday morning I engaged with God in my usual conversation about all of my shortcomings, illusions and infatuation. Usually, I ramble on and on to Him, reminding Him that the last time I felt this way was at least a year ago. But this time something different happened. This time, God spoke back.

I heard Him clear as day. The thought sequence retains its opalescence in my mind, ringing freely. The mind of the infatuated man is *inclined* to communicate with the Almighty. After all, did God not create the woman that my heart longs for? She is His creation, implying He is also connected to *her*. He must know her. He is her father, and when one longs for the woman of his dreams, does he not ask her father for her hand?

The sequence began while I was touching the petals of a wayward blossom, a peony white and pink camellia, struggling to open. I separated the petals and helped it unfurl its beauty. "Lord, who is this mysterious woman who I think about so continuously?" I laughed at myself, having said the same thing two weeks ago about Madeleine. "Why did you bring her into my life? What is her name? Who is she, really? What has she been through?"

I pause for a moment, looking at the clear blue sky. "Does she know you?," I ask my Him. And I am silent again for a good ten minutes. I look around the yard- perhaps it is three acres or more, and the trees are planted in the style of an orange grove. The grass tickles my ankles, and the sun hangs heavy on my fingertips. My mind goes quiet for a second, when I see a tree that has blossomed late in the fullness of its beauty. And then, a whisper.

It was indiscernible at first, and it felt like it had neither a beginning or an end. The softness of it was beautiful, but I could tell it was distinctly masculine. I looked for Henri, and he was not there. I stood silently, shocked for a second and certainly unaware of what was going on around me. And then, clear as day, the words formed in my mind. They were distinct and vivid, but they were not sonorous, as you would expect. It's like He wrote them there, and someone was introducing them into my sequence of thought. Why do I know this? Because they went completely against my sentiments, my thought sequence and my mindset in that moment. There was one problem. I didn't know who He was talking about, at first.

"Bring (her, them, yourself) back to me."

I had no idea who he was referring to. Who could they be? Could it be about myself, and how I had left the path of righteousness? Could it be about my friends and family? They were all good Catholics. He could have told me this before. I deduced, from my dialogue with God, and my current sentiments, that he could only be referring to one person: Nanette. This must have been the reason she came to me.

They were so gentle, and so sweet, as if God was sad, and He missed His little daughter. And now He was placing some kind of mission on my shoulders to liberate her from the life she was in. I knew nothing of her at this point, but unfortunately, this message was fertile soil for my already raging desire to be with her. From that moment on, I felt like I was supposed to be infatuated with her, as it served a purpose. All of my previous attempts served on my desire, and while I did not wish to posses or control her, I felt my infatuation, while in itself was unhealthy, could be used for some kind of good.

Like a man waking up from a hypnotic trance, I heard Henri yelling for me to come inside. I took one step forward, again wondering what God meant, and why the second word in the series was so vague. The eternal struggle of man is to try and understand what God is asking him to do. If only we paid better attention, because, as North says in his book, *we should know this already.*

Sin is not really a big deal. It used to be, but it isn't. Jesus dealt with the issue, right? I am fickle, like the waves in the ocean, building up strong, and mighty, and then breaking before I even make it to the shore. It is inevitable that I will sin again, but my next occasion of sin provided me with some sort of inclination that God had spoken to me in the orchard.

Thursday night was crazy. I was in a good mood, looking forward to the dinner on Friday, while planning for a second one on Saturday. Friday is more intimate. I am not allowed to talk, and I bring out food, and pour Champagne. Plates are absurdly expensive, and meals are four courses. A stream of regulars come in, and they sit at a large table and discuss the past, but in a gray light. The guests are older, less colorful. They drive German cars, and they don't smile as much. They are learned, but in a way that is unappealing. Their one hundred dollar plates of food are more of a means of survival for Henri. The thirty guests (the number is limited, and when Henri makes reservations for the week, they fill up in about a day) are both regular and irregular. Food critics are not allowed. Henri, one time, found a food critic among the group, and escorted him out with a pistol, or at least that's what he says happened.

When I returned home on Thursday night, I have no idea why, but I felt like looking at pornography. Some of us could say "resist and flee the temptation!" But temptation is not something to be fled. It follows you with an ever increasing grip on your thinking. It might be stronger than infatuation, at least in my mind. I always ask myself what sparks this urge, but I can never think of anything. It just appears, as if it is rooted solely in the biology of concupiscence. Henri had made me work in the wine room, cleaning bottles of Burgundy that had been sitting for a year or two without sunlight. The pairs that showed up (solitary persons were not given first refusal or early reservations- Henri preferred couples on Friday, as couples keep each other in check) would often order their own bottle of wine after dinner. Selection from the wine list was compulsory. If you showed up to dinner, you had to order at least a glass of wine. When I asked him what these cost, he laughed at me and said "I can't. You would die." He did indicate that his profit margin per bottle was about thirty-five percent, which meant that a sixty five dollar bottle would sell for a good ninety on his table. He was happy to explain to me what each was, and when I asked him if any local vendors sold the types of wines he carried, he would gently remind me that no two bottles of wine are the same, and they were not just paying for the brand, but where it came from, which year it was grown, how long it sat in his cellar, and how hard he had to work to find it. He also informed me that he chose the prices depending on the brand's current market, the forecast for the forthcoming season, and how much he liked the customer.

"What if someone doesn't like it?" I asked.

"That is his problem, not mine. I have no bad wines."

And I returned home late, tired and unfocused, after this long day of work.

When I sat down in front of my computer, and turned on the monitor, opened my browser, and began thinking about what site I would visit, I suddenly felt a chill down my spine. "Why was I doing this?" The Spirit of God was leaving me.

There was a site I occasionally visited that was based out of Miami, or something like that. The scenery was certainly Floridaesque, and in the back of my mind, I occasionally found myself looking at the videos on it, indulging in the idea that I was the man. Porn actors are anonymous, especially the men. They are referred to as "He," or "Him" in this sensual context, as if all men are the same, and the same person. You should never meet these people in real life. They do not exist, and they are not part of the rest of humanity to me. God created them, but they created what they have become. I acknowledge that this is one of those careers that cannot be contained inside the will of God, if said will has even the slightest pull on the universe. And yet, I subscribe to it, and, deep inside the layers of my mind, I am nearly thankful it exists. God never made me sign anything that said I would be perfect.

After browsing the contents of this site, I went to another one that was linked to it. That site failed to captivate me, and I went to another smaller, sketchier site. My anti-virus software flashed, and I ignored it. The animal inside of me was looking for a rush.

An anonymous woman was having sex with a man in an anonymous room. She was screaming and wailing, and I couldn't help but wonder who she was. She was face down, in the carpet, and moving her hands. In no time at all, I made all the motions, arriving at orgasm quickly, and then feeling the recession. Right as I was about to shut down the video, she turned around. At first I thought I was losing my mind, sort of like the time I discovered Lucia in that big house. But this time, I paused the computer, and looked dead on at the face of the girl. She was distorted, and her expression was almost distrusting. Seconds earlier, I would have been aroused by it, but today, it was not so.

I hit the play button again, and much to my dismay, her face seemed familiar. Her hair color was different, she was wearing contact lenses, she had a large tattoo that I could not discern, and she had a certain lightness about her. My Nanette, my dearest Nanette. Only this time, she was identified as "Kat," which I am certain was also not her real name. I was devastated, perhaps because I knew that she needed to be rescued, and I was not able to do it. However unsure I was that it was her, a certain part of my brain had identified Nanette in another identity. Perhaps God spoke to me in that moment, notifying me of Nanette's secret occupation. The suspicion arose in my chest that this might really be Nanette, and I wondered, from that moment, if she was truly a *sensual actress*. I felt very shameful, and very aware, as if God had revealed something to me. But at this low point, I felt only one thing: An immense burning sensation to love her.

Friday. It is three o'clock in the afternoon, and I am hesitantly waiting for Henri to get back to the house, so that we can begin setting up. He had gone out to receive a generous delivery of codfish loins for our dinner tonight, and had left me in charge of cleaning flutes and wine glasses. The nefarious Nanette was coming to the house after she had finished some other tasks. Henri had no issue with her lateness, but it made me nervous. Seeing her was really my only source of joy, and my main delight in this sort of meaningless work. She made the workplace sacred, much like the presence of the Eucharist makes a Catholic church a holy place. I am always fearful that she will not show up, and I will never actually get to know her. The weather is milder now, as spring begins to take hold. Next week is Valentine's day, and I am contemplating giving her some kind of gift. But the folly ceases when Henri calls and asks me how I am doing on my organizing of the utensils. As if we were preparing for surgery, everything had to be spotlessly clean. The plates, gleaming white. The glasses, crystal clear. And furthermore, the cutlery had to look unused. If a knife so much as got a scratch, it would be polished out. What could not be polished would be discarded into a bin in the cellar. I asked Henri if I could have a damaged fork, and he stated that such things could reveal the presence of his palace. I looked harder at the fork, and discerned his initials.

As I stand here, polishing like a fiend, I hear a familiar step. I struggle to address my personality flaws, and present myself as a likeable being. She closes the door, and sets her purse down in the hall. She walks slowly towards the dining room. There is a to-do list for her, attached to the door. She ignores it, because I hear her laughing and saying "Oh Henri..."

I go back to polishing, merely because I want to have something else to do other than listening to Nanette. She moves lightly through the dining room. I hear her checking chairs, cleaning little things in the room. I cannot hear exactly what she is doing, but I assume she is trimming candle wicks, adjusting the level of lighting, and folding napkins. I can see that she is a perfectionist, evident by her pairing of earrings and shoes, clothes and colors. She coordinates the dining room with the same brand of intricacy. Her pairings are sentimental; rose-colored napkins with light yellow table cloths, deep red place settings and lavender candles. The last camellias are on display in shallow cups tonight. They are beautiful, but they are weak, and perceiving them to be alive and well presents an intellectual struggle. Henri cut them earlier today, and put them on ice. Now, they sit in cold water, where they will not be observed again in their splendor until next year.

Nanette enters the kitchen, and I jump up with a start. She comes in looking for the wine glasses, and does not acknowledge my presence. She takes a hanger with ten glasses, and goes out to set them in place. I anticipate she will make several trips into the kitchen, while my heart continuously races with aspiration. I remember what Poff told me, a long time ago- n*ever say hello first*. I wonder why she doesn't greet me. It seems so selfish of her not to acknowledge me.

After her third trip to the kitchen, she finally says something. "Hey Apollinaire, you should have cleaned these a bit better."

"I prefer that you call me Benedict."

"But that's your real name. We aren't supposed to use those here."

"Well, when no one is looking, call me Benedict."

"Wash the glasses better. He will blame both of us."

She is all business. There is no room for romance in a job like this, I suppose. Henri being the European that he is, has a penchant for order, and we must honor it. Nanette continues to be great at what she does, and I continue to struggle in my focus. This is what he told me to do- to not let her interfere with my focus, and here I am, struggling. Jim told me that there will arise in me a great distaste for women after all of this obsession clears. But he also says that the next five years will be difficult, knowing the kind of personality that I have.

With several hours under my belt, I manage to complete my

195

tasks.. Henri allows me a break of twenty minutes, so I go to the car, and take out my copy of *Redeeming Sexuality*. North has outlined, in chapter three, a grand analogy, about how marriage on earth points to marriage in heaven- all of us will have a marriage to God, so he says. It seems like something to get excited about, but in all fairness, marriage to a woman seems so much more exciting and fun than marriage to a deity. There is no part of me that wants to trade this sexuality we have on earth for something that I don't know about. But it is all beyond our control, and I am forced to be accepting of it. North goes on to say that the church is an analogy of what a holy marriage is. I suddenly realize that I am part of the church, and I am part of the problem with the church. If only I had a better character, I could be part of the solution. This all makes me wonder why God gave us free will, and then certain human tendencies- sexuality, for example- that are stronger than our will to do the right thing. Our human tendencies are stronger than our desire to be "good," and so they end up leading us from temptation right into sin, over and over again. With the reliability of the sun rising, I am unable to choose chastity. With the indifference of original sin, I fail to control myself. I live out my days to suit my interests, and I do not do any good for anyone. I am indifferent to doing good- I have no desire, but the desire to love and be loved. This desire, gone unfulfilled, paralyzes the will and makes it ineffective. The only way I have been able to assuage my long suffering body is by engaging in the act of masturbation. Instead of anyone condemning me for being so pathetic and indifferent, they should have pity on me. Sexuality is too much for me. But it is in the very fiber of my being, so I might as well keep praying for a spouse, and trying to reconcile with Jesus. Jesus forgives us, and that is really my only hope.

17

Dinner that night is a whirlwind. Nanette ducked into a bathroom right before dinner, and re-emerged magnificent. She is dressed not as a hostess, but more as a *maitresse*. Her soft skin has the hues of an impressionist figure, and her hair is blonde and fluorescent. She smells like springtime. I am overwhelmed, but I do my best to focus on the task at hand. The atmosphere is hushed, with elegant personages entering. Henri demands that everyone arrive between seven and seven fifteen. Those who are late are not granted entry. The appetizer, and the first wines are served. Nanette gracefully goes from table to table asking for wine selections. It is customary for a table to purchase a bottle at this time. It may last them all night, but many of the patrons and their dates seem content to consume two or more bottles. Some guests are more modest, drinking by the glass. Any table that orders more than two bottles is watched by Henri- drunkenness is intolerable here, as it disturbs the peacefulness of the occasion. I follow Nanette from table to table, topping up water, and distributing the first bits of food. On the menu is a large variety of mushroom, which I have never seen before. The mushroom is topped with something that smells interesting. I look at the menu card- it denotes that the attractive fungi are topped with a salmon roe, on a base of caramelized shallots. Each guest seems delighted with their mushroom. Henri explains what it is after each guest has been served, and then a toast is made to a great contributor, usually for the glory of France.

"This week, I will toast the great writer Antoine de Saint-Exupéry! May his works live on in our hearts forever!"

Nanette pauses, and Henri raises his glass of Burgundy (at least I think it is Burgundy). She looks in my direction, but she doesn't acknowledge me. I pause, as if Henri is praying, and look at the floor. A number of voices respond to his toast accordingly, and then the life flows. I wait about 30 minutes, attending to our guests, and then I bring out the second course- young partridge with a sweet orange and pineapple glaze, while Nanette continues her task of making sure that everyone has wine. Henri makes me pass out a paper, on the disappearance of Saint-Exupéry, and the guests review it. The title of the paper is "Who shot down the plane?"

This curious paper goes into a discussion about whether the famous Frenchman was shot down in the war, or whether he made a

197

"graceful exit" from society, which was a recurring theme (at least in Henri's opinion) in his books.

"I would have vanished," I think to myself. I recall several circumstances where I had wished I could vanish under the pretenses of death. It is far too difficult in a time of peace. I would leave cameras behind, in hopes that I could watch people miss me. Maybe someone would videotape the memorial service. But of course, this is all stupid. And of course, someone found Antoine's bracelet off the coast of France in 1998. Somewhere out in the hidden corners of the world, though, I would like to think that there are people who have managed to escape from society.

While I am imagining running away with Nanette, Henri comes and taps me on the shoulder. "You are visibly distracted by your co-worker. You need to stop staring at her." Henri says it in a barely discernible whisper, such that I hardly understand what he is saying. I feel a chill roll down my spine, and out into my hands. He is upset, and I don't want him to see me as a failure.

I need a way to figure out who this Nanette is, and what her life like. Is she really an adult film actress? Or is she a saint? Does she live in an underworld, or is her life a semblance of heaven? I wonder what she does at night. I wonder if she has a lover or not, or if she has someone she is hopelessly enamored with. I wonder if she is religious. I wonder if she has a child. I wonder if she as been to college, and if she finished. I wonder if she knows how I feel about her. I wonder if she has dreams...

"Dammit, keep your eyes on your task!" Henri whispers angrily as I walk to the kitchen. "You are failing me! I can't serve everyone here- that's why I hired you!"

Henri's frustration prompts me to be more exact. My guilt makes me pour water like it is champagne, serve the cod like it is filet, and attend to the guests like they are kings and queens. Henri watches me with his dark eyes, making sure that I am focused on my work. Nanette moves with familiarity from table to table, and then she brings out a cart with the second wine orders. One by one, she approaches each table, bottle in hand, filling the glasses gracefully. I do not watch intently, this time, as expulsion from this workplace means I would never see her again. I make sure all of our guests are both comfortable and fully supplied, and then I disappear.

Henri begins to read about Saint-Exupéry, citing the testimonials of German pilots who shot the man down over the Mediterranean, and going into depth about the circumstances surrounding his disappearance. "Do you believe the bracelet was planted?" he asks the guests. "Do you believe that the writer, and others, made a graceful exit from society?"

I would certainly take Nanette on an old Lockheed bomber, and fly away with her into the night. She and I would go to the deserted atolls of the Pacific, where clothing was optional. She would be my lover, and I would be her hero. We would live out our days in solitude, and use the airplane's radio and a solar panel to provide a one way connection with the outside world. We could be somewhere on Midway Island, or in the uninhabited reefs of the Solomons. We could call these places ours, and no one would take her from me.

After dinner is over, at eleven thirty, Henri administers a blessing to the guests (in French, none-the-less) and dismisses them. They make an exodus to the door, and thank him for a strong and elegant meal. Henri takes the checks and the bank notes, and counts them. The average profit from each table is about a hundred dollars, with the bills approaching three hundred or so. The tips, which are split seventy-thirty between Nanette and I, are compiled and divided. In the meanwhile,. I carefully remove the table contents and dispose of any extra. Nanette follows suit, but with smaller, more delicate things. The empty glasses are hung, and the food plates are cleared with a decisive action. Henri tells me again not to break anything, and I begin to look for any items I have missed. Nanette darts around, like a minnow, or a mermaid, doing her job.

"What is your life like?" I chance to ask her. She ignores me, and rubs off the question. I wait a bit longer.

"What is it that you do the rest of the week?" I ask again.

199

She hears me this time. "Why do you want to know? It's not your affair. I'm a normal person."

"I don't know. I find you intriguing, I guess."

"There is nothing intriguing about me," she responds, glancing over he shoulder at me.
In that moment, I am paralyzed with sadness. She does not know what a great person she is. I feel an urge to affirm her.

"But you are!" I exclaim.

"I don't want to be. Is that OK?"

"You may not want to be, but you are. I can't help but notice it."

She becomes quiet, and dismissive. Her eyes tell me that she prefers I not talk to her.
I continue to clean, and wash dishes. It is nearing 12:20 AM, and I am getting tired. But before I go, Henri calls me in to his office.

"Benedict, may I have a word with you?"

I walk in sheepishly, knowing that this cannot be good.

"Your failure to observe the needs of the guests on a continuous basis is not acceptable. "

"I can't help it. It's not intentional."

"Still...you watch her too much."

"I can't help it. And I don't watch her that much. I'm looking around. I'm looking at everything!" The frustration in my voice grows by the second, and I become unnerved.
"You need to work on this behavior. Every fine dining establishment has to have an attractive hostess. It is the stuff of legend, really. It has to be this way. Consider her an objet d'art. She is essential to the presentation of my maison. You are not essential, and I can find another Benedict. I can only thank God that you are not married. But really, mon ami, she is not an extraordinary girl. She is who she is-beautiful, exquisite, charming. She is no Marie Cassat, Helen Keller, Adrienne Von Speyr. She is, rather, another beautiful girl. You need to stop worshiping her."

"Why did you hire me, then?"

"I saw you had potential. I saw you were willing to do it.

You are more akin to a suicide bomber than a highly trained assassin. I need someone to do the dirty work with an air of dignity."

"Well, Henri, I need to know who she is. I .."

"I know how you feel. When I was a young virgin, I used my camera to take pictures of women I found attractive so that I would not forget who they were."

"That's creepy." I make a frown, and then a grimace.

"No, in the period it was acceptable, even charming. But you, you have no charm. You have no accessory to attract a woman to you. You are too plain. You are unappealing. Women do not go for men who are weak and bland. Rather, they prefer those who are charming and cultured. But I do not require an expert womanizer. I require a good server, and with enough concentration, you will be one. *D'accord*?"

I nod. Then I get up, and excuse myself.

"Wait!" he yells, suddenly.

"What is it?" I demand.

"I cannot describe to you what you do not know or understand, but your mind is consumed with a first world issue. In 1976 I was traveling through the Middle East. I saw so many things there that were just sad- awful things. Few of these people were wishing some girl they were enamored with was trying to seduce them- they were too busy fending for their lives. Their homes destroyed, their livelihood demolished, their wives and children killed or injured. You understand?"

"What is the point of your diatribe?" I ask, angrily.

"You have it too easy. You should be using your energy to change the world." It was hard to argue with him.

"*Bon nuit*," he whispered. I nodded and walked forth. Nanette was gone.

The dinner on Saturday had gone a little bit better than the one on Friday. Friday blessed me with heavy casualties, at least because Henri saw what I was focusing on. Nanette, on the other hand, was more fun to be around, since we were inclined to participate. The focus of the dinner was a reading from Camus' story, *The Adulterous Woman*, which Henri and I discussed beforehand. While the woman is not unfaithful to her husband, she struggles to gain his affections, and then is drawn to the glance of an Algerian officer while she is in transit. It is a story of unfulfilled emotions and desires. I can relate to it beautifully.

After dinner, Nanette and I are again assigned to clear tables. This dinner is less expensive, so that "those of us who have a drive towards the finer things in life should not be barred access to them," says Henri. The guests of this dinner are more colorful and less elevated. They are young and affluent, but they see no need to spend three hundred dollars when they can have a fun time for a third of that. The guest list is again limited to thirty, but there is a bias towards those who are single, this time. Much like the retreats, Henri states with eloquence that there will be consequences for the "mixing of the sexes."

He also states that those who are in the business of "acquiring phone numbers for the purpose of getting a date" are forbidden, and that contact outside of the society is "frowned upon."

While some of the participants are indignant of this rule, Henri has a history of catching perpetrators, and allowing them to finish their evening in peace. He then calls them up the next day, and asks them if they have any plans during the week. "The seductive powers of such a grand dinner and such high learning can endanger the fidelity of a man's marriage. I would hate for a great event, such as my dinner, to be marred by scandal. They must not try things with other guests!" Henri tells me.

I asked him if it was always like this, and he tells me that this idea of limited contact was initiated following complaints of a woman that her husband met a new "friend" at his house. The husband and the lady friend began an affair that went on for six months. Henri felt no responsibility towards it, but he stated "marriage, above all, must be preserved, as well as my reputation. A bit of wrist slapping is good for a man. If you slap the wrist of an animal, it does no good, really, unless you do it a lot. But a man learns quickly. I might as well slap their wrists, so they don't ruin themselves. I prefer a gentle slap of the wrist, with all of its minor complaints, than having a finger thrust at me for creating a fertile breeding ground for an extra-marital affair." Such was Henri's adamant enforcement of this rule that I felt Nanette was secure. No one from this place could take her from me. There would be no dashing banker, or a politician, or a professor, or a corporate imbecile, who could thwart me. Henri's reputation as an interrupter of the extra-marital affair was certainly a greater thing to have than the opposite.

I am in the kitchen, again, and Nanette is helping me clean the glasses. We wear gloves to protect our skin from the hot, soapy water. Nanette is disenchanted. I can see it in her gaze.

"What's wrong?" I ask her, nonchalantly. I feel almost guilty.

" Nothing is wrong. I am fine." But again, I have watched her enough to see a disturbance in the symmetry of her actions. She does not have her ethereal beauty tonight.

"You can tell me you aren't fine. It's OK."

"My contract with Henri stated that I would not become *emotionally* involved with my co-workers or dinner guests."

"Henri told me it was alright if we spoke."

"Did he?"

"Yes, he did. Several times."

"Well, he told me that he preferred I not speak with you about external affairs." She looked distantly across the kitchen, like she was waiting for Henri to step in and quiet me. I though to myself "my feelings for you are an internal affair. They are disrupting my abilities here."

I think what happened after that is where my relationship with her began to take form. After dinner, I sit in my car, and the scene replays itself in my mind.

It was late, very late. I continued my tasks of cleaning the cutlery, while Nanette moved back and forth, putting things away. The plates, once removed from the dishwasher, had to be inspected for any issues. They were stored in cabinets, but the cabinets had to be checked for dust. Nanette checked the cabinets thoroughly. I glanced at her from across the room, her gray sweater hiding the curves of her upper body. She stepped up on a stool to reach the uppermost sections of the cabinets. As she cleaned, I sensed an imbalance in her positioning on the stool, so I walked up to her, and carefully placed my left hand on her middle back to balance her. There was one problem- I forgot to tell her what I was about to do.

As my hand made contact with her sweater, I felt her back tense. She turned around, startled, losing her intense focus on the cabinet. "Benedict! What the hell!" She began to yell as she fell backwards. Awkwardly, I tried to catch her, but she was a bit too heavy. While her lovely body tumbled downwards, I grabbed her arm. Her legs collapsed beneath her as she hit the floor, and I pulled upwards. She braced herself with her other arm, frightened, and afraid.

I spared her head from hitting the hard floor. Her arm was sore and bruised from where I caught it (although these bruises may have been there already), and her ankles hurt from the impact, but she had no serious issues. She got up and looked at me, her eyes boiling over with hostility.

"I'm sorry! I would never, ever drop you! Never!"

I felt horribly awkward and embarrassed from my poor judgment, and it showed. Nanette was indifferent. She picked up the stool, and went back to cleaning cabinets. No one could fault the quality of her work, and the devotion to it. In fact, it was sexy.

Henri did not hear the ruckus, fortunately, and I finished up my work, and left.

It is twelve forty five, and I am on my way home. For the first time in my life, I realize that I am a workplace hazard. How could I injure someone that I care about so much?
I arrive home, circa one in the morning, and I begin to read a bit more of Mr. North's book.

Brothers and sisters, what is it that makes chastity so hard?

Considering that sin entered the world, and "corrupted" our humanity, the greatest corruption has occurred with our sexuality. Humanity has fostered this corruption, and now, it must be undone. But what are we to do when churches, religious educators and the clergy shun our human sexuality with explicit disdain and vague spiritual direction? My earliest confessions as an adolescent consisted of awkwardly telling my parish priest about the times I looked at pornography and misused my body for sexual gratification. His advice was indirect and incoherent. "We must stay strong!" he would tell me. I would close my eyes and struggle to get through each confession as he would lord my repeated sinfulness over me.

The church still discards the gift of sexuality, leaving it as merely a "bad thing" when misused, and a "good thing" when used in a contraception-free marriage. But it makes me ask the question "Is there any use for our sexuality outside of marriage?" There is, I promise. All of our creativity, our personalities, our spiritual practice, our hope and our desire to be loved, all of them have their roots in our sexual nature. In fact, what happens inside the bedroom between married couples is just a tip of the iceberg. This sexuality that God has bestowed upon us is really what binds us to Him. The marriage we yearn for on earth shows how God yearns to be united with us.

So why do we dilute it with all of these grotesque abominations, namely the use of the body for actions of great perversion? Why are there orgies, and ads on the internet for casual encounters? Why is it that these are subtly introduced into our minds on a daily basis?

Because Satan is doing whatever he can to stop us from true unification with God. He does not want that to happen- it would mean that he loses the war. What must we do, then, to help the cause? I assure you, my brothers, and my brothers especially, that we must not give up. Go to confession, even if it is every week. Do not leave the faith on account of your weaknesses. God will not stop loving you for the crosses that you can't carry. In His passion, Jesus exemplified that carrying the cross means a painful and reoccurring fall. The act of reconciliation is vital to our relationship with God, no matter how ugly the sin. Remember, there is no sin that Jesus cannot forgive. All we have to do is ask. And there is no cap on His forgiveness. All we have to do, again, is ask.

His love is for human beings, and in His mind, no one human being is better than another. Jesus doesn't say "Oh, Joe, you've carried your crosses so well! You have outperformed eighty-nine percent of humanity! Good work, old boy!" No, no. He rejoices when a sinner returns to Him, even after that sinner has sinned week after week after week. Take heart, and forget about your sinfulness. Love Him, and do good in His name. You will never be sin-free, but you can still be full of the Holy Spirit. The greatest Christian is the one who does not let his sinfulness mar his relationship with Christ.

Olivia, Progenitor to Lucia

I feel as if he spoke to me. I have persevered week after week, where chastity for me has been a daily battle. What the Catholics in my group don't understand is that in my daily life I am either running one of two directions- towards Jesus or towards sexual temptation. I think my bipolarity originated in high school. I became acquainted with porn relatively late in the game, at age eighteen.

I used to drive a K-car until I was accident free for a year. My dad handed me the keys to the Saab, and said "be good. Don't get in trouble!"

The first day I had it, I was clocked at sixty four miles per hour, in a forty five zone. The consequence was that I had to go to traffic school. My friends were amazed, considering that the speed of my ticket was a descending speed. I had been going nearly ninety, because one of my friends had dared me to go twice the speed limit. The cop busted me while I was slowing to a more reasonable velocity. Two weeks later, I found myself in a driving re-education class at a dingy strip mall in Pensacola. The room was full of all sorts of derelicts, most of whom had to take the course to keep driving. But there was an open seat in one row of plain plastic tables and garish chairs next to a girl whose beauty could only be described as unforgettable. Perhaps this could be attributed to the unremarkable setting, but for some reason she appealed to me in a different way than any girl had previously. Her hair was dark brown, and she had blue eyes and pale skin. Her body had a certain delightfully presence, something possibly nefarious. She wore her cunning like she wore her light blue shirt, and her freckles stood out on her pale skin. She had her CD player out, and she was nonchalantly waiting for class to begin. Oh, and her body was sculpted exceptionally well.

She looked over at me five minutes later, and took the CD out. She was listening to the Ataris. "I like them" I whispered in her direction.

"Yeah? I'm friends with them. They are pretty cool." When she said that, I got the feeling I was sitting with an extraordinary girl.

"Why are you here?" I asked her.

"I got three speeding tickets in the last few months. The big one really set it off though."

"What do you drive?" I asked.

"A 3000GT turbo. What did you do?" She asked me blankly, like she didn't really care.

"Speeding. I was doing like a hundred in a forty five." I have learned that if someone can't go back and see the event, a small exaggeration doesn't hurt anything.

"Oh yeah?" she looked at me with vague interest.

"Where did you get the 3000GT from?" I asked.

"My boyfriend gave it to me. He flies helicopters. It was a gift for my eighteenth birthday. It has special turbos on it."

"What did you do?" I asked. Any intelligent male would know that by now I felt seriously depressed because she had a boyfriend who could afford to buy her the holy grail of entry level super cars.

"I got pulled over racing some guy in a turbo Supra. He told me that if I lost to him, I had to give him a BJ."

I was shocked and appalled.

"Did you know him at all?" I stuttered.

"He never had a chance." And she smiled to herself.

The attractive girl continued. "I showed his flop bitch ass. We got up to like 130, and then backed off. I got nailed a half mile later doing 105. I was arrested, but then my boyfriend bailed me out. The court ordered traffic school."

"That's quite a story."

"Yeah. What do you drive?" Her self absorption was becoming more evident by the second, but she seemed to acknowledge my presence.

"I drive a Saab 99. It's like a rally car. It's pretty sweet."

"Is it fast?" She asked with a little bit of interest.

"It got me here, didn't it?" I was ashamed to tell her that it had 108 horsepower.

I stared at her the duration of the class. We passed notes for the next three hours. On break, she went out and pulled out a cell phone. She called someone quickly, and then went back into class.

"Are you a senior?" I asked her, sheepishly.

"Yeah, you?"

"I am. Where do you go?"

"It's not important. I'm almost done. I don't hang out with high school kids, anyway." She obviously fancied herself a bad-ass.

"That's cool. What are you going to do after school is over? College?"

"I'm going to start a pay site."

I was curious. "What's a pay site?"

"It's live porn. It pays well, and you don't have to touch anyone." I felt a mixture of fear and wonderment. "And then what?"

"I'm going to party."

"What's your name?"

She threw me a sidelong glance. "I'm Olivia" she said, and extended her hand, elongating the "a" with a low tone, and a sexy, scratchy, girly voice.

"I'm Rad."

She rolled her eyes, and giggled a little bit. "Cool."

"Where do you live?"

"Gulf Breeze," and a detached grin wrinkled the corners of her mouth.

After that class was over, I walked her to her car. The 3000GT was black, with stickers on the back windshield. She started it, and I could hear the turbos whistling nervously under the hood. She gave me her AOL screen name, and I gave her a hug. Funny, hugs are about as close as guys like me ever get. I have this blockade, in my mind, that a hug is the stopping point, and I will never get closer. This spilled over into my relationship with Lucia. I never even tried to kiss Olivia, or thought of it. I never tried to kiss Lucia either. I probably won't try to kiss Nanette.

The next two weeks, I wasted a bunch of time on the internet looking for her, just to see if she already had a pay site. I would go to nightsurf.com and search "Olivia Pay site."

One day I chanced to ask a friend of mine, who was from Gulf Breeze, if he knew an Olivia who liked fast cars and had dark hair and blue eyes. To my surprise, he had heard of her. "She was a bad girl," he told me. "She hooked up with a lot of people. Most of the guys she was with were dicks. They were the kind that drove fast and partied hard, and didn't give a shit."

"What else do you know?"

"She dropped out of high school at the begining of the year. I think she strips now, actually."

You get these feeling sometimes, and they always begin with "what if." I wondered "what if" about Olivia pretty often after that talk. I would think about her having sex with strange men, and say a little prayer for her. Something never seemed right to me about situations like these.

I was even more enamored by her. She never went on AOL

messenger, and so I had no way of learning about her. I forgot about her for a bit, but then, out of the blue, she resurfaced.

It was the first week of July. I saw a newspaper mention a terrific car accident, where the victims, nineteen-year-old Olivia Brittany Neumann, and her passenger, one Brittany Thomas, were killed when that very fast Mitsubishi 3000GT flipped over on Interstate 10, rolled across the highway, and caught fire after coming to a rest, gasoline spilling all over those hot turbos. Neither girl was wearing her seat belt. The kids in Gulf Breeze that I knew made a startling revelation. Olivia really was a stripper, and she had been found HIV positive the month before during a mandatory drug test related to her "job." After that, she started living recklessly. I was at the beach two days after the accident, and I ran into some people who knew her. They were talking about the accident.

"She was so fucking hot!" One prick said. I wanted to cut his balls off and feed them to him. I really did.

After that, I began to view porn. It made me forget how sad I was that this strange and beautiful creature had died, and, in an indecent way, I used it to honor her distant memory. My porn addiction is not Olivia's fault, but somewhere in my mind, it is linked to her. She spawned my fascination with it, and I began to believe that the bodies and orgasms of unattainably beautiful women were at least partly accessible in the dark corners of the world wide web. I went to college with an on and off struggle under my belt. The desperation I felt of not being able to be with Lucia reinforced my behavior. I was never open with myself about how much I liked it, and how often I viewed it, but one thing was always certain- I couldn't give it up.

I think the death of this strange and beautiful creature inspired a change in me that let a certain darkness in. After I am done indulging in my guilty habit, I become lost in thought, wondering where her soul is, and if God had mercy on her or not. On my way to my parents house, I drive past the accident site on the interstate. There is a little cross there. One time it was knocked over, so I pulled over and fixed it. Two other times, I stopped and left flowers by it. They were for both girls. None of the guys she slept with ever left flowers, dammit. Only suckers like me, who long for and pine after these girls, leave flowers. We get nothing, and we stay, because our love is pure and our hearts are clean. If Lucia died, I would do the same for her.

When I met Lucia, there was a rawness in my being that desired some sort of intimacy to heal me of the impact. With that rawness came vulnerability, and that vulnerability allowed so much to set in- Lucia, porn, religion, depression. I wonder if Joseph North's theory of the heavenly marriage encompasses Olivia...

Of course, then I wonder what would have happened if she had not died. Or if I had never met her. I might have still started looking at porn. It's impossible to say what could have happened.

The sunset drew to a close as Lucia and I sat on the beach in Apalachicola, less than a year after Olivia's death. The waves gently lapped the shore, and the panoramic red sky began to draw to a soft fluorescent color. The twilight was still and surreal. The cloud beach and the upside down ocean met and reflected the colors, throwing them to the north. The eastern sunset made the gulf look a million miles deep. The greenish hue of the water promised adventure and romance. There was no one here for miles. It was like Olivia's beauty went back to the earth. I had seen these things so many times, and never before had they looked so perfect.

I pressed my hand against Lucia's, and she did not move. I felt her fingers quiver with life.

"The sunset is so beautiful," I murmured. She was silent.

"Like you..." I continued.

She looked at me and smiled. I wished for a second that she would reciprocate something. A touch, a kind word, maybe even more than what I gave her. I played with her fingers, and she moved closer to me. I placed my arm around her shoulder, and stroked her hair. She laid her head on my shoulder- sort of. Her hair was dark and soft, and she smiled at me. Drunk on her beauty, I began to ask questions. "Are you happy here with me?"

"Yes, I am. I like being around you."

I had known her for about a month at this point. I was crazy about this quiet, beautiful creature. I was certain that she felt the same way. I loved her, and it was remarkable. When I woke up, I thought about her. I thought about her all day, and when I went to sleep. My mind never rested. I was only peaceful when I was next to her, and I had just held her hand. What a glorious feeling. While other kids were losing their virginity, I was holding hands with this amazing girl. I just needed to initiate a relationship with her.

The sun was all but gone, and we got up and walked to the car. I took one last look at the water. I imagined Olivia being peaceful.

"I need a ride to this place..." she said flirtatiously. As she said it, she touched my arm.

"Sure...where?" I was already starting to have a bad feeling about this.

"This guy's apartment. He's having a party."

"I didn't know we were going to a party. I thought we were going to hang out all night."

"We are hanging out...but you'll take me, right?"

"I'll take you anywhere."

She smiled. "Thanks...I will be done at two-ish...you can come get me then."

"I thought we could both go."

She looked at me pitifully. "Sorry," she said sheepishly, elongating the "o" and the "r."

I understood why she had dressed up. I didn't understand this at the time, but Lucia was a parasite. She could convince a man to do anything for her. When she was with me, she knew she was beautiful and convincing. When she was with those losers, she felt low and undesirable. She tried so hard with them, and for what? I was here. I was all she needed.

That was the first time I dropped her off. After that, it was a routine. The only way I could reconcile the fact that she was using me was by looking at pornography. This was reinforcement. This was what my relationship with Olivia would have been if my "what if" was answered.

Sunday night was my new weekend night- sort of. I would go to Henri's, and we would get things in order. He and I would talk about culture, and language, and history. He would teach me about things that I needed to understand. We would never discuss women, or sex. I could tell that it visibly upset him.

It is Sunday, three weeks and one day after Nanette has fallen off the chair. Henri excused me around eight, and Poff has invited me to see the Burning Drugs and another band called the Lemon Dreams with him. So I am on my way to meet them at the Wild Mustang, another bar downtown. Poff is waiting at a table with his buddy Hamilton.

"What are you doing, Rad?"

"What are *you* doing, Poff?"

"I'm getting girls pregnant in Georgia." Hamilton laughs irreverently. "He probably has a whole trailer park full of illegitimate kids."

"Rad, what's this new job you have?"

"I can't tell you. It's kind of a secret. But I am a waiter."

"Is this like a place where the mafia meets?" Hamilton asks.

"Exactly. The Tallahassee mob meets at this place. They are all Cubans."

The Burning Drugs take the stage. Good old Billy Hollis is wearing a Sex Pistols tee-shirt. Billy plays a Gibson Les Paul something or other, and he is belligerent and stupid. His lyrics have a bunch of swear words, and most of his songs are a euphemism for sex.

213

"I can't wait to get you baby, I wonder if you'd like to rape me." I can hear him, even though I am trying not to.

He certainly has his fans, the bastard. There are a few girls on the floor dancing, most of whom are drunk. The bar is sweaty and hot, with no oxygen left.

"Oh that girl, she's a chatter box- she likes to yell, she likes to scream, but she really likes to talk..." I get angry just seeing him.

"Meet any girls lately?" I ask Poff.

"Yeah, duh! Georgia is full of girls. The only problem is that they all have kids."

"Ever get to Atlanta?" Hamilton queries.

"Yeah...it's wild. There are a bunch of crazies in Atlanta. One time, I saw some guy in a parking lot at a bar breaking into a guy's car. He used a crow bar, and broke the glass on the rear window. At least five people saw him. He took the stereo and some other crap. No one even stopped him. That's how they are there. No one cares. It took the cops fifteen minutes to get there. Another time I was at a club, and this girl was totally on drugs, She started to grind on me..."

Halfway through his tale, I look over, and lo and behold. My breath leaves my body.

In the far corner, sitting with two or three girls, was a blonde head of familiar proportions. She was angelic and airy, with a familiar lightness. She was in her own world, tilting her head all directions.

I watch her for at least forty five minutes. She doesn't even look in my direction. I am waiting for what happens next.

"What are you looking at?" Poff demands, with an undertone of arrogance.

"I should be hanging on every word you say, huh?"

Poff laughs. "Absolutely. For your intelligence I am going to reward you with another Newcastle."

"Thanks."

"So who are you looking at?" He asks again. I lean over and whisper in his ear. "I can't tell you in front of Hamilton."

"Ok." He looks over at Hamilton. "Rad and I are going to the

214

bathroom, like girls."

Hamilton makes a gesture that looks phallic. We walk to the bar and he orders me another beer.

"Ok, tell me!" He yells.

"So this place I work at. It's really strange, and different. I can't tell you more, but the important part is sitting right over there." I point at Nanette. Poff laughs again. "No more Madeleine, huh?"

He looks at the modestly attractive bar tender. "I don't want a Newcastle. I want a Sam Adams."

He looks at me. "Keep talking, cowboy."

"Ok, so, her name is Nanette. But that's not really her name. We all use aliases. Anyway, she's like..." I struggle for words that accurately describe her. "She's like a goddess."

"What do you know about her?" Poff asks.

"Well, I think she does porn."

"Who told you that?" Poff's eyes light up ambiguously.

"I saw her. On the internet."

"Holy shit!" Poff yelled.

"I like her. I'm not into the whole porn thing." Poff laughs like a prick. Hollis finishes his set earlier than expected and starts to unplug his pedals.

"Let's move." I tell Poff.

"Move what?"

"Move our table, so I can watch her."

The Lemon Dreams start setting up, and Hollis jumps off the stage, after making an obnoxious gesture about the other band's key-tar. Hamilton and Poff move all of their crap to a table closer to Nanette. Hollis walks over to our direction, but doesn't notice us. Instead, he marches over to Nanette, and taps her on the shoulder. I smell vanilla.

"Hey!" He yells at her.

"Oh, hey!" She says, and gets up. He hugs her, but while he is hugging her, he smacks her on the butt.

"Goddammit!" I growl subversively. "What a dick!"

She kisses him, to my surprise. Or at least that's what it looks like, it's possible that it is too dark and I am too drunk to really tell. He then walks away from her, and heads to the bar.

"I'm going to shove his balls up his ass."

Poff laughs at me for the hundreth time. Hollis is crazy. If he heard us say that, he would start something.

I dump my bottle out into Hamilton's glass of Guinness. "What the heck are you doing?" Hamilton asks.

"You'll see."

"You're drunk as shit." Hamilton mutters. I have had at least four beers.

"Are you going to talk to Hollis?" Poff is seriously concerned.

"No. No talking." I get up, and march (or maybe stagger) across the room, right to the bar. Hollis is about two inches taller than I am. He has black hair, tattoos, and blue jeans. He looks half redneck and half hardcore kid. His skin is pale. He is ugly.

Hollis is ordering something, but I'm not sure what. I hold my bottle in my hand.

I walk up to him, sizing him up carefully and slowly. "Hey, Billy. Remember me?"

He turns around. I was disgusted. He had taken the beautiful angel and desecrated her sacred body. I love her in a way that is dignified and chivalrous. This piece of shit needs to be taught a lesson. Hollis turns around.

I swing the bottle and hit him in the face. I feel the glass make contact, and I get ready for the next swing.

"What the..."

Bam. One more time, directly in the left eye.

Billy tries to punch me, but I hit him over the head, angry like a bull in heat. The bottle breaks when it makes contact with his skin. He grimaces in pain, and I hit him again in the jaw.

Hollis is pissed off, and he charges at me. There is blood in both his eyes, and I throw a chair in his way. He trips on it, falling on his face. People are rushing to his aid. Poff comes up and grabs me. At first I think he is restraining me, but he and Hamilton drag me out to the back lot. Hollis's hooligans attend to his needs. I don't even see the nymph.

"What the fuck are you thinking?" Hamilton yells.

"He's drunk" Poff snickers. "Let's keep moving." We hide in Hamilton's car until the bar cleans out. Some guys come out and are looking for us. They start checking cars, but after a minute they give up. The Ford Crown Vic (Hamilton's) we are hiding in is comfy and safe.

"You do some crazy shit for women," Poff says. He isn't exactly wrong. I have some history, to say the least. At a retreat, back in college, there was a girl that I was attracted to (Another Madeleine, perhaps?). I followed her around the entire weekend. There was another guy that was interested in her too, but he actually had the nerve to talk to her. She was very kind to him, but she acted suspicious of me. Poff smuggled some vodka into the retreat. After I had more than I should have, I stumbled across this guy, and let him have it. My impaired inhibitions did not serve me well. While I was yelling at this guy, the girl who inspired this mess walked up. Horrified that I was calling him a "fucktard" and screaming in his face, she started crying and ran to the chapel. The Blessed Sacrament was displayed a hundred yards away there. I was amazed they did not send me home.

I am stunned but I am proud of myself. I wonder if Nanette saw me beat the crap out of him. I hope she was impressed. She probably didn't notice. I feel like taking a nap. The last thing I hear is Hamilton starting the engine.

18

"Rad, wake up."

I open my eyes and then close them again.

"Wake up! NOW!"

"Who is it?"

"It's me! Stephen!"

"Where am I?" I open my eyes and I can't see.

"We are at your car."

"Huh?"

Somehow, Poff helps me out of the Crown Vic into the Saab. I feel my hands in my pocket and I remove my keys, sort of. Poff drives me home. Poff forces me out of the car and parks it. I stumble into the front door.

"That was difficult!" Poff yells.

"Why are women so...so damn difficult?"

"You're the difficult one."

"All I did was give that guy what he deserved."

"You're a fucking eighth grader." I lay down on the couch. Poff kicks me. "That was pretty bad ass."

"I'm an eighth grader."

"Yeah, you are. I bet Hollis is going to kick your ass."

"I bet he's looking for me." I really think he is. Poff just laughs at me. He rolls me off the couch, and I stumble to the bed.

I wonder what Mr. North would say about my assault on Hollis. I was standing up for Nanette's beauty. I was standing up for what was right and just. I was the instrument of God.

"Hello, Hello. God? Hello. Why is this so difficult? What do you want from me? Why can't things just work out? What are you trying to tell me? What are you trying to make me do? What is the issue with me? What did you do to make me so weird? Is there a reason? You make everything so difficult and impossible. You make me feel like I am flawed and poorly made. Poorly made. Dammit, poorly made...God."

The sun comes through the windows with a deliberate inflection of light and perfection. I roll in the covers, and look at the clock. It must have been two when I dozed off, and now it looks like it might be nine. My heart is racing, and I feel like the room is spinning. I have a brilliant hangover, and the sun is giving me a headache. I had a dream about Madeleine last night. I dreamed she was angry at me. She leaned over and yelled in my face. I think that I see everything in my dreams as it should be in real life.

Madeleine's anger should have been expressed to me. But now it is routed to my subconscious, to be manifested in my dreams. Like a tiny bleep on the radar, my brain begins to register my current situation. My mind re-enacts the situation of last night, and I become a bit nervous. What is Henri going to say? What will Hollis do when he finds me?

I stumble into the living room. Poff is grooming himself in the adjacent bathroom, leaving the door open. He leaves his hair all over the sink.

"Want some breakfast?" He mumbles.

"I guess. What happened to me?"

"You got in a fight, and we pulled you out before the shit really hit the fan."

"Wow. You guys are awesome."

"You owe us."

"What do I owe you?"

"A thank you would be nice, maybe."

"Thanks, buddy!" I smile, trying not to be sarcastic.

"I think that you should be dead right now."

I shoot Poff the bird. He laughs irreverently. I take a quick look at myself in the mirror. I was certainly somewhere last night. "Was I drunk?" I ask Poff.

"You were drunk, but you were certainly *composed*. I mean, the way you walked up to Hollis, and smacked him in the face with that bottle, and then did it again...I was wondering if you lost your common sense and kept your reflexes."

A long time ago, when I first started drinking, I used to talk a bunch of crap, but I could get up and fool anyone into thinking I was still sober by maintaining a steady gait. I still had good speech, and good reflex, but boy did I lose my shit. My common sense was the first thing to go, and then the passivity. I would go from being passive-aggressive to just being plain old ready to fight someone. Much like my incident with Anthony, my lack of sobriety did not help me in this case. Of course, I am willing to admit that Hollis deserved it.

Since it is Monday (Poff has a day off), we go get breakfast again. Poff and I drive to downtown, so he can retrieve his car. He doesn't drive the vintage Saab down here anymore. In fact, he has had a bunch of things fixed on it. His "modern" 9000 sits in a parking lot, having escaped the dangers of the previous night.

"I wonder if they called the cops?" Poff yells as he gets in. I shrug, and we drive off to the Waffle House.

Henri requests that I come by the house during the afternoon. He is making me and Nanette watch *Andalusian Dog* to prepare for our dinner topic on Saturday. I sit with a sort of nervous grin on my face, while the movie unfolds in no particular order. Indecently, I imagine that the eye being slit belongs to Hollis, and that I am doing the cutting. Nanette and I are to watch the film separately, in isolation, so that we may generate unique ideas and opinions about its meaning and content (or because he is trying to separate me from her). Henri has me come at three O'clock. In all fairness, I am fascinated by the idea of seeing Nanette. I want to know how she feels about my interaction with Hollis the night before. Immediately after I view the film, I elect to do some work in the kitchen.

"I must make some desserts for Friday- perhaps you can come up with an idea. I will have madame Nanette assist you when she gets her. I expect she will be late, the wayward coquette," Henri chuckles.

For about a half hour I flip through all sorts of glorious cookbooks that describe tortes and tarts, cakes and custards- perhaps some not as easy to make as others, but all delicious. Prudently, I ask Henri for the main course.

"Young rabbit, stuffed with wild onions, barley and other provincial herbs, in a horse radish reduction."

"I don't know what goes with that."

"Anything you want. We are not *Le Cordon Bleu*. We make the rules here. If I tell my guests that one thing goes with another, they obey me."

I select a simple cake with strawberries and fresh cream. "This should last a week, and it will be easy to make," I think to myself. Henri glances over my shoulder. "This looks far better than the extravagances that Nanette has selected. *Bon idée.*"

Henri and I get to work, making *gateau àu créme frâiche* for thirty people. Henri removes all of the utensils and shows me the measuring implements. He pulls six cake pans, good for five slices each, from his cabinet. He bestows upon me a baker's apron, and hands me a hair net.

She does not show up on this day. I waited for hours, holding my breath. After the cakes are made, Henri dismisses me and I go to the chapel to pray. I fervently look to heaven, wondering if God is listening to me. My desire for intimacy is beyond my own understanding. If intimacy is a gift from God, why does He choose not to give it to me? I have a vendetta against Him, because He has shown me all of these things, planted them in my heart, and then withheld them from me. I think back to my life as a child. I recall being a blossoming adolescent, full of wonderment. I recall being so *optimistic*, so hopeful. I don't know where I lost hope, mainly because it happened so gradually. Disillusionment is a process, not an event (not so much *when* I became disillusioned, but *as* I became disillusioned). I *started* to become disillusioned about the time everyone else did- at age fourteen, maybe fifteen. I was certain that something good would happen- the world was vast and beautiful. It was full of promise and expectation. If God had withheld expectation from me, I would never have become disillusioned in the first place. But you see the things that happen *around* you, and you want them to become part of your existence, and they don't. No, no one likes you, no one kisses you on the cheek, or holds your hand. You feel handicapped by your own self, and your own awkwardness. You do your best to ignore it, but it keeps on making itself apparent. I learned a long time ago that there is really nothing you can do about this sort of detached sentimentality, and while it is certainly not enticing, you get used to it, and eventually, you start to enjoy it.

My apparent disconnection with female phantoms such as Nanette is nothing new to me either. She has a very distinct something or other that echoes all my other infatuations. Perhaps her allure is in the fact she's unattainable, not because she *actually is*, but because I have decided that she be so. I have done much the same to God, saying that He can do nothing for me, and that my love for Him has only to do with the fact that He has blessed me with this miserable existence. After all, a miserable existence is still an existence, is it not? I have no reason to be truly upset with Him. I am only frustrated that He gave me desires that He refuses to help me fulfill. Perhaps I have disappointed Him to the extent that He has decided to withhold them from me. But none of us are perfect, rather, all of us are equally imperfect. Why should He permit someone like Robbie, whom I saw with Lucia, an entry into her heart of hearts- while barring me from such fulfillment. At least the dates that I took her on were not to a shooting gallery.

I am not a confrontational person, but the attitude Nanette conveys suggests that she is more accessible outside of Henri's, and that is where I am going to have to meet her. If Henri fires me, the only thing I will miss is getting to see Nanette so regularly, and being called "Guillaume Apollinaire." Of course, be that as it may, I am too much of a coward to approach her in real life, and there is no existing circumstance under which I might do so, thus I can only pray that an opportunity presents itself. The part of me that loves an adventure is stirred.

Oddly enough, while adoring Jesus, I am more or less forced to ward off thoughts about sex. Joseph North states in his book that the "most inappropriate of sexual thoughts seem to surface in the presence of Christ." I was not sure of why, but I did not have these issues when thinking about Nanette. My Madonna-Whore complex towards her is exactly the opposite of the one I felt towards Lucia. I was jealous because I desired Lucia's body. In this case, I desire only to love Nanette as she should be loved, more in the style of what Mr. North writes. My mind does not go to her body, but rather, I want to hold her, and tell her how much I love her, and watch her smile as I tell her so. The jealousy I feel is more a reflection of seeing Hollis mishandle her, as if she were *his* object. Of course, I go back to the event now, and everything is fuzzy. I admit that I really didn't have a clear motive. I should have at least told Hollis that I was angry at him for touching Nanette.

Of course, I can't have Nanette anyway, so why risk my own self? I think that the underlying selfishness that motivates me in this area stems from two things:

1. If I can't have her, no one else should be able to.
2. *Women control the relationship.*

My thoughts constantly revolve around sex. I cannot fulfill my desire for it in a moral, constructive and fulfilling way, so I have to run away from it. Either way, it is always there. There will never be resolution, so I have to self medicate with pornography. But these two things are making the problem worse.

Thus, there are two things I really want to change. I recall the first time I went out with Lucia. She made her plans seem so out of sync with her current situation that it actually scared me. She had some extravagant ones, too. She wanted to move to Los Angeles and become an actress, and wanted to have a perfect husband, and be rich, and famous. She liked attention. Certainly, though, she was kind to me and sent me some ambiguous, but pleasant signals. It was so convincing and sweet, like she was a free spirited, innocent girl. But I should have understood that even then, she was not intended for me. I harbored such an instinct, but instead of hoping for the best for her, I wished that she would drop dead right in front of me. I shuddered at the thought of her being with another man, in some distant city. This was unhappy for me, and unpleasant to imagine. It would be easier for me to imagine a resigned form of grief at her funeral. Certainly, I felt threatened by, and even jealous of, her future lovers. I would have to accept them, but I felt a secret and perverse comfort with the thought of her dying suddenly from unprecedented natural causes.

Women control, and have always controlled, the relationships that I have entered into with them. It's not definite until they say "yes." It's not OK unless they say it's OK. I don't feel empowered enough to try to make them change their minds- the possibility does not exist. And besides, someone should not have to be convinced to like you. I am not certain how some men convince women to like them. It is the most depressing form of manipulation that I have ever seen, but I don't want to become that way, either. I can't compromise my values in such a manner. So in my mind, I equate "having control in the relationship" to "manipulating the woman into getting what you want." I can't seem to compromise the idea of having some sort of say with giving someone freedom. I could always tell them what I want, but they usually don't listen. And for some reason, I don't think they are even aware that I am speaking out of desire when I tell them what great people they are, and how much I enjoy their company. I have lived too long in the space of not being able to express myself. There is certainly the likelihood that this will be the case with women for a long time, but God has given me the gift of prayer, and I express myself to Him. The sexual and romantic expressions that I long to release fall on deaf and beautiful ears, but the ability to contain them permanently is lacking. They must be expressed, even to a woman on a monitor, having sex with a stranger. As for my purity, God will fix me when it is time.

When I was young, I had an irrational belief that ties into this whole mess. I would go off into the pine forest near my house and look for evidence of God. He would leave little things for me- a leaf twisted into an unnatural form, A morning glory with extra petals, a rivulet bursting with life after a rainstorm. His presence was felt in the winter sunshine, in the summer rainstorms, in the upside down ocean. He was so real, so apparent then. His love for me was strong, and it burned brightly. I was His child- His *little child.* Now I feel as if I am His struggling adolescent, unhappy with myself and with Him. He has done such wonders for me, allowing me to have such a great life, and here I spend it looking at my singlehood through a kaleidoscope with a crack in the lens. I recall there being a time when I was not even interested in women. I was fascinated by God, and the world that He had created. It was me and Him, and nothing else was on my mind. I ran into the forest, screaming and yelling, letting His spirit saturate me. He was so open and clear then, so apparent. He would talk to me through the trees, telling me the secrets of the earth, letting me know that there was time for me to grow up. He blessed me with dreams, where I was naked and isolated, in a field of sunflowers. I couldn't see Him, but I knew He was there. In these reveries, I promised Him that I would never leave Him, and He would always be with me.

But the life that I have led has distanced me from my Father, the love of my childhood. Now I idolize women, and dwell on them. Is worshiping the creator encouraged through adoring his creation? Is worshiping the creation blasphemous? I try my best to pretend, but this sort of pursuit has led me into the throes of sinfulness. I do not consider viewing pornography as a form of worship, but I am sure my brain has tried to make the argument. The Benedict in the dark room, in front of a computer, is far removed from the child in the woods, playing underneath the gray clouds coming off of the coast, in the high grass, under the watchful presence of a perfect and beautiful God.

The tiredness of the day is lulling me away, back to my home. I thank God for providing a place for me to find Him.

Poff has this idea. He calls it "carnal synchronicity." It revolves around the idea that two total strangers can meet each other and have a magnetic sexual attraction, completely out of the blue. This sort of phenomenon leads to all sorts of weird things- marriages, divorces, unwanted children, one night stands, bad dreams and maybe even true love. But more than anything, Poff adores the concept, and makes sure that everyone knows about it.

Poff first became aware of it when he met a girl at a gas station. He was driving up from Camilla to Atlanta, and stopped at this place in the middle of nowhere- he didn't even recall the name of the town. It was on highway 520, and it was later in the day. The girl that worked there was of medium height. She was pretty, sort of in a way that he says was "good enough to make him check to make sure she was actually pretty." The girl was drawn to him, and he felt an odd pull *towards* her, like she knew what he was like. She conversed with him using a certain familiarity, as if they had met at some point in the past. She liked his car, and began to ask him questions.

"What time do you get off work?" He asked.

She rolled up her sleeve to reveal a tattoo and a watch. "In about an hour."

"Want to do something?" He asked.

"We could go back to my place," she said. He claimed that she was devouring him with her eyes the whole time. I was not certain of whether he was telling the truth or not, but Poff tends to make himself look more desirable in his stories. Girls look at him, but not like he wishes they would.

Poff hung around that little town for about forty minutes, trying to decide if he should let anything happen with this girl. I wonder at times if he knew better. He says that he had a degenerate desire to have sex with her as soon as he saw her. Poff does not have morals. He is about as religious as a plastic crucifix. He acknowledges God, but he loves himself more. Poff decided, ultimately, that this girl was too low for him. He rationalized it all kinds of ways-

"Who knows what kinds of STDs live in the Georgia backwoods."

"She might have had kids."

"Where would I buy a condom in Deliverance, Georgia?"

"She was too far down the socio-economic ladder. I don't want to end up attached to someone like that."

His so-called faith was never a factor.

Naturally, he asked me what I would have done in those circumstances. I responded with a shrug of my shoulders. And I would have driven the interstates. Poff gave me the usual long, hard look, and subsequently laughed in my face. Sometimes I think he is my friend because he knows I am a more pathetic human being than he is. I secretly find him repulsive- we could be girls in some kind of unspoken early adolescent rivalry. One day he will find another girl that he has carnal synchronicity with. He will get married, and the world will go on. Poff is a dick, though, and he will ruin it. If she's nice, and she's pretty, she won't stay that way. Poff will ruin that for her, too.

But this concept fascinates me. I think Lucia had a similar distraction. She was always looking for guys that she experienced this kind of super chemistry with. I have no idea what flowed through her head, but I wanted it for myself. She met this guy one time, and I overheard her speaking with a friend of hers about it. She said that she wanted to tear her clothes off and rub her body all over him. I suppose that she and Poff should have met. I have a counter notion that this whole thing is spiritual. It is entirely possible that this occurs among people who are possessed. I suppose I won't know until I experience it. Poff swears it is not a supernatural occurrence. I believe him, because no demon would ever possess Poff. His personality is too irritating, and he always avoids taking action. He's also clumsy, the bastard.

Ok, so if I were to meet a girl and "sync" with her, how would I know? I am quite oblivious to even the most obvious things. I once stepped on a nail and didn't know it until the blood coming out of my shoe caught the eye of my mother, who panicked. I had no clue...

Poff, being the mastermind behind all of this, said that some people just don't "sync." He was implying, in a nice way, that I should not count on it happening to me. In the back of my mind, I believed he was right, but I did not want to let Poff decide my fate. The idea of proving him wrong was too appealing. The pitfall that he cited was that I become drawn to girls whom I have no connection with at all. I am so busy chasing these girls that I am not open to meeting anyone on a whim. He is right. I am afraid of cheating on a girlfriend that I don't have. I also enjoy being alone. They say that misery loves company, but I prefer my solitude. Solitude makes misery comfortable and pleasant. Perhaps I give off a misery signal that acts as a foil, so I don't "sync." In any case, this is what my life is, so I might as well embrace it. I will never find out if carnal synchronicity is real or not. I am Benedict Radmeier.

The sunshine lights up Henri's front yard. No sooner had I arrived, than Henri handed me a number of envelopes. They were all stamped and addressed, with his miserable script detailing their destinations. I noticed that one had been returned, since its address was illegible.

"Can we rewrite some of these?" I asked. Henri sensed I was being helpful. "I suppose that you could rewrite some of these."

Henri hands me the stack, removing one item from it. I sit down at the desk in the salon- I would call it a living room- and begin to rewrite the letters. I innocently take a glance at all of them, noting that many are bills to wine merchants and truffle importers. I look at each one, doing my best to discern the script. I pick out a few of the more interesting ones, and begin by sticking labels over the old addresses after copying them down on a separate sheet of paper. I then rewrite each address on the label. Hopefully, Monsieur wine merchant and Herr truffle importer will not be offended if I misspell their excessively complicated European names.

Henri steps in and thumbs through the stack of letters again. He grabs one, but before he removes it, I glance at the name:

"Sarah Temple."

I know not ask questions, as Henri will tell me to quit being meddlesome. He tries to be nonchalant about it, but he saw my eye connect to the address on the letter.

"Ms. Temple used to work here," he said. "You replaced her. She and Nanette did not get along."

I continue to undo Henri's poor penmanship.

"I only write this badly in English," he tells me as he goes back to his office. I see one of the hairs from his beard laying on my workspace, and I brush it off.

This task consumes roughly forty five minutes, and when I

finish, Henri permits me to take the DS to the post office. I couldn't help but wonder who Sarah Temple was. Perhaps she could tell me more about Nanette. The rationalist in me was certain that Henri sent her off for a good reason, although this job was certainly strange.

Upon returning from the post office, I enter the house, looking for Henri. The familiar RX7 is sitting in the driveway, next to my car. I hear some noise out back. It is nearly two o'clock in the afternoon, and this is the time that Henri waters his flowers.

"Henri!" I yell. "I'm back." I venture around the house, looking for him. Instead of Henri, Nanette is there. She is watering the flowers, wearing a red sash on her forehead. Her light brown hair makes the sash look royal. She gives me a disdainful look.

"You can't go anywhere without being excessive," she chides. I don't know what else to say, so I mutter an indistinct apology. I turn around and go back into the house, but I stop and turn around, and walk back towards Nanette.

"I have a question," I ask her nonchalantly.

"Go for it." She does not even look up from her task.

"Who is Sarah Temple?"

"It's not important."

"If it's not important, why did Henri make sure that I couldn't mail a letter to her."

Nanette looks up at me, slightly irritated. I feel like I have pushed some invisible barrier.

"Please, Nanette."

Nanette stares at the ground for a bit longer, and then shuts off the water. She does not dismiss me, but I know she wants for me to go away.

"I have no idea who Sarah Temple is," Nanette responds carefully.

"You could have just told me that. Henri told me she used to work here, with you, so you must know her."

Nanette is visibly irate now. She drops the hose, instead of curling it up, and walks away from me. Dismissal is the most arousing form of rejection. Right when she is about to go back into the house, she turns around. "Henri would appreciate it if you would leave myself, and Sarah, alone."

Right now, I feel a mixture of hurt and oppression. This sting of rejection is characterized by a lack of sympathy from all of these women I have liked. But of course, in the world of Nanette, even a little bit of privacy must be fought for, and I suppose that with all the men she has been with, a certain hostility dwells in her that makes her unapproachable. If I were a dictator, I would line them all up and shoot them. Perhaps she might converse with me afterwards.

It seems unreasonable to me that she should meet me with such hostility, and even more unreasonable that her story and Henri's story do not match. Of the two, I trust her more than Henri, because she has been brutally honest, and Henri would likely mislead me so I have no idea who Sarah Temple is. I decide to go in and look for Henri. I go through the front door, so as to avoid Nanette. A list of small jobs with my name on it is attached to the wall with a piece of tape:

Replace the light bulbs in the dining room
Wax the tables
Turn the champagne refrigerator down
Drain the blood off of the lamb
Come see me in my office when you are done

Henri has a cabinet full of necessary items. I fumble around, looking for bulbs. There is a small ladder in the shed, and so I go and get it. There is a rain shadow on the horizon, and I sense the presence of another cold front.

As I wax the tables, I wonder if Nanette's real name is Sarah Temple. But what a plain name it is. I can't perceive her as being a "Sarah," and so I dismiss the idea in my mind. What seems more rational to me is that she may have been Henri's lover of sorts. He often says me that "taking a lover is taking an extra burden of grief." She may just be an unmentionable whose life has gone away from Henri's.

230

Nanette's real name should be more exciting than that. She should be a "Celeste" or a "Diana," or perhaps a "Rebecca." I have often imagined her as a girl, aspiring to be something great. It seems she has gone down a path of disillusionment, like I have. If we could only find a way to make things work, I could help her restore her dreams. She could become the person she dreamed of being, and I would be happy, knowing I brought about positive change in her life. I want to be her hero. That way, she won't have to keep company with people like Hollis. She won't have to make pornography. She will know what it is like to be loved.

Henri interrupts my thoughts. "You need to work harder on those tables," he remarks. I busy myself with waxing tables, and admiring the swirl marks, while he takes a seat.

"Nanette told me that you had to ask who Miss Temple was," Henri states after he has sat down. "I find it useless that you are so curious now. For the sake of my own affairs, such things should be left alone."

I go back to waxing tables, surreptitiously. Henri watches me for a bit longer, and then alights from his chair, and goes back to his office.

I am more curious now than ever before. I suppose that this will keep me distracted from Nanette, at least for the time being. Of course, in the midst of all this, Nanette walks into the kitchen, and my eyes follow her. There is no relief from this sort of trivial existence. This infatuation is an anticlimactic empty promise. Perhaps she will.

The "Andalusian Dinner," thus far, has been a mixed bag of success and distraction. Contrary to the norm, the Saturday group is coming tonight. Henri was certainly nervous about me paying too much attention to the wrong things. He ushered in the guests, and as the film played, I went from table to table to fill drink orders. Nanette flitted about like a butterfly in the dark, hardly aware of the film. She was like a phantom, with her black clothes. It's reminiscent of how the women in my life have been elusive. The closer I get, the more translucent they become. I have always wondered what sort of negativity drives them to be so. In hindsight, perhaps Nanette has several good reasons for avoiding me, but her close bond with other men makes this complex and inexcusable. She should get to know me. I am a much nicer person than any of the guys she's been with. What irritates me even more is her jovial and fluorescent lightheartedness on this evening. There are some guests here who she addresses with a sort of intimate familiarity, mostly men in their forties and early fifties. I was unsure of why she noticed them, and inflected a sense of kindness and happiness towards them. I would watch Lucia with her friends. When a guy would pass by who she found appealing, she would laugh, and giggle, and her face would capture the moment, as if it were on film. She never did that for me. She had a special glance for me. It was highly conditional, meaning that she was only happy to see me when she needed something. This sort of extroverted infatuation, where Lucia and I were seemingly among friends most of the time (or at least my friends knew her and knew how I *loved* her), pales in comparison to the stark loneliness and introversion of my fixation on Nanette. In this case, Lucia represents a sort of cathartic love, which feeds off of late night gatherings and the sort of things that take place in the life of a college student. The dichotomy is that Nanette, or rather my infatuation towards her, amplifies my feelings of isolation. The fact that I have fewer friends, many of whom I feel little closeness to, make this sort of feeling more insufferable. Her relative lightheartedness in this plane of isolatory suffering makes me feel even more desolate, because it denotes that there is no connection at all. Having this sort of infatuatory depression leads one to believe that they are to continue in a trajectory of hopelessness, with no relief.

Jesus and I have become very close in these moments, perhaps because there is no one else to turn to. Henri certainly would not want to know about this. Poff is tired of it, Francis has more meaningful things in his life. Kevin is too preoccupied with being perfect. The rest of the Catholics, particularly the women, would want me to appeal to Jesus for a complete spiritual overhaul.

In all fairness though, when I fall into this trap of depression, there are only two ways out. I can pray and wait for Jesus to alleviate my suffering, or I can turn towards porn. I usually choose the latter in the moment, but I think that over the course of my life, I have ultimately chosen Christ. Otherwise, I would not even see Him as an option. I could choose him *perfectly* every time, but there would be no value in it for me. I must experience the ultimate low to appreciate the high that I get from reconciling myself with Christ. Suppose one of these women were to materialize into something- what would I do? Lose sight of Christ? I am fearful of this sort of issue overtaking me.

Henri thrusts a plate at me with little white cards. Each has a word on it, which is a possible theme of the movie. I am to present a theme to each guest, at random, and they must state whether it is present in *Andalusian Dog* or not. Henri will make each guest argue his point, and if said guest proves their point, they get a free drink. I glance about the room, passing out the tiny cards, to the figures of Camus, Monet, Lawrence- all of them might as well be who they say they are. I look again at Nanette. This time it hits me. I have sabotaged myself. In a theoretical perfect world, if I were to have a true friendship with Nanette, I would sabotage things on a whole other level by telling her how inadequate I am. I would not make a conscious decision. I would simply slip it in here or there- why I am no good for her, why I am not ready, why my bad habits in the realm of my sexuality render me unfit. I could go on and on, but every conversation with her would look like a messy confession of sorts. What woman would want that kind of mess?

I used to do such things with Lucia. When we were out, I would begin to talk. Always about myself, never about her. I would praise her, and make her apparent weaknesses sound trivial. She would receive an endless stream of unfounded accolades because she was who she was. But I would impale myself with vague allusions to my past and present sins.

"Lucia, you would find me to be a terrible person. That's what I am. There are unmentionable things I have done that make me so."

"Lucia, no one should *ever* love someone like me. There would be no hope."

"Lucia, I go to confession often. Not because I am content to go, but because without it I would perish."

"Lucia, The only person that will ever truly love me is Jesus. I am so damaged that I am unrecognizable as a good human being."

Perhaps she heeded all of the allegations I imposed on myself. Maybe that is why she never wanted me. No woman wants a man who is constantly in need of affirmation. But whether I like the idea of being affirmed or not, I am in need of it, and it spills out of me blatantly. If only she told me I was good enough, I would be good enough.

People who are not suffering from the pathogen believe that it is simply an immense feeling of love and desire. Really, it is like someone has amplified all of your negative emotions, so that they are huge, and you experience them all at once. This is the way that I experience it, so that it keeps me down, a prisoner to feelings that I neither want nor need. In this instance, my feelings are flaring up, reflective of the aggressive nature of this incessant illness. If I am not thinking about Nanette, I am thinking of Lucia. If I am thinking of neither one, I am beating my own person up. If I am not doing this, I am praying.

"Benedict, get the main course ready!" Henri yells. The loudness of his voice really irritates me, and I cringe as I walk across the floor to the kitchen. The distress reflected in his voice makes me feel sorry for him. I have been useless and distracted, again. I wheel the dinner cart from the kitchen into the dining room. Nanette simultaneously takes the plates and sets them before the guests, most of whom are talking amongst themselves. After the tables are set, and the food is served, Henri starts the discussion.

"The surrealist aspect of Andalusian Dog from the perspective of …Guillaume Apollinaire!" His voice trails off near the end. He hands me a little white card with the word *surrealism* on it.

I am surprised that he has called upon me to present Apollinaire's viewpoint. All eyes turn towards me, so that I am nervous. However, I was attentive to the film. I move towards the center of the room, and begin to think.

"Andalusian Dog is a film with no plot and purpose. It is a creative exercise with no point, and no motive."

Henri looks at me inquisitively. "What is your point? What does this film contain for *Apollinaire*?"

I look around the room. A smirk has formed on Nanette's lips, indicative that she is paying attention to what I am saying. She was otherwise standing still, minding her business.

"I feel that as a surrealist, I would find the film to be insubstantial. Surrealism is, in and of itself, a joke. An exercise in futility. It has no value, in and of itself. It is an escape from substance. The insubstantial qualities of this film make it a true masterpiece of surrealism."

"And what does it make you think of, Mr. Apollinaire?"

Nanette has made it known to me that she finds my answer weak and stupid by nodding her head.

"It makes me think of death, really. There is no substance in death. It simply is." Henri dismisses me, and I pull a chair out.

"Does anyone agree with him?" The old man pouts.

An older Gentleman, representing Charles Baudelaire, raises his hand. "I agree because if we were to analyze it, it would take up too much time. Time we could spend drinking with the prostitutes, perhaps? I know that it has substance, but that substance means nothing to me. It is too substantial, and that nullifies its meaning. The analyses would be a vast amount of rambling. It means nothing, thus." While he is speaking, he turns to Nanette and winks at her. I am illuminated with quiet rage.

"Another glass of wine, *monsieur*?" I ask as I approach him. "It would be customary of Baudelaire to finish that comment up with a drink!"

"As the great poet lives, give me another glass of Beaujolais!"

I enter into the kitchen, grab a glass, and pour it full of wine. I take a large gulp and swish it about it my mouth, then discharge it back into the glass. I inspect the wine for any bubbles, and after it has settled, I deem it to be sufficient as a punishment for the old bastard. Disdainfully, I bring it back out to him, and set it before him.

"Thank you, good Apollinaire!"

"You're welcome, but please keep in mind that our waitresses are not whores at this maison." I finish up my dissertation with a roll of the eyes. He takes the first drink, and I beam with delight, knowing that he has ingested a generous portion of my saliva.

Meanwhile, all of the other dead writers and artists share their opinions about what it is, and is not. The eventual discussion escalates to an argument, much to Henri's delight, and then the argument progresses to an uproar. Henri laughs hard, and drinks more. Contrary to the natural order of her role, Nanette is handed glass after glass of wine by the guests, and they keep flagging me for more drinks. She has become a guest at this party. Henri orders me to crack a case of cheap Merlot, and the wine flows. Everyone is slowly growing merrier, and the banter about Dali's film turns into organized chaos. The rearmost part of the dining room is an open floor, quite large, and Henri suddenly goes to a closet and removes a record player. He begins to play Chopin, and Verdi, and in the most ungraceful fashion, couples begin dancing dances that do not fit the music even at a stretch. Those that are not drunk are merry. Those that are merriest are usually the most reserved. Nanette is passed from gentleman to gentleman as they dance about the room with her, over the hardwood floor. During the festivities I put glasses and dishes away, and clear the tables. On each table, I place a slice of cake. Nanette, still drinking more, is brought back to a table with some of the guests, who keep drinking. Nanette does not drink to excess, but she sips her merlot gregariously so that the patrons may see it. They laugh at everything, and beam with delight. The fresh bulbs that I installed illuminate their gray beards and bald heads. Their faint tan suits and black coats are suddenly lively. The room spins with energy, and the couples are beaming with the youthfulness that their biology no longer exudes. The colorful porcelain pieces on the mantles shake, the candles on the table flicker, and Henri engages the wives of several guests. I bring the rowdiest ones napkins to wipe the sweat from their brow, and they thank me by handing me dollar bills. The first world atmosphere is antiquated and contagious, possessing a sort of thrill that has escaped modernity, leaving behind an afterglow that lingers where each happy being has danced. Nanette is laughing vivaciously, with a graybeard on her left and her right. She twirls her golden hair, and makes wild hand gestures, her seriousness diluted with intoxicating liquids. One old man smells her, and she tells him of her Shalimar or her love of pure Bulgarian rose oil. Another touches her hair, which looks like apricots with lavender petals in it. Another one, across the table, kisses her hand and leads her to dance. She walks past me and smiles at me, laughing about something that I cannot quite make out. Her heels click, and her black skirt and blouse are as deep as the night sky over the ocean. She peels back the cork wrapper of another bottle, and leaves the older man to dance with a silver fox in his early fifties. He touches her with a near familiarity, as if he knows her with some degree of intimacy. She looks nervous, but keeps laughing, and then sits down after taking two or three swigs from her fresh bottle. Henri is laughing, sitting at a table with a woman ten years his junior, and another couple. He is less drunk, but he is reflecting on the humorous issues of French socialism, and the nuances of the French language, and its cheese, and how they are all related. Henri smiles at me, beckoning me to the table.

"You're doing well," and looks at the woman, saying "I will make a Frenchman out of him!" I smile awkwardly, and fill their glasses using the bottle under my left arm. I go about, making sure that everything is good and right, and do my best to ignore the phantom who glides quietly about the room. Her eyes are glowing faintly, and her aura is pure white. I cannot abandon my post, lest I let Henri down.

After the party winds down, and the guests convalesce for a spell, they begin to exit quietly. Taxis pick some up, others choose to drive home under the spell of possible intoxication. Nanette is lying on the couch in the foyer. She smiles faintly as I walk past her, with my plates and bottles, picking up the debris that the guests have left. I smile back at her. Henri gets up with a heave and addresses me from the kitchen.

"Monsieur Radmeier!"

"Yes, coming!"

Henri is clearly in the company of a lady. I can tell what is in store for him. She is still quite lovely for her early sixties, and she and Henri are both immodestly intoxicated. She fingers the belt loops on his trousers, and he touches the hem of her dress. It was both depressing and majestic at the same time. Perhaps even a bit saddening, but I have no clue as to why.

"You must drive *mon lis* home, yes?"

Henri calls Nanette "his lily" when he has a bit more to drink than he should. It's used most often after dinner is over. I suppose the circumstances are favorable for this excursion, as Nanette is in a positive mood, and I am too tired to be elated.

I finish up a few tasks, and Henri and his lady friend go to bed, hanging on to each other. He turns around and smiles at me. "They used to call me '*Reynard*'," he states firmly.

His lady friend places her hand on his posterior, and they promenade the last few steps before opening the door to his chambers.

The last two guests leave in their cars, so I go towards the couch and sit down at Nanette's feet. She looks up at me. "What time is it?"

"It's a quarter past two," I respond after glancing at a clock on the wall. She opens and closes her eyes, slowly, several times.

"I have to drive you home."

She tries to sit up, but can't muster the strength. "Why do you have to drive me home? I can't stay here?"

"Henri has a guest tonight. He didn't say anything, but I think he wants the house to himself." She makes an unpleasant face, and then giggles.

"My purse is on the big table in the dining room. Please get it."

I obediently get up and grab the purse. I walk back to her with great docility. She extends her hand, and I help her up. When I touch her hand, a warm electricity flows through my body. She breathes in and out two times, and sets her purse on her shoulder. She extends her hand again, and I help her to her feet. She leans on my shoulder, and we walk step by step to the door. The merlot is strong, diminishing only slightly in the cold night air when I open the door. She asks for her coat from the coat hook, and I take it in my free arm. I support her with one hand and slip it over her. She holds steady on the wall, and waits for me to finish. She grabs my arm again, and I walk her to the Saab. This could very well have been Lucia. I walked her out of many houses when she was too drunk to function on her own.

I seat Nanette in the car and fasten her safety belt. I quickly enter the other door, and remove my keys. I take a look at her. She has closed her eyes. I reach between the seats and start the engine. The cold start injector kicks in, and the motor lights off after a second or two.

I rouse Nanette. She looks over at me. "Yes?" She whispers.

"I don't know where you live."

She laughs a little bit. "If you drive to the end of Henri's street, take a left. After you drive two miles on that road, make a right. Then drive four miles and you will come across an apartment building called "The Nest." It has a big hedge, with a lot of brown and yellow, and the fronts have big windows." Her voice wanes in the last sentence, and she drifts off. I drive carefully so as not to disturb her. We glide over the hills under a canvas of stars, my heart racing with anticipation of something that will never come. The engine hums and blats, and the brakes squeak at each stop.

Nanette sleeps so peacefully. He smile is faint and opalescent, and her fingers move slightly. I am deeply moved by this image of her. Her arm hangs freely by her side, and by all the strength of God, I resist grabbing it. She moves her head to the right, and extends a finger forward. The light casts a glow on her neck, and I see a faint marking there, like a bruise partially healed. I see a chip in her dark purple nail polish, and I study her earrings at the stop signs. It is as if she is a dead corpse, and I am performing the autopsy.

I glance at her chest, hidden by her coat. While she is not voluptuous, her form is perfect and ideal, like a flower or a rainbow. The pink and peach hints on her skin are not marred by exposure to sunshine, but rather they continue to the secret places underneath her garments. Her breathing is slow and steady, and she is certainly asleep. I see a strand of hair migrating into her mouth, and I reach over and brush it out of the way. She acknowledges having been touched, and places her hand on the strand of hair and makes sure it is clear. She extends her leg forward, and touches her hair one last time before going back to sleep. I am in the home stretch, and I slow down considerably so that I can extend my time with her.

The Nest is old and charming, with three stories and a little garden. The moon illuminates it enough so that I can see what sort of place it is. I would expect most of its residents to be quiet, maybe older or at least situated. It has a mature air to it, with nice, clean cars, a well-kept lawn and a number of trees. It sits about 30 feet above the road. Nanette, almost innately, wakes up and tells me where to turn.

"Make a right here," she suggests sleepily.

I turn sharply, and go up a hill. I notice a row of thick bushes that border on the street, below the sliding glass doors. "Any idiot could see in!" I think to myself.

"Now turn here- left," she points.

"Now turn right and there's the stairwell." I park the car, and gingerly exit. I walk to the passenger door and open it, so that she might exit. She struggles to undo the seatbelt, so I assist her, and then extend a hand to help her out.

"No, I'm fine," she whispers as I touch her fingers. She takes her purse, and lifts herself out of the car. We walk up the stairs. Other than her using the hand rail, she has recovered her sobriety in an astoundingly short time. We approach her apartment. On the door is a wood carving of a swan, with a bell around its neck. She rings the bell. "It's a doorbell, see?"

But my attention is on a small, yellowed piece of paper attached to her door knob with a piece of tape. Noticing it, she grabs it and takes a quick look at it. She then crumbles it up, and throws it over the railing into the night breeze. She laughs to herself.

"You function very well when you're intoxicated," I muse.

"Well, it certainly helps me perform certain tasks." I take it at first that she is being lighthearted, but her face is completely serious. My mind begins to analyze what sort of tasks would require, or maybe even encourage, a functional alcoholic. Nanette walks through her door. "Good night. Thanks for the ride."

She closes the door without even waiting for my response.

Immediately my mind goes to the note. I must retrieve it, so I can find out who sent it to her.

I run down the stairs, and follow the wind. There is a strong wind from the west, blowing in gusts every five minutes. I look about in the moonlight for the small piece of paper, scrambling from bush to bush, getting on my hands and knees. For over ten minutes I look, soiling my pants, getting dirt beneath my nails and even getting cut on a piece of glass in the parking lot.

It seems to no avail. Just when I get up, losing hope, and start walking back to the Saab, something catches my eye. Right below Nanette's door is a dormant rosebush. The crumbled up little yellow ball is caught in a vine behind the bush. I carefully pull back its branches, getting cut on the thorns, until I see my desired object. I grab it, and walk back to my car, clutching it in my fist so in case she looks down, she will not see it.

Of course, she will have seen my other antics, so why even bother. I start the engine and pull out of the parking lot. About a half mile down the road, I pull over under a street lamp so that I might read this letter. I quickly notice that the handwriting is in neat but nervous cursive. My generation does not practice this sort of writing technique.

Butterfly,
I am extraordinarily lonely for you. You have not returned my calls or my letters for two weeks now. I felt the need to drive to your residence to see you, but you were not there. I left you this note.
Your silence confirms the worst of fears- that I have upset you and you do not wish to see me anymore. I know that our liaison was doomed from the start, given that we met under such questionable circumstances, but I cannot deny my love for you.
I apologize for attempting to film our intimacy, as I knowingly violated your privacy. I did not understand at the time that this had happened before. You had told me you were not camera shy, and I misinterpreted it. I apologize for upsetting you thus.
My wife does not know, but in the near future I plan to bring up the topic of divorce. My work here ends soon, so we might flee somewhere to one of those places we discussed, like Amalfi, or Tuvalu.
I hope I have given you an incentive to think about things. Please do not stay angry with me. There is no one that I love more than you.

I will be waiting to hear from you, as always. Please find it in your heart of hearts to accept my apology. In the meantime, I shall wait patiently.
Forever yours,

BJR

When something is doomed, sabotaging it makes no difference. It is only a form of putting it out of its misery. So, in the context of myself and Nanette, sabotaging any relationship I have to her would be an act of mercy. She does not suffer, but I do.

I always had a fantasy with Lucia that I should die in battle to save her. Not in a war zone, but in an act of self sacrifice where the true nature of her lovers was revealed through my heroic efforts. These heroic efforts, although revealing, would serve to extricate me from her life. I would leave with a permanent stigma that would make it impossible for me to be part of her world again. But I would also leave with the knowledge of having defeated all of those unworthy pricks, with her open and finite acknowledgment that I was not only worthy of her love, but I was her *Hero*. After this, any outcome would have been acceptable, even death.

The Illusion of Heroic Virtue
"He that is jealous is not in love."
-St. Augustine
19

Men hold onto a myriad of irrational beliefs when it comes down to winning a woman over. Ignoring the pretense of natural selection, they resort to a near barbaric cognitive process. A man frequently surmises that if he proceeds forth with the following follies, a woman will love him:

> *If he buys her things, she will love him.*
> *If he rescues her from some sort of difficult situation, she will love him.*
> *If he constantly proves himself, over and over again, she will love him.*
> *If he is a perfect gentleman, she will love him.*
> *If he shows great responsibility in his work and in his life, she will love him.*

243

No matter how much we tell ourselves that it is not, romance is a disjointed offshoot of natural selection. This is the only valid explanation for the woman choosing her mate. Nice clothes certainly don't hurt, though.

Anyhow, I find it confounding when women develop feelings for, and attachments to, the following perpetrators:

Men who are married.
Men who have a history of treating women badly.
Men who are superficial.
Men who only care about themselves.
Men who have bad personalities, who are overweight, and who don't try until it's too late.
Men who don't give a shit.

These men are my nemeses, and I have always felt that I have been fighting a battle against them. And beyond a shadow of a doubt, the person that left this nice letter for Nanette is most likely of the second variety.

If there's one thing that I hate more than the *existence* of these sanctimonious assholes, it is having to *compete* with them. It seems that my whole life, I have always had to prove to the women I have liked that I am better than some prick that they think they like. The worst part of this is that I always end up losing. Women only want what is bad for them anyway, and this is yet another irregularity that I want to fix.

I drive home, contemplating this note over and over again. It certainly has diminished my feelings of being victorious in Nanette's presence, knowing that she has slept with some jerk who even bears my initials. He is obviously well off, making this situation even more unfair. The miraculous evening I shared with her, which made me feel special, and even happy, has been decimated. While I know that I should accept Nanette for who- or what- she is, I am quite tired of accepting *these* people for who *they* are.

The Saab hums merrily along the parkway as it closes in on 3:30 AM. Clutching the note in my hand, I wonder how I am going to establish its originator, and ultimately eliminate this menace from her life.

It is Sunday, and I am exiting the church after going to Mass early. Dinner the night before was anticlimactic, being low key after Friday night's event. Nanette was her usual unfriendly self. In my combined sentiments of righteous anger and convoluted misery, I went to confession that Saturday, and confessed *everything* to poor Father Phillip, who was suffering from laryngitis. He simply nodded when I confessed to him about looking at pornography, and when I told him about my feelings of hatred towards the anonymous adulterer, he simply nodded his head, absolved me quietly, and jotted down a penance on a piece of paper. It was quite simple-practice not hating people, and pray for them instead. This was typical of him, but the penance was a bit much for me. Putting such a vague directive into action would require a major mindset shift for me. A disproportionate number of hate-based relationships exist in my life.

Nanette, being her normal busy self, stopped only once last night and thanked me for taking her home. She asked me if anything strange had happened during our car ride, which I thought to be a peculiar question. I wanted to remind her of the note on her door, but I figured that she had remembered it, and wished it gone. The main course, venison with wild herbs and potatoes, was sanguine and acidic, and not to my liking. More so, Henry only served a *tarte aux framboises* for dessert. Still, no one complained. The guests drank liberally, and tipped well, resulting in a spectacular profit margin for Henri, and a larger paycheck for myself.

The sun is strong today, with only a few clouds dotting the sky. The weather is warm for February, meaning that it might be nice on Valentine's Day. The Catholics are meeting for a picnic this afternoon, so I have elected to drive over to the park where they are meeting.

I stop off at Publix to get a dessert, and park out of view of the group. As I walk towards the crowd, Kristen sees me and waves. I did not show up for our discussion group Tuesday, so I am waiting for the questions to start. Instead, though, she embraces me, telling me she missed seeing me and wishes I would come around more. I remind her that I don't have her phone number, and then she immediately laughs and smiles about another topic. She doesn't mean to be insincere, just like I don't mean to be creepy.

She and I don't really talk anyway, and for the rest of the afternoon, I sit on a blanket with Xavier, Kevin and Patrick, talking about Mr. North and his fantastic text- at least until I get bored.

Halfway through our lunch of pre-made hamburgers, baked beans and other questionable delicacies, I elect to change the topic.

"Let's say you guys were trying to find out who someone was. All you had were their initials. What would you do?"

Xavier, since his life is so boring, immediately takes interest in my question. "How did you find out about this person in the first place?"

"We'll say he left a note at my friend's house."

"Maybe you could ask your friend who left the note?" He laughs, like this whole thing is funny.

"She won't tell me."

"What do you have to go by?"

"His initials, which are, strangely, the same as mine."

"So it's a she?"

"Yes, but that's irrelevant."

Patrick chimes in. "Is this that girl you work with?" I nod my head.

"Who left her a note?" He asks.

"I don't know, which is why we are having the conversation- but it wasn't a good note."

Xavier reverts to his holier than thou persona. "Perhaps you should distance yourself from her."

"In Catholic land that works great. Here, not so much."

Patrick and Kevin laugh at me. The grass is cold and a little bit wet. I don't know if any of them realize what this is like, but it's not much fun. I look over to my right, and see Madeleine and Anthony, together. Patrick notices that I'm staring.

"His wound is recovering nicely, don't you think?" Offended, I get up and leave my small group. I march off, angry to have seen Mr. and Mrs. Perfect together. I decide to leave the picnic, because I cannot tolerate seeing them.

It's usually in situations like this that I resort to looking at porn, so I know I should not go home tonight. My copy of *Redeeming Sexuality* is sitting on my front seat, so I think about going to a quiet place and reading it. My heart longs for some alone time with Jesus. I hop in the Saab, and drive to St. Paul's, hoping that I can get into the adoration chapel.

I arrive at the church, and sneak in. The sun is low in the sky, and it is approaching five o'clock. I knock on the door to the chapel. A nice lady opens it and lets me in. I go to a spot, kneel for a minute or two, and then I begin to read.

Chapter Five

Celibacy and the Heavenly Marriage

I am writing this book, not so much for the theologically learned, but more so for the masses. I am sure many of you have asked why priests are celibate, and why this sort of behavior has not been phased out. To be perfectly honest, I believe priestly celibacy is a good and healthy practice. In our limited understanding of our relationship with our Creator, we believe that He created all of us for the same purpose- to find love with a member of the opposite sex. We should all want this, right? While I cannot argue with the Church's teaching on marriage being good and holy, for some people, life is better without it.

I can see all of you young, single optimistic men getting flustered by this statement. If you are worried, I send my condolences. God has a different set of plans for some of us. He needs some of us to serve Him on earth, in the same sense that Jesus did. How does this work? I am happy to explain if you'll listen.

A man can only do so much with his time. If he must take a wife, and bear children, his first duty is to his wife and offspring. I see often in various non-Catholic denominations a breakdown in the family unit, where children are often led astray by the world while their father tries to lead the community. It is very difficult to have a ministerial career and a healthy family unit. The priest has no duties in this sense, but instead his family is the parish he is part of. He is responsible for his flock, and celibacy frees him from the responsibilities of having a blood family.

Is this a calling? Absolutely! I cannot understand it, as my calling was to marriage and theology. I do not understand what it is to be "called" to be celibate for the kingdom because it has never happened to me. However, those I have spoken with who felt that calling were eager and enthusiastic to speak with me about it. These are men that have been joyfully celebrating masses, baptisms and weddings for years. They are connected to their parish families, much like good and adherent fathers in blood families. While some of these men were immediately present to their calling at an early age, others had to undergo a great deal of suffering when they were in their young adulthood before they knew what God wanted them to do. I have no idea why they had to suffer so much, with mixed signals from women, feelings of depression, loneliness and abandonment, but God had something special in store for these young men.

One young seminarian I spoke with, Dunstan, was especially eager to share his experience with me. Dunstan was a struggling young adult, with a college degree, a job that required a lot of effort, a small wish and a big question- what did God want him to do with his life? Now this is a big question, and a clichéd question. Every young man and woman asks himself this in some way. I cannot iterate how many of us are disappointed with the response God gives us. In His infinite wisdom, He often forces us to find the answer. Dunstan had awful luck with women. One of his girlfriends actually cheated on him. Another left him out of the blue after being with him for a year. He said that he largely based his happiness on how his love-relationships were working, which left little room for God to make a difference in his life. Finally, after a cycle of repetitive ups and downs, he took six months to listen to God, stop pursuing women and stop worrying about what his life was supposed to be like. It was in this desert that he heard the Lord ask him to try seminary for a year. Dunstan unhappily left his job after four years there, and at the age of twenty five, became a seminarian. He told me that the first year was a struggle, and the second year was only a little bit easier, mainly because he had gotten used to that way of life. However, he began to really try to open up to God, letting his frustrations with celibacy and seminary out in prayer. Ultimately, God sent the Holy Spirit to Dunstan in a remarkable way, affirming his purpose and giving him a vision. It is this vision that gives Dunstan joy today, and helps him want to become a priest. When I asked Dunstan what his expectations for priesthood were like, he gave me a simple answer. "I have no expectation, other than I know God will call me to do things that are out of my comfort zone."

Certainly, this not always the case, but I think all of you understand how God works. He may not affirm our calling overnight, but we need to give Him a chance.

Inflamed, I shut the book. North has no business suggesting I become a celibate.

Father Phillip has taken a seat behind me, and is watching me, with a smile on his face. I turn the other way. I do not like to contemplate the idea of celibacy. John Paul II said that in order for a man to understand what he is embracing, he must understand what he is giving up. I have never experienced love (from a woman), and therefore, I must experience being loved before I can even choose celibacy. God reaches out to me in this moment.

"Do you believe that you are loved?"

"Yes, but not in the way I want to be. I want to be desired."

"Do you believe I love you?"

"Sometimes, but you created conflicting desires in my heart. I desire you, and a woman. If you loved me, you would give me both." The Lord is silent after that.

I look behind me. Father Phillip is still sitting there, with his rosary in his hand. He looks up, and I smile nervously. He smiles back. "What are you reading?"

"*Redeeming Sexuality*."

Father Phillip nods. "I have heard of it, but I haven't read it yet."

"It's pretty intense. It has helped me with a few things."

"Should I be reading it?" He laughs.

"I guess so. I was looking through the section on celibacy, and I thought about you."

"What do you mean?" He asks.

"Well, you're really unpretentious, for a priest. And I was wondering how you developed a more outgoing personality than your peers."

Father Phillip beams with delight. "I was always like this."

"Even before you went to seminary?"

"Certainly. I went to seminary when I was twenty six. I think before that, I might have been a ladies man. I mean, I saw a lot of girls. I always respected their boundaries, but there were certainly a good number of them."

"No priest I know would ever respond to a question like that with your degree of honesty."

"What do you want to be, Benedict?"

"I want to be someone's hero."

Father is silent for a bit, like he is wondering if he should tell me something or not. Finally, after a moment, he speaks up.

He holds out his left hand. "I was engaged when I went to the seminary. It was hard, but I never even thought about it until she and I had been together for a year and a half. I was sort of nursing a sick puppy, I suppose. She was a very nice girl, but she had been with a number of men before me. I really, truly loved her, but we could not be close. She was afraid of kissing, afraid of intimacy. The closer we got, the more she pushed me away. I asked God, often, if this was to be my *cross* in life- being with a woman that had been with so many men that she could no longer love someone who truly loved *her*. I had more than enough money, and I had a good job. That was never the case. Rather, I couldn't do it. But, convoluted or not, I truly cared for her, and I could not serve another woman. I couldn't leave her and just be with someone who was better. But I also couldn't keep trying to be her hero. Christ is her hero. Being a *hero* is an emotional dead end, with no promises attached. It gets you nowhere. *A woman can only be rescued by her Creator*. And so, despite how hard it was for me, I acknowledged that the only way I could really practice heroic virtue was by serving the Lord. If I truly wished to be someone's hero, then I needed to be a hero for the church. She needs heroes to take up her battles. If you want to fight for something, fight for what is right, not for what you *want*. Just because you have strong feelings for someone, or something, doesn't mean that you should lay down your life for that cause. Rather, being a hero is about ignoring how you feel, swallowing your pride, not giving a damn about your future, and going head on into it, whether you like it or not. A hero fights for a noble cause, not a self motivated one. In the long run, the only way that I could get revenge on all the men that emotionally handicapped my fiancée was by fighting the battle for Christ. The revenge motive has been transformed by Him into a desire for me to stand up for, and fight for, what is right and just."

Moved by his dissertation, I was silent for a good minute or so, before I had any response at all. He just sat there, with a big smile on his face, contrasting to his black shirt and white collar.

"What happened to her?"

"I said her wedding mass a year after I made it out of seminary. I have only been a priest for three years, but they have been the most meaningful three years of my life."

"That's big of you, to say her wedding mass. How did you feel?"

He laughs, big and strong. "I felt awful, but it had to be said. She asked me."

"Did *she* know how you felt?" I asked.

"She did. She saw it on my face. She even apologized." I noticed that he was smiling. This intrigued me. How was he so comfortable with something even I was uncomfortable with? I could never see myself looking back on a relationship, giving it up for seminary, and moving forward into life as a priest. I do not know if I could stand a full circle moment like that. I look over at Jesus, on the cross. I feel His presence.

"I don't know if I could do that…see Lucia married." Or any girl I loved. I secretly acknowledged that I was glad that Olivia had died. She couldn't be with anyone if she was dead. Perhaps I even wished death on Lucia, or Nanette. After all, death is the only way we can be reunited with God, isn't it?

20

February fourteenth came and went. I spent the majority of Valentine's Day by myself, in bed, imagining what it would be like not to be alone. Since my encounter with Nanette, she grew less hostile, and less distant. While she had no clue about the virtuous romantic endeavors that plagued my thoughts, she still instinctively displayed an uneasiness around me. She would say hello now, and she would smile once in a while. But her gestures of kindness were still never good enough for me. February fifteenth I wrote her a note, showing how much I aspired to be her friend. However, as I closed it, I recalled how she threw away the last love letter she had, and by the implied intonations of said letter, it was distinct that she even had feelings for the bastard. How, then, would she handle a note from me, someone that she despised?

I concluded from this event that I would have to show her that she needed me. I could certainly be a hero to her, and not just some pathetic romantic.

There is a sort of desolation in the city today. It is hot for the winter, reaching eighty degrees. The big trees hang low over the roads. A dry wind forces its way through the canopy, and the sky is clear, but not terribly blue. It reminds me of the summers that I spent by myself, thinking about Lucia. In the heat of July, the thunderstorms would roll in over the horizon, and the wind would be weak and paltry. Black men selling watermelons would set up along the side of ninety-two, and I would suffer in the heat all day, waiting for the sky to crack. The humidity would sky rocket, and I would sit on my porch, in my underwear, sweating while the flies would dart. The house I lived in my second year of college was very old. It was built in 1927, and had no air conditioning, no fans and no electrical sockets in the bathroom. The depression era shanty would be my house for a year and half, from age nineteen into age twenty one. I paid for it what I would have given for a nice apartment in the area by the college. But in this place, I would smell the gulf, which was about three miles away, and think about my long lost friend Lucia, and wonder who she was with. I would take a bite of watermelon, and the rains would come, like clockwork. Big drops would contact the barren yard, and with a thud they would land. One more, after the next, would plop down on the ground. I would count the drops that I could see for five more minutes, and then it would become impossible.

During the school year, Poff would come over and we would play chess on the front porch, sweating all night in the dirty Florida heat. I was very lonely then, feeling like I had no real friends. A stray dog would wander up my street every few days, and I would feed it, and give it water. Those summers went by slowly. I would take one class, but I had trouble making meaningful acquaintance with anyone in it.

A stream of present day Madeleines and yesteryear Lucias would eat into my sleep. I only knew that I had to forget about Lucia in order to keep on in the right direction.

I had a neighbor on that little street. She was a young girl, married to a man with red hair and a red beard. They had a child together, and he was no older than four years of age. I surmised she had conceived this child in her adolescence. He had a dumb look, and a poor haircut, and he would stand by the fence and watch me while his mother would try to hang laundry or cook. This impoverished family looked miserable. The man would go to work at six in the morning, and he would come back at seven or so, and he would start drinking. He looked older than his young wife by at least six years. I could tell that at one point she had been exceptionally beautiful, and she was still quite attractive. Her adolescence was disrupted by this brute, who had no real aspirations. He swore at her, and they yelled, and the poor, dumb little boy ran and hid in the trees on the back lot.

One day, while I was out walking, I saw a small flowering bush of similar exceptional beauty. I had no idea what it was, but I collected about a dozen blossoms, and left them on her mailbox. I watched as she went out later, and saw them. She was delighted at their innocent perfection. Perhaps she could relate to them, as they had been cut from their life giving bush, and she had been prematurely severed from the vines of her girlhood innocence.

I made this a practice for the rest of the hot months of July and August, several times a week. I knew this was the only joy that she received during the day, knowing that someone saw her and thought she was worth a few small blossoms from a flowering plant. While I never aspired to take her from her husband, she was a precious human being in her own right, worthy of being shown love.

Perhaps this is where my heroic designs really originated. I wanted to bring something extraordinary into the picture of this woman's life. If only I could operate out of love, perhaps I could be a hero in more people's lives. But my selfish ambitions, and my insufferable desire for Nanette, endeared me to be her hero, and her hero only. Now, more than anything, I wanted to stand up for her, and win all of her battles. She is a woman in need of a hero, and I am a man in need of a fight.

Henri opens the door for me as I arrive at his house. He carries an air of delight, as his lady friend from the other night has returned on several occasions. He is wearing a robe and slippers, while his chest is exposed at the top. I look about the room, and I can tell that he has not tidied up.

"She was here last night?"

Henri nods with a slight smile. I follow him around, as he picks things up here and there.

I muster up the courage to ask him something that has been on my mind for a week. "Do you find you have to choose between God and woman, Henri?"

"What a bizarre question," he mumbles. "Go straighten up the kitchen."

I proceed to the kitchen, and while I am wiping down the counter tops and polishing the crystal, he comes in, still wearing his robe, but with pants on.

"What is this question of choosing between God and woman?" He asks.

"Well, I would feel morally culpable sleeping with a woman, especially at your age. I mean, it's a conflict of interests. You can't be a good Catholic and indulge in a mortal sin."

My theological point of view bores Henri. "In my former years, I would have discussed this with you, but I will let God determine the penalty for my shortcomings. I will say, however, that you don't choose God. Rather, God is immersed in everything, so that you can't separate Him from anything."

"I agree-"

Henri silences me. "Let's avoid a discussion of subatomic particles. I need for you to scrub the inside of the bottom cabinets."

I (finally) reach the kitchen, while Henri goes and puts normal clothes on. He stops half way down the hall.

"Benedict!" he yells.

"Yes!"

"There is no such thing as a good Catholic. I certainly never claimed to be one, and neither should you!" I don't respond, and I get down on one knee and begin to scrub the cabinets. They are certainly not dirty, but perhaps it is the constant cleaning that keeps them this nice. My mother used to say I should clean things before they get dirty. I have always thought to apply this attitude to myself. Perhaps going to confession when I feel the least bit sinful would be a good exercise, or praying for wisdom, before making a bad decision, rather than praying for forgiveness afterward. I am so short sighted though, that I operate out of that damnable theory of permanence.

I am no more than five minutes into my task when Nanette enters the kitchen. I can see her sexy little tennis shoes gliding across the floor. She sets down her handbag and collects her list of things to do, which Henri has left on the table in the foyer.

Henri, hearing her enter, rushes down the hall, with hurried steps. I straighten up and take a peek into the hall. He looks dismayed. I keep cleaning the cabinets, pretending like I don't notice anything. I take an upward glance as he walks past me, and stops.

"Did you need anything?" I ask.

"No. Where is the wood nymph?"

"She is in the foyer looking at her list."

He turns, and yells. "Nanette!"

She rushes in, looking concerned. I keep cleaning, and turn my head to my work. Aside, I hear Henri angrily at the entrance of the kitchen.

"Nanette, A man named Byron…Byron Rose, called for you."

She is silent.

"Was the rule to let no one know you work here?"

"He used to eat here, if you remember."

"Still, I have enough men in this house who can't keep their eyes from you. We don't need anymore affairs under my roof. I sent him away to preserve his marriage, *n'est pas?*"

She sounds agitated as she acknowledges the statement.

Secretly, I am delighted, as I thought Henri saw her as being beyond fault, even though he made a comment about my fixation on her.

"Anyway, he called and wanted to know if he could come see you here."

Instantly, Nanette tries to respond, but Henri silences her. "You *are not* to allow him this place, ever. Now go back to your work, *mon framboise*."

She marches into the kitchen. I take one look at her face. It shows overtones of unhappiness and embarrassment. She begins to remove several pots from the walk-in closet, and arranges them on the counter. One by one, she checks to make sure they are clean, and then looks at the ingredient list for the dish she is making. She darts from one cabinet to the next, industriously, like a small bee, and gathers all of the ingredients. She then proceeds to get the utensils. Much like me, when she is admonished, she works more fluently, with a sort of urgency in her step. She contemplates the nature and mystery of nothing, feeling she must make good on her breach with Henri. She is small and defenseless. Now is the perfect time to ask questions.

"Who is he, this Byron Rose?"

She looks over at me. "Must *you* also meddle in my affairs, Benedict?"

"No, I was just curious."

She goes back to working on her culinary projects, turning the stove on to heat a large pot of water. She speaks without turning around. "He wasn't supposed to call here, but when we started seeing each other, I told him that only in the event that he could not get a hold of me for a prolonged period of time, I might be here. It was not wise on my part."

"I see," I mumble as I keep cleaning the cabinets.

"Focus on your work. I think we have irritated Henri."

My reaction to this statement was mixed. I was both curious to see how recent it was, and also irritated because she kept lovers. She should not have to even think about her lovers anymore. I wish it was that I, and I alone, occurred to her, not these older men.

Naturally, this deep and irrational desire is merely a result of that damnable pathogen. The parts of my brain that are still resistant keep me focused. Nanette blows all else aside and concentrates on dinner.

Henri has demanded that tonight's menu be rustic- In this case a pie of venison, with vegetables in it. He has a whole doe that he is preparing- purportedly he shot it a few evenings ago in the back yard of a neighbor. Henri has lapsed into a quasi-insane whimsical state since he has begun his recourse with this woman he has met. He is quicker to anger, and he also laughs more irreverently. Our topics for the last few weeks have been more entertaining- the love affair of Fernande Olivier and Pecasso, for example. Myself, as Apollinaire, had also been with mme. Olivier, and I was to read a bit of her memoirs in character. It was fitting, I later learned, as Apollinaire *had* been a waiter at various times in his short life.

Nanette rolls thirty six pie crusts. I peel carrots, onions, potatoes and fennel, while Henri stands over a giant stew pot. We cook the crusts first, and then the insides are filled. We run a bit behind tonight, such that the last pie comes out of the oven when the first guest arrives.

During dinner all I can think about is this Byron Rose and my utter disdain for him. I wonder if he knows Billy Hollis (who, I have heard, is looking for me, hence why I have not ventured out in a while), and the other men that Nanette has been with. Although he muttered some garbage about working in the capital in his note, I have conjured up an image of him as a discreet director of pornography. After all, many of these white collar political types are involved in questionable lucrative endeavors. Knowing that he has been a contributing agent in the corruption of beautiful young women, notably the one I am so intoxicated with, motivates me to dislike him so much. I was attacking *him* in my movements towards Hollis and, to a lesser degree, Anthony.

Henri interrupts me. One of my tasks had been to wash the glasses, which, given my proximity to Nanette, may not have gone so well. Henri is walking up to me, holding a crystal upside down, much in the way one would hang a prisoner by his feet before killing him.

"*Helas*, look at this glass!" Sure enough, the glass is cloudy.

"What did you do, Guillaume? Drink milk out of it?"

The guests are silent, as the confrontation, much to my dismay, is occurring right in front of them.

Henri drops the glass in front of me, staring me in the face with red, angry eyes. It shatters on the floor. I feel little pieces hit my trousers. He walks to the kitchen and tells me to set down my bottle of champagne and wash everything again.

Nanette assures everyone that it is just a part of tonight's show, as she sweeps up the broken crystal.

In the meantime, Nanette and Henri distribute the script for the evening. The subject of tonight's other topic, which Henri chose at the last minute, is a synopsis of the French Grand Prix in 1914 and how it contributed to World War One. He begins a brief slideshow describing all of the adversaries- Mercedes, Benz, Peugeot, Louis Wagner and his Fiat, Victor H- something, and their exciting drive to world domination.

I wash the glasses slowly, feeling embarrassed. The hot water burns my hands, and I keep my eyes focused towards the sink. I feel like an adolescent child who has been caught masturbating. Henri walks to the Kitchen and gently closes the doors, so that I might be forced to do my work in solitude. The good part of all of this is that there is no extra noise. I can actually think.

While I am nearly done with the glasses, the phone rings. I am not allowed to answer the phone, but I feel a strong urge to. I keep moving, drying the glasses. The guests are mumbling to themselves, while Henri steps in to the kitchen. I hide a glass of wine that I have been sipping on.

"I am about to serve the main course. *Allez!*"

Henri wheels the cart out, which Nanette has prepared. I open the door for him, and he walks out into the dining room.

The noise quells, and I begin to put the glasses on another cart. As I put away the last few, the phone rings again.

Henri has never told me *not* to answer it. The phone sits on a table in the hall. It rings miserably, but the dining hall is too noisy for Henri to hear it. My temptation gives way to action, and I venture out into the hall. The phone has rung about seven times, and being the lightweight that I am, I feel inebriated enough to answer it. I grab the phone, breathing heavily, nearly forgetting that it has a cord.

"Hello?" A voice crackles on the other line. "Is this the *Maison Rosengart*?"

"Why?" I ask, suspiciously. I already know who it is.

"I must speak to an employee of yours."

"She is busy." I answer flatly.

"It is very necessary."

"This must be Byron…Byron Rose."

"How do you know who I am?" He speaks slowly and carefully.

"That is unimportant. What is your business with the girl?"

For some odd reason a great dislike for her welled up inside my chest. I hated her strawberry hair, her large sunglasses and her big, soft eyes. I hated her for being *unobtainable*. And I hated her for being involved with this schmuck.

He is silent for a moment. "Is there anything I can do to speak with her?" He says tersely.

"I can take your number. You are not supposed to call her. I will pass any message on for her. Failure to disclose any information will result in you having no access to her. If I tell our proprietor that you phoned us, she will be fired. Then you will have no chance of speaking with her."

He breathes deeply. "You may reach me at eight five zero, nine two five, six seven three one."

"What is the purpose for your call, Mr. Rose?"

I can tell he is nervous. I try to be as firm and mature-sounding as possible. I even try to deepen my voice. From the kitchen, Henri shouts for me.

"Benedict! We need you! Now!"

"Mr. Rose, I need a statement now."

"It concerns the state of my marriage."

"Very good. I will pass it on to her. By the way, How did you get this number?"

"From Miss Sarah Temple." Although I am dying to know who miss Temple is, I have to go.

I click the phone off, and run into the kitchen. Henri wants me to apportion *Mille Feuille* for the guests. I carefully place each little bit on a small plate, and decorate it with a raspberry stripe. I wonder how he knows Sarah Temple.

Nanette and I are alone in the kitchen for a moment. I can't let her know that I have read the note and have a prior knowledge of Mr. Rose.

"You had a phone call."

"Another one? Did you answer it?" She seems concerned.

"Better myself than Henri. He would fire you."

She is not happy. "Did he leave a message?"

"He did, and a number."

"What did he say?"

"It concerns his marriage."

She nods. I can't read her face, but this is certainly more emotion than she has ever expressed around me.

"I need to speak with him. Please give me the phone number."

"I will, but you need to tell me what the nature of your conversation is."

"Or what?"

"Or I will tell Henri that he called."

"You fool. He used to come here. Before my time, but he did."

"Henri does not give the number to the guests." I hand her the piece of paper, and go back to work.

"Henri has before."

I am about to respond to her statement, when I hear him yelling for me.

"Speak of the devil..." Nanette says. "You might as well

261

attend to him."

He yells at me, mostly about supplying more alcohol to the guests, so I obey and go get a case of wine. The rest of dinner goes quietly, with the usual outbursts from Henri. I am careful to avoid Nanette.

Henri takes me aside after dinner.

"My friend, I must tell you, my new lady friend and I are anxious to travel. March fifth, she and I are going away for a bit. At this age, you never know how long it will last."

"What am I going to do when you're gone?"

"I am giving you and Nanette the responsibility of keeping an eye on the place. You must be civil towards each other. And respect the rules."

"I will be happy to."

Henri opens the kitchen door, hands me a check, and bids me good night.

I follow Henri out. "How long will you be gone?"

"Two weeks."

"Will I be working while you're gone?"

Henri assures me that I will be fine, and closes the door to his quarters.

Nanette is folding the napkins. I watch her from the kitchen. While I am looking, I am not looking. While I am observing her, I do not allow myself to observe her. While I block my brain from processing her, I cannot stop taking her in. She has manifested herself with a distinct magnetism. She has dragged me into herself. I have to eliminate her, make her fall in love with me, or eliminate myself. There is no apparent relief from the feelings that I have for her.

21

It is a cool evening. The moon is clear and bright, and I park the car in an indiscernible spot on the side of the road. I walk the three blocks or so to Nanette's apartment building, again under the cover of darkness. I had acted on this urge last week, ironically on Valentine's Day, but I was afraid and I went away, shivering from fear and cowardice. It is certainly cold.

I have to find out who she is. I can't just become infatuated with this woman and then pretend that who she is does not matter to me. I need to know if she is still involved with Byron Rose. I need to watch her. I need to see how she behaves, if she leaves the lights on at night, or if she has a lover who comes over. I need to experience who she is beyond her façade at work. She is surreal to me, but I will have to establish an idea of her- a realistic idea. If she has a lover, it will be easier for me to tear myself away. If I can't tear myself away, I can at least establish all his weak points and be better than he is.

I walk slowly towards her building, eyeing the shrubbery beneath the balconies. The terraces seem like a secure place, and I can blend in with the plant life. I count the balconies, one by one. Hers is the second from last. I look at my watch. I can barely make out the dial, but I think it says ten o'clock, or thereabouts. Her lights are on. The lights at the end of the row are also on. I wonder if I have her place mixed up. I wonder if any men live down the hall from her. I wonder if she slept with any of them.

One time Lucia did that- she was infatuated with a guy in her building. She went over to his place one night, and something happened. I never asked her any questions, really, but I knew exactly what was going on. There was an instance where I confronted her about it, and she got angry. She was quite far gone then- this was sometime in between when I saw her with that guy at the mansion, and when she started dating Alex.

I know I shouldn't assume anything about Nanette, but she just seems like the type to have careless relationships with guys who are ignorant and stupid. I carefully hide myself in the rows between the condo and the road, feeling the prick of tiny thorns on tiny branches. This miserable place is cold. No bugs are crawling, but I am still feeling the ill sensation of being crawled on. The dirt is grainy and smelly. I wonder why I am putting myself through all this trouble.

Infatuation is not glorious. It's an ugly thing. It will always be an ugly thing. But I am not indulging in a romantic whim. If I ask myself honestly, I am on a rescue mission. I am only doing what God has told me to do, and even if it is ugly, socially unacceptable and uncomfortable, it is what it is.

In high school, there was a girl named Vivian Chandler. Vivi and I were close, sort of. In ninth grade, I developed a serious crush on her. She mistook my kindness for something sincere, when I knew it was laden with ulterior motives. Through the rest of the year, she and I became close friends. I was sufficiently able to mask my jealousy towards her suitors for a reasonable period of time. When we came back to school next year, much to my dismay, Vivi had acquired a boyfriend. They had been serious all summer long, leading him to bestow on her a promise ring.

I don't know how *other people* feel about promise rings, but I personally loathe them. They represent an unfair claim staked upon a woman's heart, when there is nothing substantial that can be offered to her at the present time. Show me a woman's hand with a promise ring upon it, and I will vomit all over it.

In the real world, the adult world, the promise ring is viewed as a pacifier to rid the mind of the difficulties of the emergent adult world. It is a symbol of both existing and latent chemistry that *consumes* everything but produces nothing. It is an unexpressed symbol of selfishness, saying "your heart is mine. I can't offer you food, clothing, shelter or even protection, but I can offer you this stupid ring."

It was for this reason that I got so bent out of shape when, in the first few weeks of tenth grade, Foster, Vivi's boyfriend, gave her the damn thing.

I told Vivi that I liked her and I didn't think she should

promise herself to Foster at such a young age. Life doesn't make any sense when you're sixteen. You don't even know what will happen in six months. Vivi was *disappointed* that I liked her. She almost pleaded with me –*"Benedict, please don't be hurt. Benedict, please don't be upset!"* She would say urgently.

It was two weeks after she got the fucking thing that I told her my plan- I was going to starve myself until she gave it back to him, and she was not allowed to tell him why she was giving it back. "I'm doing you a favor, trust me. In the future you'll be glad you gave it back." My exact plan was for Foster to get upset and break up with her. Then she would be devastated, and run back into my arms. And I would be her hero. If you can't find a situation to be a hero in under the auspices of real life, then you must create one.

Nanette's lights flash on and off a few times, and I see nothing. I stare at the ceilings of the balconies, like I am walking in a big, big city. I am hidden. The cold air is heavy. I can see my breath. I check my shirt to see if it's dark enough. I look at my watch, and it looks like 10:50. I struggle to remember what day it is. I am beginning to wonder if I should come back another night, and I am trying to make up my mind, when I see her come to the window. She looks out, over the stars, and then shuts the blinds. She moves into the living room. I can see her outline in the room. She lights what might be a candle. She dims her lights, and makes sure the shades are closed.

In about five minutes, I see headlights coming down the road. In the wake of the light, I stand up, and move to the shelter of a near tree. She comes to the window, and draws the shades, as she looks towards the headlights. Her face is illuminated, and I can see that she looks quite nice. She replaces the shades, and turns on another light in the house. The faint growl of an engine intensifies, and I see a black BMW turn into the parking area. The car parks, somewhat obtrusively. A shadowy figure briskly exits from his vehicle, with some kind of overnight bag in hand. He rushes up the stairs.

I move into the parking area, from the east side of the building, where I can see her door clearly. He doesn't see me, but he behaves as if someone is watching him. He knocks on the door, carefully and softly. She opens it, easing it backwards and peeking out. He enters, keeping with his discreet nature. I never really get to see his face.

I reinstall myself in my place in the bushes. I watch the living room, but I see little more than a few shadows. I am too tired to really feel anything, but I know exactly what is going on. They drift into what could be a bedroom, and the lights go on. I hear no noises, and I see no movement, but I know why people drift into bedrooms, and I know what happens when they settle in.

In my discomfort, I abandon my vigil and leave my post. I walk back to my car. It is 11:28 PM. My brain has stopped analyzing all of this. It is too painful. I wonder if the man in the BMW was Mr. Rose himself. I should have apprehended him, but I didn't have the courage. In all respects, I am a coward, and cowards make terrible heroes. I do not have the courage to do any of this. I get to the car, and I put in my *Promise Ring* mix tape. It is certainly cold- forty one degrees. Only when I shift the gear lever into reverse, do I realize I cannot feel my fingers…

It is Monday. After my escapade last night, I am exhausted. I sleep in until noon, and then I awake to noises in the kitchen.

I have missed our small group for a few weeks now, and for a good reason- I dislike seeing Madeleine and Anthony together. It's not so much the idea of two people being together that irritates me. It is more so that they spend all of their time together, holding hands and laughing. Of course, one session of any small group like that and you can bet that the negatives will denigrate anything I receive from it.

Francis and Kevin are in the kitchen. There is a sandwich on the counter, and they look excited.

"Hey guys…how are you?"

"Oh, hey stranger! Did you hear the big news?"

"I don't know if I want to know what it is."

"Oh, ok. Then we won't tell you."

"No, no. Tell me. I need more shit to be upset about."

"Ok, well, Anthony and Madeleine are engaged. He proposed to her yesterday."

While I understand that these things have to happen, I wonder what separates me from them. How is it that some guys find great jobs, meet amazing women and seem to live perfect lives? I must have done something wrong. I stand there silently with a mild frown. While it is quite the opposite of the spiritual ecstasy that the saints experience, it sure felt like I was placed in some deep, melancholy trance.

Francis taps me on the shoulder. "Rad? Are you ok?"

I am clearly out of it. "They met like…two months ago…"

"You don't know that for certain. But isn't it cool?"

"No. It's stupid of them."

"Marriage is a good thing though, when you understand how it relates to-"

I don't let him finish. "It's only good when it works."

Francis looks disappointed. Kevin simply ignores the whole thing.

"Where are we in the book?"

"It's irrelevant…you don't read it anyway." Kevin responds.

"I do read it. I read the chapter on celibacy!"

"And how about the one on not being pissed off all the time?"

"All of you are pompous asses."

I pull a package of cheese out of the fridge, and take it back to my room. I would be susceptible to looking at porn for the moment, but my desire to shove cheese in my mouth is overwhelming. In a few minutes, I get up and walk down the hall. I grab the cordless phone off of its charger. I dial Byron's number. The phone rings aimlessly for a bit. Whether or not this is a bad idea is irrelevant to me.

Finally, someone picks up. "Hello?"

"Hello, yes Ma'am…is this Mr. Rose's house?"

"It is."

"Is he available?"

"He is not."

"Who is this?"

"This is Mrs. Rose."

"Do you know where he was last night?"

"He has not been home in several days."

"Did he give any indication of where he went."

"No, but when he would visit..." she stops suddenly.

"Visit? Where? Who?"

"Stop meddling. What is the reason for your call?"

"I was making conversation"

"Who is this?" She asks.

"It's unimportant. I was calling to confirm his reservation."

"Where?"

"It's a secret."

"Why is it a secret? Does it involve another woman?"

"That's not my responsibility. I must go."

"You cannot. I am his wife! I am entitled to knowing."

"Does it usually involve other women?" I ask. This was complicated, as I knew that if he was seeing her, Mrs. Rose might know. But I didn't want to tell her too much either.

"Again, what is this one's name?"

"It is not with a girl. Is there a recent record of him casually seducing anyone?"

"He never says her name. When goes to see her, he leaves for two or three days, like this. I know he goes to work, but he resides at her house. I found out about it a few months ago."

"This is beyond my duty. Let him know his reservation at the Maison is ready. I assure you it does not involve a woman."

I hang up the phone. After I finish off my cheese, I go for a walk down the hallway. I beat on the door to Francis' room.

"Francis...are you busy?"

"I'm not. What do you need?"

"Nothing, I just wanted to apologize."

"For what?"

"For being so negative towards everyone and everything."

"That's nice of you. You must be having a difficult day."

"I am. And I didn't enjoy hearing about the engagement."

"Do you like us, Rad?"

"What do you mean?"

"Do you like us- our group of *friends*?"

"What makes you think I don't?"

"You're always unhappy."

"I am always unhappy."

I *am* always unhappy.

Henri has us come in Tuesday. He is ardently preparing for his junket with his lady friend. Nanette is there. She does not know of my visit Sunday night. She is wearing a mango colored top with spaghetti straps. The high is seventy three degrees. She wears her hair up in a bun. I can see the tiniest outline of a tattoo on her shoulder. There is a dolphin swimming in the silky-smooth sea of her skin. It plays in the dim light of the kitchen. I have never seen this much of her.

I sit down in the dining room for twenty minutes and fold napkins. Henri and Nanette go outside and begin to unload the Citroen. While they are on their third or fourth trip out, the phone rings. I go to the phone, and I see a note by it, in Henri's script.

"If it rings, don't answer."

Against Henri's will, I go and answer it.

"Hello?" A familiar voice crackles on the other line.

"Mr. Rose?"

"Yes, this is he. I tried calling earlier."

"State your business."

"I received a message from my...er, wife, that you had called."

"Yes. The timing is bad. May I call you back later this

evening?"

"Is there any point to calling me back?"

"If you wish to see your butterfly, I suppose there is."

"As you wish." Right as he finishes, Henri walks in. I hang up the receiver violently.

"Who was that?" He demands.

"It was a telemarketer."

"I don't get calls from telemarketers."

"This was from a telemarketer. I swear!"

"I don't have the time to argue with you, Benedict."

"Nor I with you." He growls at me, like an angry carnivorous animal. Nanette comes in a moment later, carrying a bag of groceries. I open the door to the kitchen for her, but she ignores me completely.

Henri weighs a brick of Romano cheese. "Look, the bastards. This was supposed to be a two kilo brick. It doesn't even weigh one and three fifths!" The people at the *fromagerie* always rip Henri off. They are supposedly communists one week, Jews the next, and always bastards.

"Communist bastards," he mutters as he weighs another brick of Roquefort.

Nanette accosts me from my perch at the door. "He is pissed off today. I think you should go."

"Why do you care if I leave or stay?"

"Before you, Monsieur Apollinaire, he would get like this. I would tell him stories to calm him down, but he wouldn't feel comfortable with it in your presence. Besides, you might add to the problem."

Her somewhat sinister and mocking intonation made me want to *take* something away from her. It made me scornful almost, towards her and Henri, like they wanted time alone together, without me there.

"I'm leaving!" I yell, as I go grab my jacket. There is no response. I head to the restroom, where I left it on the sink counter. When I return to the living room, the front door is open, as if he is gesturing me to leave. I look into the kitchen, Henri glares at me, as if he knows I am up to something. Feeling uneasy, I leave on my tiptoes. I start the Saab up, and drive off.

I decide that I will go see the Catholics tonight, as it is time for their weekly meeting. I pull up to the convent, and, certainly enough, the green Corolla sits in the driveway. While Madeleine is almost a distant memory, I still feel great antipathy concerning her recent engagement. I see evidence of Kevin being here also.

A familiar figure opens my car door when I park.

"Where have you been?" I look up. Jim is smiling down on me.

"Chasing girls. Don't hate."

"Seriously. You just disappeared."

"I do that from time to time."

Jim sneers at me. "What's her name?"

"Actually, I don't know."

"Do you know anything about her?"

"I know where she lives."

"And...?"

"I'm pretty sure she's in porn- like an actress."

"This doesn't sound too good."

I open the car door, and I scan the area around the porch. I have a feeling that it is early, but I don't have a device to tell the time with. Jim and I walk up to the house together. He opens the door, and I glance around the living room. I turn to Jim.

"What chapter are we on?"

"Nine or Ten. It has to do with defining God's purpose in your life."

I had seen this chapter, and looked upon it with mixed emotions. It was entitled *God Has A Plan For You.*

Being very apprehensive about seeing this group, especially because I have been hiding from them, I come in bracing myself for the unwanted attention.

I look through the door. To the right is Paul. He looks at me, but he doesn't say anything. If you don't have anything nice to say...

I am about to walk up to him and say hello, when I get a tap on my shoulder. I turn around, and, believe it or not, it is Madeleine. Needless to say, I am amazed.

"Hi, stranger." She is actually smiling. I have never seen this Madeleine.

"Hello." I try my best to smile while I say it.

"How have you been?"

"Good...I heard you will be getting married."

"I am!"

"Don't you think it is a little soon?"

"I have known Anthony for a lot longer than most people here think."

My brain translates this as "you never had a chance. I didn't even have to talk to you."

"Oh, so he was in the picture before you came here?"

"Yes, yes he was."

Because I don't care anymore, I ask honest questions.

"How's his lip?"

"It's healing up OK. He didn't need any surgeries."

"What brings this elated mood upon you? You seem happier, excited."

"I was always this way."

"Not towards me."

"I know, I'm sorry. I guess it's just the joy of knowing you have met the person God has meant for you."

Translation: Not even someone as creepy as you can pop my bubble of happiness.

"Are you nervous?"

"About getting married?"

"No, about seeing me."

"I don't know why I would be."

"Yeah, me either, I suppose."

"So what have you been up to?" She inquires.

"Nothing. Nothing at all."

272

I am appalled that she has the audacity to be so *nice* to me. She has never treated me kindly. The only explanation for her kindness might lie in the fact that she is wearing the rose colored glasses of eager anticipation. I suppose if I met the love of my life, I would be the same way. I might even like everyone around me. However, it was unfair for her to never even tell me she was seeing someone. The retrospective is chilling. I hate the idea of pursuing a woman who was in love with someone else the whole time. It made Madeleine not all that different from Lucia. Madeleine was Lucia with Jesus. Take Jesus away, and all women might be the same, for me at least. I take a seat on my favorite seventies sofa, and crack open my copy of the book. I have missed several chapters. This book was supposed to have all the answers. It probably does, but I don't want them. If there is a secret equation to being a good person and getting the things you want out of your life, I don't want it.

Last year, I made a pilgrimage to Lucia's hometown to pray for her. She was from Destin, a small town of cute craft shops and nice beaches. After I went to her old home parish and said a Rosary for her, I sat at a restaurant in downtown, looking at the passing cars. It was summer, about this time, and there were fewer people than normal. The Saab was parked on the street. I know she used to hang out here. Part of me wished she would pass by here, with Robbie, or Alex, or whoever she was with. In my mind, our eyes meet. I tip my hat to her, and she smiles at me. Not an obvious smile, but a tiny, subdued, reassuring smile. A smile that contains a certain lightness, where the past melts away, and all you have left is that feeling that occurred when you first laid eyes upon each other. A smile that signifies an acknowledgment of well being. A smile that suggests we are both OK, and that everything is fine. No words or emotions are expressed, no contact is made, and no intentions are catered to. I cry a little bit at the thought, and a chill runs down my spine. I don't want to be loved. Love is not tragic. I am a tragedy of a human being. I wish to slip into the folds of history, and die in a state of loneliness. For me, it would be enough if Lucia saw me, for a split second, so she could see that without her, everything was fine.

The mindless chatter of the crowd is silenced by Paul's nasal, alkaline voice. Jim plops down next to me. Anthony comes in, holding a coat. He sits opposite of me on a chair, next to his future bride. She looks over at him and smiles, and in a few seconds, he takes her hand. I look over at Jim. He is flipping through his book, and seems unaware of what is going on. My personal choices always catch up with me in these situations. I wonder what all of these people would think of me if I kept my tongue tied and my hands to myself. Jim moves towards me, as Xavier sits down. He greets Jim and ignores me.

I have not even looked at the chapter on vocations. I am not terribly excited about a chapter in a book dictating the rest of my life to me. But so many of these Catholics let that happen. For example, Madeleine has been *told* she should marry a man like Anthony. I would be hard pressed to say she doesn't love him. She has been told to love him, and so she most likely does. The chances of her waking up and pursuing some sort of misaligned desire that has even a tiny bit of conflict with the Church lies outside the boundaries of her consciousness. As I am thinking these thoughts, Paul begins to pontificate about what a vocation is, and how it is discovered. As usual, he cannot be brilliant or creative, so he relies on third party texts from more competent theologians. We read and pray, and read some more. It goes on for about thirty minutes.

"Our vocations are part of God's plan for our lives. They are reflected by the innermost desires of our hearts. If one deeply desires children, it might well be said that his vocation is marriage. If one deeply desires to serve the Lord, it may be said that his vocation is celibate life. But our desires can be misconstrued, so that we do not know what our true vocation is. For instance, a strong desire to pursue wealth does not indicate that one should take up a secular job in a big company. Neither should a woman believe her vocation is to celibacy if she is unable to bear children."

I raise my hand and interrupt Paul. "What if one looks at pornography...does that indicate he should take a wife? I mean, that's what the apostle Paul says."

Paul frowns. "Sort of like that."

My statement is too blunt for him, but he acknowledges its theological validity.

Xavier chimes in. "Paul says that if we can restrain ourselves, then we should not get married."

I get angry at his comeback, even though it is true. My recent conversation with Madeleine burns inside me.

"Does that mean that Anthony and Madeleine should not get married, but for some reason, they can't restrain themselves?" I feel both relieved, and self-immolated. The room is silent. Paul's jaw moves a bit. Kristen is looking down. I don't dare look at Madeleine or Anthony. I can smell my own bad breath.

Out of nowhere, Jim speaks up. "It means you should stop looking at pornography, you idiot."

I hang my head in shame. "I can't. I have a problem. I have a problem with all of you. I feel like *all of you are constantly judging me*. All of you are hopelessly insincere, especially all you girls. You are the ones that drive me to keep struggling with these vices. If one of you women would only love me, maybe then I would stand a chance. But I can't- there is no hope for me. I am one of those people from the fringes of society. None of you love me. None of you are really my friends. None of you care about me. I am one of those people that is marginal- outside the group, or the clique. Outside the thoughts of others. Many of you wish I would go away. I am a nobody to all of you. And now, the only reason any of you have noticed me is because of my admission of sinfulness!" I begin to cry, but instead of sitting there and continuing to make a scene, I decide to leave.

Paul stares down at me. I get up, without looking at anyone, and run out of the room, towards the door. However, I take one glance back at Kristen. She seems very sad. I give her a forlorn stare.

Everyone is so restless. If they could, they would stone me. I would be the woman caught in adultery. I am begging for mercy, constantly. There is no rest and respite from this affliction. I reach for the door knob, and my hand shakes as I open it. I think at this point, I feel hopeless. My life, for what it is worth, is worth only what I use it to rectify. I have stopped trying to rectify myself. What now?

I drive to my house, and not knowing what else to do, I redeem an old honey jar and make it a flask. I add the remnant of a bottle of cheap vodka that Poff purchased several weeks ago. I will need something to keep me warm. I look at the phone. Mr. Rose was supposed to call me back. I call the Rose house again.

His wife answers.

"Mrs. Rose?"

"This is she."

"Is your husband available?"

"He is out."

"Out to where?"

"How should I know?" I can tell she is quite upset.

"You have a troubled relationship, don't you?"

"That's not your affair."

"Every woman who has had her heart broken by a selfish man is my affair."

She is quiet for a minute or so, but she finally speaks. "We do, sadly. He has been seeing this young girl. They are off again, on again. He will say it is over, and he will say they are going to end it one week and that he is going to leave me the next."

"What are the current circumstances?"

"This week he is going to leave me!" And then, she sobs loudly for thirty seconds. I stand there, listening to her, feeling awful.

"My apologies."

Why did you call?"

"Oh, the dinner I invited him to. It will be Saturday. It is unrelated to his..."

"Affair?"

"Yes. That. It is for an old friend who is moving."

"I shall let him know." She struggles with the last words.

I decide to go drive by Nanette's apartment, and see if anyone else is there. I am certain she will see me. It is close to eight thirty when I get there. In my typical fashion, I park the car near the lamp posts about a block away, and I walk briskly towards her building. As I see it in the distance, I notice that the place is relatively well lit for the hour, and there are a number of cars in the parking lot that are not indigenous to the complex. As I stand facing the parking lot, I see the familiar black BMW. I take a glance upwards at Nanette's apartment. It is faint and more dark than light. A certain boldness rushes over me. I hold my new flask and bring it close to me. "If now is not the time to be bold, then under what circumstances will one act courageously?" I ask myself. I twist the lid off the jar, and take a swig. I wait about two minutes, and I take another one. First I go to the mail boxes, but they are all locked and I can't figure out which is hers. The vodka is strong and warm, and I stand in the dark, glaring at the BMW.

My inhibitions now partially diluted, I begin to walk towards the big car, looking for any sort of indication that it belongs to Mr. Rose. I can see a parking sticker, low on the rear windshield. Although it is unfamiliar to me, I have a suspicion that it might be downtown parking, near the parliamentary buildings. Upon close inspection, I see that this car is a very dark blue, and not black as I formerly thought. I look into the windshield. It is clearly a man's car, as the interior is devoid of anything that belongs to a woman. In hopes that someone might actually come downstairs and enter the car, I hide in the hedge that faces the car's front bumper. It feels like twenty degrees, but I know it is in the forties. I take another swig, but even as I am slowly becoming intoxicated, I realize that he is here to stay the night.

I notice that the wheels are very dirty with brake dust, and then I shut my eyes for a minute. I feel tired and heavy.

I wake up and look at my watch. It is nine fifty one, and that car is still here. They are most likely indulging in their passions, that damnable pair. I lay there for a second, swishing vodka in my mouth, feeling it burn my gums. I am irritated, imagining what Byron Rose looks like naked, with this woman who has me captivated. He is a charming fellow, I am sure. These thoughts leave me feeling more hopelessly inadequate. I hoist myself to my feet, and, without paying attention, I draw myself out into the moon light. I walk across the parking lot, with some difficulty. I am cold, and my body is stiff as a board. I take another drink, and try to walk more, but it doesn't work. I get back on my feet. I count the steps across the parking lot, and I make it to the edge. I turn around, and to my left I see the row of buildings. I take three more deliberate steps towards the street, and then a voice stops me short in my tracks.

"What are you doing here?"

Every idea I have is a bad idea. This was a bad idea among bad ideas, and I am a failure among failures. Nanette is standing twenty feet behind me, by herself. I cannot see what she is wearing, but she keeps a loose fitting jacket close to her. Her beauty is plain as day. I am instantly overcome with fear, jealousy and sadness, all at once.

I have no good response, but I have an honest one. "I am merely taking an inventory of your friend's car." I point to the BMW. She makes a face, but I can't see what it is. She is certainly not happy to discover me here. This is it. My cover is blown. She knows I have feelings for her that I cannot control.

"Go home."

"I am." I begin walking. I am terribly embarrassed. Thank God I am somewhat intoxicated. This moment is certainly God's way of telling me that stalking is bad. I am sure she has concocted a new set of personality flaws about me. I don't dare look back. She must be thinking the following:

Benedict is a seriously damaged individual.
Benedict is psychologically disturbed.
Benedict is disgusting to me.
Benedict is a creep.

Needless to say, any chance I had to make myself look even the least bit good to her has been demolished. Now there is nothing to lose. I wanted it this way, though, from the first day. I have to destroy the chance, even if the only place that a chance exists is in my own mind.

Again, every idea I have is a bad idea. There are no good ideas.

22

Dear Diary,
I don't know why this book should still have any residual value to me. I am tired of it, to say the least. It's funny how I still believe that everything he says is the truth. It is terrifying that the truth seems so far away. Christianity is a great sequence of "in order to's," the first of which is that you have to want to be one. I don't know if I even want to be a Christian anymore.

I hurriedly call the Rose phone number. The buttons are out of reach, and I struggle to hit them. The phone rings. A male voice answers. This is my third attempt today.

"Mr. Rose?"

"Yes."

"Have you made amends with her?"

"You might say that."

"She requests you."

"On what day?"

"This Saturday, at seven thirty. It is at the *maison.*"

"How do you know this?"

"I convinced her."

"Thank you, but she does not need to be convinced."

I begin to get angry, but I am sure I will have my revenge some other way.

"She will be delighted to see you."

"She should be." His voice is dull and arrogant, but somewhere in there lies is a sort of desperation making itself heard.

23

I have hid from Henri and Nanette for all of Wednesday, and all of Thursday. Tonight is his final dinner before he leaves on his trip. I sneak in Friday, a half hour late. Henri has left a list of chores for me to follow. I take it and I begin to accomplish various mindless tasks that have become so routine. Henri has ordered me to take home several plates of food from tonight and the previous week, lest they go to waste. Nanette has been given similar orders, but her portions are still in the fridge. I begin laying out the silver ware in the normal fashion, keeping tabs on the slightly longer guest list.

As of late, and late being the past two days, I have experienced a resurgence in my desire for Nanette, and my admittedly excessive disdain towards Mr. Rose has heightened. Instead of running from her, I observe her from afar. She knows I am here, and we both share a discomfort in each other's presence. Mine is derived from the hazy incidents of failed contact. I cannot speak for her, but I can see she dreads me now. My lustful fantasies about her have intensified, being a continuous struggle for me. I have no idea who she really is, but her body and its associated behaviors are eroding my soul. And to think, God has instructed me to save her from some sort of vice.

I catch myself following her gestures and pondering her behaviors with the men she has been with, married to a plethora of emotions, but always with a certain hateful envy and a venomous curiosity. I force my mind between fits of lust, and fits of sadness where I imagine all that has taken place between her and Byron. It is very likely that his may not be the car in front of her apartment, but he has been with her in the past, and for his past transgressions I seek revenge. He is the scapegoat for all the men that have wronged the women in my life.

Nanette pops out of the kitchen. Her positivity confounds me. She seems as light as the day that I met her. Why should she change though? In spite of me, she has not rendered her lightness.

And still, when I am with her, I am at a loss for myself. I feel so good, just with the idea of being near her. I study her minute features- how her hair falls, what color the skin on her upper back is, how many red hairs she has. I watch her steps, imagining that they are directed towards me. I look at her bare arms, wondering what they feel like to the touch. I look at her fingers, and think of all the electromagnetic charges waiting to happen between us. She knows I am looking at her, but this is now normal for us. I wonder what the invisible barrier was, the one that existed from the beginning and keeps me apart from her. I wonder why it is that the harder I try, the further away I am pushed. I wonder who wished it so, and why. I wonder what drives me to thinking about her at night, wishing her present with me.

And suddenly, I am made aware. No, she is not that beautiful. No, she is no one exceptional. No, she has never done anything worthy of my admiration. No, she has no truly vibrant features. No, she should not have held my heart captive this long. I keep repeating to myself "Nanette is no one special."

And this is the mystery of infatuation. Infatuation makes a woman beautiful and exceptional, when she is neither one. Infatuation is the unfair imbalance of pent up affections that were never released. I am still amazed at what a strong hold it has on me. I look upon her again. I am so tired of longing for her, desiring her and needing her. I am so crippled by these overpowering emotions that cannot be satiated. I need to rid myself of them, because I will always be beneath them. Perhaps even death is better than a life where the object is a predetermined goal that cannot be met.

She rises to her feet, and looks in my direction. "There is a chef coming tonight. He is preparing a dish for Henri."

What sort of dish would Henri need help preparing?"

"He does this at least twice a year. You'll see." She vanishes into the kitchen.

At four, a Japanese man appears at the door. Henri comes out of his office, where he has been camping out all day. He addresses the gentleman in French, and he proceeds to the kitchen. Consequently, I begin to rewash and polish the crystal. I watch as Henri appears with the mysterious package from the freezer. The Japanese man enters, carrying a small knife, and begins to survey the area. Henri appears, and chats with him in French. He looks at me, nods, and exits the kitchen. And there it is- the little package I had noticed before, with the Japanese script on it. Henri has removed it from the freezer, and it is thawing in the sink.

"What are you preparing?" I ask the Japanese chef.

"I'm preparing *fugu*."

"How do you know Henri?"

"We are old friends. I trained under a close friend of his about five years ago."

"What is fugu?"

"Fugu is a Japanese delicacy, a type of puffer fish. It is toxic, and requires special training to prepare."

"What happens if it is prepared wrong?"

"You loose control of your muscles. You eventually stop breathing, and you black out, and then suffocate."

"What part of the fish must you remove?"

"Well, the poison is usually in the ovaries and the liver. They have to be disposed of responsibly, so when I remove them, they are frozen, and someone comes and gets them."

"Does fugu taste good?"

"Oh yes! I had fugu very often while I was in training, and I never got tired of it. I would eat it in front of my guests so they would know it was safe!"

"So I suppose Henri enjoys it?"

"Once a year, especially before a trip. It is his way of making sure that everything goes well for him. Like a good luck charm."

"What is your name?"

"You can call me Hai...it's my nickname."

"Why is that your nickname?"

"It is unimportant. The preparation and sale of *fugu* is illegal in this country. Who are you?"

"They call me Apollinaire, but my real name is Benedict."

" Ah, the surrealist."

"Oh, Henri mentioned me?"

"Of course he did."

Hai takes the package and unwraps it, carefully laying the fish out on a cutting board. He surveys the fugu, and begins to section it. He then asks me to leave the kitchen, as he demands total silence while he prepare the deadly fish.

After a good twenty minutes, he allows me to come back in. He gets a bag, and begins to put the organs of the fish into it. Meanwhile I assemble the dishes for the main course- octopus, with fresh "aquatic herbs." Henri has requested that Nanette and I come in Saturday to make sure everything is orderly before he goes away. He has left each of us checks to cover our expenses for the time he is away. The nymph organizes the dining room, while I watch as she darts in and out of the shadows.

"Mr. Apollinaire!" Hai calls.

I look in his direction.

"These are the organs of the fugu. They must be placed in this container. Please hold the container open while I drop the bag in. Then put it in the freezer inside another bag and label it." I hold the lid off the container as Hai sets the poison fish parts in it. I then put the lid on, slide it in a brown bag, and place it in the freezer. I look about for Henri. I put a label on the bag that says *fugu-danger*.

Hai begins to cook the delicacy, and I sneak into the dining room.

"Nanette?" She looks up at me, without saying a word.

"Henri says he wants you and I here and dressed tomorrow

night, in case anyone shows up by mistake for dinner."

"He would say that," she mutters.

"There is a very special gentleman who may drop in tomorrow," I continue. "If he arrives, we are to be prepared to serve him."

"Henri does not make special accommodations for anyone."

"He does for old friends."

"Which old friend of Henri's is coming?" She still seems doubtful.

"A friend of Camus' son." I exit the dining room before she can respond, and go back to the kitchen for a bit. I wait until Nanette brings the glasses in and then I walk to Henri's office. I knock on the door.

"*Entrez, mon ami!*" Henri exclaims.

"Nanette says she would like to have a guest tomorrow for a meal. He has attended before, so she is not bringing a stranger in."

"Is it the man who keeps calling?"

"This one is not married. He goes by Verlaine." I recalled seeing the Verlaine personnage talking to her a few weeks ago.

"I'm OK with it- this is nothing new," he muses nonchalantly. "Mr. Verlaine is quite old and harmless."

"Really? This has happened before?"

Henri perks up at my interjection, almost like he has divulged too much information.

"It's fine with me," he says, and returns to his paperwork.

"Where are you going?" I ask.

"I am not sure. Europe? This may be the last time I do this. It is hard to meet women at my age." His words were painfully ironic. I thought it was supposed to get easier as you get older.

"Don't they get more reliable with age?"

"Benedict, it will always be the same. It is you who defines the situations. If you are waiting for something to change, then stop. It is aimless. Nothing will change."

"It won't?"

"If you do not attract love now, you never will, my friend.

Not with your methods."

"Did she tell you?"

"She told me. I see your desperation for her."

"So now what?"

Henri sighs. "I am going to provide you with the resources to find new work. You have a month or so. When I get back, it will be best for Nanette that you not return here."

The thought of never being able to see her again petrifies me. I am beyond words, so I start to cry.

"B-b-but I- I love her!"

"No. No you do not." He is stern, cold.

"H-how c-can you s-say that?" The tears well up in my eyes and run down my face. Henri focuses on his work.

"She is all I think about!"

Henri ignores me.

"You can't! You can't do that! She is the source of my hope! She is the only thing I want!"

"Even I still place my hope in God." He whispers.

"God has done nothing for me! Nothing!" I yell. Tears fall down my face, and on my shirt. I look down at my pale, hairless chest. I wipe my eyes.

"Benedict!" Henri yells.

I look up. He extends his arm, and slaps me clean on the cheek. "Be a man. Men realize that not every battle ends in victory."

I perk up a bit, stunned by how hard a man of seventy years can exert force.

He looks into my eyes. "When she has her guest over tomorrow, be good and attend to them."

"Why should I do that?"

"Because it is your job." He opens the heavy door, turns me around and pushes me out. "Oh, is my Fugu ready?"

"It should be."

"On Saturday evening, a man will come and get the organs."

"What time?"

"Who knows."

Henri comes into the kitchen at seven, and the guests start to arrive. He waits for all of them, and then tells them that he is leaving for a fortnight or so.

I pace about the living room. Each guest comes in, and hands me their coat. I walk them to the dining room, and announce the menu. Henri sits by himself at a small table. He picks up the bits of the poison fish, examining them. Hai sits down for dinner. I begin to serve the wine.

During the night, I realize that if this stays the same, I won't be able to bear it. But I feel powerless to change it. If this is what it is, I am truly stuck here. I wonder why things are so dim. I look at Henri, snacking on his *fugu*. He loves this existence. I look at Nanette. Men have loved her her entire life. She has no reason to ever desire me. I wonder what Byron is doing. I am sure he is thinking about Nanette, and how he can use his power and money to win her over again. I am envious of him, not for having her, but for the fact he does not fear her. He can request anything he pleases from any woman he wants to.

She walks towards me, never smiling, She walks right by me, and straight through me. I look at her and smile. She does not notice. I wonder if there is anything that would make her notice me. I look at how she interacts with other men. She is so gracious and kind to them, as if it were sentimental. I wonder if she has a soft side to her at all. I am more determined than ever to bring it out of her.

After dinner is over, I walk up to Henri.
"Please give me a key. I will return it when I come back."
"Nanette has the key."
"Can't you give me one?"
"There is no reason for it."
"I will give it to her tomorrow night. It will not be an issue again ."
"Why do you need a key?"
"So I can prepare things for Nanette and her guest."

"Give me a moment." He disappears and goes to a drawer in the kitchen. He produces a key.

"This is for a side door," he says as he hands it to me. Somehow, I feel that Henri pities me just a little bit. He knows as well as I do that I cannot succeed, but I believe he wants success for me. I look for menial tasks to perform, while I watch the guests leave. A man in his forties is still lingering. He hands Nanette a business card.

"Why did he hand her a card?" I ask. Henri ignores me.

"I thought contact outside the maison is not allowed!"

"She will be responsible about the rules. I have a trip to be ready for."

I put the plates in the dishwasher, and I begin to clean the crystal. I will miss this place. Even if I have to chase Nanette for an eternity, I still want to be here in this antiquated kitchen, with its vintage fridge, stained stove tops, innovative floors and tiny spaces. I did not want to go anywhere, but my actions have created this.

I get home at eleven P.M. and Poff is sleeping on our couch. I don't know where he came from. I push him a little bit.

"What are you doing here? Are you asleep?"

"I'm napping. Just got in. I'm going out later, I think."

"I am not going to be working at that place when the owner gets back from his trip."

"The one with the girl you like?"

"Sure."

"I heard about your outburst at the convent."

"What did that sound like?"

"I would expect it from you, actually. Were you drunk?"

"Surprisingly, no."

"They said you admitted to looking at porn."

"Maybe I did."

"They feel bad for you. They didn't know you were struggling so hard." I feel anger well up in me.

"You look at porn,too, Stephen Poff."

"I *used to.*"

"How long did 'used to' used to be? A week?"

"I don't know why we are friends," he states blankly.

"You're not a real Christian. Your version of Christianity is horse shit."

"Rad, you can be a judgmental little fuck. How do you know that I don't struggle? My struggles consume me, too. Do you think you're the only one who struggles? We all have struggles. Some of us just struggle more gracefully than others. Struggling doesn't have to look like a bitchy, whiny little mess. Yours is messy. Mine is what it is. Stop judging." Poff punches me in the arm, very hard. I am tired of people expressing their frustration towards me with violence.

"I'm sorry. You're right. I've been a terrible friend." I don't know what is wrong with me. I start to cry uncontrollably, and I sit down on the couch. Poff comes up and gives me a hug.

"I love you, buddy. I do," he says politely.

"I-I'm just sick of girls- treating me like shit all the time. I just want- want to be loved." I feel the tears hitting my arms and fingers.

"I'm sure there's a gas station gal in lower Georgia with a 'Ben' tattoo somewhere."

We both laugh. I look at Poff through my tears, and feel overwhelmed and sad. I have never been as fun for him as he has been for me. I am always falling into the trap of "nothing is good enough."

I struggle to get myself together, and Poff suggests we go out for a drink. I don't feel better, so I opt to stay home.

I go lay in my bed, and open up my copy of Redeeming Sexuality. I skim through the book, realizing it is too painful for me to read it. A passage on the very last page catches my eye.

"There is no trick to this kind of pursuit. The truth is that we must set aside our desires, no matter how attached we are to them, and ask God what He truly wants from us. When our desires become clear, we will see that there is goodness in them."

I honestly do not want to set aside my desires. I want only to be with a woman. I understand that I cannot accomplish this dream anymore. I am too broken and too messy for a woman to love me. If God has something else for me, I do not want it. If I cannot have what I want, I cannot destroy or terminate those desires. The solution is lost on me, but if I cannot satisfy my desire for love, I will at least satisfy my desire for revenge.

24

I unlock the side door of Henri's house at five o'clock on the nail. I go into the kitchen and select a wine. I prepare some steamed halibut and a side of left over seaweed, among other delicate and barely edible things. I use an exquisite blue china plate, with little silver tassels on the rim.

I go to the freezer, and remove the box marked *"fugu"* from the bottom shelf. I allow the package to thaw, noting that it smells fishy, but not repulsive. My theory is that the taste of the seaweed will offset the taste of the fugu, so that it is not noticed.

I take a sharp knife, and I mark the plate on the right so that I do not get them mixed up. On said plate, I rub the liver of the fugu on the base, so that it is sufficiently *coated.* I then take the rest of the organs, and squeeze their juices into a small cup. I mix the extract with vodka so that the taste is somewhat masked.

I begin to set the table, making a place for Byron on the right, and a place for Nanette on the left, such that they are close to each other. I place the white linens down, with the silverware in what I consider appropriate positions. I light a long stemmed candle, and place it in the middle of the table. The floor is cold, so I walk to the thermostat and turn it up to seventy degrees.

I suddenly become nervous, because I have not told Nanette what time to arrive. She must arrive before Byron does, so that she does not see his car. I go back to the kitchen and stare at the sauce cups. There is a bottle of Merlot open, so I decide to use it. In the mean time, I take more *fugu* scraps and smear the inside of one of the sauce cups with them. Using an oyster splitter, I nick the base of the cup so I don't get the two mixed up. As I nick the rim, I place a finger in the jaws of the splitter, and I unintentionally cut it. It bleeds substantially. As I just start to attend to my finger, I hear the front door open. I hurriedly set everything down and hide it, rushing to make sure no one sees what I am doing. I run to the foyer, holding my bleeding finger in a towel.

She enters, looking nervous and irritated.

"What's wrong?" I ask.

"I have had a terrible night. It was a bit much for me."

"What happened?"

"Nothing, nothing at all. Just a rough night."

"I see."

"What am I supposed to be doing here?"

"Nothing, just relax."

She strolls into the dining room and immediately notices the spread. She looks perturbed.

"Is this for us?"

"No- not for us. For an old guest of the house. Remember?" She looks exasperated, and I want to take her into my arms and console her about what happened, but all I can think of is Nanette and that scoundrel, Byron.

I hand her a glass of wine. She takes it. She doesn't say anything. She walks to the couch in the living room, and she sits down. I must keep her out of the kitchen at all costs, so I go in and lock the doors. Nervously, I take the few remaining scraps and feed most of them to the garbage disposal. My hand has stopped bleeding, so I throw the towel away. The stench is heavy, and I use some bleach to chase the remains down the sink. I wash my hands after all of it is done.

I then take the damaged sauce cup, and pour the vodka and *fugu* extract in it. I add some merlot, some brown mustard and some horseradish paste. I duplicate the mixture for the other cup. I taste a bit of the concoction. It certainly isn't bad, but it is nothing marvelous either. Henri has a habit of creating these somewhat unappealing science projects, and then encouraging his vassals to consume them on the grounds that it is in keeping with "the finest European traditions of taste."

I place the dishes in the microwave for a moment, and carry the wine glasses to the table. I top off Nanette's wine glass. As I do so, there is a knock on the door. I set the sauces on the counter, and I walk to the door. It occurs to me instantly that Nanette may try to answer it.

"Nanette, I will get it!" I yell.

"I wasn't even going to," she replies, and heads to the dining room. I walk to the front door, aching to catch a glimpse of my adversary. He knocks again.

"Give me a moment!" I use my elevated voice.

I peer into the peephole, and there he is, a miserably expressionless man in his later forties or early fifties. He takes the appearance of wealthy anonymity, with an exaggerated brow ridge, rife with stress, graying hair and opaque skin. He stands six feet one or two inches, a good bit taller than me. I see nothing in his expression that would incline him to be a romantic. His hands are firm. Mine are shaking.

I open the door.

"Mr. Rose?"

"Yes." He does not shake my hand. Rather, he walks to the coat rack, and stretches out an arm. "Aren't you going to take my coat?" he demands. I peek outside, looking for his car. I don't see any BMWs. I am now very confused.

I seize his coat. I make myself aware that his keys are in the breast pocket. He stands watching me, staring me down a bit. I lead him into the dining room. Nanette sits there, quietly. She sees Byron, and an expression of disappointment sets in. She rises to her feet, on her short heels. She throws me a sidelong glance. I feel slightly ignominious, having led her into these circumstances, but I realize that there is nothing to be lost from her feeling upset or happy. If she is so unhappy with him, I will be doing her a favor. If she is so glad to see him, I will bestow the satisfaction upon myself later. As she rehabituates herself with him, I slip back into the foyer, remove his keys from his coat pocket, and hide them in the couch. They are not car keys, much to my dismay. I will have to fish the keys off of his person later.

In the true fashion of an anonymous society, no names are used. I strain to hear their exchange.

"Miss Nanette, how good to see you." He bows low.

"And you also." She looks grim, but not angry. She embraces him with a hug, indicating that there may not be any hard feelings. She quickly pulls away, and he lingers just a bit. I am even more confused. Does she hate him or not? Both possibilities are emminent.

She excuses herself, and walks into the foyer. Nanette drags me aside. "You invited him here, didn't you?"

"He invited *himself*. He had to see you. He gave me an incentive."

"How typical of him, thinking he can *buy* whatever he wants."

"Will you sit down? He pressured me into having him here. Henri approved this."

"I did not want to see this man- ever again."

"He told me that you and him had planned this, last time he called. Henri approved it. What harm can come of it, anyway?"

"I suppose it can't hurt anything."

"When was the last time you saw him?" I ask her.

"Not your concern."

"You know I am leaving after this. Henri has fired me. Just get through this. You'll never have to see me again." A look of relief decorates her face, but she tries to subdue it.

"Good." She marches into the dining room, and holds light conversation with Byron. I catch words like 'divorce' and 'Italy' and 'secret.' A long time ago, Poff told me a secret. He said that people will follow orders if you put them in a situation, because people cannot think for themselves.

After five minutes of this nonsense, I enter the dining room and I walk Byron to the table, haplessly breaking up their conversation. He pulls the left chair out for himself, but I stop him.

"The floor is colder on the right. It is the gentleman's seat."

He moves his chair, but Nanette glances at me again, skeptically, as if she knows something is up. I go back to the kitchen, looking for my wine glasses. I figure it is best to let them get reacquainted. First, I offer a flavorful wine with a high alcohol content, in hopes of at least breaking the ice a bit. I happen to know, from Henri, that Nanette enjoys a good red zinfandel. I go in, and ask Byron for his wine selection.

"Do you have a red zin?" He asks. "If I recall, there was a type she really liked." He looks at Nanette and smiles. " Was it the Coppola?"

I suppose he *would* know what kind of wine she likes.

She smiles back, and begins to lighten up. I run back to the kitchen, but I linger around the corner for moment.

"I missed you," he says. "I know it is against the rules, but I pressured them into allowing this."

"I suppose it won't hurt us," She mumbles with the traces of a drunk smile emerging.

I am merely taking advantage of a situation to carry out my own designs. He has set the trap for himself.

Henri had ridiculed her once or twice for her overtly American preference for wines. I come in with the first bottle. "Is this acceptable?" I ask, pretending to be humble and timid.

Nanette nods. Her expression stipulates that she prefers something that will speed up her escape from this situation. I am hesitant to give her *too much* wine, as she lightens up when she drinks. Nonetheless, libations are urgently required.

I pour the wine into their glasses while they sit silently. I excuse myself for the time being, leaving the bottle on the table. She does not utter a word. I crack the kitchen door, hoping to hear more of their small talk.

"How have you been?" He asks her.

"I am well," she replies coldly.

"How is your wife?" she asks.

"She is fine. She took her maiden name back."

"When?"

"She stopped using my last name two months ago."

"So it's final?"

"It is."

They are silent for a good five minutes. I busy myself by making noises in the kitchen. I put on a low playing CD of inappropriately gay sounding waltzes. I think to myself "I am tired of telling women that they are beautiful. They only care about hearing they are beautiful from men who don't care about them."

Byron speaks up. "It was not you who inspired the divorce."

Nanette is quiet.

"I know that it was more or less a last straw, but it was not you."

"Fidelity is an impossibility," she replies mockingly. "You would always say that."

"It is a challenge."

"I don't see a reason why a woman should be faithful to you then. Did you honestly think that I would be moved to want you again because you were unfaithful to your wife, and then, on top of that, left her on account of your own weakness?"

"I figured it was best for both of us."

"Best for you, mostly."

I can't help but observe their discussion.

She downs her glass of wine, and then pours another. Byron drinks his more cautiously.

"Why are you here, anyway?" She asks.

" As I said, I pleaded to come and see you."

"Did Henri *specifically* approve this?" She questions.

"According to the headwaiter, he did." And he points to the kitchen.

"We have no headwaiter."

I hear their comment, and come out under the pretensions of bringing salad. "Henri absolutely approved this. Otherwise he would not have given me a key." I show Nanette the key. She frowns upon seeing it.

"Did you speak with Henri?" She asks Byron.

Byron looks at me.

"He spoke to Henri," I state.

Byron is no stranger to lying. "I spoke with him a week ago, and he approved it, on the grounds I was a guest here."

Nanette concedes. "Very well. Mr. Apollinaire, do you have any pinot noir?"

"I do. I will be back shortly."

I come back with a bottle of pinot I am unfamiliar with. She inspects it, and hands it back to me. "Find something more expensive. If Henri approved this, we will drink his wine."

"Is there a bottle of Nesting Duck 2001?" She demands. Henri had mentioned this wine before, saying it was his favorite pinot, even if it was from the wrong continent.

"I don't know where it is."

"It is in the office. He keeps an unopened bottle in there." She smiles just a bit.

I run to the office, and sure enough, upon his desk is a bottle of the Nesting Duck. I come back to the table, open it, and pour it.

"We might as well enjoy ourselves," she asserts.

"Cheers," says Byron, as he raises his glass. I excuse myself and go back to the kitchen, while they eat salad of arugula and spinach and drink their pinot.

She and Byron become slightly less hostile towards each other.

"Do you recall our trip to the Barcelona and Madrid?" He asks.

"I do. Why?"

"The salad reminds me of the salad we had when we were having lunch in old Madrid, The one with the anchovies on it. You said 'Euw! I have never had anchovies on a salad!' And then I convinced you to eat one, and you liked it."

"This salad could use anchovies," she responds with a slight laugh.

"Monsieur, please bring us some anchovies for the salad!"

I am irritated that they are starting to lighten up, but it is necessary. I go into the cabinets and fiddle around until I find a can of the anchovies. Perhaps he will not mind the rest of the fish in the main course.

I arrive with a small plate of anchovies. He places three on her salad, and five on his.

"You enjoy the fruits of the sea?" I ask Byron.

"Always."

I excuse myself again, listening even harder.

"That was a fun trip," Nanette quips. "I remember when we saw a bullfight. That was something wild."

"We can always go back."

She blatantly ignores his comment, instead reminiscing over the bullfight some more. "Do you remember when the matador fell? I thought to myself 'he will never get up in time!' And yet, for some reason, he did. And with not even a second to spare."

"I was on the edge of my seat."

They are silent for a bit, and they drink more wine.
"And then our trip to the coast. That was memorable, also." Byron waxes nostalgic for a while about it, and then bites his lip. Nanette is smiling about something.

I am struggling about whether or not I should go through with my plan, but after a moment the conversation shifts.

"Do you remember the Moorish castle in Alhambra?" He asks.

She smiles, but only partially. "Of course I do."

"That was truly a feat."

"It certainly was."

"Do you remember the ceiling in the hall of Abencerrajes?"

"The gold, brown and red tiles, and my wonderment of how

they got there?" She laughs.

"Do you remember what I compared *it* to?"

As soon as I hear the word "it," my ears perk up. What could *it* be?"

"You said that the colors of my birthmark and the colors of the ceiling were exactly the same."

"I did," he whispers.

"I liked my birthmark after that. I never thought it was beautiful, until you said that."

She smiles dreamily about it, and touches her stomach, just below her bust, gently. I boil with envy, from my hiding place in the kitchen.

I will never enjoy the sight of this birthmark of hers. Ignited, I go to the container and scavenge the rest of the fish guts, using my bare fingers, pouring them into the mortally wounded sauce cup. I must get him to consume this foul tasting concoction. "I will call it a 'fine delicacy of the Iberian peninsula'," I mutter to myself.

A few minutes later, I present the Halibut, with its potato compôte and 'aquatic herbs.' By this time, her attitude has improved to some degree. She is almost happy to be with him tonight. Byron takes a bite, and is quite impressed.

They still have never addressed each other by their birth names. It is now irrelevant, anyway. For her to have a normal, common name would betray her quiet elegance. Knowing who she is makes no difference to me.

I serve the sauce, nervously, and as I do so, I begin to notice a tingle in my arms. A slight numbness occurs, which I attribute to my willingness to follow through with this endeavor.

"A delicious horseradish sauce for the halibut!" I exclaim. "It is in the finest of European tastes." I set the chipped cup in front of him. I am not being a follower of Christ right now.

Nanette looks at her sauce cup and grimaces, while Byron studies it with curiosity. I contemplate the texture of the swill myself, and see the tiny bits of *fugu* in suspension in his cup. She smiles at him, and they laugh together, but suddenly he becomes very serious.

I excuse myself, and retreat to he kitchen.

"Why did our love have to end?" He asks her earnestly.

She is silent. She pours the last of the pinot into her glass, and takes a drink.

"I think about you every day," he groans. "I miss you at night, I long for you. I think of all the time we spent together." I am beyond any doubt that the consumption of so much wine has induced this sort of honesty.

Byron raises his glass, and says "To our love-"

Nanette stops him. "I must impart something on you, Byron."

"What is that?"

"I have to tell you why it ended."

"It was because I filmed us, wasn't it?"

I was angrier than ever now, waiting for him to finish his toast.

"No. It was not. It was me, not you."

"How was that so?"

"Well, Byron, you are impulsive, and selfish, but those things are unimportant. You see, you are part of my *business*."

"Business? What sort of business?"

"I have clients. I did not take a pension from my you. I was always well funded by you without any request, more so than others."

"Do you mean that there are others?" He coughs, like there is something is his throat.

He, and, of course I, are both aghast. I look at his face. It is pale and sad. He is choking slightly. I feel a greater numbness in my arms. I look at his plate. He has not eaten off the bottom of it yet.

"There are others," she states blatantly.

"At the same time as...me?"

"Yes." She is silent for a minute.

He does not breathe for a good while.

"Did you ever love me?"

"I enjoyed our time together. But I could see that you loved me. I had to end it, for both of our sakes. When you, or anyone, paid me enough, I would do things with them- travel with them, talk to them, dine with them, sleep with them. You gave me a credit card, which was very generous. Do you understand? I thought you did."

There is some silence, and then she speaks again: "I was never your girlfriend. I lived off of your generous 'gifts'. I run a business. You were my client." She is very cold and matter-of-fact, almost numb to the fact that she has mortally wounded his person.

I shed a tear for Byron, as he falls apart in his seat. Women do these things, where they seem to think an understanding exists where one never did in the first place. He, despite his more advanced years, is still getting the short end of the stick, despite his wealth and his accomplishments. He cuts his halibut, and turns away from her. "I suppose all we can do now is finish our dinner. Thank you for your honesty," he says.

Trembling, his hand moves towards the sauce. I cannot allow this. At this moment, all the emotions from Nanette are pulled back into my self. At this moment, I am fleeing the big house, where Lucia is quietly being objectified- with her under my arm. I am holding out my leg for Anthony- and drawing it back in so he does not get injured. I am thanking Kristen- and realize that I have left her no choice but to be insincere towards me. I am crawling up the cross- and hanging myself upon it.

I am telling myself that the only way to undo all of this selfish damage is to offer myself as my own penance. It might have been easier for Byron had he died in that moment, but it will not be so. I calmly walk into the dining room, grab the sauce from him, and hold it to my mouth. He looks confused, and gestures towards it.

"No, Byron." I turn away from him, holding the cup.

I consume the disgusting swill, trying to keep from vomiting it up as I down it. My throat burns from the horseradish. I set it down, and I take Byron's plate and walk back into the kitchen.

"What are you doing, *Benedict*?" Nanette yells.

I keep silent, as my arms feel heavy and my chest wells up. I take a seat in the corner, by the counter where I first watched my Nanette decorate the cakes with a *fleur de lis*. Feeling nauseous, I hold my stomach. Byron looks over at Nanette and begins to cry. "Why? Do you not realize I love you? I can give you anything you want."

"Give your wife those things," she says.

They sit there in extended silence for what seems like a long time. I keep waiting for her to say something, but she does not. I begin to cry. Byron is truly no different than I. Who is to say that after a lifetime of the sorts of things I endure, I might turn out differently? I can see my adult self in his weak, mournful shadow.

After the longest ten minutes of my life, Nanette comes into the kitchen, presumably because she cannot stand seeing the results of her lie. I wonder how much she charged the credit card for, or how their process of lovemaking went. Is this all there is? Dissatisfaction? All of these men are so weak, and so tied down to their obsession with beautiful women. Even Henri has wasted a lifetime on it, and to think, I looked up to him. I want to be a real man, a man who does not need or depend on sex for fulfillment. I do not want it, for it is repulsive and pathetic to me. I would rather be loved by no woman than have to engage in this ritual of subjugation. For the first time in my adult life, I am free of the desire for a woman. And here I am, about to die for it.

I am still angry. I look up from my stomach ache. "How did you and Byron meet?"

"Here. Two years ago."

"And Henri...?"

"Henri knows. He introduced us."

From that moment forth, I despised Henri Rosengart. I looked at Nanette. The beautiful woman, a farce. Her body is for sale.

"What is in that sauce you made us?"

"Yours is safe." I struggle with the words, noting that I am starting to feel cold all over.

I get up, and take four very heavy steps into the dining room.

I am overcome by a feeling of immediate lightness, and I crash to the floor. My knees hit the hardwood, but I do not notice it.

Nanette stands behind me. "What have you done to yourself?"

"This is my fault. I should never have fallen for you."

She will never be able to have me. That is my final satisfaction. I lay on the floor for another ten minutes. I want to get up, and I want to crawl to my feet, but it is useless. This is what it feels like to take one's own life from one's self. I keep thinking to myself "Did Henri sell her services? Was Sarah Temple another one of his girls? Is he an old, senile pimp? May God punish his sorry ass."

At that moment, there is a heavy knock at the door. I want to get up and answer it, but I know I can't. Nanette runs to the hallway to phone the paramedics, and Byron goes to the door.

I am astonished. I rotate my head slightly to the left, and Henri rushes in. I cannot see him, but I know his walk. When he appears, he is looking cold and frustrated. He looks at Byron, who follows him, but he says nothing.

"Nanette!"

"I am on the phone with the ambulance."

Henri runs into the dining room. He stops short and looks down, and only then does he see me lying on the floor.

"Did she leave you?" I ask.

"Benedict!" Get up!"

"I will not, you bastard." I struggle to yell.

"What happened?" He shouts.

"Did she leave you?" I ask a second time.

"She may have, but it is not your business. Get up."

I laugh and, very weakly, point at him. "You deserve it, corrupter of...virgins!"

"Get up!" He yells, this time with authority. My gasps for air have become audible.

Byron speaks up, trembling. "He has done some kind of harm

to himself."

"Why did you not tell me she...was a...a...*coquette*?" I rasp.

"It is not your affair! What have *you* done to *yourself*?"

"You are an abominable old man!" I take a deep, difficult breath."Byron!"I yell.

He steps over to me, still in shock.

"Please tell them...when they come..that Henri...*poisoned* me."

Henri yells at Byron. "I did not! I did not poison anyone!"

Byron keeps silent. I feel my breathing getting weaker.

"Byron, he is the one...who set you...up. He is satan, father...of lies."

Although I feel tired, I hear everything. I struggle to talk anymore, but some how, I get the words out.

"Good Byron...tell the nymph I loved...her, and her only."

I turn my thoughts inward. I realize that I have compromised myself. If I make it to purgatory, I will be fortunate.

"Henri...please...pray a chaplet...of...Divine Mercy."

In my mind, I begin to pray. "Lord...should you choose to spare me, give me a new purpose for my life." I realize I am forcing God to spare my life, not for my sake, but for His purpose. Byron stands there, looking miserable. Nanette comes in. Her demeanor is calm.

"What has he done to himself?" Henri asks her.

"Oh, he poisoned himself. But let's agree it was an accident." Her lack of compassion is disheartening.

"I did this...because... of you." I whisper. She does not hear me, or possibly cannot understand what I am saying.

"They should be here soon," she says, blankly. I want her to make a commotion of this, but she does not. She is the last thing I see before I loose vision. What a life I have led, pursuing only women instead of God. How selfish I have been. I hear Henri, as he begins to pray.

The first paramedics enter. I hear someone say "I think he had an allergic reaction." As they come in, Henri begins to pray, slowly. "Eternal Father...I offer you the body and blood, soul and divinity of your only Son, our Lord, Jesus Christ..."

I try to reach for Nanette, and I thank God I will die a virgin. My breathing is very slow, and my body is paralyzed. I cannot feel much now, and I struggle to inhale. It feels like a half hour has gone by. I try to talk, but I cannot. My thoughts are occurring in a purple haze now, with soft lights. Nanette is no longer a human, but a brand new color, exempt from the known spectrum. Henri is a talking old, white and gray storm cloud, all rained out, but still thundering with vigor. I think of my Saab, and how my dad will take good care of it. Lucia comes to me in this semi conscious state, as young and innocent as she once was, with a flower for me. Is she, too, part of this world of departure? I touch her, but there is nothing to touch. She is an abstract ideal, as she always was.

I hear human voices, and someone picks me up. I realize I have seconds now until I slip into darkness, as I cannot breathe. "Lord, please give me a purpose. Anything. I will do whatever you ask of me, in this life, or the next."

This is the process of conversion. This is how the greatest sinners become the greatest saints- by abandoning their own lives and letting God take control. The prom night fantasy will die with me, and I am left standing there, alone, on the dance floor, after everyone else has left.

As I fade out of life, I think of all the times I have loved. I pray to meet the girl from my driver's education class, but I cannot recall her name. I pray to see Jesus, and I hope He still loves me. "Please forgive me, Lord. For I know not...what I do." He is near, and He reaches for me, or perhaps it is just the sweet feeling of the freedom that comes in dying to one's self.

The Afterglow
" God cannot give us a happiness and peace apart from Himself,
because it is not there. There is no such thing."
-C.S. Lewis

25

It is a beautiful day. I feel so ready. I feel invigorated and refreshed after a good sleep. I look at the church. It is beautiful and clean. There are smiling faces, men in clean suits and women in nice dresses. All of them are young and bright. Several of them wave and smile at me. I wave and smile back. I walk around the church, admiring the art work. The echo of my shoes is pervasive and crisp. I step up to the altar. Under all of my clothes, I feel a bit warm, so I stand with my sleeve up to air out. The sun is high, brighter than ever. I am more and more excited by the minute. I dress quickly. I run back out to my faithful Saab for a quick phone call, and I snip a stray eye lash with a grooming kit. I spray myself with cologne, and I adjust my collar. I look at the landscape. There are all varieties of flowers blooming in the nearby garden. The Saab sits there proudly. Recently I treated it to a cosmetic makeover, in its original hues. It is an old friend in a new suit.

After fifteen minutes, I proceed to the front of the room, and the service begins. I cross myself, and sing with the beautiful choir. I process to the front, with altar servers and well- clad lectors. And then the church erupts into a joyful expression, as the bride comes in. She glistens, in her long and lovely dress, with her father at her side. He is a man of some years, with a mustache and a remnant of hair. He walks slowly with her to the altar, and she bows before stepping up. She faces me, looking towards me with big, brown eyes. At this moment, she has placed her future in my hands, with total trust. She carries herself with adulation from the congregation, looking upon Jesus and kneeling for a moment. We sing the *Gloria* in Latin, followed by the liturgy of the word. A sharply dressed young man reads the first reading from Song of Solomon. I marvel at the beauty of this work, as I dwell upon the beauty of our sexuality and marriage. She smiles at me, as sing with the responsorial Psalm. A girl in her early twenties reads the second reading. Her voice is powerful and declarative, as she speaks about the husband being willing to die for his bride, in true Christ-like fashion. I shed a tear, thinking of the beauty of this analogy.

We all rise for the Gospel, and we all hear the words that Jesus speaks to me, day after day- "I am the bread of life. He who eats of me shall not hunger." And then, the moment I have prepared myself for all week.

"In the name of the Father, the Son, and the Holy Spirit..." I pause momentarily, thinking of what it means to be happy. I keep my hand at my sternum for a moment, and then I begin to read.

God is good. God loves us. We keep telling ourselves this over and over again. We feel Him in the silence of our hearts. He moves in and out of the shadows, watching. He has created in us a vast love. His ways are not our ways, and His timing is not our timing. He can choose whatever He wants for us, without our consent. His love extends to the worst parts of ourselves, beyond the places we open up to Him. His forgiveness gives us a place in His plan. He uses the weakest ones to carry out his greatest deeds.

God is good. God loves us. But none of us really believe that. None of us really get what we want without enduring some sort of painful process. God fails us over and over again, so we say. He has planted within us desires that lead us to all sorts of bad events. He is a great being, but we are such weak and pathetic people. Who is to blame then, Him or us? Shouldn't we receive these desires that we long for so badly? What was His intention in creating such things in our hearts?

God is good. God loves us. He is always on top of everything. Even when we lose hope, He still has control. God is not just there- He truly is good.

Or is He? When a man indulges in his carnality, is God still good? How about when a young woman dies in a car wreck after a short life of poor decisions? What about when a man's spouse leaves him for someone else? Or when the woman of your dreams chooses a night of anonymous sex over being truly loved? If God were truly good, wouldn't He stop these things, at least sometimes, when we cry out to Him? Wouldn't He work with us to undo the damage? Wouldn't He at least say something? But God is silent. He gave us the ability to communicate, so He must have it also. But He remains a mystery. What then, do we do? How do we bring goodness to our families? And how do we bring kindness to our friends? How do we help our neighbors? How do we turn around our humanity? How do we show the world that hope exists? How do we love ourselves? How do we know God really loves this, all of it. How do we form a relationship that appears to be so one sided?

There is only one way- we must choose love. Choosing love involves bringing the action to the situation that is missing. When we feel angry at another person, or jealous, or hateful, we must forgive. When we feel depressed, alone or vulnerable, we must be courageous. When others make us hurt, we must empower them. When we loathe ourselves, we must glory in who Christ has made us. When the world challenges us, we must take up the challenge. When we are blessed with mediocrity and boredom, we must be the adventure. When the situation looks hopeless, we must bring hope. Choosing love means not choosing to make things worse. Choosing love means that we are choosing God. Only then can He work.

And yet we ask "does God really ever intervene? Does He get His hands dirty?" He gets our hands dirty for His will. When someone stops to help at a car crash site, or to clean the floors of a hospital, God is there, working. When one man feeds another, God is working. When a team of doctors flies into a remote corner of the world, God is working. When someone survives against all odds, God is working. When two people fall in love, God is working.

But we want Him to do all the work for us! And when He asks us to work alongside Him, we plug our ears, close our eyes, and just say 'no.' We have said "no!" for so long, we don't even know how to say "yes" anymore! "Yes" begins with sacrifice. Saying yes means giving up what you want to do where sacrifice is required, no matter how hard it looks. Saying yes means being unselfish so that another person can feel God's love. God's love comes in different forms- a bed to sleep in or food to eat, a kind word, an end to suffering, or freedom from sin. We cannot give these blessings to others without sacrificing something. The bigger the sacrifice, the bigger the blessing for the recipient. There is no way to escape from this- marriage, family, vocation, work, spirituality- all of these will only arrive at perfection after sacrifice becomes a way of life for you. People often ask "How can one keep sacrificing so much for the good of the world without replenishing your own self?"

It is simple. God will fill you. God will overflow inside you. You will love the act of sacrifice, because you will find the greatest sustenance you have ever known inside of it.

God sustains those who sustain humanity. Priests, nurses, doctors, spouses, parents- all of you must make daily sacrifices for others. Let God love you in the midst of your sacrifice. Let Him be the life inside you. And share that life with others.
God is good. God loves us- but we must prove that love through sacrifice, so that others may see it. Amen.

I look into her eyes, and I see true love there. This is the greatest day of my life, where two people, irregardless of where they have been, or who they are, are brought together by Jesus, in holy matrimony.

And there it is.

"Do you promise to be faithful to each other, in good times and in bad?"

"I do."

"Do you promise to love each other in sickness and in health? To bear children in a loving, Christ centered household?"

"I do"

"Do you promise to love each other, until *death* do you part?"

"I do."

"I pronounce you man and wife."

The Eucharist is consecrated, and I feel more alive than ever as I take it. I kneel before Him and thank Him for my life, and for this beautiful woman, who has blessed me today with her "yes" to a life guided and filled with the Holy Spirit. I kneel down, praising and thanking Him for sparing me, so that it might be fulfilled. I recall trading my desires for His desires. His desires for me were good. They have brought me happiness beyond description. There is nothing in the world I would trade for it.

I watch, solemnly, as communion is distributed. The choir sings the "Ave Maria," and the pipe organ joyously spills its bubbly notes. When I see the entire front row come and receive, each person kneels. I have so much to look forward too, with this up and coming generation of reverent Catholics.

The church becomes a party, as shouts of joy capture the moment, and bells erupt. A tearful bride and a confident, yet compassionate groom exit the church, and make their way to a canopy. Photos flash, and friends, young and old, hug and cry. Kisses are exchanged, gifts are given, children are fussed over and all the fixtures are embellished with flowers. I take a moment, and kneel towards Him, recognizing that He is the source and summit of my existence. My eternality is a function of His forgiveness and mercy. What would I ever want for? I look at the ring on my own finger- my promise of faithfulness and fidelity, and I realize that there is nothing between me and Him right now. The bride and groom kiss, and kneel. They look so holy together. I feel better about humanity every time I witness a moment such as this.

Christ's quiet perfection repeats, and repeats, more enticing each time. I can only stand back and admire it. He is real, and I am His.

The crowd walks past me. "Father, thank you for such a great homily!"

"Father, you must be a doctor of letters. I hope you don't mind, but I recorded it!"

A beautiful woman clutches my arm, and smiles. I feel a warmth beyond anything I could have experienced without Christ. The bride and her husband greet me, and give me a hug. Just hours ago, I saw him in confession. "Your only sin, my friend, is not trusting Him enough! Be courageous!" I told him.

He thanks me for what has been the most beautiful confession he has ever had, and the bride sheds tears of joy when she thanks for being there for them. She is St. Claire, Mary Magdalene or Gianna Molla. She could have been any of the women that I loved at any given time. They are the body of Christ, together, and I have been God's assistant in this process. I still keep a battered copy of Joseph North's book. I hand it to him. "Read this and return it to me when you have finished it. It will change your life." They thank me, and they enter a limousine waiting. I beam with delight, and reach for my keys. I turn to the parking lot, and place one foot in front of the other, with a little bit of difficulty.

As I begin to walk back to my car, I see a young man admiring it. "Is this yours, Father?"

"It is- I have owned it for fourteen years, believe it or not."

"I have never seen a Saab like it before."

"It certainly is something special. A lot happened in this car."

The young man turns and starts to walk away, but then he stops dead in his tracks. "Hey Father-"

"Yes?" I stop looking for my keys.

"That was a great homily. What inspired you to write it?"

"My own conversion."

"What was significant about your conversion?"

"I guess you could say I was restless. Restless for *something* to happen. Or else, things would keep repeating themselves. I suppose you could say I was a hopeless romantic."

"So you needed to be *converted* from that?"

"Yes, yes I did. I absolutely needed a conversion. A specific conversion for hopeless romantics."

"Was it that bad?"

"It was. Giving up the desire to be with a woman could only have come from God. That's why I identify it as a conversion."

"So after your conversion you decided you wanted to become a priest?"

"During, actually."

"Very interesting. How did that happen?"

I feel the tracheostomy scar on my neck, and look at him inquisitively. "Would you believe that this decision was made in a life or death situation?"

The young man scratches his head. "I suppose that would make sense. How did that come to pass?"

"It was the effect of a bad decision. A reaction to several things."

"And God used it to get your attention?"

"My dear friend, God will do whatever is required to bring us to Him. In this case, He spared my life because I asked for Him to- for His own purpose."

The young man looks uncertain, and then he asks a powerful question: "Father, what did you mean in your homily when you said that God will provide you with sustenance? I think it seems a bit optimistic!"

"I mean that if it wasn't for that sustenance, I would not be able to do this kind of work."

"What would you do then if you weren't a priest?"

I stand there quietly for a second. I shudder to think of what my life would be without this concentration of spirituality. "Do you ever think about women, marriage, and the affiliated set of expectations?" I ask him.

"Yes, yes I do," he states with obvious consternation.

"This job is far more productive- for me, at least."

I open the car door. "I must depart. Keep your head up!"

The young man smiles, and waves goodbye. I raise my hand, and bless him. As I turn the key, in between the seats, I think for a moment about Lucia, and I say a little prayer for her. You see, after all those months in the hospital (after the near-death encounter with the *fugu*), I made good on my promise. I chose the one institution that had kept me together for my entire life up to that point. I would like to think I chose the path that allowed me to love- and fight for- all women. I am now hope for the hopeless, a friend to men who struggle, and a man who admires himself. The rush you get from being a warrior- a real hero- is all I want, and I am sure it is better (to me, at least) than sex. So sure, in fact, that I don't need to find out.

The Saab buzzes like a little hummingbird when I race it through the gears, as I head off to the wedding reception. As I drive away, I keep thinking to myself "God is good. God loves us. But the burden of proof rests upon our shoulders."

fin